D0755650

She had to agree, she couldn't wait any longer for him to give her more proof of his love!

They must really and truly be made for each other, who else would have found out her password – treefrogs5!

RETOUCHED
and
STORMY PARADISE

-SHEILA SMITH-

RETOUCHED

and

STORMY PARADISE

Copyright © Sheila Smith 2013

All rights reserved

ISBN 978-09569349-5-6

First Published 2013 by
Sheila Smith

Printed by
www.printondemand-worldwide.com

I dedicate Retouched to my husband Geoffrey.

He has provided me over many years with facts, information on places, events, and interesting characters living in the Lake District.

Previous Books by Sheila Smith
Valley of Stone
Rural Haven
Restitution
Aftermath
Demons and Daffodils
Mother Goddess
Synergy
The Whispering Tarn
Hermit of Hesperia

RETOUCHED
A soldier returns from Afghanistan to share the last few months of his father's life with him. He is thrown into a life and death situation with a young student and her mother, and it is some time before their problems have a chance of being resolved, even in the beautiful English Lake District.

STORMY PARADISE
Morgane Maine lives at Smugglers Cove, near Hamilton on the beautiful islands of Bermuda, where she takes in a few guests to help retain her home.
Joe Lawson is a well known portrait painter who arrives on the islands from London, and it transpires that he has secretly left the UK. He stays at Smuggler's Cove and they get on very well, until he finds out her name and then everything changes. Morgane is adamant that his beliefs are untrue.

"Coffin Stone" or "Resting Stone"

Before "St Mary's" Church in Ambleside was consecrated, coffins had to be transported along the "Corpse Road" from Ambleside 4km to "St Oswald's" Church, Grasmere for burial. This route is now the present day Bridle Path to Rydal.

This stone along with others along the way was used for supporting the coffin while the bearers rested.

Another Corpse Road over Hunting Stile and Red Bank was used to bring coffins over for burial from Chapel Stile, Great Langdale, until "The Holy Trinity" Church and grave yard was consecrated in 1821.

Note: The above information is taken from a sign on one of the Coffin Resting Stones. Presumably the last paragraph applies to the Chapel which was on the site before The Holy Trinity Church, Chapel Stile was built in 1858.

St. Oswald's Church (Grasmere)

RETOUCHED

CHAPTER ONE

The coffin was built of oak, and the splendidly marked wood had been waiting to be used just for that purpose. The oak had been seasoned slowly over the years in a well ventilated barn, since the tall tree had been felled on the old man's small hill farm near Rydal in the English Lake District in 2004. Scott Peterson stared at the coffin lovingly created by an old friend of his father over the last six months since his father had contacted a life threatening illness. Scott was a tall lean man, with dark short hair, with military bearing and distinctive grey eyes. The expression in those eyes was one of loathing but not for the man inside the coffin, his father, but for what had transpired in the last few months, but mostly and in particular in the last few days - he loathed and abhorred himself!

He had been on his way to a military hospital, when he had been informed of his father's illness, and had managed to persuade the powers that be that he should be at home as soon as possible. He had thought that he was well enough, but perhaps they knew more than he did, but his insistence had allowed him to spend with his father the last two months of his life.

They had talked for many hours, and he now treasured that time together, as all through his childhood his father had not had much time to spend with his only son, as he had been running the small farm, and also a slate quarry that had taken up most of his time. The quarry had been closed upon his retirement, and that had left only the farm to be cared for, by his son and Scott hoped with the *help* of his sister Adele. However, she had been married to John Simpson a local farmer for the last eight years and had two boys under five - Elliot and John junior, and they took up most of her time and energy. When last he had spoken with Adele he had been made aware that she was pleased that her brother had been left the quarry and small farm. She had been left a handsome sum of money which she planned to use for the education of her sons, and to help with her husband's farm, should that be necessary in the future.

Scott's father, Elliot Scott Peterson, in the two month's before his death had understood his son's desire to go back to Afghanistan to rejoin his friends and colleagues and had said so often enough as that was the wish of his only son!

But now Scott was feeling undecided, as he had done three years in the Army and had survived two blasts from improvised explosive devices (IED), and had been much luckier than some of his colleagues. Oak Tree Farm, named many years ago when the oak tree had stood tall and proud in the front garden but just to the right of the house in order that the view of the valley was not impeded, was the only real home that Scott had known, but it was empty without his father. He had only left it to finish his education, and that seemed a long time ago. *Should* he return to the Army if he was to get a clean bill of health – his health would surely determine whether he even *had* a choice? He looked normal, and he hoped his behaviour was too, but if he *was* still suffering traumatic brain injury (TBI), would he know? He was aware that the medics now made a point of investigating this as it had become very common in the last few years, and was not identified until sometimes it was too late. He was getting really fed-up with having initials used with most actions in the Army, but that was probably because of mobile telephones, text messages and the like, and like many other things in the army he would just have to put up with it like everyone else on active service!

Scott now followed the funeral director and coffin, leading his sister, her family, and their father's many mourners from St. Oswald's Church, Grasmere. St Oswald's was named after the seventh century Christian King, Saint and Martyr of Northumberland who it was believed had preached on this site. The present Church was the fourth built on this site, the earliest remaining parts dating from 1250AD, and the Church had a musty comfortingly old smell. They proceeded to the cemetery for the interment, with Scott wondering if seeing his father there in the grave would at last help him to *accept* his loss. He sighed heavily, as his father had been a wonderful father and a good man who had made many friends over the years. He heard the Vicar's words as if from afar, and was slightly shocked when he was asked to throw soil onto the coffin, as he had not seen it being lowered into the grave. He now *focused* his attention onto what was happening around him, and apologised briefly to the Vicar and his sister Adele, and as soon as the other people present slowly filed passed the grave he moved to one side wondering how he would get through the rest of this traumatic day.

Scott received heartfelt condolences from all his father's friends, and a few quite distant relations, but he felt very much alone. Only two people had enquired where his girlfriend Samantha Brown was, but he had merely said that she was away on holiday. He could not very well have told them the truth!

His mind was a whirl of almost unbelievable regrets, and he felt a tormented disbelief at his own recent behaviour, which was totally alien to his nature, and had only a *little* to do with the absent Samantha! His time in the forces which had been proof of man's inhumanity to man, and the battering that his previous belief in the goodness of men of all races had taken whilst there, had taken its toll. This had made him cynical and scornful of almost everyone, and in particular himself!

As for women, he was of the opinion that he could do without them in the future. Why couldn't they all be like his sister, loving and loyal to her husband and family? Perhaps *Adele* was the only decent woman in his circle, as that was how it felt at the moment.

He walked back towards the Churchyard, and was rather exasperated to find numerous visitors queuing to view the area under the yew trees where William Wordsworth had been buried in 1850, over a hundred and sixty years ago, in the family plot. *How* had so many people managed to *get into* this village, as the river beside the Church was still full and still rushing as powerfully after the latest tumultuous rain storm towards the already flooded lake, and yet two days ago the roads had been impassable?

The floods had closed the road from Rydal, and he had decided that it was of the utmost importance to get the coffin to the Church immediately in case the flooding continued. This had meant that the coffin had to be carried along the old coffin route from the town of Ambleside and into Grasmere in the still very heavy rain. His father's last wish was that he *must* be buried in St. Oswald's Church, as he had been baptised and married to the love of his life Mary, in that Church. Mary, the mother of Scott and Adele, had died ten years ago when Scott was sixteen and Adele eighteen, and now Elliot Scott Peterson had sadly joined her in death.

The coffin route had been in use for hundreds of years before there was a consecrated Church in Ambleside. Two days ago it had been deemed a more suitable idea to use that fell side route, with the help of three of his father's ex quarrymen and an old fashioned wheel-bier (a polished wooden frame to hold a coffin, with four large wheels) rather than try to get the coffin through the floods by vehicle. Old Joe Smith (Ald Smithy) had been his father's foreman, and although as old as the deceased, had insisted upon carrying his old friend - today and also two days ago. The narrow road across the valley was also flooded and impassable, and there were also floods over the other side of the pass towards Keswick.

Now Scott felt a touch on his shoulder, and turned to shake the hand of one of his father's close friends.

"I'm really sorry Scott that you and Adele have lost your father. He was one of my greatest friends as you know. Please let me know if there is anything I can do." Daniel Sharpe said with compassion. His handshake was firm, and Scott knew he meant exactly what he said.

"I may have to take up on that offer if I go back into the Army, it depends on my next medical," Scott replied gratefully.

"Oh, how remiss of me, I should introduce my companion, her mother Charlotte Howes couldn't come because she is ill, and her daughter Zoe here, has kindly agreed to accompany me," Daniel said apologising for his oversight. A very pretty girl who nodded briefly was revealed as Daniel moved to one side, and Scott suddenly turned pale and sweat stood out on his forehead, and the girl moved quickly away towards the hotel. "Scott you are not well, let me take you back to your sister," Daniel finished speaking, and took Scott by the arm and moved towards Adele and her husband John Simpson.

"Adele, your brother is not very well, I think the doctors were quite right in saying he was not well enough to travel home to be with his father," Daniel said worriedly. As Adele turned and took Scott's arm, as her husband took the other arm solicitously.

"Thank you Daniel, we'll take over now, and see you at the hotel shortly. Please make sure everyone is made welcome at the hotel for something to eat and drink," Adele said quickly putting her hand on Scott's forehead, which annoyed her brother intensely! She should act like his sister not his mother!

"Don't worry Daniel, I'll be fine in a moment, and Adele please *stop fussing*, today we are meant to be saying *goodbye* to Dad. John please take your wife to the hotel, and Daniel too, I'll follow in a few minutes?" Scott said hating the fact that some of the people standing around were looking towards them with a great deal of interest.

Adele looked at her brother closely, and worriedly let go of his arm as she noticed his look which plainly said 'leave me alone or else.' When he had come home a couple of months

6

ago she had been very worried about her brother as he appeared to be on a short fuse, but since then he had seemed to improve, probably just for the sake of his father, and she now decided to keep a closer eye on her only brother, but with all these people around she had better do, for now, as *he* wished.

Scott turned away, and walked slowly to the small park where he walked on local slate tiles, each with a name carved on it, all of which had paid for the privilege of being a friend of Grasmere, and others who had planted a daffodil. He moved on down towards the river which was still over the top of its banks where it made its way under the road towards the lake. He sat on a bench and leaned forward with his head in his hands. Thank goodness no-one had followed, as he needed to be by himself. He thought his headaches had gone away, but just at the moment his head pounded uncomfortably. He delved into his pocket and extracted two pills from a foil strip swallowing them quickly.

If his doctor at the coalition medical facility had been here he would have been certain he was suffering from a traumatic brain injury, which was the most pervasive combat injury suffered in the last few years on active service. Maybe he *was* suffering from that affliction, he had most certainly been too close to two improvised explosive device detonations, but he could not get out of his mind, the surprise evident on the face of the young woman he had just been introduced to by Daniel Sharpe. Her blue eyes had almost turned to green showing that she was emotionally involved, and he remembered with self loathing and regret, those lovely innocent eyes changing colour once before due to circumstances brought about by *his own* need and instability.

CHAPTER TWO

Zoe Howes accompanied Daniel Sharpe to the hotel, where together they assisted Adele and John Simpson to welcome to the funeral tea the many relations and friends of the late Elliot Scott Peterson, who had been appreciated as a man dedicated to anything local, in particular the quarries and quarrymen of the area, all through the slow demise of that industry during the last few decades of the twentieth century. Daniel looked towards Zoe with a worried frown. The usually quiet and pragmatic young woman was looking a little ragged around the edges, as her distinctive blue eyes looked troubled and she appeared to be suffering from lack of sleep or a hangover, if he had not known her better that was what he might have considered. She had only known Elliot Scott Peterson (the deceased) as a friendly neighbour and so this occasion should not bother her *too* much. She had informed Daniel that those little chats with Elliot had often brightened her day, as Mr Neil Brown was usually arrogant and unhelpful, and always reminding Zoe (when she was unable to avoid him) that she was living in *his* house with *her* mother on sufferance! However, her mother whom Daniel knew very well was quite ill, and Daniel was also very worried about *her*.

"Zoe you are very quiet, are you alright?" Daniel enquired worriedly, as Zoe had not really wanted to leave her mother to attend this funeral. Perhaps Charlotte had been hiding something from him! Or maybe it was just the occasion, because one so young had probably not attended many?

"I'm fine Mr Sharpe, but I'm worried about my mother, as you know she was too ill to accompany you today. I think I should walk back to Rydal and make sure that she's alright. As you are aware Mr Brown is really put out that she's ill, and I have been doing some of her work just to keep him sweet. I think I'll walk back before he starts to want his tea and expects Mum to get it," Zoe said quickly.

"You do too much Zoe, but it isn't up to you to do your mother's work, and she can't help being ill. If Neil Brown gets too unbearable and unpleasant you must give me a ring, as I would like to help if I possibly can?"

"I might do that, but I want to get something prepared for tomorrow then Mum hasn't much cooking to do, as I have to go back to University, thank goodness I only have eighteen months still to do. Mum might be better tomorrow," Zoe said with a worried sigh. Daniel Sharpe looked at the worried young face of his friend's daughter, and wondered about their rather odd circumstances. Where was the husband of Charlotte as she never mentioned him was he dead or had they divorced? Also why did she have to do a living-in job, as she seemed to be a well educated and pragmatic person? She was certainly at the moment a sick woman, and he worried about them both!

"Zoe you must go back on the higher road if you must walk, as the road by the lake as you know, is still partly submerged in flood water," Daniel Sharpe instructed.

"I'll do that as it won't take me very long. Thank you for your support with mother, and I feel much better knowing she has you for a friend," Zoe said pulling on her anorak, as it had now started to rain once again, with the rain beating against the hotel windows and obscuring the usually fantastic views.

She pulled up her hood and dug her hands deep in the pockets, and slightly bent forward against the rain she left the village and walked passed the Wordsworth Centre and the coffin resting stone on the hill, and moved along the road towards White Moss car park, as it was very wet underfoot. She was informed there by an ice cream sales man that the road further along beside Rydal Water was still underwater but just passable by vehicles, and so she moved upwards to rejoin the rest of the old coffin route. She was quite wet when she came to the last coffin resting stone, and sheltered under the overhanging branches until the rain almost stopped. She felt wet and miserable, and not just because of the rain today, she should never have come this way, even if it would have meant begging a lift, or walking through the cold and possibly dangerous floods!

Zoe shivered as she thought about her mother Charlotte who had been live-in housekeeper to Mr Neil Brown for eight years now, and at first her mother had been relieved to find a live-in position, and Mr Brown had not seemed to be too demanding. She had suffered from ill health recently, and she was worried that if she could not keep doing her job then she and her daughter would be moved out of Mr Brown's home. Zoe was studying at Lancaster University doing a degree in English language and literature, and only had eighteen months left to do. She had run up quite a debt on course fees, living and travelling expenses, but that would all be an unwarranted waste if she *left now* to help her mother! Her mother had helped as much as she could, and was very proud of her daughter, and this made Zoe even more determined to do well, and finish her course and hopefully end up with a reasonably good degree.

As soon as the rain abated then she would move on and maybe rest for a minute in the hollow oak tree in the next wooded area where she had rested with her mother three days ago.

Zoe wished she could forget the look of dismay and chagrin on the ruggedly handsome face of Scott Peterson when Daniel had introduced her at his father's funeral. She had been wondering if he would remember her, after all it was only three days ago that they had first met, and even the weather had not improved! Although Scott Peterson was the son of a neighbour, over the last eight years whilst visiting this area to stay with her mother, she had never met him! She *had* expected him to get in touch with her after their first meeting, even if it was just to apologise, as she also wanted to apologise to him! If that happened then it might be possible to put the whole disastrous meeting behind them for ever!

Three days earlier in a fine misty rain, Charlotte and Zoe dashed into the shelter of the hollow oak tree, as Charlotte had suffered a coughing fit, and her breathing was shallow, with a pain in her chest and throat which made breathing very difficult. In the confined space Zoe lowered her mother onto a stone just about seat height and rubbed her back comfortingly, but her mother continued to gasp for breath, as she searched through her pockets and looked helplessly towards Zoe. They were almost a quarter of a mile from the house, and Zoe was desperate to get help, there was no way her mother would make it in time even with Zoe's help, and she had obviously forgotten her glyceryl trinitrate spray which would have relieved her angina symptoms. Zoe went through her own pockets and they were bare of anything useful, like aspirin.

Zoe heard voices and rushed out of the hollow oak tree, and the four men carrying a coffin on their shoulders almost dropped it as she suddenly appeared before them shouting desperately for help, her voice both frightened and demanding, and therefore not something to be ignored. At the time she didn't think it was an odd thing to see in the twenty first century, but it would have been quite normal two or three hundred years ago. All she needed was help to get her mother home as quickly as possible. She noticed the strange wheeled contraption which was being towed along behind the men carrying the coffin, and wondered if she could push her mother home on that, as home was only a few hundred metres away.

"Please help me as my mother can't breath," she gasped and grabbed the arm of the younger man at the back corner of the coffin.

"Yes, just a minute, we'll try to help you," the young man said quickly. "Can you men carry on to the resting stone, the path is a bit easier walking here, and we can put Dad on the wheeled-bier. Wait at the resting stone, and I'll catch up with you."

The men looked very concerned, particularly the elderly man who had been carrying in partnership with the much taller young man at the rear of the coffin, but they nodded slowly, and as soon as the young man had helped them to place the

12

coffin on the wooden wheeled-bier, they awkwardly moved off on the uneven path in the direction of Grasmere.

The tall young man looked at Zoe warily, as though her actions were rather odd!

"Have you brought any medication with you for your mother?" he asked and looked even more annoyed as Zoe shook her head, and took his arm to pull him towards the hollow oak tree. "I'm Scott, so what is your mother's first name?"

"Charlotte and I'm Zoe, but we are only a few hundred metres from where we live, if we can get her there she can use her spray, and I'll ring for the doctor. Mother works for Neil Brown, and lives in."

Scott took in the position at once as he gazed down at the frail woman gasping for breath, as he put one arm around her shoulders and one under her knees, and lifted her up and carried her feet first out of the hollow oak tree and into the fine rain. Charlotte tried to speak but couldn't manage it, and Scott set off at a good pace followed by Zoe. As they came to the many gates across the path Zoe ran ahead and had them open for Scott to walk straight through without slowing.

"I know where Mr Brown's house is, I think you should ring for the doctor on your mobile, if he is in Ambleside he might even get to the house before us with a little luck," Scott told Zoe as she ran back and forth opening and closing gates, and moving any obstacles from his path such as broken branches from the trees due to the recent high winds and rain. *His* voice was now little more than a gasp, as he was still hurrying as much as he could, and even the weight of this slight woman was beginning to take its toll over such a long distance, and of necessity Scott changed his hold on his burden into a fireman's lift, moving Charlotte slowly onto his left shoulder, and he was able to pick up his pace slightly.

Zoe made the call to the local doctor, and then ran passed Scott and her mother, to open the gate to Park House, and then she moved around the back of the house, and Scott followed wondering why they hadn't gone in through the front door. Scott rested to get his breath leaning against the open door and holding Charlotte's head with one hand to make sure that he didn't bump into anything, and then followed Zoe into a bedroom where he placed his gasping burden on the bed. He was very relieved that they had not encountered many visitors to the area walking the coffin route because of the weather!

Zoe was riffling through a bedside cabinet, and as soon as she found the spray she put her arm around her mother and Scott opened Charlotte's mouth, as Zoe sprayed the back of her mother's throat. Scott propped some pillows behind the woman, and stared at the daughter for the first time. She really was worth looking at even though she was quite out of breath and anxious about her mother. She was about five foot four, slim and agile, had vivid blue eyes and dark blonde hair and at least for the moment she was totally unaware of herself or him, as she gave all her attention to her sick mother.

"You can leave your mother with me, go and keep a look out for the doctor," Scott instructed briskly.

"If you think I should, I'll go and open the back door," Zoe said, taking her hand from her mother's damp forehead. Her breathing seemed to have improved, but only slightly.

"Use the front door, it's nearer, and if Neil Brown has any objections send him to me," Scott said imperiously, realising for the first time that Charlotte's room was on the ground floor, and he wondered where her daughter slept in this apparently Victorian household, probably in the attic!

He realised that she was a very caring girl, and he really hoped that the mother would recover very quickly. He compared this young girl to the one he had gladly returned to this country to see, and the circumstances in which he had found *her* had shocked him to the core, but he caste aside this memory, and concentrated on the way the young girl was with her mother. He was very touched, and he now told her to stay with her mother as *he* would await the doctor on the front step!

This he did, and soon ushered in the doctor, who took a while examining his patient, and then he found Scott, and thanked him for his timely intervention, which had probably saved the woman's life. When the doctor returned to the patient Scott left the house, to make his way back to the coffin of his father, and the men waiting for him.

Vaguely he realised that he was worried about the woman, but mostly because of her daughter. However, now that the doctor had taken charge he was free to undertake the unpleasant task of getting his deceased father to St. Oswald's in Grasmere in order that *his* wishes would be fulfilled in the next few days. The rain which had ceased whilst Scott was carrying the woman home, now started again and he felt a sudden paroxysm of grief, for the last ten minutes or so he had *forgotten* his father! He hurried to catch up with his fellow bearers. It was *his* father in that coffin, and he had been called away, *he ought* to be with his father on his last journey. He arrived at the coffin resting stone and realised that the men had obviously been waiting a while, by the number of fresh cigarette ends that were strewn about the area. He was disgusted and started to pick up the cigarette ends, and then realised he would not mention this to the other bearers, as they were after all carrying to the church a loved and missed colleague or good friend, and were probably missing Elliott Scott Peterson, almost as much as was he! They must have decided to carry on without him. He slumped onto the coffin stone in despair, was there anything he could get right during this traumatic part of his life. He was twenty six, and felt like a raw youth, unable to cope with everything, and his head was beginning to ache with the stress of it all.

"Scott, please wait, you didn't give me a chance to thank you for what you've done for mother. Please wait I really need to talk to you," Zoe was running along the ancient pathway to try to get to him to thank him for saving her mother, and he was glad, as he too needed someone. She came close to him, and stopped and slipped on a moss covered stone. He caught her and held her close as she clung to him, both were soaked to the skin with the heavy rain, but for the moment they were almost unaware of their surroundings, as in this location at this particular time in their lives they were completely alone, and each of them needed someone desperately for different reasons. Scott because of his grief following the death of his father, and his cynical beliefs regarding his time in Afghanistan and his shock at his girlfriend's recent shocking behaviour, and Zoe for very similar reasons and her sick and unhappy mother. They both needed the comfort that the other gave with a growing desperation, without a thought that they might not see each other again, or failing that, that they might meet again and that would be even less palatable than the alternative!

CHAPTER THREE

After the funeral, Scott spent a couple of weeks with his sister Adele and her family at their farm High Stile, and arranged to have Oak Tree Farm cleaned and closed up until his return from the Army. He had left everything belonging to his father just where it was, and he hoped that he could tackle the sorting out of belongings and papers upon his return. John Simpson had already moved any stock on the farm across to High Stile farm across the valley, and he had agreed to keep an eye on things until Scott's return.

Adele's real interest in the business with her husband was the Riding Stables which adjoined their farm High Stile. She had been running the stables herself before they were married, and had always maintained that she would *never* marry a farmer, and it had taken a tumble from her horse, when John had come running to her aid, for her to change her mind and her life. Now they had two wonderful sons Elliot and John junior.

Adele was very annoyed with the friend who worked for her, Samantha Brown, who had taken a week off without informing her! Adele was doubly surprised, because a few weeks ago Samantha could hardly wait for Scott to return home on leave, she had talked of nothing else since Scott's last leave. Before Scott had joined up, Samantha and he had been good friends, and as he was going to be away for long stretches of time, they had decided to put their relationship on hold. On Scott's last leave they had become very close again, and Adele was mystified as to why Samantha had suddenly decided to disappear now that Scott was home! Her note said 'a week,' but at the end of that week there was still no sign of her.

Scott's gear was all packed and he was waiting for a taxi to take him to the station. Adele had insisted that she would take him, but he now came to find her in the stables, where she was trying to arrange for the two young stable girls to take over from her for an hour.

"Scott is it time to go, I won't be a minute," Adele said obviously stressed out with trying to arrange cover whilst she took him to Windermere. "I'm sorry, but Samantha taking off like she did has left me very short handed, and I am very disappointed in her acting the way she is, not being reliable and not bothering to get in touch."

"Don't worry about it Adele, I've ordered a taxi and have just come to say goodbye, as it will be here soon." He pondered for a short while looking at his sister's harassed face, and realised that when it had happened a few weeks ago he had thought he was devastated, but now he realised that it was just as well things had happened as they had. He was a free agent, and he liked the feeling, it was almost as though he had been released from something unpleasant. Their relationship, his and Samantha's, had been quite satisfying at the time, but he didn't feel as though he had lost anything. "I think I can give you a little explanation as to why Samantha might have been so uncooperative." Scott said with a twisted cynical smile.

"What, are you saying that Samantha told you she was going to take time off, and why, I am the one that has to provide cover for her, it's not on Scott?"

"Not exactly Adele, but I did decide to *surprise her* when I found I had a little time free because Daniel Sharpe had come to spend time with Dad just before he died," Scott said enigmatically.

"Samantha has done nothing but talk about you since you were sent home from Afghanistan. I know you and she have something going on between you. Did you surprise her?"

"Not as much as she *surprised me*! I came into the stables and couldn't see her for a moment, and then I saw her startled eyes looking at me from a pile of hay. She was looking at me over the bare shoulders of one of your middle aged clients and was presumably, quite satisfactorily pinned to the floor, as I guess he comes here quite often! Well often enough to get to know her very well indeed. I didn't recognise him from behind and he was far too involved to notice my presence, but he was certainly enjoying the ride."

Adele suddenly sat down on one of the grooms' steps, as she gazed with wide eyes and open mouth at her brother. He must have been shocked and devastated but now he was making a joke of it!

"Oh Scott I'm so sorry, I had no *idea* that Samantha, well you know, I didn't think she was that sort of girl."

"Well luckily Samantha seemed to have a good idea of how to *please* your client or clients. It is up to *you* what you do about your staff, dear sister, when and if she returns. I won't be waiting around to see her, and you never know, she might be in *love* with the man, if he is the *only one*," Scott finished cynically, and then suddenly seemed quite startled by what he had said!

As Adele looked into his eyes she was sure that after the first shock, he was not *at all* interested in his ex-girlfriend's work *or pleasure* activities. But she couldn't set aside the information that had come her way - that she should keep an eye on her *brother*, who might be suffering more than he thought with regard to injuries sustained in the last few months. As he was going back to the army that would be *their* problem for the next few months, or until he finished his time with them. He certainly would not expect, or want his sister's interference.

Scott opened his arms and Adele moved into them for a hug.

"Please Scott don't forget to write, ring, text or email, and let me know where you are and what you are doing. I do hope they give you a clean bill of health. If not, come straight back home, there's more than plenty for you to be doing here and at Oak Tree Farm. You haven't touched Dad's things yet, have you?"

"No, there's plenty of time for that sister dear, you look after John and the boys, and don't worry about me." He turned and left her before she started to cry, or *he* became a bit of a wimp. For some reason he felt there was something he must do, some unfinished business he had to attend to, but other than the girl Zoe introduced to him at the funeral by Daniel Sharpe who had erupted into his previously straight forward life, he thought he had kept all bases covered.

The taxi arrived at the station twenty five minutes later, and he realised the train was in, and he had to get a move on, luckily he had a return ticket and could board straight away. The train seemed to be full to bursting, and he wondered where he could stash his kit bag. He saw one seat free, the three other seats around the table were taken, and he pushed his way through and sat down, placing his kit bag across his knee. Luckily there was no ticket on the back of the seat proclaiming that it was reserved. He now endeavoured to push the kit bag under the seat, and looked apologetically at the window seat, and went still with shock. The blue eyes staring back at him were equally shocked and she seemed to have difficulty breathing.

"Mr er Peterson, are you returning to the Army?"

"Yes, as you can see, Miss er Howes?"

"Zoe, as I think you know."

"Just as you know my name is Scott, as it seems ridiculous to say Mr and Miss after what happened," he stopped speaking, feeling stupid for *reminding* her of *his* stupidity!

"I thought it was tacitly understood that some things are better forgotten, I thought we were agreed on that, even if nothing had been said." Zoe replied, and rather than look at him as she felt she could not at the moment, she looked out of the window without seeing the countryside passing by, but totally aware of the man sitting beside her!

"I have been intending to apologise, so much has happened and it is difficult to explain." Scott said evenly, wondering why he was acting like a young boy instead of the man he was, and fully aware that he had thought about this young woman just about every day or night since he had met her!

"No apology is needed, as I have already said, we were both at fault for different and private reasons. And I must just say again, thank you for helping my mother." Zoe never turned her head from gazing unseeing out of the window.

Scott wished she would turn towards him he wanted to know what colour her eyes were at this very moment. However, she plainly wanted nothing to do with him. He felt pressure building up inside him, as he wanted to say so much, but did not have a clue how to do it. She looked really lovely and he wondered why she was on the train.

"Are you travelling far?" He asked, trying to say something normal and hopefully put them both more at ease with each other.

"To Lancaster, I am studying there," she said quietly.

"What are you studying?" He really wanted to know!

"English literature and language."

"I studied, well that's a long story." Scott said and laid back and closed his eyes, as she obviously was very embarrassed to see him, and he wanted to make things as easy as possible for her, as he was certainly aware of her youth and *inexperience*.

He could hear her breathing, and now and again she gave a little sigh, but she was finding it difficult to sit still, she seemed troubled, as indeed so was he! He relaxed after about fifteen minutes, as he was very glad to be sitting next to her, and as far as he knew, he might never see her again, or sit next to her again. He opened his eyes and glanced at her but she was still gazing out of the window, and he wondered if she could see his reflection, because he could! This was ridiculous, but how could they converse on the train, there was too much to say, and not enough time or privacy to say it! Why was he leaving today, why had he not searched her out, as he knew where she lived with her mother, for at least some of the time?

"Is you mother well again," he asked at last.

"She is doing quite well, but the angina comes and goes, but both of us are very grateful to you for your help." Now she turned towards him, and he didn't want to look away. "If you will excuse me, I must get ready, as I am leaving the train in a couple of minutes," Zoe said, and seemed reluctant, as he stood and moved into the aisle for her to pass. She looked up and he realised she needed to get something from the locker above, and he opened it and when she indicated a bag, he lifted it down for her, and it was really quite heavy, probably full of books. He wanted to look into her blue eyes so that he could remember them whilst he was away, and their glances held for an awkward moment.

He stood beside her as the train was slowing for Lancaster Station. People were pushing passed them, and at the last moment she stood on tiptoe and reached up to kiss him on the cheek, and he was mesmerised and could smell her very pleasant but subtle perfume, and wished he had moved so that the kiss landed on his mouth.

"Thank you again, and please keep *safe* and well," she said quickly, and her hand held his upper arm tightly, and then she moved off along the carriage.

He was in the way of other people, but he didn't care, as he watched her move out of the carriage, glad for once that he was tall. She soon disappeared amongst the thronging people on the platform, and he felt a strange twist or tugging sensation in his chest which he had never felt before. Just for a second he wondered if *he* should also vacate the train. Zoe Howes had been a revelation to him, she seemed so honest, and not for one moment had she tried to put the blame onto him for what had so suddenly erupted between them. It had been so very unexpected, devastatingly needful, and somehow inevitable.

CHAPTER FOUR

Zoe in a kind of daze somewhat reluctantly returned to the flat which she shared with three other girls. They were good company, and she was glad when Emily was in, and she received a pleased welcome. Emily had no home to go to at weekends and holidays, except for an elderly aunt, who was pleased to have a visit but she had never asked Emily to stay with her for more than an odd weekend. Zoe regretted that as her own mother 'lived in' with the arrogant and sometimes beastly 'Cruella de *Neil*' (as Zoe had christened him remembering The Lady and the Tramp) and Zoe was only allowed to visit her mother on sufferance, as she would have loved to invite Emily to go home with her.

Emily turned from her computer screen after saving her work. "Did you have a good time with your mother, and is she any better?"

"Yes, she had a very bad episode whilst I was there, but she is fine now."

"I was hoping for something exciting, as I have been really bored out of my skull for the last few days," Emily said grumpily. When she was happy she was a very pretty girl, but just at the moment she had not taken any pains with her appearance, only expecting to see her friend Zoe, and her hair looked as if it needed a good brush, and a dash of lipstick might have helped her appearance.

Zoe nodded with a slight smile, and went to switch on the kettle. She was feeling ashamed of her recent behaviour and was not about to share her thoughts with her friend, but now she was back in the flat, and having her work to attend to she was hopeful that she would now get some sleep, not waste her time wondering *if only*, and get on with her studies. After running up such a bill it would be disastrous if she didn't get a good degree at the end of it!

The other two girls arrived at the flat, and they all worked hard for the next two months, and they were all looking forward to Christmas. Now the nights were dark the girls spent a lot of time together, with just the odd night when other friends joined them for the odd glass of wine, and in some cases *whine*. Zoe was particularly pleased when Jennifer and Mary, sisters from Richmond in Yorkshire, asked Emily home with them for the festive season. When the girls had left, she was tidying up the flat before going to get her train to Windermere. She glanced at the calendar and thought what a good thing it was that they all recognised the handwriting of the other three. It was scribbled on from top to bottom, and it was just as well that a new year would be coming in very soon.

She suddenly grabbed for a kitchen stool, and managed to sit down on it. She gazed intently at the calendar and was grateful that the other girls had already left the flat. She suddenly walked in a daze towards the sister's room, and started to search through the bedside drawers. She was aware that they were quite sexually active both having steady boyfriends, and she managed to find what she needed and could later replace it with a new one!

Fifteen minutes later she was in a quandary as she waited for the result of the test, she couldn't make up her mind what she really wanted the test to show, whatever the answer was it had been determined over two months ago! It was positive, and she felt shocked and worried. The morning after pill which she had taken, must have been taken too late as she had been looking after her mother who was confined to bed. Also *Cruella de* Neil had been most officious and unpleasant, although Zoe had been running around after his needs most of the day *and caring* for her mother!

Two hours later as she travelled along towards Windermere in the train, the wheels seemed to be saying 'three months pregnant, three months pregnant' in a never-ending chant, mocking her and the strange thoughts she was having about the father of her child. She thought she was probably over the time to be able to have an abortion and she didn't even check that fact, and she believed the decision had been made for her! What was worrying her was how could she tell her mother? How could she finish her studies, and work to pay off the thousands of pounds worth of debt that she would have run up by the end of her pregnancy, and look after a child? Other young mother's did it, and she started to wonder if there was a nursery at the university!

Her eyes filled with tears of frustration, she must concentrate on herself, her mother and the baby, and stop wondering if

Scott Peterson was safe and well in Afghanistan. Presumably he could have stayed at home as he had, apparently, already been injured and sent home. Selfish pig! No she didn't really mean that, she didn't know what she meant! There was no way that she could tell her mother who the father was, it would show both herself and him in such a bad light, they had only met twice, and seen each other once on the train, days after the burial ceremony of his father! One thing she knew for certain was that he had ruined her future, because she did not, or would not want, any other man!

As she left the train in Windermere she saw Daniel Sharpe, a good friend of her mother's. He was a good man probably in his fifties and had brown sympathetic eyes, but just at the moment she could not bring herself to see anyone. She ran to the bus stop, and luckily a bus was ready to leave. She had to walk from Ambleside to Rydal, and sighed with relief when she arrived at the house where her mother worked. Even the garret room under the eaves of the house would be very welcome, and somewhere she could hide away and lick her wounds, God she was pathetic!

She went around to the back of the house as usual, and was very surprised when the door was locked, and so she went around to the front to ring the doorbell. It was now dark, and she hoped it would be her mother opening the door to her and not her employer Neil Brown!

In fact, Zoe was surprised when the door was opened by a young woman. She spoke good English but with a strong east European accent. Fancy Mr Brown getting help in the house, help had been needed for years, and she was relieved that her mother was now getting some help!

"Yes, what do you want," was the unhelpful enquiry.

27

"I have come to stay with my mother the housekeeper."

She was however shocked when she could not gain admittance as apparently this *girl* was now the housekeeper, and she was not aware *of anyone's* daughter coming to stay!

Zoe was mystified and in shock, what was going on! Eight years her mother had worked for the unpleasant Neil Brown, where could she be, as the young woman did not even register the name Charlotte Howes! She calmly closed the door and turned the key in the lock, concluding the interview. Zoe felt really hurt and angry, and lifted her fist to bang on the door, and then changed her mind.

The only person she could think of who might know the whereabouts of her mother, was Daniel Sharpe, but she had seen him on Windermere station and hidden herself away from him, too ashamed to make herself known, and now he was the only person to whom she could turn. If Daniel Sharpe was not home then she would have to ring the police, as something must have happened to her mother! She truly hoped that Daniel had not gone away on the train on which she had travelled to the Lake District - that would be just her luck!

The outside lights were on at Sharpe House, and she truly hoped that he was home, but perhaps they left on the lights just to make anyone passing think the house was occupied! She ran up to the door and urgently pressed the bell.

She heard Daniel's pleasant dark brown voice, and sighed with relief. The door opened and she was bathed in light and she blinked, whether with the light or because her eyes were stinging with suppressed tears, she wasn't sure.

"Zoe, thank goodness, please come inside," Daniel said taking her rucksack from her, and closing the door behind her.

"Mr Sharpe, do you know where mother is, I've been to Mr Brown's, and the young woman who answered the door had never heard of Charlotte Howes, how can that be?"

"Your mother was taken into hospital again, and she didn't want to worry you. Anyway, she wouldn't let me get in touch with you. When she returned from hospital, her bags were all packed and in the garden shed, together with a black plastic bag of your things. I brought her here to stay, and my cousin came over too, so that nobody would talk. Now that you are here my cousin Janette will be glad to get back home, as she often looks after her grandchildren. Earlier I came to the station to pick you up from the train, but I must have missed you." Daniel said putting Zoe in the picture, and relieved that she had now turned up at his home, as her mother had become very anxious. And she Zoe, had not wanted Daniel to see her at the station, how stupid was she!

A woman probably in her sixties came into the hallway, and smiled a welcome to Zoe. "I'm Daniel's cousin Janette, come on let me have your bag, and I'll show you to your room its all ready for you, and then I'll take you in to see your mother." Janette said thoughtfully, and then took Zoe's arm as she threatened to burst into tears. "Come on let's go in to your mother right now, I think that would be best. Try not to worry so much, your mother is doing quite well, and you are very welcome here with Daniel and me, there is nothing for you to worry about, the best thing for your mother is that you just make yourself at home here."

CHAPTER FIVE

Zoe followed Janette up the wide stairs from the hallway, and into a beautifully furnished large room at the front of the house. Her mother was sitting on a chair beside the bed, and looked better than Zoe had seen her for a long time. The room was comfortably carpeted, and the curtains on the tall windows were obviously tailor made for the room, with an elegant pelmet and tie backs. Zoe could see the evening light shining on Rydal Water, and it was slowly disappearing as the setting sun went behind Loughrigg fell and the Langdale Pikes.

"Don't look so worried Zoe love, I have just got ready for bed, and I have been up and dressed for part of the day. Daniel kindly insisted that I should move in here, and he is adamant that there is room for you too when you come home at weekends and holidays, he *insists* that this is now our home, and I cannot believe how kind and thoughtful he is. I'm afraid Mr Brown does not require a housekeeper who is ill part of the time, and I can't blame him. At least during the eight years I was there you were able to finish *most* of your education, and most of the jobs that I couldn't do!"

"Oh Mum, I'll have a look around and see if I can find us a flat or something, and I will have to travel to Uni every day." Zoe said wondering how this could be arranged, because she really didn't want to take advantage of Daniel Sharpe's kindness. They would have to pull their weight, as Daniel had already said that his cousin was anxious to get back home to enable her to help look after her grandchildren. He didn't need a housekeeper as he had a cleaner who came in twice a week, and Zoe was already aware of this from earlier conversations with their kind benefactor. He was a very kind and old-fashioned man in a way, who else would have thought of getting his cousin to chaperone them in this day and age. Her mother had worked for Mr Brown living in and no-one had made anything of that situation. But then most of the people hereabouts knew Mr Brown by his unpleasant reputation. For the moment Zoe was pleased to accept Daniel's offer of accommodation because her mother really needed to be settled so that she might get well again, but she was determined that they would not take advantage of his kindness for too long.

At the end of the following week, Janette returned to her family, after saying fond farewells to Charlotte and Zoe, and her cousin. She had overseen the preparation of most of the Christmas fare, and left realising that both Charlotte whose health was much better and her daughter Zoe, could manage perfectly well.

In actual fact it was the best Christmas that Zoe could remember. Her mother seemed to blossom with Daniel's kindness to them both, and she was grateful that Zoe had also been made welcome in the home of her friend for the last eight years. The best part of it had been that Zoe had been left to decorate the Christmas tree bought from a local garden centre, and also to choose a number of new decorations, together with a new set of tree lights, it was a first and she really enjoyed herself as the Christmas spirit seemed to be all around them!

Daniel had a lot of Christmas cards, and together with the few that Charlotte and Zoe received from friends, they created a very festive atmosphere, or maybe it was just that they were all happy and not used to that feeling! Zoe also thought about Emily and was really pleased that Jennifer and Mary had invited her to join their family for Christmas.

Zoe had now stopped worrying quite so much about taking up Daniel's time and his home. He seemed really happy, and even invited some of his friends in for drinks on Boxing Day. One of those families John and Adele Simpson, and their two boys, Zoe really liked and hoped she might see more of them.

As her mother was so obviously very happy, Zoe did not inform her of her own news, which she would not be able to keep to herself much longer. She already felt some of her clothes were getting slightly tight and uncomfortable. She had worked out that the baby would be due in June, and she made an appointment with the local doctor after the New Year festivities, and he confirmed what she already knew.

Zoe was to accompany her mother to the hospital in Kendal for a consultation with her Consultant, and she was able to make an appointment for her first scan which was, of course, overdue. She decided that would be a good time to tell her mother, and they would be in the *right place*, if the shock was too much for her! She was much more worried about how Daniel Sharpe would take the news because he had even asked his cousin to chaperone himself and Charlotte!

As it turned out, Charlotte *was* very surprised, but also very intrigued, and when she saw the photograph of the scan, she was very happy and excited at the thought of becoming a grandmother, but Daniel was very *surprised* as he was aware that Zoe was a sensible girl, and did not believe she slept around, but when he saw how pleased Charlotte was he seemed to accept the inevitable. Although being so morally strict it was hard for him at first, but he made the effort for his friend Charlotte as he had never seen her happier.

During the next six months Zoe kept on with her studies, and she saw her mother blossom from the quiet and unassuming woman she had been after her husband had left her. The divorce had come as a shock to her and since that day her confidence had disappeared almost entirely. Now in Daniel's company she was a different woman. Zoe had high hopes that they would get together eventually, and was really pleased when her first visitors to the hospital after the birth of her son whom she named Joss, were her mother and Daniel Sharpe. It wasn't until she spent time with the other young mothers that she realised how lucky she had been to have such an easy pregnancy and birth! She was also overcome with the love she felt for her son together with the smell, the sight and feel of him when she first held him in her arms. She could not believe how protective and bursting with emotion she felt in those first few days, and it was only because she was so busy looking after her son that she felt able to carry on with her usual life. She tried without much success to put any thoughts of Scott Peterson out of her mind, as she would probably never see him again.

After four weeks she resumed her studies, and missed her son every day she was parted from him, although she was aware that Daniel and Charlotte between them took great care of him.

Joss was three months old when he finished his bottle of milk, and suddenly stared up into his mother's eyes, and it was a shock to her system as she recognised those eyes as identical to those of his father. Her heart thumped and she looked around quickly, but there was nobody else there to see, and she wondered if anyone else, who was even slightly acquainted with Scott, would notice the likeness. However, this was unlikely as according to Daniel, his deceased friend's son was not due back for another year at least, and she breathed a sigh of relief, and decided that by that time she together with her mother and son would be long gone from the area.

Charlotte Howes and Daniel took Zoe and Joss out for an early dinner. Joss was quite well behaved now he was nearly into his second year, and once or twice they had been out for a meal in a restaurant. Today was different because Charlotte had at last agreed to marry Daniel, and when they informed Zoe of their news, she found it hard to take in. However, they were so very happy and she hoped that now her mother felt more confident she was ready to take a step forward with her life. Zoe now found out that Daniel had *often* asked her mother before, but until now she had not felt ready to enter the matrimonial state for a second time.

Zoe had finished her degree course, and was in the market for a job, preferably teaching, but in the meantime, she was taking on any jobs that came along. She had to start paying for her keep, and as soon as possible start paying off her rather large student debt.

It was the following Sunday afternoon, when Zoe and Joss arrived home after spending a very happy afternoon with one of Joss's friends and family, that Daniel met them at the front door and immediately Zoe knew that something was terribly wrong. Without waiting for Daniel to say anything she took Joss to his room, where he started to play quite happily. She walked back down the wide stairway, and followed Daniel into the drawing room. Daniel was sitting on an easy chair with his head in his hands, and she realised he was quietly crying.

"What's wrong Daniel, where's mother?" Her heart was beginning to sink, and she wanted to rush to hold her son to her, but Daniel needed her just at the moment.

"I'm so sorry Zoe, just after you left your mother had a massive heart attack, and I got the paramedics, but they couldn't help. The ambulance came and took your mother to hospital, but it was too late." Daniel said sorrowfully, and stood and opened his arms as Zoe moved into them, as much for his comfort as for her own.

"She managed to speak to me, and say she loved me." He gulped, "and I made her a promise that I would look after you and Joss. I need you both Zoe, as I've never been happier than when you and Charlotte moved in here."

"Oh Daniel, poor Joss he is too young to understand. His granny loved him so much. I'm so sorry that your happiness with Mum has been cut short. I've never seen her happier, and *you* did that for her."

"I promised her I would look after you both and I will, but the only way I think I can do that properly, is if you will marry me then I can protect and look after you both. Then I will have Joss to inherit this lovely house, as I have no close family left."

Zoe suddenly sat down in a chair, with her hand at her throat, was she mad, and why had she immediately thought of Scott. She hadn't managed to forget him, as she looked into his eyes every day, every time she looked at Joss! Her heart twisted in her chest as she thought of her mother, who had lived with an unhappy marriage, and when she found the right man, she had so little time with him, and none in a biblical sense. She was certain of this as Daniel was a wonderful man, but so very straight-laced and moral which had been proved with his care of her mother, even getting his cousin to chaperone them. She really grieved for the happiness that Daniel and her mother could have had if her mother had accepted his proposal earlier. She knew both she and Daniel would miss her mother every day, and regret the fact that she had been looking forward to being with Daniel, and having at last a real family around her.

Zoe knew that her mother's savings would possibly pay for the funeral, but that was all. What was she to do, she must work to pay off her debts, look after her son, and she couldn't just leave Daniel who had been so very good to her mother, her son, and herself.

"I've rung my cousin Janette, and she will be coming over to stay until after the funeral. You can't stay here full time Zoe, unless we get married. It is for the best."

"You have *Janette* and her family Daniel, so you have *family* who could inherit."

"They are well provided for, and your mother was to become my much loved wife, and you would not have objected to her getting this house, she loved it and deserved it. Besides that Joss has never known anywhere else, and it is bad enough for him that his grandmother will not be here, without having to move. My name Daniel is Hebrew for God is my Judge, and I could never live in sin even in the eyes of our good or bad neighbours who *know* us."

"I presume by the 'bad' you mean Neil Brown, but for now I must think, and first I must say goodbye to my mother, as for many years there was only the *two* of us." She tried to smile for Daniel's benefit because the last thing she wanted was to hurt him in any way.

CHAPTER SIX

Zoe tried very hard in the next three days to get a flat or even a couple of rooms in the immediate area and then she could stay near to Daniel, who had been like a father to her. There was nothing available and if there had been one, the letting agent had informed her that she would have to pay the first month in advance, *and* provide a bond of £600. She badly needed a teaching post at once preferably with a nursery attached, and very well paid at that, as she also had to repay her student loan, although she knew that would not be necessary just yet, but she hated owing money to anyone.

On the morning of her mother's funeral, Zoe found Janette in the kitchen washing up the breakfast dishes. She joined her and started to dry the dishes.

"Janette, has your cousin told you of the strange idea he has formed with regard to mine and Joss's future?"

"You mean that he has suggested he should marry you so that you and Joss can live here?"

"Yes, of course, I can't do that Janette he has promised to leave the house to us, well Joss really. People will think it very odd if I marry him, when he was about to marry my mother!"

"Joss's father, is he likely to come back on the scene, are you expecting to see him again? As I am sure that you must know who it is, according to Daniel you have never played the field?" Janette said finishing wiping the sink down, and then turning to lean against it with her arms folded, and her kind eyes enquiring but not as embarrassed as were Zoe's!

"Janette, I have only had a couple of *friends* who were boys, and then Joss's father *very* briefly, and I don't expect to see him again as he left before I knew I was pregnant, and it was a mistake and that will never happen again. I don't see why I can't lodge here, and help Daniel with the loss of my mother, the house and garden, and get a part time job."

"You are missing the point Zoe, as Daniel will not have you living in the house because people would talk, and that is the last thing that he would want. He has always taken pride in his good reputation and lifestyle, and I *can't* stay here indefinitely as I have my own family to look after."

"I'll just have to leave Daniel and this lovely home, the council will have to house me and Joss, until I can get a good job," Zoe said with tears in her eyes.

"And you would break Daniel's heart, he has made a solemn promise to your mother to look after you both, and he wants to do just that. Would you take his money if he offered it to you Zoe, and leave?"

"No of course not Janette, he is a wonderful man and I love him like a father."

"And he loves you like a daughter, and Joss like a grandson, he has only us distant relations, and he has never had someone to share his home before, and he is really happy sharing it with you and Joss, I can tell, and he truly loved your mother and will miss her terribly."

"But *why* must we marry, what does it matter what anyone else says? I have always thought I would marry, but for love, not just for convenience," Zoe said, and accepted the paper handkerchief passed to her by Janette to wipe her eyes.

"It matters to Daniel, as you well know. He promised your mother he would look out for you and Joss, just let him do it *his* way Zoe. What else are you going to do, little Joss loves it here and he also loves Daniel."

"But I don't think I can take advantage of him like that Janette, I'll have to struggle on somehow."

"Perhaps if I tell you something in confidence Zoe, you will be able to at least consider things, and then make up your mind." Janette said, and put on the kettle to boil, "we'll have a nice cup of tea."

Zoe and Daniel were married by special licence at the Registry Office in Kendal, three weeks after they had walked up passed Alcock Tarn with young Joss to scatter his grandmother's ashes in the bracken which overlooked Rydal Water and Grasmere, and Zoe had broken down and sobbed her heart out as Daniel walked Joss a short distance away. What she really mourned was the wasted years when she and her mother had just managed to exist, and then her mother had enjoyed such a *short time* with Daniel and Joss, both of whom her mother had loved dearly. She gazed at the roses that Daniel had cut from the garden and made into a small posy to leave beside the ashes. He was a wonderful man, and she would do her very best to see that he enjoyed a good and fulfilling life with his new family. Late one sleepless night, watching the moonlight on the lake, Zoe had come to the conclusion that to marry was the right thing to do, both for the sake of her son and for Daniel. She had briefly known how it *could* be between a man and a woman, but only because she had been going through a really bad time in her life, and she had not been alone in that. Now she was determined to make Daniel as happy as she possibly could, because she knew that it was the best thing she could do for him and most of all for Joss.

The months passed happily at Sharpe House, and at first Zoe had wondered if things might become difficult with Daniel, because of her likeness to her mother and their proximity, but never was she made to feel wary or unhappy. She was treated as the daughter she would have been, and she relaxed, but wondered if Daniel had ever been married, as he was a man in his late fifties, so that certainly was possible.

She found a nursery where Joss could mix with children of his own age, and she started to look for a job in earnest, as she was determined to pay off her student loan herself, without any help from Daniel. Unfortunately the local teacher training college in Ambleside had recently closed down due to the recession, and cut backs in funding. So there was nothing in the immediate area, and to teach younger children she would have to take a teacher training course, even with her degree.

There was only one thing that tarnished her newfound happiness, and that was overhearing a conversation about herself, in the Post Office. The conversation came as a surprise, having married Daniel she thought everyone would leave them alone. Apparently there were a few discussions in the immediate area where some people were of the opinion that

Daniel must be the father of her child as he had married her as soon as her mother had died! She was hard pressed to stop herself from answering this innuendo, but she decided it was nothing to do with these gossips, and she hoped none of this rubbish would reach Daniel's ears. He had promised her mother to take care of her and Joss, and this he was doing to the best of his ability.

A few weeks later Daniel came home from a ramble around the countryside, with what he hoped was good news for Zoe.

"Zoe, I called at the riding school to see my friend John, and he tells me that his wife Adele needs someone to help at the riding school in the office and greeting customers. If you really want to work as you keep telling me, what about that as an interim job. I'm sure the hours would coincide with the nursery hours. But even if they don't I could look after Joss."

"It sounds a good idea, I need to be working, and we can work something out about Joss," Zoe said thoughtfully. Daniel loved Joss, and Joss loved Daniel, but now that Joss was running around and some days going through the 'terrible twos' now that he had a mind of his own, she thought it might be too much for Daniel alone. But they could work something out to suit everyone she was sure, and if Daniel's friend and his wife had made the offer it must be because they thought she would 'do' or perhaps they were *desperate* for some help. When she had met them at Daniel's home on Boxing Day she had liked the Simpson family.

A couple of days later Daniel drove Zoe and Joss to the stables and reintroduced them to Adele Simpson, and then went off to look for John Simpson whilst waiting for them.

"I'm pleased to see you Zoe, please come inside I have just made a pot of tea," Adele offered, and led the way into the farmhouse. She was very surprised by the young and lovely girl whom Daniel had married. She had not been aware that he had married the young girl they had met at his home, and now meeting her again she seemed very young.

They all sat around the kitchen table, and Joss was at first shy and very quiet, but he gradually cheered up as he saw the puppy chewing something on the rug before the open fireplace, and looked at the shortbread biscuit in his hand.

"Give puppy biscuit?" he asked beguilingly, and Adele smiled at him, and then looked a little stunned and was quiet.

"No Joss, I don't think Mrs Simpson lets her boys feed the puppy," Zoe said surprised that Adele was so strict.

"No, I mean yes you may Joss, but eat most of it first, and just give Flash, that's the puppy's name, a little bit." Adele said and looked a bit bemused, as Joss quickly ate most of the biscuit with a big grin on his face. "It's a pity my boys are at school Joss, you would like them I'm sure, but they are five and six now and both at the infant school, or *big* school as they say when they move from nursery."

Half an hour later Adele waved off Zoe and her son, as they made their way to join Daniel beside the car. Everything had been arranged to suit all parties, and Zoe was really pleased, at last she would be earning and able to start paying off the student debt, as Daniel would not allow her to give him anything towards their keep in Sharpe House.

Adele had other things on her mind just at the moment, and wondered if she had done the right thing, but was now certain she needed to keep in touch with Zoe, and in particular young Joss.

She could hardly wait to speak to her husband John, but then decided that perhaps this was not the correct thing to do as he was very friendly with Daniel Sharpe, and she had to agree with her husband, they had never seen Daniel happier! Perhaps she was imagining things, she would wait and see if John came to the same conclusion when Zoe came to work for them, because she had agreed that Zoe should bring Joss with her when it was necessary.

CHAPTER SEVEN

Daniel was very pleased that Zoe obviously enjoyed her days spent at High Stile. She enjoyed taking the bookings for riding lessons, and helping in the farm office. Quite often at the end of the day she had to prise Joss away from the farm, because he loved the animals, particularly Flash the puppy, and also had made firm friends with Elliot and John junior. Although the boys were considerably older they were very patient with Joss, and also very good a keeping an eye on him near the animals. At first Zoe had insisted that he stayed in the office with her, but somehow that didn't seem to work very well, there was far too much that interested him outside! He was very good really, he was not allowed near the car park, or outside the farmyard and garden. John was very good at informing Zoe when she must keep him inside, if machinery and animals were being used or moved around.

Daniel really enjoyed being in Sharpe House now, especially when Zoe and Joss were there, but only on one or two occasions he had really enjoyed the silence that meant that Zoe was working and Joss with either with her or at nursery, and he was able to concentrate on his Telegraph crossword, and he could savour the quiet companionship that he had shared with Charlotte for such a short time. He had thought of Charlotte and her quiet yet unconditional love as a bonus for him late in life. Unfortunately April every year brought to mind just how much he had lost, as on the 12th April every year he remembered the riding accident that had caused the death of his friend Elliot Scott Peterson's much younger sister and his own beloved fiancé Nell. He still bore the scars from his endeavour to save her, and he and Elliot had spent many hours for the next two weeks at her bedside, before she had left them. Elliot had been devastated as he felt he was to blame for not being able to stop his younger sister by twenty years from riding the black gelding. She had been very headstrong and independent, and Daniel often wondered each year, if she had survived that accident then there would most probably have been something else to take her away from them! Only occasionally did he feel his true age which was now fifty five, and it was hard to believe how so many years had gone by so very quickly? He and Nell had had such plans, all of them exciting, mostly travelling the world, and then settling down to bring up a large family, but it was not to be.

Daniel looked at his watch and set his paper aside, he would drive over to High Stile to pick up Zoe and Joss, because usually she had rung to say she was ready by this time, it was almost five o'clock, and he would enjoy the short ride, as the spring evenings were slowly lengthening.

Zoe was finishing up the diary entries for riding school bookings, and keeping her eye on Joss who was drawing a picture of Flash, with both of them sitting on the floor of the office, but neither seemed able to keep very still! She noticed a taxi drawing up in the farmyard and assumed it was someone for the farm, as all the expected clients had already arrived. Her heart seemed to jump in her chest, and there was a thumping in her head, she felt hot and certainly bothered. Surely she was wrong, it couldn't be Scott Peterson, what was he doing here? She needed to sit down but dare not miss a second of what was happening outside! Her life for the last few months had been going along very pleasantly, so why had that feeling of complacent conformity to be so rudely set asunder?

"Mummy, Flash won't sit still hold him," Joss said grumpily, he was quite tired after being at the nursery, and now his mummy was ignoring him!

"Get your coat quickly Joss, we'll walk home tonight, let Flash go now," Zoe said hurriedly opening the door to let the puppy have the freedom of the farmyard.

"Not want coat Mummy."

Zoe picked him up, threw her shoulder bag back over her shoulder, picked up her own and Joss's coats, snapped the lock on the door, and together they set off home, with Joss dragging behind angrily as she had been forced to put him down as soon as they got outside. She pulled him along behind her, and then stopped to pick him up again and give him a cuddle.

"Sorry Joss darling," she hugged him and he put his arms satisfactorily around her neck, and gave her a wet kiss. "Can I have chocolate now?"

"You little imp, you're trying to manipulate me already, and you are not yet three years old."

"Maniplate chocolate," he said beguilingly.

"Chocolate, but only one piece after your tea."

Daniel pulled in to a stop at the sight of Zoe and Joss, just outside High Stile, and reached across opening the passenger door.

"Sorry did you ring, if so I missed the call?"

"No Daniel, I thought we'd walk, but thanks, I'll just put Joss in his seat." Zoe said, and fastened Joss in his seat in the back of the car quickly, and then got into the front passenger seat. She had found from experience that Joss was better without her beside him in the back, he settled down much more quickly. Daniel leaned back and tickled Joss in his tummy, and realised that Joss had been waiting for that as he laughed out loud, and Daniel drove off carefully with his new family around him.

"Daniel, the man that helped get my mother back to Mr Brown's when she couldn't breath, Mr Peterson's son I think, he came to the farm today, is he a keen rider or something?" Zoe asked. She had *seen* him when he helped her with her mother, she had seen him just for a moment at the funeral of his father, then on the train in his Army uniform, and she had hoped he had gone away for good. In view of his occupation she was really pleased that he was home and well, but now her pleasant and *safe* little world with Daniel and Joss seemed to have been turned upside down. With luck he was only back in the valley for a holiday!

"Oh is Scott back from Afghanistan, how wonderful. His sister must be so very happy and relieved, even if he is going to open up Oak Tree Farm." Daniel's voice had a happy smile in it, and Zoe now really started to worry.

"His sister? Afghanistan?" Zoe asked holding her breath, she hadn't *known* where he was going, but why would she?

"Yes, Adele of course, she is a couple of years older than Scott, and she married John about eight years ago."

"John Simpson!"

"Of course John Simpson, didn't you know?"

"Why would I, I'd never seen Adele except fleetingly at Mr Peterson's funeral and on Boxing Day, if you remember I went back to be with mother on the day of the funeral. Oh, I think Joss is sickening for something, I might keep him off nursery tomorrow, so I'll not be able to go to work," Zoe said quickly, she had to get her mind around this news, and she would rather not go to work tomorrow. She felt rather guilty because Joss really liked going to nursery.

"That's alright, I'm not doing anything, I'll look after Joss for the day," Daniel offered.

Zoe sank back in her seat, as she had a strong suspicion that Joss might make a very quick recovery by the morning. Not because she didn't trust Daniel to look after him, but because she thought Joss would be a handful if not allowed to go and join his friends at the nursery, being so fit and well!

Joss did go to nursery the next day, and Zoe was intent on finishing work early in order to look after him at Sharpe House, rather than High Stile Farm.

During the night Zoe had had very little sleep, and was awakened in the morning by Joss jumping on her bed. Daniel had been up with him for quite a while it transpired, and so after dropping him off at nursery Zoe was determined to get everything up to date at the office, and leave early to go to the nursery to pick Joss up herself. Only once did she see Scott, he came into the yard riding a large horse, and she was not surprised when it took *two* female and very young grooms to attend to him. Luckily he strode across the yard to the farmhouse without even one look towards the office, and she sighed with relief.

It was just before three o'clock when Adele, John and Scott were enjoying a cup of tea on the terrace, as the afternoon was balmy and quite warm for early spring. Adele was admiring the first flush of daffodils, and her gaze lifted and she looked with interest as she saw Zoe locking up the office and making her way out of the yard. She was almost transfixed as she watched her brother. He too was looking into the yard and had seen Zoe, and the fingers holding his tea cup almost turned white, and he placed his cup on the saucer with a little clatter, which also alerted John that something was amiss. Zoe looked tall and slim in her jeans and low heeled boots, with a sparkly T-shirt and a lightweight fleece over her shoulders.

"What is Zoe Howes doing at High Stile? Does she work here?" Scott asked with a frown.

"Do *you* know Zoe?" Adele asked replacing her cup carefully on saucer, trying to school her expression so that she didn't show how interested she was in his answer.

"Not really, I helped her with her mother when she was ill. At the time I was here for Dad's funeral. She was also at the funeral I believe, but I only saw her for a few seconds." Scott said with a frown furrowing his brow.

"Zoe does work in the office for us, she is very good at her job, but she is no longer Zoe Howes," John said thoughtfully. "She is now Zoe Sharpe. Quite soon after her mother died she married Daniel."

"Good Lord, he is old enough to be her father," Scott said finding it hard to believe what John had said.

"Yes well, but he is a very young fifty-five, and I've never seen him happier." John replied watching his brother-in-law carefully with a frown on his forehead and puzzled eyes.

"Well good luck to them both," Scott said in disgust. "I'm surprised she is bothering to work, Daniel must be quite well off, as I believe he retired early."

Adele was rather worried by the scowl on her brother's handsome face, and was disappointed because that made her think that she had been quite right in what she had surmised on the day she gave Zoe her job in the office!

"I don't believe she was after his money Scott, how could you think such a thing. She said she wanted the job to enable her to pay off her student loans herself, which I think were quite big because her mother wasn't even able to provide her daughter with somewhere to live, except at weekends."

"Did she finish her course, if so she could get a much better job than working in your office?" Scott sounded quite annoyed, and he had now also annoyed his sister!

"What is wrong with working here, she has a good job which she enjoys, and she is able to bring her son Joss with her after nursery when necessary," Adele said quickly sounding really aggrieved. She almost wished that Scott had moved straight into Oak Tree Farm, rather than staying here with them until the house had been cleaned and decorated as necessary.

"Where are you going Scott?" Adele said quickly as he moved away from the garden table, and moved off towards the office purposefully. So purposefully that he trod on a daffodil plant which also surprised and annoyed his sister.

"Oh no, it looks as though Zoe has forgotten her handbag it will have her mobile phone and keys in it." Adele watched as her brother arrived at the office door at the same time as Zoe.

"What do you mean 'oh no' what is wrong with you Adele," John said at a loss to understand what was going on.

"Sit back John, and I'll tell you what *I think*, and if I'm right things are in a hell of a mess," she replied, and he was worried by the apprehension he could see on his wife's face, besides that she never swore, even when the children with not with them!

CHAPTER EIGHT

The farm range-rover arrived, and stopped in the yard, where Elliot and John junior climbed out excitedly, and a few seconds later Joss was lifted out by the driver. Joss moved off into the garden with the Simpson boys, where they all grabbed a biscuit off the plate on the garden table, and then moved off to the rear of the house to play.

The driver shouted to Zoe informing her that he had brought Joss home from nursery as was usual, as she was standing in the doorway to the office after pulling out a key from her pocket to open the door.

Adele moved off to follow the three boys, giving her husband John a rueful look as he sat at the table looking shocked, then he settled down to wait as he saw Scott move slowly towards the office, what was said looked interesting, but he couldn't hear.

"We meet again Zoe Howes, although I understand it is Zoe Sharpe now? It appears you always move very fast when you get involved with someone, as you now have a son Joss with Daniel Sharpe, it's just as well I returned to the forces."

"One incident Scott Peterson, you can't build a life on one incident, and anyway I didn't know you were going away, nor can I remember you mentioning that I should *wait* for you!" Zoe was really angry, and upset at having to return to get her bag and keys, she should keep her mind on what she was doing, and now particularly, on what she was *saying*!

"I've never been described as in *incident* before. However, I was not in a position to ask *anyone* to wait for me at *that time*," Scott remembered how he had wanted to get off the train and follow her after she had kissed his cheek and told him to keep safe and well. But that would not have been right either!

"In the last three years I have been married, and have settled into this very nice job, and before you ask I *didn't know* Adele was your sister, and I need this job. And here *you* are ruining things for me and my son." She couldn't stand here talking to him, as he was just as she remembered, and with Joss's distinctive eyes!

"I have no intention of making you leave your employment as I understand you are very good at it. I will be back at Oak Tree Farm soon. But I will be visiting Adele, John and the boys, as she was my *sister* before she was your *employer*." He sounded and felt like a raw youth, and he put out his hand towards her, but then drew it back suddenly.

"We sound like children arguing. I'll do you a deal Scott, you keep out of my way, and I'll keep out of yours when you're visiting your sister and family. Why did you have to come back and remind me of my mistake, as I'd forgotten what happened between us?" She suddenly stopped speaking and tried not to look into his enigmatic and yet penetrating and coldly remote grey eyes.

"Liar," was all he said as he left the office, and walked off towards the field inhabited by the horses and leant against the fence with his elbows on the top rail. She was just as attractive as he remembered, but she now seemed fully grown up and confident!

Zoe's heart ached and seemed to twist, and she thought it was a feeling of guilt. She felt the pressure rising in her body and wanted to stamp her foot and shout, and took a deep breath.

She did neither, and quickly went to collect Joss who didn't *want* to be taken away from his friends, and they moved off down the lane towards the gate. Daniel was waiting in the car, and they moved off towards home, with Zoe apologising to her husband for forgetting her handbag, in which were her mobile phone and house keys and all the bits and pieces that young mothers and young boys need.

"Its fine Zoe, I just thought I'd come along anyway to pick you up, you have had a long day. You also seem rather frayed around the edges." His tone of voice sounded indulgent, and for the first time it annoyed her. She was becoming an ungrateful cow, and she didn't like herself very much!

"No I'm fine too Daniel. Joss didn't want to come home just yet, he was playing with Elliot and John junior," Zoe replied, and then wondered if she should have taken the opportunity to tell Daniel she wanted to finish her employment at High Stile! But he was aware how much she enjoyed her work there, and would probably require an explanation as to why she had suddenly changed! She felt a fool for believing that she had seen the last of Scott as he had been born in this valley, and his only family still lived here, of course he would return at some time, but she wished it had not been until Joss was much older. It was the very first time that she now wondered if marrying Daniel even for the sake of her son had been the right thing to do. But of course it was the right thing, as Daniel was really happy now, and seemed fulfilled, and was thankfully very well!

Zoe looked out of the window as the beautiful scenery passed by, Rydal Water, with still reflections of Loughrigg Fell perfectly calm except where dark cormorants dried their wings, and swans and geese slowly paddled leaving a wake behind them, totally at odds with her own feelings! She was familiar with the bird calls, which she could not hear now because the window was up and Joss was chattering to Daniel, and she worried that they would not be able to stay here in this beautiful countryside. Her main problem was not the fact that she was working at High Stile frequently with this being the home of Scott's sister Adele, it was the fact that Oak Tree Farm was less than half a mile from Sharpe House! She started to wonder what Scott had meant when he had said that he had been 'not in a fit state to ask anyone to wait for him.' Perhaps he was already married, which was very likely as he was not unattractive to *other* women, and he must be nearly as old as his sister Adele, and she must have been married to John at least for seven or eight years.

As soon as they arrived at Sharpe House, Zoe prepared and served the evening meal, after which Daniel retired to watch television, and Joss was bathed and put to bed. He always wanted a story and tonight Zoe lay on the bed beside him, and read to him, when she started to think of something else, he quickly told her 'wrong silly mummy', and she realised that he almost knew it by heart, and since meeting the puppy Flash at

High Stile, whenever she read the name of the tabby cat in the story, he would always say 'not Tabby mummy, Flash.' She rolled towards Joss and smoothed his hair with her hand, and felt a rush to protective love as she looked into his familiar smiling grey eyes, so like those of his uninformed daddy.

Her eyes filled with frustrated tears, why had everything become so complicated, and would Daniel, or even worse *Scott* suspect the truth, and if they did find out would *they* hurt as much as she was just now. It was her fault entirely!

Daniel was a wonderful kind man, and he had promised Charlotte to take care of her daughter and grandson, and that he had *done* in the only way he felt he could by marrying her to give her a home, and Joss an inheritance. Zoe wiped her eyes with a tissue, and kissed Joss again and left the bedroom, determined that Daniel should not find out that the father of her son, was the son of his friend and neighbour for as long as he could remember, and the result of a coming together which was hard to understand and difficult to forget. Zoe was determined to do as she had told Scott she already had, forget what had happened.

She went to say goodnight to Daniel who was now watching golf on his large screen television.

"Is there something you would like to watch Zoe, I don't mind switching over." Daniel smiled encouragingly.

"No thank you Daniel, I could watch upstairs. I think I'll have an early night."

"Good idea, you do seem more tired than usual. If Joss wakes up, don't you worry I'll attend to him," he said and she kissed his forehead as a thank you, and decided to leave him alone with his television. Tiger Woods was just putting for a par. "You'll be back on par tomorrow Zoe," Daniel finished with a smile. "And I am going to go up to the old quarry to have a look around tomorrow as the weather forecast is quite good, so you can take the car. Perhaps we should think about getting you one of your own?"

"Oh I don't think that's necessary Daniel, but thank you for the offer."

He was so very nice and good to her and Joss, but just for today she would have liked him to be unpleasant to her (not to Joss) but *she* would have deserved it, just for her thoughts!

The next morning Zoe supplied Daniel with a flask and sandwich for his lunch and he walked slowly up the fell road to the old quarry. It was a wide road, but it had become uneven and was not a comfortable ride, and he preferred to walk.

During her work day Zoe managed to get through without any contact with Scott and she started to relax, and after picking Joss up from nursery in the car she took him for a walk along the old coffin route, as it was his special walk, because he kept finding places where he pretended to find the tabby cat out of his book, and more often than not Flash the puppy. Strangely his favourite place was the hollow oak tree, in which he pretended to live with Flash and tabby cat. When they returned to Sharpe House Daniel had returned home, and he suggested that he should take both Zoe and Joss out for a meal. This had occurred from time to time, and Joss was now quite used to eating out, and was usually very good. Today he was anything but good, and Zoe and Daniel decided on only one course, and they were making their way to the car when Daniel saw John, Adele, Scott, and the two boys eating in the next room.

"Daniel you go and speak to them, Joss is really playing up, and I'll take him back to the car and wait for you." Zoe said quickly before Joss saw the boys, or they would have had considerable difficulty in getting him to go home! Her wayward heart had done its usual twist and painful tug on recognising Scott, she assumed mostly because she wanted to keep Joss away from him, and not because he looked devastatingly attractive in his lightweight grey suit and white shirt.

Daniel joined them in the car, and looked thoughtfully towards Zoe. "Guess what Zoe, I have the germ of an idea of what I would like to do with the quarry, and I'm going back up there tomorrow, and so you can have the car again."

"OK, thank you Daniel. Please remind me in the morning to make you some sandwiches and a flask to take with you, and please take your mobile phone with you just in case you are going to be late back," she smiled at him, because he didn't really like his mobile at all, and was always forgetting it, or forgetting to use it *if* he had it with him!

During the following morning whilst in the office, Zoe saw John driving out of the yard with his large tractor, and on the back Scott lounged comfortably, and she sighed with relief, hopefully they would be working at the other end of the farm. She began to realise that she hadn't a clue what they might be doing, sowing seed or something, or digging drains perhaps, anyway she was happy as she never saw them at all during the rest of her working day.

In the evening she noticed she had one missed call on her mobile, but something was wrong, as there was no number or name showing.

Joss was very overactive, and throwing his toys around which was not like him, and Zoe wondered if he had been eating too many sweets or chocolate, or was he just being unbearable this evening. She decided to take him for a walk, of course, that had to be along the coffin route to the hollow oak tree. As he played in the oak tree, Zoe sat and stared at the still reflections on Rydal Water, and watched the visitors to the area as they walked along the shore path. They were in small groups and couples, some with dogs, and some with excited children. Quite likely most of them had visited the cave (it was really a 'close head' (old working chamber) the floor of which was partly covered with water which seeped in from the hillside. Sometimes if was closed to the public if it was deemed to be unsafe, but it was exciting for the little ones to look inside, with their imaginations running riot. She smiled at the conversation going on inside the hollow tree and stood, as it was time they were getting back. Daniel must be back home, and would be wondering where they were, and she didn't want to worry him.

"Before you say anything, I was not *aware* that you were here," Scott's distinctive voice said quietly. Zoe had been looking down towards the oak tree and she literally jumped at the sound of a voice so near. She moved her eyes to the right to see a pair of scuffed walking boots, then lightweight jeans, and when she came up to the T-shirt, she didn't lift them any further, she would rather not meet his expressive grey eyes.

"Well don't let me detain you, I must get back home, enjoy your walk," she replied, looking towards Grasmere, hoping that Scott would continue with his walk, as Joss was still playing in the hollow oak tree, and praise be he was at the moment silent!

"I once apologised to you Zoe, as did you apologise to me, can't we have a fresh start and try to be friends, Daniel is a close friend of John and Adele, and there are other reasons why the Peterson's and Sharpe's have a close connection?" Scott asked, wondering why she wouldn't even look at him.

Just then there was a loud howl of pain, followed by shouts of 'Mummy, Mummy.' As mother's do she had forgotten who was beside her and why she didn't want him around, and she set off at a run.

Scott reached the hollow oak tree first, and picked up the crying boy, and drew a handkerchief from his pocket, and wiped the tear stained cheeks, and the crying stopped magically, as Joss looked up with surprise at the man holding him secure and safe. The next few seconds felt like hours as Zoe held her breath, and felt her eyes fill with tears.

Scott was completely silent and ominously still. Zoe knew she would never forget the sight of the tall man holding the child with his arms slightly bent as they stared at each other, and her jumbled feelings were hard to define just at that moment, as most likely were theirs!

"Give me my son," Zoe demanded angrily, her voice sharp as Scott continued to stare at Joss.

"I will Zoe, but I now *know* why you have been avoiding me. Does Daniel know that you were pregnant when you married him? He is *my* son, he has *my* eyes, and *my* little dimple," he said, and then sighed. "That accounts for how strange Adele has been behaving since I returned from Afghanistan, I guess she knew right away that Joss is *her* boys' little cousin." Scott never took his eyes away from Joss, but when Zoe tried to take him from his arms, he moved to one side to avoid her, but placed Joss carefully on the ground.

"Scott you are frightening him as he is very young, please give me my son." Zoe pleaded. "Joss calls Daniel by his name, as do I, and he has no idea who his father is, as Daniel married me *after* Joss was born."

"Are you *sure* Zoe that he doesn't know?" Scott sighed deeply knowing Joss was the spitting image of himself at that age. "I think I can work out to within a few days how old he is!"

"If Daniel knew he would have said. I don't know *why* things got so out of control between you and me, so quickly and unexpectedly, but…" Zoe was stopped from finishing her sentence as hard lips pressed against hers in a punishing kiss, and then softened almost without volition, as Joss struggled to get close to his mother, and held his little arms up to her.

"That is why Zoe, and it won't go away, damn you." Scott replied, and pushed Joss towards her and when she held him, he moved away taking big strides as though he couldn't get away fast enough. She watched with a thumping, aching heart, as Joss started to cry again quietly, and she hugged him close, and for the first time mourned the fact that Joss would never know Scott as his father. How strange that Joss loved the hollow oak tree, and loved to sit on the coffin resting stone dangling his little legs! He couldn't *know* that he had been conceived there!

CHAPTER NINE

Zoe rushed Joss back along the footpath towards Sharpe House, her husband and normalcy, longing for time alone to go over in her mind the ramifications of Scott's recent discovery. Surely he would not cause trouble for her and Joss by informing Daniel? It was obvious that Scott liked Daniel very much, as he had been a good friend of his father and the whole family. And she had believed him to be a really good and helpful man when he had been so caring and helpful when she had demanded that he should help her mother get home for her medication! The trouble was that she had been so worried for her mother, and he had been immediately good to her, and such an attractive man, who probably also had issues. One of which was the recent death of his father that he wanted to blot out from his mind, and they had certainly done that, if only for a short time!

She remembered parting from him on the train to Lancaster, and that had been painful too. There had been so much that should or could be said between them, but she had been embarrassed and most probably he had too.

It was all beyond her understanding, as she had never previously acted in such an uncontrolled way, and she believed neither had Scott! They had both been shocked, embarrassed, and regretful when the euphoria had subsided, and they both came back to their senses.

Zoe didn't start to worry until about seven o'clock. She had bathed and put Joss to bed, read him a story and turned off the oven where their evening meal was keeping warm. She was surprised that Daniel had not returned in time to watch Eggheads on the TV at six o'clock, which was usual. She had watched it and then put Joss to bed, where he was now sleeping. She checked the house phone and noticed a missed call, but there was nothing recorded, and then she checked her mobile, but was not surprised to found nothing there. Daniel hated using his mobile phone. The only people that might try to reach her by mobile were her student friends, Emily, Jennifer and Mary, also Adele – but she had been at work today at High Stile, so that was not very likely.

The evening was still quite light, and before dark she had better *do* something, instead of thinking about it. Perhaps John and Adele had seen or spoken with Daniel. She quickly rang the farm, and was quite relieved when John answered the phone.

"John, have you seen Daniel at all today? He took a sandwich and flask for lunch as he has quite often lately, and said he was going to check the quarry again as he did yesterday, as he was mulling over some idea. Perhaps you know something about it, because it's now gone seven and there is no sign of him and it will be getting dark soon."

"Sorry Zoe, I haven't seen him today. Do you mean the old quarry workings on his land?"

"Yes John. I think I'll get Joss up out of bed, and walk up there, is it far?"

"No not very far, but you should stay at home. Wait there, I'll arrange something, and see if I can get old Smithy to come, he knows the place like the back of his hand." The phone went dead, and Zoe wondered what he was going to arrange.

Rather than do nothing, she got Joss out of bed, and he wasn't very pleased as he had been fast asleep. But she could not leave him in the house alone, and she had to go and find Daniel, the man who had been so good to her and Joss. No wonder her mother had fallen in love with him, but much too late in her short life! Zoe tried to put Joss in his pushchair, which he now hated, wanting to walk everywhere that he wasn't driven in Daniel's car. How could she search holding his hand all the time? She shouted at him to 'be quiet' and as he wasn't used to her raising her voice, he burst into tears and so did she. That was how John found them as he strode into the kitchen through the back door.

"Stop crying Zoe, Daniel will be fine you'll see. Adele and the boys are getting out of the car, they'll stay here with Joss, and I'll take the Range Rover as far as I can, and you will no doubt want to come too?" John said as she wiped Joss's eyes and then her own. Miraculously Joss was now fully awake and eager to play with his friends Elliot and John junior!

Zoe was persuaded to change her fashion boots for wellingtons, and she pulled on an old waterproof. She was then allowed to accompany John to the range rover where old

Smithy was waiting. He was quite small, perhaps he had wizened up with age, but his eyes were bright as he looked at Zoe as his lined face crinkled into a sympathetic grin, and she realised that she had seen him before when *he had* been carrying Scott's father along the coffin route.

"Don't thee bother lass, we'll find the ald coot, as always our much thinking, not enough doing. Silly ald bugger should be looking after his sel. Bin badly lately." Smithy gave Zoe a wide encouraging smile, showing that he had a number of teeth missing, probably where they had worn away from having his pipe held in his mouth from morning until night, according to what Daniel had said about Smithy over the months. For some reason Zoe started to feel better, Daniel had good friends, and *they* seemed to know what they were doing, even if she didn't! Then she pondered upon old Smithy's words. 'Bin badly lately,' she was sure that he meant that Daniel had not been well recently, but if that was true surely *she* would have noticed, since her mother's death she had always made certain that Daniel took the few pills that he had been prescribed!

The range rover had managed the rough road very well, and on the quarry bank it did a full circle in the hands of John and came to a sudden stop facing back down the fell road.

John handed a torch to Zoe and Smithy pulled up his trousers by putting on his yorks (leather thongs tied around just under the knee).

"Is that to keep them dry?" Zoe asked. She wasn't sure whether to believe him when he replied with a grin. "Nay lass it's to keep t' rats from climbing up inside me trouser legs."

He was wearing sturdy boots, and Zoe started to worry how she would manage to follow the men in her fashionable

Wellingtons, which looked even less robust as the others got ready to go into the quarry level.

"Thou will hev to stay here m'lass, we only hev two hardhats, John'll hev to hev yan as he's big, and I'll hev to hev yan even though I'm small and most likely won't bang me head, but *I* know't way." He finished with a grin, and Zoe realised how kind he was trying to get her to relax.

"I must help I can't wait here, Daniel might be hurt," Zoe replied wondering why he had let her come if she couldn't help.

"You can listen, and when I've whistled six times, you can listen, for't reply. An if Daniel has a whistle or't torch, he'll reply with three whistles or three flashes. You stay here w' your new gadget," Smithy said and moved off towards the entrance to the quarry level.

Zoe looked nonplussed, and John smiled at her. "He means your mobile telephone, but there'll not be a signal in there." John said indicating the dark entrance to the quarry mouth, as he patted her shoulder comfortingly, and then he moved off and was soon out of sight.

For the next half hour according to her watch she waited, but she believed she must have been there much longer as she listened and watched for any flashes of light or whistles in the dark interior of the hewn out rock in front of her.

She was really waiting for Adele to ring her and say that Daniel had turned up at home, but nothing happened, and she realised that she did love Daniel, but as her deceased *mother's* fiancé. Suddenly she nearly jumped out of her skin as a mountain bike slurred to a noisy stop beside her, and her heart raced, and she was glad it was nearly dark, as she recognised the rider.

"Scott, what are you doing here, have you come to tell me Daniel is at home?"

"Sorry, no, I've come to help look for Daniel." Scott said pushing the bike to one side. He looked even taller than ever in his dark cycling shorts and top, and she worried he might not be warm enough inside the quarry. She was getting very worried about Daniel, and the fact that Scott made her feel something she shouldn't angered her.

She was *really* worried for Daniel, and could have done without having Scott around at the moment upsetting her equilibrium.

"*You can't* go in there, as there isn't another hard hat."

"Thank you for worrying about me Zoe, but the cycling hat will have to do. I've just seen *our* son on his way to bed." Scott replied irritably as he had been surprised at how much he had been troubled by watching his son with his sister Adele beside him watching *her brother's* every move. It seemed as though she knew Joss was his son, but as long as neither of them said anything it could be ignored, but he knew that was not true at all. Why had Zoe to be here, he could have done without seeing her, as she looked wonderful even in Wellingtons and an old raincoat, and her eyes were green today as she was emotional with the disappearance of her husband! Stupid he was, she was looking for her *husband*, and of course she didn't share a room with her son as he had hoped, he had noticed *that* as his sister had tucked Joss in to bed! And *he* must help look for his father's good friend, and his own good friend Daniel! He strode away full of determination, Daniel must be found and quickly.

68

"Be careful Scott," she shouted after him, and he walked back towards her and she looked so devastated that he put his hands on her shoulders and wanted to comfort her.

"I'll need to take that torch, if you need any light you can put on the range rover lights," he said, "but let us hope we have found Daniel before dark."

When it became dark Zoe went to sit in the range rover, and waited, and waited. She felt almost dizzy with staring at the mouth of the quarry level into which apparently, four men had disappeared. She started the engine, and put on the heater, Daniel would be very cold when they found him, and he would need the heat on. Whilst she was doing this and checking that there was enough petrol to keep the engine ticking over, she never saw anyone come out of the quarry.

The door opened and Scott joined her in the front seat. He was covered in a dark green sludge, and he looked cold and enigmatic, and she tried but couldn't tell from his face what he was thinking.

"Give me your mobile please Zoe." She passed it to him silently, staring at him. "Daniel is alive, but hurt." She started to speak but he put up his hand asking for silence, as tears filled her eyes he stared out of the front of the vehicle.

"Police? Can you get the Mountain Rescue please, and send them to Sharpe Quarry, near Rydal. They will need lights, a stretcher for one casualty namely Daniel Sharpe, a paramedic, and an ambulance. There is room on the quarry bank for all the necessary vehicles, and there will be someone ready to guide you up to the quarry. Thank you." Scott glanced at Zoe and saw her worried face only slightly relax.

"Is he going to be alright Scott?"

"I hope so Zoe, I'll go back down on the bike, and direct them from Sharpe House, when the paramedic, mountain rescue and a stretcher get in there I won't be needed."

"Please don't leave me alone Scott." Zoe said desperately, and put her hand on his. He turned his hand and held hers tightly, that was all he dare do just at this moment, she looked so lonely, and he thought she must love her husband very much, even with the vast age difference. They sat in silence until the sirens and vehicles were heard in the distance.

"You'll be alright Zoe, Daniel might need you here. I'll go down on the bike now, to direct them. Daniel has a head wound, but it's probably not as bad as it looks. There was a slight rock fall," Scott said briskly, but could not leave without giving her a comforting hug, well it *might* have been comforting for her!

"Tell them that Daniel has been taking medication for angina they will need to know. Just like Mum, and look what happened to her." Zoe replied in some distress. "Please check with Adele that Joss is alright, I am going to go to the hospital with Daniel."

Scott was soon down at Sharpe House, and was met at the door by his sister, but his mind we still with Zoe on the quarry bank waiting for news of her husband.

"What's happening Scott, I've just put Joss to bed for the *second* time, and the boys are watching television." Adele said really hoping for some good news.

Just then the Mountain Rescue and a paramedic car arrived, and Scott stopped to show them where to go, and then looked at his sister.

"Take the boys home Adele, and put them to bed. John will be a while yet. I'll stay here until Zoe comes home from the hospital I think John will also want to go through there, perhaps he will bring her home when they have seen to Daniel. If not, I'll bring Joss over to High Stile and he can have a day off school," Scott said worriedly. He was worried about both Daniel and Zoe, but he was determined to have just one night in the same house as his son! Adele looked at him closely, and then agreed. Although the fact that Scott *knew*, and his sister *believed* that Joss was his son, nothing was said and she nodded sagely and gathered up her sons, and left for High Stile, with a sense of foreboding, and an ache in her heart for both her brother and her friend Daniel.

Adele immediately called Zoe on her mobile.

"Zoe, are you alright, have you seen Daniel yet?"

"Yes, I have Adele, and I am going to the hospital with him, he is not very well and needs me." Zoe replied to her friend and employer. "Can you take care of Joss please, I don't know where they are taking Daniel yet, and John says he is coming in his vehicle, just in case we are able to come back quite soon? John says he is going to ring you as soon as we get there. Thank you both, and Scott for all that you are doing Adele, it is good to have such good friends." Zoe finished hurriedly.

"Don't worry about Joss, I have already kissed him goodnight for you, he is fast asleep, and looking forward to having the boys to play with. Please give Daniel our love, and say we look forward to seeing him fit and well in the very near future."

"Thank you Adele, see you soon," Zoe finished the call and walked slowly to the ambulance to join her husband, thinking how lucky she was to have found such good friends, and for the time being she would give all her attention to the man who had taken her and her son into his home, because in their own way they both loved him.

CHAPTER TEN

Zoe felt the grip of Daniel's hand slacken slightly, and she was relieved as he had just received a painkilling injection from the hands of the doctor who had arrived with the Mountain Rescue team. He had seemed agitated and unable to fully explain in full what had happened inside the quarry. He had also sustained a slight head trauma, but the Doctor didn't seem as worried about that as he was about the state of Daniel's heart.

She remembered Daniel's lovely cousin Janette and was determined to try and remember to get John to get in touch with her as soon as they found out how badly Daniel had been hurt. Janette had fully agreed with Daniel that for him to marry Zoe was the easiest and best way to fulfil her mother's wishes that he should take care of both Zoe and Joss. Janette had also informed Zoe that Daniel was not a well man, mainly suffering from angina as did *her* mother, and that as time went on he would need someone to take care of him, and Zoe had then agreed to the marriage as she would be able to help Daniel in return at some time in the future. It seemed that now was that time, and she was determined to do everything in her power to keep him safe and well. Fleetingly she thought about Scott and realised that she must make an effort and try to make friends with him, as Daniel was closely involved with the Peterson and Simpson families.

The next hour and a half seemed interminable, and when they arrived at Lancaster Royal Infirmary Daniel was rushed into Accident and Emergency, where they started to do various tests as Zoe waited in the waiting room whilst the tests took place, and the rest of the time she was allowed to sit with Daniel. She had moved into the corridor to get a cup of tea when the consultant asked her to accompany him to see his patient.

The consultant then told them both together that Daniel was to be moved to Blackpool in the morning, and he was to have an emergency heart operation. It seemed that the angina had been covering up a more serious condition and it was imperative that this operation was undertaken as soon as possible, he also said that if this trauma in the quarry had not warned him, then he could probably have died at any time, as he urgently needed a quadruple heart bypass. Zoe felt devastated, but was surprised at how well Daniel had taken this information.

"Stop worrying Zoe, it is a blessing really at least I now have a possibility of becoming well again," Daniel said to his young wife. "Now please can I have the consent form to sign as we need to get things moving. And Zoe you had better go home with John who I can see is waiting outside, your son needs you, and I will be getting all the care that I need."

Zoe waved to John indicating that he should come into the room, and told him everything. As she finished she looked directly at Daniel. "Daniel, I am coming with you to Blackpool until after your operation. John will go back to Adele and his family and tell them what's happening, and I am sure that she will take care of Joss until I can get home. I know you have your wallet with you, and you won't mind paying for a room for me, so that is what we'll do." She sounded adamant, and both Daniel and John looked at each other briefly and agreed.

"Whilst we get your husband ready for the move to Blackpool, I suggest you get yourself something to eat, and anything else you need," the consultant said with a smile at the young woman who looked young enough to be the patient's daughter.

"I'll take Zoe to get something to eat, and be back in about half an hour, and we'll also ring Adele and put her in the picture," John said to his friend who looked both pleased and surprised by his young wife's determination.

After eating in the restaurant at the hospital, Zoe was amazed to realise it was eight o'clock in the morning, and when they rang Adele, she said that Joss was eating his breakfast with the boys, and was looking forward to seeing his mummy. Adele handed the phone to Joss, and he looked at it and when he heard his mother's voice, he smiled and asked if he could go to school with the boys in Adele's car.

"Sorry Zoe, he has now run off to get ready for school." Adele said breathlessly, "and don't you worry about him, you know he likes it here at the farm. I'll have to follow him, but please let us know how Daniel progresses. Give John back to me please I have a question about the farm," Adele said hurriedly.

Zoe smiled and handed over the phone to John, and he spoke with his wife quietly, as Zoe sighed and waited for John, thinking that Joss wasn't missing her at all!

"I might as well get back home now Zoe, I'll just come in for a word with Daniel. Have you plenty of money on your mobile, and is there anything else you need before I go home."

"No thank you John, I can get anything I want on Daniel's card, and he has a little cash anyway. Thank you for everything you have done, both you and Adele. Also Scott when you see him and Mr Smith too, or should I say 'ald Smithy.' I do hope Joss doesn't give you any trouble."

"Ald Smithy, he doesn't *answer* to anything else. Don't worry Zoe, Daniel will soon be in the best place. It's marvellous what they can do nowadays."

As she waved John off in his vehicle, she wondered why Daniel's condition had not been identified earlier, they might have lost him at any time, now that he had started going up to the quarries for some reason – and they still might.

It was five thirty in the evening when the surgeon came to speak to Zoe, who had been waiting for hours and hours it seemed, he cleared his throat and she couldn't tell from the look in his eyes whether it was good news or bad!

"Please sit down Mrs Sharpe, you look exhausted," the surgeon said briskly, and Zoe thought she was going to faint and wished he would get a move on with whatever he had to say.

"It was touch and go for a while," he paused as the door opened behind him and Scott walked in without knocking.

"And you are?" the surgeon asked enquiringly.

"Daniel Sharpe's godson, I promised Daniel to be here for Mrs Sharpe, whatever the news you have." Scott sat down beside Zoe, and took her hand firmly in his, as they both stared at the surgeon, and Zoe realised how much better she felt with someone holding her hand tightly, even the hand of Scott. She and Daniel needed him at this particular moment.

"As I was saying Mrs Sharpe, it was touch and go for a while, but for the moment he is quite stable. The next few hours will decide if he comes though the operation, but I have high hopes of that outcome. It is good that you have someone with you. I suggest you go and get something to eat and have a rest if you can, and when you return you will be able to sit with your husband for a while, he is in Intensive Care at the moment," the surgeon said tiredly, and then smiled briefly, "and then you can inform other people, as I understand you have a son."

"Yes, we do have a son," Zoe replied with a smile, as the surgeon tiredly left the room.

Scott sat perfectly still holding on to Zoe's cold hand, and wondered if she realised what she had said, and was she thinking of *him* or Daniel when she had said *we* have a son.

"Could we get something to eat Scott, then I think I'll come back and wait until I can sit with Daniel. You can use the small flat I have been staying in outside the hospital. And thank you for coming here to me and Daniel, having you here is being a great help. Was Joss alright when you left the farm?" She finished and glanced at Scott's haggard face, and she realised just how much Daniel meant to them both!

"Yes, I could rest there for a while, we could get a take-away and take it back there, as it would be quiet there, and I could tell you about Joss." Scott suggested briskly.

"Alright, just a sandwich or something, or *you* could get some fish and chips or something, I couldn't eat very much." Zoe replied tiredly. "I didn't know you were Daniel's godson, he never mentioned it, but then why would he, as he could have a number of godsons and daughters? Joss and I have been such a small part of his life, or so it seems." Zoe said quietly, with a furrowed brow. She stood up, and started to walk away.

Scott looked worried, and followed her quickly. "Where are you going Zoe, as I thought we were going to the flat you stayed in last night after getting something to eat?"

"One of the other women went to a Chapel or something before, when she was waiting for news of her husband, and I thought I would too, Daniel needs more help than I and Joss can give him, and you should come too Scott, I'm sure Daniel would appreciate it."

"Yes I will come with you Zoe, if you promise me that you will then get something to eat, rest a while, and then you will be able to sit with Daniel when the powers that be suggest it." Scott wondered if Daniel and his little family went to Church each week, what did he know of Daniel's beliefs, but it seemed a good idea to go along with Zoe for the time being anyway. He still hadn't told her that he had stayed the night in her home, to have some quality time with his son, and he had not taken young Joss to High Stile and his sister until the morning! He quickly decided that this was not the time to make her aware of Joss's movements, as she was aware that Joss was safe and sound with Adele at High Stile at the moment, and for now she had enough to worry about.

They found the Chapel, and it was comforting, in that it was quiet, with only a couple of other people there, and they were quietly communicating with a higher being with great success, or so it seemed. Scott sat beside Zoe, and bent his head as did she, and after about fifteen minutes Zoe stood, and her brow had cleared, and she smiled at him, as they left the Chapel. As they left the hospital Zoe decided she might be able to manage a small slice of the pizza that Scott had bought, and they arrived at the small flat, and Scott let her deal with the pizza as he called Adele on his mobile telephone. He spoke with his sister for a few minutes, and then realised that Zoe was standing beside him, looking eagerly towards the 'phone. "Do you want to speak to Adele, she can tell you about Joss?"

Zoe nodded, and Scott gave her the phone and pressed her down onto the small settee in the quite pleasant and functional living room. He went to put the kettle on to boil and listened to Zoe's conversation with his sister. He was seriously thinking of leaving once more the area of his birth, and his nearest family, namely Adele, John and their boys, as it was becoming increasingly difficult for him to stay around Daniel and *his* family, why and how had things become so difficult, and was anyone else to blame, or was he the only one? He really believed that he should leave Zoe and Daniel to get on with their lives, but Daniel has asked him to be there for Zoe, particularly at the hospital. The trouble was that being here with her, had brought to the front of his mind various things that he needed to ask her, mostly with regard to their son Joss. Spending the night in Daniel's home with his son had been a mixed blessing, as he now realised how much he loved his son and how difficult it was going to be to leave him and his son's mother to get on with their lives with Daniel. He truly loved Daniel as a godfather, and he had prayed in the Chapel with Zoe that Daniel would recover from his serious operation. He was a good man with high ideals, and he had already suffered momentous problems in his life, and deserved some good luck for a change!

Later after eating and resting for a couple of hours, two hours forty minutes in fact, Scott had awakened to find Zoe asleep on the small settee in the living room, because she had insisted that he, with his six foot plus, needed the use of the double bed. He had given in to her because he needed a little space, as it would be a few further hours watching for some recovery signs from Daniel, before Scott would be able to return home, and he must fulfil his promise to Daniel.

They returned to the hospital to find that Daniel was still in the intensive care unit, and it was with misgivings that he agreed to leave Zoe at her husband's bedside, and return home. Zoe had promised that when Daniel was returned to the ward, which should indicate some improvement, that she would ring and either Adele, John, or Scott would return to visit, and take her home to be with her son.

It was in the early hours of the following morning that Daniel awoke to find Zoe asleep in the chair beside the bed, covered by a blanket. The nurses did not waken her until Daniel was ready to be moved to the ward, and it was a dreadful moment for her when she woke to find a freshly made up empty bed. The nurse was there very quickly with the good news that Daniel was back in the ward, and ready to see her. Later the consultant informed both Daniel and Zoe that they expected him to make a good recovery with the patient eager to improve, and his wife keen to take care of him. However, he would not be out of hospital for a few days, and would be taken home in an ambulance.

For afternoon visiting John arrived to visit his friend, and Scott arrived in his own car to take Zoe back, as John was travelling in a horse box as he had to collect a new horse for the riding school from the midlands, and would not be back until the following day.

Daniel insisted that Zoe should return home, as Joss was missing her very much according to John, and if she insisted on visiting the next day, she could drive herself in Daniel's car, and Scott and Adele would take care of Joss once more, but he insisted that he was in the best and safest place at the moment, and he would rather she spent more time with Joss, than sit worrying about him in the hospital!

Zoe was quite sleepy, and the journey back to the Lake District in Scott's Rover car was travelled in silence for the most part, until Scott took courage and looked at the tired girl beside him, and asked if she was too tired to talk.

"Of course not Scott, what would I have done without the help of you, John and Adele, since Daniel's accident? You will have to excuse me if I dose off, as I want to spend time with Joss today, I have felt as though part of me was missing the whole time I have been at the hospital."

"I shouldn't ask you now Zoe, but there is rarely a time that we can speak privately, there is always someone else around."

Zoe sat up straight and stared at him, as he glanced towards the passenger seat and she now looked both tired and angry, and her eyes flashed at him. He looked almost as tired as was she, and she almost put out her hand to smooth back his dark hair, which was a little untidy as the window was open a small amount and the wind was cooling the inside of the car.

"We don't need time to speak privately Scott, and I have a family to think about." She clasped her hands on her lap, to try to stop them shaking. Scott has been so very helpful, and now he wanted to ask questions, and she realised that he had every right to, as he had not expected to return from Afghanistan to learn that he had a son! In this day and age he must have assumed that she would have taken care of things, as they had both agreed that they had made a dreadful mistake, and had apologised to each other. He must have believed that was the end of the matter - that is if he had thought about it at all!

"I am not blaming you for anything Zoe, I just want to understand what happened after I left the UK? You have been so understanding about what happened between us, although you must have felt as mystified as I did, it was so out of character for both of us, at least that is what I thought at that time."

CHAPTER ELEVEN

Zoe looked like she was considering what he had said, and Scott returned his eyes to the road ahead and waited with a kind of dread rather than patience.

Zoe was unable to look towards him and kept her eyes on the mountains in the distance and after a little while she seemed to relax her hands, sighed, and then raised her shoulders in a hopeless gesture.

"The day you helped me get mother home, the doctor instructed her to stay in bed for a couple of days for complete rest, and the next morning Mr Brown was a pain in the neck, he was horrible to me and mother, and it was afternoon before I could get away to the chemist. I did get the necessary pill and took it, and assumed everything was alright, as I worked it out that I had taken it after approximately sixteen hours, and the paperwork said that it was best before twelve hours, but usually effective if taken within three days. It was after ten or eleven weeks later that I realised that something was wrong, and I took a test and I was pregnant, but by that time I believed it was too late, and I decided I couldn't do it, as however small it was, it would now be a baby. I'm sorry if you are upset Scott, but I think it was the best and the only decision I could make."

"That baby was Joss, and I'm glad you made that decision Zoe, he is a wonderful little boy, and you can plainly see how much Daniel dotes on him." Scott said quietly.

"Scott, about Daniel you are right he does dote on Joss, and he is a wonderful father."

"That is yours and Daniel's business Zoe, nothing to do with me but if you need anything let me know," Scott interrupted quickly.

Tears filled Zoe's eyes and she stared out of the side window of the car, after swallowing quickly. She had been about to say that Daniel was a wonderful *father-figure* for Joss. Obviously Scott had received all the information he needed, and she already knew that Scott loved his godfather! He obviously thought that Zoe had been in an awkward situation and she had taken advantage of Daniel's goodness, and determination to do the right thing, and he had *married* her, and he assumed that she was Daniel's wife in more than just name! As things were there was really no need to explain anything further, but she had thought he might have given her the benefit of any doubt!

The rest of the journey was travelled in silence, until they left Ambleside.

"I will take you to the farm to collect Joss, and then to Sharpe House." Scott said tiredly.

"Thank you Scott for coming to fetch me home, I'm sure Daniel will be grateful. If I need to visit Daniel in the next few days, I should be able to get Joss into the nursery, and perhaps Adele will let him come to the farm with the boys as usual, but

I will only go there, stay with Daniel for a hour, and return home to look after Joss."

"There is no need for that Zoe, you know that Adele, John and I will do everything we can to help. Stop thinking about yourself and think of Daniel and Joss." He was still brooding over what he thought she had tried to tell him, "that Daniel was a fine father and husband."

"I do, all the time, and I thought you *knew me*, but judging by your comments, I can see that you think I have coerced Daniel into marrying me because I have a child to take care of. If that is what you want to believe, then do so, but leave me and Joss alone, and allow me to take care of my family responsibilities."

"Is that how you think of your husband and son, as just responsibilities?" Scott said, realising that things between them were getting out of hand, all because he felt so hurt, lonely, ineffectual and powerless in these circumstances, as perhaps, so did she!

The car drew to a stop in the farmyard, and Scott left the driver's seat but before he could open the passenger door, Zoe was out of the car and running towards the farmhouse. The farmhouse door opened and Joss almost jumped into his mother's arms, and Elliot and John junior stood watching on the steps with Adele.

"Welcome back Zoe, someone is very pleased to see his mother," Adele said smiling at Zoe as she cuddled her son, and glancing with a sinking feeling as she saw her brother's grim expression. Surely Daniel's condition had not deteriorated!

"Is Daniel doing alright Zoe?" Adele asked as Zoe reluctantly released Joss and stood him on the steps.

"He is doing well thank you Adele, or I wouldn't have left him. John is with him for an hour or two, and as soon as I get back to Sharpe House I'll be ringing Daniel. He might be allowed to use his mobile occasionally. He will be coming home by ambulance, and I'll need to get things ready."

"Scott bring mummy home," Joss said with satisfaction, and Adele rushed into speech.

"That is good news. I have managed to get someone to help out in the office here, so you needn't worry, you can come back to work whenever you want."

"Thank you Adele I appreciate all your kindnesses. Joss darling, say goodbye to Elliot and John, Mr Peterson is going to take us home now."

"No Zoe, I have prepared some lunch, Scott will take you home when we've eaten. Joss and the boys have been waiting for you to get here, and they have been getting the table ready," Adele replied quickly.

Zoe's eyes filled with tears, and Adele took her hand and pulled her gently into the house, thinking that things were getting on top of her friend, and wondered whether the tears were because of the strained look on her brother's face, or the thought of the boys getting the table ready for Joss's mother!

"Adele take the boys in we'll follow in a moment," Scott said briskly, and Adele looked at him for a second, and then nodded and shepherded the boys into the kitchen.

"Zoe, look at me," Scott said with his hands on her drooping shoulders. "Truce?'

She nodded, and wiped her eyes, and he gave her a quick hug, and then followed her into the kitchen. Perhaps it wasn't a good idea to ask her *why* she had married Daniel, as he might not like the answer Scott brooded, and with a concerted effort he lightened his dark expression, and was touched when he followed Zoe into the kitchen, as the boys had decorated the table with balloons, and half a dozen Christmas crackers and Zoe was wiping her eyes and thanking the boys. Joss was really excited, and after a moment asked when Daniel was coming home!

A few days later Daniel arrived home from hospital in an ambulance and the district nurse came in each morning for the next couple of days. Daniel was looking surprisingly well, but it was Zoe who looked drawn and tired, with all the travelling she had been doing back and forth from the hospital over the last two weeks, although Adele, John or Scott had all taken turns to visit to give her a rest. On the third morning, about seven thirty in the morning the doorbell rang, and Zoe rushed to answer it, not wanting it to disturb Daniel or Joss, as she was enjoying a quiet time with her first cup of tea of the day.

She opened the door, and on the step stood a small, rotund woman with a smiling face, with wisps of salt and pepper hair peeping out from under a navy blue hat, which matched the serviceable coat she was wearing. Her cheeks were rosy with the early morning cold air, and her pale blue eyes sparkled merrily.

"Good your up and about m' lass, don't want to disturb Daniel, or the young un. *The morning hour has gold in its mouth, let sleeping dogs ..*" she didn't finish her sentence as Zoe interrupted her.

"Excuse me, what do you want, it seems you have come to the right house, but…" Zoe, stopped speaking as the little women moved into the hallway with a bag she picked up off the step. Zoe was not frightened or worried by this small, voluble and interesting woman in fact, she rather liked her on sight.

"I'm Maisie Sharpe, Janette and Daniel's cousin by marriage to my Bob, God rest his soul," she said placing her bag on the floor, she opened the door to the lounge and looked inside with undisguised curiosity, then did the same to the dining room and last of all, the kitchen. "Any tea in't pot, I'm parched?" She remarked sitting down at the kitchen table, and taking off her hat, as Zoe hovered around behind her, and took her hat and placed it on the kitchen counter.

"Of course, and the toast is fresh too, I'll get you a plate and cup and saucer," Zoe replied in a bemused voice, "Can I take your coat."

"Please lass," Maisie said and shed her coat and handed it to Zoe, "and I'll just freshen up this pot o' tea with a bit of boiling water." She moved the kettle and lifted it, and happy with the weight of water, she switched it on and returned to the table, as Zoe sat down opposite her still with a bemused smile, after taking the hat and coat into the hallway.

"The things you say are rather, er different," Zoe said hoping she hadn't upset her guest.

"Aye lass, m' mother was full o' sayings, for every occasion, and I guess it caught on." Maisie grinned, *"deeds are fruits, words are but leaves."*

"I'll think about that one," Zoe replied in awe, but with a smile.

"Now lass I hear stirring upstairs, an' as its quiet I guess that'll be Daniel." She paused and looked closely at Zoe, and then continued. "I'll go and see to Daniel as that's what I've come here for, now that t' district nurse has stopped coming. I know you and Daniel are married, but he was worried that you would be embarrassed helping him with personal things, as he truly thinks of you as a daughter and *you* love him like a Dad.

Don't you worry lass, *nobody knows* but Daniel, me, cousin Janette, cousin Janette's daughter an.." she burst out laughing as did Zoe, who forgot to be embarrassed by this strange conversation so early in the morning. For some strange reason Zoe wasn't worried about Maisie knowing their secret, or her family, as long as Daniel wasn't hurt in the future by other less friendly locals who might cause unpleasantness for Daniel who was in a way, straight laced and definitely conscious of what was 'right.'

Zoe was complacent as she watched Maisie quickly take a large white apron from her bag, slipped it over her head and tied it at her waist as if that was something she did every day, and it probably was!

"You alright to fetch up Daniels breakfast in half an hour, or will your lad be wanting yer?"

"I'll get Joss up now, get him washed, and he likes to dress himself, sometimes with a bit of help. Then I'll bring up Daniel's breakfast, as usual, as Joss likes to see him as soon as he's dressed and every day before he goes to nursery."

Maisie smiled, "As I said *deeds are fruits, words are…*"

"..but leaves," Zoe finished for Maisie, and they both laughed.

Joss was playing in his room in his pyjamas when Zoe looked in and she washed him in her en suite bathroom, and as he cleaned his teeth, she decided she had better prepare him for Maisie. Who could be prepared to meet Maisie? *Amazing Maisie* she thought and shrugged her shoulders, as to tell the truth it was a relief to have her here. Daniel was the most thoughtful man imaginable, as at first it *would* have been difficult for her to look after him all the time in personal or wifely matters, but she had been determined to do it, wasn't that one of the reasons she had married him? Janette had told her that Daniel was not a well man and would need help in the future, and she had married him because she thought she would be able to do something meaningful for him in due course, but now she realised that Daniel didn't want that, he wanted things to go on as before. Not many men would have been so thoughtful and caring. But it made her feel rather superfluous!

Also the reason for her marrying Daniel was fast disappearing as if he made a full recovery as his surgeon had suggested the reason for that marriage as far as she was concerned would have gone! She truly hoped that Daniel would not regret their marriage, as his reason for marrying her had been to give her a good name, and care for her and Joss because her mother had requested that he should. Although she had saved she had been unable to pay anything off the fees for her education, but in a couple of years Joss would be in full time education and she truly hoped that she would be able to get a full time, well paid, job as befitting her hard won degree. She fully appreciated how lucky she was to have a fine home for herself and Joss, and a very helpful mentor in Daniel.

Daniel was out of bed and sitting by a table in the bay window of his bedroom when Zoe took Joss in for his morning visit, and he went to Daniel and leant against his knee and looked towards Maisie as she poured Daniel's tea at the small table. Joss watched, and then removed his thumb from his mouth.

"Are you Daniel's mummy?" Joss asked, and Maisie pretended to think about it!

"Do you have friends at nursery, and are some of them girls?" Maisie said trying not to laugh out loud, as Joss was so very serious.

Joss nodded thoughtfully, and put his thumb back in his mouth, only to have it gently removed by Daniel.

"Well, I was at school when I was little with Daniel, and Scott and Adele's daddy, and we played a lot, and are still good friends."

"That's OK," Joss said in agreement, and took his mother's hand ready to get his breakfast and go to nursery.

"I'm so sorry Maisie," Zoe said moving towards the door, as Daniel and Maisie burst out laughing.

"I told you he was a bright lad," Daniel said proudly, and gave a worried look towards Zoe, but she seemed quite happy with the situation, and it was a great relief to him. Maisie had told him she would sort it all out, and it appeared that she had! He had thought of a way to make it up to Zoe, as she could have been very hurt by his high-handed decision to ask Maisie to join their household, as she had taken good care of him in the last couple of years without any embarrassing incidents. He would get John or Scott to find a small car for her and that would give her some independence, as it was she always felt she had to ask if she needed to use his car. As it was her first car, perhaps she would like to choose it herself, he would get on to that matter as soon as John or Adele came to call. He was surprised that Scott had not looked near since he came out of hospital, perhaps he was now getting down to sorting out Oak Tree Farm. He smiled thinking of one of Maisie's mother's old saying, *ill luck comes by pounds and goes away by ounces,* he would have to be very careful and make sure that the few things he could do to help Zoe and Joss, were only 'ounces' then she might accept the small things that he could do for her now, as she had in the last two years. As his health improved he worried that she would again think that she was taking advantage of him, but she was now and had always made his life so much more worthwhile, since she and Joss had come into it.

CHAPTER TWELVE

Within a couple of weeks Maisie had settled in at Sharpe House, and between her and Zoe everything was running smoothly. In fact Daniel was feeling better every day, and soon would be able to drive once more. Maisie appeared to be a fixture and it suited everyone. The house was often filled with the enticing smell of fresh baking, and Maisie and Zoe were in the kitchen quite often in order that Maisie could pass on her culinary skills to Zoe. On one of these enjoyable days, they were enjoying scones and jam in the kitchen, as Daniel had asked Scott to come over from Oak Tree Farm, where he now spent most of his time. They had elected to have their afternoon tea outside in the warmth of the June sun.

"There is something I have been meaning to put to you Scott, with regard to the old quarry workings." Daniel smiled at Scott and wondered if he would be surprised by his ideas.

"I guessed that you were not wasting your time idly up at the quarry when you had your accident, is that what this meeting is about? Are you thinking of opening it up again to supply slate or stone?"

"No, according to ald Smithy there is not much metal left worthy of being quarried, that's why it was closed in the first place. I was there when the small rock fall occurred with a view to having it converted, if it is safe, into a kind of museum. You know, showing what was there in the old days, and how we managed to bring any slate or stone out, and how it was processed before supplying it for sale. We still have a small amount of slate, and most of the tools for getting the slate out are there. Although we don't have any of the new machinery as in a modern quarry, such as a frame or band saw. I think with only a little work, it would be an interesting and informative place, if visited by schools and visitors to the area. If it got under way then it might be a part time occupation for one or two of the old quarrymen. Just showing how slate was riven, and dressed into slate, or supplied as cladding to buildings. You know the thing I have in mind."

"I did notice when I came to help find you when you were missing, that you still have some of the rails in place, and the odd wagon or two used to bring out the rock, and the close head is quite spectacular, just like an enormous man made cave, which of course it is, that would be an interesting place to visit if nowhere else!" Scott replied with an interested smile.

"Well you seem interested. Did you ever go up to your old quarry workings Scott, with your father when you were younger?"

"Well yes, and I did find it very interesting, that is why I decided on doing a geology degree. A fat lot of good that has done me, with me going into the Army. The Army had always

94

interested me because of my grandfather being in World War Two."

"Well ald Smithy has convinced me that there's only a few feet between your quarry workings and mine, because of the way the seam of slate is situated, what do you think Scott, are you interested in joining up and joining in?"

"Well it's worth thinking about, you do realise both quarries would have to be surveyed, and health and safety issues would be of paramount importance. I realise that your accident was caused by a piece of loose rock which you bumped into, but I think it would be worth taking a further look." Scott replied, sounding interested, and Daniel was relieved as he had been thinking about doing this for quite a while, and only since he had married Zoe and now had Joss to think about had he been spurred on to do something about it. He was feeling so much better in health after his operation, and other ambitions held for many years, were also often on his mind, things that he had *always* planned to do.

They both left the table on the small lawn, and stood looking up at the fellside behind the houses, which faced out over Rydal Water, just as Maisie came out around the corner of the house from the kitchen area.

"Do you two men want another pot of tea?"

"Yes please Maisie, and perhaps two more of your scrumptious scones?"

"Not my scrumptious scones, your wife is very adept at making them now," Maisie said with a pleased smile.

"Well you are an excellent teacher then Maisie," Daniel replied with a laugh. He glanced at Scott and saw that he had moved further away to get a better look at the hills above them, and by the frown on his face he wondered if Scott was having second thoughts about his plans.

Joss came running full pelt from behind the house laughing loudly as he was pursued by Elliot and John junior, he bumped into one of the metal chairs that had been moved back from the table, rolled over and scratched the side of his cheek with one of the home made wooden arrows that he had been holding in one hand, and the home made bow snapped in two and his knee landed on the severed end. He howled loudly, mostly in shock, and Maisie went towards Daniel, who was now holding his chest and she moved one of the metal chairs so that Daniel could sit down. Meanwhile, Scott gathered up Joss in his arms and headed for the kitchen area.

Zoe who had heard the shouts and Joss's frightened cry, met them in the doorway.

"Scott what has happened, oh darling Joss, come to mummy," she reached for her son, and he reached for her with tears running down his cheeks.

"Instead of messing about and laughing with Maisie you should be looking after your son," Scott said angrily. "Where is the first aid kit?

Zoe pointed to the drawer next to the sink, and sat down on a kitchen chair with Joss on her knee. She kissed Joss on the forehead, and looked at the scratches on his cheek and knee. Over the last three years he had suffered much worse little accidents.

Scott looked on angrily as Zoe sat Joss on a chair and then poured some boiled water out of the kettle into a dish, and cleaned up the cuts with cotton wool, and then antiseptic wipes, and stuck a plaster on his knee. Joss looked on with interest, then looked in the shiny steel of the fridge and felt proud of the reflected knee with a plaster on it, and he smiled at his mother and ran out of the kitchen to show his friends.

"He could have put his eye out Zoe, and besides that Daniel is quite shocked, and Maisie had to get him to sit down."

"He can't be watched twenty four hours a day Scott, he has to have time to play and be a boy. Don't you remember what it was like to be young, and how exciting it was to make bows and arrows." Zoe asked, moving towards the kitchen door to find out how Daniel was, and Joss met her in the doorway.

"Daniel said I should say sorry mummy, and to Scott." He turned and ran back into the garden.

"There at least your husband is teaching him some manners," Scott said angrily.

Zoe turned angrily, "What are you doing here Scott? I am quite capable with Daniel's help of looking after my son."

Scott held her by the elbow, and she looked angrily into his face, and realised how dangerous it was to lock glances with Scott as she was aware that underneath the surface hardness in his grey eyes there was a depth of sensitivity, and how easy it would be to forget to keep the awareness between them under iron control. They both stood back suddenly, and Maisie walked into the kitchen with a relieved smile.

"Daniel is alright now Zoe, and I've come to make a fresh pot of tea. Can you do a couple of scones and bring them out in a minute?"

"Of course Maisie, and thanks for looking after Daniel, Joss of course has been kissed better, and run of again." Zoe said, and watched as Scott moved out of the kitchen with down bent head, and for some reason she ached a little. Why had he to come here to see Daniel, he kept away most of the time so she assumed that Daniel had invited him, but why?

Zoe delivered the scones to the table, and Daniel smiled at her.

"I have asked Scott to look out for a car for you Zoe, you always ask when you want to use mine, and that's not right, you need a car of your own."

"But Daniel, I don't need a car, soon you will be able to drive, and Joss will be at the big school. And if I change my mind, I can choose a car for myself."

"Do you know anything about the mechanics of a car Zoe, could you pick one that you were certain was safe for yourself to drive, and safe for Joss to ride in." Scott interrupted her. "I understand you only passed your test in Daniel's car, when your mother was still with us, and that is the only car you've driven?"

"Whatever, if you *both* believe you know best," she said angrily, and shrugged her shoulders and walked off towards the kitchen, at least she would be able to get off by herself sometimes she thought, and then realised she was being ungrateful, Daniel was such a generous man, and most of the time she wouldn't allow him to be his natural self!

"My, my, that's not like Zoe," Daniel remarked with raised eyebrows. "Perhaps she is worried about driving something else other than *my* car as you pointed out Scott, or maybe Joss's little accident is bothering her more than we think."

"Don't worry Daniel she will come around. If we let her choose something she likes, and get it checked over by a mechanic, that should please her," Scott replied ruefully.

"I hope so Scott, I have offered to get her a car before, and she has always said it was an unnecessary expense. And she has always objected every time I have said I would pay off her university overdraft. She also said she could manage to look after both me and young Joss without any help, but she *has* become good friends with Maisie."

"I bet Maisie said "*a friend in need is a friend indeed,*" Scott said ruefully, he was upset because both Daniel and he had upset Zoe, and for some reason he felt much better knowing that Maisie was staying here in Sharpe House.

"Not that I know of Scott, but she did say to Zoe '*out of debt, out of danger*' but that didn't have any effect either, anyway she didn't change her mind."

"*Little and often fills the purse*," that is another of Maisie's many sayings whilst quoting her mother," Zoe said beside them, and she looked really angry, as they both jumped in surprise as they were not aware that she was there. She turned abruptly, and moved of to gather up the three boys, and walked off in the direction of High Stile. Her cheeks were flushed and striding off with the boys she tried not to flounce in her anger, as she must appear to those two men as calm and in complete control. It was a great pity that the only person to whom she could run off to was *Scott's sister* Adele!

It was three weeks later that Zoe walked out in the early morning to discover a small Fiat car, the type that she had remarked one day on the road with Daniel that she thought it was quite small, and would be easy to park. It had a wide red ribbon attached to the driving door. She stopped in surprise, as she was intent on taking a short walk before the rest of the household awoke. She looked at the ribbon, and saw an envelope. She turned the envelope and saw 'Zoe' written in very tidy writing, beside another signature, which was hard to read, but she eventually realised it was 'Happy Birthday mummy," and there were two keys inside.

She took a tissue out of her anorak pocket and wiped her eyes, and turned as she heard a rustling noise. Daniel and Joss were standing behind her, and Joss looked really excited.

"Mummy, mummy happy birthday," he moved over to put his arms around her knees and give her a hug.

"We don't want to spoil his pleasure do we?" Daniel said looking extremely worried. All he wished was to make things easier for her, not to annoy her.

"How did you know it was my birthday?"

"You did have a few birthdays with your mother you know, and she and I were friends for about seven years, and for a year much more than friends, and possibly it was in the marriage certificate, I don't recall." Daniel said and looked upset at having to remind her of those occasionally unhappy times when her mother had worked for 'Cruella de Neil Brown.'

"Thank you Daniel, and you Joss," Zoe smiled through her tears, "shall we take a ride in this lovely new car?" She kissed Daniel on the cheek, and lifted up Joss for a cuddle and a tickle, and when she opened the back door Joss climbed in and fastened himself into the new child seat in the back with a pleased smile.

"Oh Daniel, you have thought of everything. Is it insured and taxed?"

"Of course Zoe, and actually that was Scott, he delivered it last night with the child seat, now you can use it right away."

"I hope you didn't mention my birthday to him, a woman never wants people to know their age."

"Only when they are much older than you, Zoe, so just get in the driving seat and familiarise yourself with the controls, and we'll give it a spin, Joss already loves it, he looks so proud sitting there in the back. I'll just move the passenger seat back to make room for my legs. Where do you want to go Joss."

"High Stile," Joss answered.

"Perhaps on the way back Joss, for now mummy can drive us to Grasmere, or even to Keswick."

CHAPTER THIRTEEN

Scott was in a quandary, or deep dilemma, not knowing what to do about Daniel's suggestion with regard to the old quarry workings on his land. He had been thinking about everything that Daniel had said, and he thought it was an excellent idea. In addition he had come up with a few ideas himself, with regard to his degree in geology, he realised that they could make some very good displays of various types of rock, and have talks on geology in general and how the slate quarries fitted into this category. Also history could be brought into it too, informing how the earth was formed and what part had been played by the ice age, and everything before, and how the slates were formed from metamorphosed volcanic ash containing chlorides, which impart a beautiful green colour and in some areas these are beautifully marked with fossils. The options were wide and all very interesting. He realised that putting the two together, his and Daniel's quarry would make it more feasible. Could he stay here in this valley in the Lake District, living near to where Daniel and Zoe lived with *his* son?

Scott was quite sure that Daniel had not sussed out the connection, and it worried him as to what would happen when and if he did! Also if he did depart this valley where he had been born, he would not see anything of his son, or see him growing up. What was the easiest option, it tore him apart seeing Zoe and Joss with Daniel, his very good friend, but *not* to see them and *not* to see Joss growing up would be an even more traumatic scenario! If he did leave he was sure that Adele if asked would keep him up to date on what was happening, although neither of them had *voiced* what Scott knew for certain, and what Adele had believed since she first saw Joss!

Scott had settled in at Oak Tree Farm, and he had spent hours sorting out his father's belongings, with the help of his sister Adele. He wanted to renovate the house, and get new furniture, but could not pluck up the necessary enthusiasm. The house had been fine for his father, and now it would be fine for him. Adele was always telling him to get it renovated or he would never get himself a wife to share it with, but he know that was not possible at present. He had been wondering about a new occupation, either using his degree in geology, or perhaps using his skills learned in the Army, but nothing had really interested him before Daniel's recent suggestion regarding the two small quarries.

Zoe and Maisie were both really pleased with the progress that Daniel was making. He seemed to have plenty of energy, and in fact he was much better than he had been for years. It seemed that the accident that he had suffered was a blessing in disguise, and it had given him back his life, as he was no longer an invalid. They were sitting at the edge of Rydal Water, watching as Joss and his two friends Elliot and John junior played at the edge of the tarn. They had brought sandwiches for lunch, and a chair for Maisie to sit on, and a blanket for the rest of them to use. At the moment Zoe was the only one using the blanket and she felt very relaxed for once, as there was no chance that Scott would put in an appearance, as he and Daniel were showing the surveyors around the quarries.

Maisie was sitting on the folding chair, wearing a voluminous cotton dress and short sleeved cardigan, and every now and again tucking up the strands of hair into a tight bun on the top of her head. Zoe was reclining on her back, with her hands holding the back of her head and her ankles comfortably crossed with bare feet, wearing white cut off trousers and a lilac T-shirt. She knew that at any moment she would have to slip on her sandals and rush to be there for the boys but just for now they were playing in the gravel with sticks and some larger stones as Joss had a little plastic digger truck and the boys were moving the sandy soil with their hands for him to move. The sky was very blue, with only a few wispy white clouds slowly moving up above her, and there were at least three white vapour trails from aeroplanes having passed overhead.

"Maisie, it was wonderful that you were able to come and help us with Daniel's convalescence. He is much better as you know, and I'm worried that you'll decide to leave us."

Zoe really didn't want to lose Maisie's help and advice, and she hoped that she would be able to stay with them for a long, long time, as it made it so much easier because she was the only other person aware of the true situation between herself and Daniel, in that the marriage was in name only because of Daniel's strict beliefs in a good name, and that had been necessary to give Zoe and Joss a home. It also meant that Daniel and Zoe could be their natural selves.

"I have mentioned 'my Bob, God rest his soul.' I only lost him eight months ago, and I was and am missing him terribly, as we had bin together for forty five years. We've only had each other since't lisle lad died when he was nine. My Bob, God rest his soul, was a lovely quiet man with nowt much to say, but we had each other. I'm fairly lost wi' him gone," Maisie replied quietly, wiping her eyes with a tissue.

"Oh I'm really sorry Maisie. I have heard you mention 'my Bob' but I didn't think it was so recent that you lost him."

"Aye lass, but it was a great relief when Daniel asked me to come and help out here. I was a nurse before I married my Bob, God rest his soul, but when we married we had t' little un quite soon, and as he was a gardener, and had to follow't jobs. We got a nice job with a gardener's cottage in Windermere, it was right grand with a real good lady, Mrs Jameson. I helped in't house and they were a really nice family."

"Does that mean you would like to stay here?"

"Aye mebbie I will sometime come back, but I promised Janette's daughter I'd be there when't second baby was born, and I'll have to be 'cos I promised. Only eighteen months between them, and they tell me this one will be another lad."

"When will that be Maisie?"

"In about four weeks I think, anyway Daniel is fine now, and doesn't need any nursing. You'll be able to manage fine." Maisie finished with a smile, as she saw her young friend's face drop in disappointment. She often worried about Zoe, she had Daniel as a father figure, but other than that she only had Joss and there was no possibility that there would be a sibling for him. What if she fell in love with someone, that would leave Daniel all alone again, and if Zoe couldn't or wouldn't follow her heart, she would be very lonely when Daniel (over twenty years older) died, and Joss grew up and went away, as they all seemed to these days. Maisie sniffed, knowing there was no good in worrying, Zoe had her own life to lead. After losing her only child, Maisie was all for the maxim, an heir and a spare, as she still ached for her lost child. A second child would never have replaced the loss of the first, but she would still have had someone to love and nurture. She was getting morbid and that wasn't any good, she might upset Zoe.

"I'll be back when I'm needed lass '*to him that is ready all is well',* as my mother used to say."

"I would have loved to meet your mother Maisie, she must have been a wonderful person," Zoe said, having regained her smile.

"She was that! Now can y' manage to get these lads out o't water and back home. I promised young Scott I'd call and have a look at some things of his dad's, we were at school together you know, and I said I'd go and put the kettle on for a drink and piece of cake for them surveyor people at Oak Tree Farm, they didn't know how long they'd be, but if I say I'll do something, I will."

"Of course Maisie, see you later."

As she watched Maisie gather her things, including her folding chair, she wondered if Scott was trying to poach Maisie away from Sharpe House, although she was aware that she had been at school with both Daniel and Scott's father. Who could blame him his house would be well looked after and so would he. On the other hand Adele had let slip, unintentionally she was aware, that Scott had had a thing going with Samantha, a girl who had worked at the riding school, which had not ended

106

well. Perhaps Samantha might have second thoughts and return, as Scott was certainly a good catch, he had a lovely home, or it would be one day according to Maisie, and it was situated in a very desirable area.

"Mummy, come and see," Joss called excitedly.

Zoe moved over to the boys and helped to put the finishing touches to a kind or fort, built with odd stones, and the help of Joss's small plastic digger. They had put pieces of fir tree here and there and it looked as if they were trees, and not only were Joss, Elliot and John working on it, but a number of other children has joined in. Zoe moved to one side enjoying the sight of all the children working together, and Joss even let one or two of them use his plastic digger!

Zoe took her digital camera out of the bag, it had been her mother's last present to her, and took a few photographs, which she would be able to get printed and which would go in the quite substantial album that she had already collected. She never showed these photographs to anyone, and she wondered if she was doing this because she believed that one day she would need them to help her remember these happy times. Very little in her life had gone well, except for having her wonderful son, and unfortunately, she only had one photograph taken of her mother before she died. Her mother had lost or got rid of anything from her first marriage, except one photograph of Zoe as a baby, and another when she started school.

At Oak Tree Farm, Maisie was putting the last little touches to the table in the dining room. It looked very nice, there were home made scones, jam and cream, together with a jam sponge cake and shortbread. She would brew the tea when the men arrived back, as they had all gone in one car up to the quarries more than three hours ago according to Scott's hastily written note on the kitchen table. Also on the kitchen table were a number of old photographs for Maisie to look through, as Scott had found a large box filled with photographs covering over forty years, and Scott and Adele hadn't a clue as to who some of the subjects in the photographs were, and they didn't want to throw them away if they portrayed local people or family. In the past not everyone had a camera in the house as seemed to be the case now, and some people might appreciate and enjoy unexpected photos of occasions and subjects to bring back memories. If Maisie hadn't any success or Daniel at some other time, then Scott intended to send them to the local library, for them to deal with as they saw fit.

The men didn't return for tea for over thirty minutes, and by then Maisie had a few different piles of photographs for noting names on the back, for local occasions and families. Some of the photographs of the annual Grasmere, and Ambleside Sports were very old. Maisie heard the vehicle arrive in the yard, and she went to switch on the kettle, and the photo in her hand caught her intensive attention in the bright sunlight from the kitchen window over the sink. It was a photo of Adele at about six years old, and of course Scott, a few years younger, Adele with the blue eyes like her mother, and Scott with the distinctive grey eyes of his father, for an old photograph the colour was quite good, and the image of the children was very clear. Maisie was still staring at the photograph when she realised the kettle was boiling and filling the kitchen with steam.

They had almost finished tea, and the conversation was quite lively, as all there were pleased with the afternoon spent in the quarries, and enthusiastic with the suggestions that had been made, when Scott left the table after excusing himself, as his mobile was ringing. He looked at it, and apologised again saying he must take the call, and went into the kitchen.

"Maisie it's a friend of Zoe's, she says Joss has cut his foot quite badly and needs to go to the doctor's he is bleeding rather a lot and might need stitches, will you explain to Daniel when the surveyors leave. I'll ring as soon as I know anything, I said I would pick them up at the roadside near the bridge, and take them in to Ambleside. Will you ring Adele and ask her to come for the boys please Maisie, just in case Joss has to go to hospital?"

Maisie nodded at Scott, as he looked quite shocked, and watched as he got into his car and left with a scattering of dust and pebbles off the drive. Did Scott know what she had just surmised about young Joss? If she had had her wits about her she would have told him they would need a child seat, or three, as his nephews were also with Zoe and Joss! She wasn't sure of the regulations regarding child seats in cars, and she doubted that Scott would either.

She sighed heavily, and then decided she would ring Adele in about ten minutes, as she assumed that Scott and Zoe *might* need a little time, and she would not bother Daniel and his visitors, she would tell him as soon as they left. What should she do? She assumed that Zoe had asked her friend to ring Scott because Daniel was here at Oak Tree Farm with him, as Daniel still didn't like carrying his mobile phone. Maisie pondered long and hard, it wasn't for her to meddle in other people's business, however close they were. Her mother would have said '*never trouble trouble, till trouble troubles you.*'

Twenty minutes earlier whilst Zoe was folding up the blanket, and putting it in her rucksack with the rest of their picnic things, Joss screamed loudly, and she turned in alarm towards the three boys on the shore of the tarn.

"Zoe, please come Joss has cut himself, there's lots of gory red blood everywhere," Elliot said with a great deal of relish.

Zoe dropped everything and rushed to Joss who was crying probably mostly because he was frightened, not with the pain he was feeling. Her heart was pounding, and she picked him up and placed him on a big stone, in order to examine his foot. One of the other mothers with a group of children came over to help, and between them they put a large wad of paper tissues over the cut which looked clean but very deep, but it would not stop bleeding.

The young woman looked worried, and glanced at Zoe who looked as if she might faint. "Hold his leg up, and we'll see what else there is to wrap around his foot to help stop the bleeding, have you a towel?"

"No it's alright thank you." Zoe said handing over Joss's foot that she was holding to the young woman, whilst she removed her cut off trousers, as she was wearing a pair of shorts underneath, and wrapped them around his foot as tightly as possible, tying them with the waist cord as well as she could.

"It looks as though it will need a number of stitches, shall I ring someone for you. I'm Jenny by the way."

"Thank you Jenny, we walked here, could you get my mobile out of my shorts pocket, and ring for 'Scott' as my husband is with him, and ask him to bring a car, Joss won't leave go of me, and I think we should set off towards the road, tell him I'll move towards the bridge and the Badger Bar, it's just too bad you can't stop there, but he'll have to. Thank you Jenny, I'm Zoe, and I think I've seen you at the school gate."

Jenny was walking along with Zoe as she made the call, and Elliot and John had picked up everything they had taken with them, and followed on rather quietly carrying the bag and plastic digger. Jenny returned the mobile by putting it in the pocket of Zoe's T-shirt. "I'll have to get back to my girls, as they are just a little bit older than your brood, but can't be left alone for too long."

"Thank you again Jenny."

By the time they had walked through the wood, and a field to the wooden bridge, Joss was becoming very heavy, but at least he had stopped crying, and was in fact, beginning to enjoy being the centre of attention, but the white trousers had now almost turned to red! Joss was losing an awful lot of blood. She was hurrying but the boys behind her had to be checked and she had to turn around and wait as they caught up with her.

"Hurry up Elliot, and you'd better help John junior, he isn't looking too well." Zoe said as the boys trailed behind her, and she now realised that she should have rung Adele and told her what was happening, because Joss would need to get to the doctor's or possibly hospital. It was all her own fault, she was to blame, as Adele had asked her to return to work at the stables and she had decided to spend the last two weeks of the summer holidays with Joss. If she had been at work this would never have happened!

They arrived at the roadside just as Scott drove around the corner and parked partly on the pavement on the opposite side of the road. The traffic slowed to a stop, and Scott left his car and came across to take Joss from Zoe's arms, and he quickly put him in the back of the car, with the other two boys, his face turned white as he saw the wrapping around Joss's foot, and he looked very angry.

"Get in Elliot, John, and put on a seat belt. You had better put Joss on your knee Zoe. I've arranged for Adele to come to the doctor's surgery to pick up the boys. I hadn't time to get your car Zoe, or Daniel's, Daniel will probably come on later with his car and the seat for Joss. Maisie said I should come on and she would tell Daniel as soon as the surveyors get away."

Zoe climbed into the back of the car and took Joss on her knee, and put the seat belt around them both. Scott waved a thank you to the stopped traffic, and set off rather faster than the thirty mile limit to get to the doctor's surgery. Zoe's bare legs felt damp and sticky with the blood from her makeshift wrapping around her son's foot. She closed her eyes, and hugged Joss close. With the amount of blood he had lost, it was probably best that she *and* Scott were with him, just in case. Poor Daniel he would be so worried!

CHAPTER FOURTEEN

"Uncle Scott, look what I brought, it's the piece of broken bottle that Joss stood on. Do you think the doctor will want to see it, it's big and sharp, and has a bit of blood on it?"

"That's very thoughtful Elliot, now put it on the floor of the car, and *cover* it with the mat. If we want it we'll know where to find it. Now will you keep quiet because I don't want to waste any time getting to the surgery, I need to concentrate on the traffic."

"Uncle Scott, I know what I'll do to be quiet, I'll think of what we have to tell them at school about the holiday, I bet nobody else will have such a good story."

"You do that Elliot, thank you." Scott said with a sigh, as he turned the car off the road and into the surgery parking area. "Stay in the car boys."

"Yes Uncle Scott, can we have the radio on." Elliot was ignored as Zoe passed Joss to Scott, and followed him into the surgery. Zoe was amazed at Scott's patience with the boys and began to realise what Joss was missing! And true to form as soon as Scott moved into reception, one of the nurses was talking to the receptionist, and moved quickly to his side!

"Oh dear what have we here. Straight into the nurses room and we'll have a look, and get a doctor down. Perhaps your wife would like to sit down, she looks a little pale," the kind nurse said, and she started to remove the wrapping around Joss's foot. "Ah your cut offs I guess, do you want to take them with you, or do you want us to get rid of them," the nurse said drawing attention to Zoe's long and sticky bare legs, and brief shorts, and Zoe felt guilty for having such uncharitable thoughts about the young nurse.

"Get rid of them please," Zoe said staring at the deep cut on the bottom of her son's foot, she suddenly swallowed, and when Scott took her hand in his she left it there, as she needed something or someone to hang on to. Poor Joss, he looked so frightened.

The doctor came to look at the wound, and the nurse assured him that it had been cleaned and there was no further glass in there, and he left instructions for the nurse to put in five stitches, in such a tiny foot. He looked at the amount of blood on the trousers, and nodded thoughtfully. "I don't think he'll need a blood transfusion. Just keep him quiet for a few days if you can, and make an appointment to get his stitches out, and I'll have another look at it then, but bring him any time if you think it necessary. A light bandage nurse, and if he hasn't any slippers, get him some to keep it clean. We need not disturb it until the stitches are ready to come out. Give the boy a lollipop." The doctor ruffled Joss's hair, and smiled at Scott and Zoe. "If there's any more outside you'd better take a lollipop for them, but don't make a habit of it. Sorry, lollipops I mean!"

Zoe blushed and Scott stared at her face, as she looked beautiful and about sixteen years old in her shorts and sandals, and he noticed that she must have been wearing shorts for a while, because her legs had a lovely light tan. Daniel was a very lucky man, and he had better think about something or someone else!

Whilst the nurse did her work, they each held one of Joss's hands, and he was very brave. He didn't make a sound except when she gave him a local injection to numb his foot.

When Scott carried Joss out of the surgery as Zoe seemed to be slightly wobbly on her legs, Adele met them with the boys who were very interested in how many stitches Joss had in the foot, and had it been bleeding again!

"Boys don't ask so many questions, leave Joss alone. And I see Uncle Scott has brought you a lollipop out of the surgery, this is a one off you know only to keep Joss company," she smiled ruefully, as she tried not to let them have too much in that line. "Oh, I've brought your car seat for Joss, now will it fit in your car Scott? The boys still have one because it is easier for me, but they will soon be able to use seatbelts I hope as they are growing so quickly. Have you rung Daniel Zoe, he was very worried."

"I'll do that now, but we'll be home in a few minutes, if we can fit the car seat quickly." Zoe said, feeling rather stupid for being so needy and holding on to Scott's hand earlier. Adele helped Scott with the car seat, and within minutes they were drawing into Sharpe House driveway.

"Thank you Scot, I thought Daniel would come, but I do see that after his heart problem, and only just getting well again, it was better for you to be there."

"No, I thought he should finish with the surveyors they were very helpful, and quite excited by Daniel's idea. And I must say that I think it would work. I had better stay in the vicinity, as you never know when Joss might need a transfusion, as he is so accident prone. And don't say that you hadn't thought of that, because I know you had." He said with eyebrows raised arrogantly, and she began to wonder why she had felt so needy just a few moments ago!

Scott received a really angry look from Zoe as he was quite right and he knew it, but it was still annoying. "I would be obliged if you could remove Joss's seat from your car," was all she could think of to say. She walked to join Daniel who was standing on the steps with the door open.

"See you tomorrow Scot, we have a lot to talk about, and thanks for picking up Zoe, the boys, and in particular young Joss." Daniel watched as Zoe struggled with Joss who wanted to be put down on his feet. "It won't be easy to make him stay off that foot. Come on Joss be very good, because Maisie is making your favourite for your tea, sausage and mash."

Zoe paused, still holding Joss closely. "Thank you Scott for all your help, we all appreciate it. Oh, don't forget to take the child seat out of your car," she finished as he looked rather upset, and she knew he was on the point of driving away as soon as possible.

"Don't worry Zoe, I'll help Scott with the car seat, I am used to it now. Take Joss inside, Maisie has been worrying about him, she has been acting rather oddly, she forgot to put milk in my tea, and when reminded she put it in and put in sugar as well. I've never taken sugar. Maisie just isn't herself at the moment," Daniel said with a wry smile.

Zoe went to find Maisie, and she wasn't the only one that was behaving rather oddly, Daniel thought and shook his head as Zoe rushed away with Joss. She was besotted with her son and rather off hand with Scott, who had kindly done everything he could to help! He brought to mind Nell, and realised that Zoe was much more pragmatic person than his Nell, she was always kind and thoughtful, and had never had an *easy time* in her short life. Nell had been unpredictable, but oh so very exciting. Nell had, of course, no need to work and had only thought of travelling the world, and she had thought of the world as her oyster, to do with as she wished. In truth she had been a bit spoilt and selfish, but when she was around he had never thought of anything or anyone else!

Joss was able to start school again with the rest of his friends, as his foot heeled very quickly, and he soon regained his usual robust energy. Zoe again started work at the High Stile riding school, and it was a relief to get back into a certain and enjoyable routine.

Maisie went off to be with Janette's daughters to be there for the birth and the first three weeks thereafter. She kept in touch by telephone. There were no surprises, as they had been told to expect another boy.

Maisie's busy presence and amusing or useful maxim's passed down via her mother was missed at Sharpe House. Daniel's health had progressed for the better, and he was living a normal life now, and had much more energy than previously enjoyed when he had been thought to be suffering from angina. He got stuck in with Scott dealing with the plans and hopes for the two quarries, and the necessary permits or licenses with the powers that be. Ald Smithy had been co-opted into the team, and he and an equally aged colleague were dealing with the joining up of the two quarries. The surveyors, Daniel, Scott and Ald Smithy and his friend were all of the opinion that it would take about two weeks to join up, and they could do it without any problem. In fact a hole had been drilled, and light was there at the end of each of the joined tunnels (drill holes).

Zoe took Joss up to the quarry, on one of the days when they were showing people around, or at least there was nothing dangerous occurring, and Daniel was waiting for them on the quarry bank.

"Daniel we decided to walk up here, but had to suddenly step aside when a small four by four came down unexpectedly, I think you will have to have a speed limit in force on the quarry road."

"That's a very sensible idea, I can see we will have to let you know what is going on, and get your input, ideas like that would be invaluable. I'm sorry if you had a fright, as I believe the young woman driving is a good friend of Scott's, she used to work at his sister's place, with the horses, and they were good friends for a while before he went back to Afghanistan."

Zoe held on to Joss's hand, as her heart began a gradual contraction, and she felt a wave of guilt wash over her, she swallowed realising what Daniel had said had nothing to do with her, she had no right to feel this pain, which must be jealousy! Was Scott in a relationship with that girl when his father died, and when he had fathered Joss? She had not thought that what had occurred so unexpectedly and irrevocably, could have affected anyone but the two of them, she felt a little sick, and had to pull herself together or Daniel would wonder what was wrong with his young wife, who mostly seemed really happy.

It was the first time that Zoe had been back at the quarry bank since Daniel had been missing, and it took her a while to get her equilibrium back, as she suffered a slight anxiety attack on seeing the tunnel mouth where she had waited for Daniel to be found, she sighed deeply, she was being a bit of a wimp today. Far too emotional, and she should get a grip of herself.

"You went quite pale Zoe," Daniel remarked as he put his arm across her shoulder. "Are you feeling alright now?"

"Yes thank you Daniel, it was just seeing the tunnel again, it brought everything back, it was a long wait for us as well as you Daniel, but everything is more than alright now. What are you doing with the old quarry sheds, they seem very different, and I didn't think there was a roof on that one." Zoe pointed where two sheds were in the process of being renovated, and in fact one had a sign above the door proclaiming 'office,' and the name of the company.

Scott walked from one shed to the other busy reading something as he walked. Daniel waved and shouted to attract his attention.

"Scott, can you show Zoe and Joss what is happening over there?"

Scott paused for a moment, and then shouted "Of course any time they are ready." He moved on then to the other shed, and Zoe felt that they were being rather a nuisance. He seemed to have his mind on what he was reading, or possibly the very attractive young woman who had just left driving quite dangerously, Zoe thought disdainfully.

"It's alright Zoe, Scott is a bit preoccupied at the moment, you will see why when you've been inside the tunnel for a little bit, and I'll show you the progress made, most of the tunnels will be lit with electric light and the rails for moving the heavy weight of slate will be renewed, as will the wagons, but everything really old will be used in the museum shed."

"Are you going to make it into a going concern again," Zoe asked surprised.

"Not really, but we will produce a small amount, in order that we can let visitors see all the different processes, leading to the finished articles, such as roofing slates, or slate for cladding buildings."

As they arrived back into the light after the tunnel, Joss was not very eager to accompany them, but he did, with a promise from Daniel that Scott would show them what he was doing in the sheds.

"Then can we go in the tunnel again," Joss said although whilst in there he had clung to his mother's hand, and sometimes hidden behind her slightly, and he really loved the little blue wellingtons he had acquired since cutting his foot, as they were great for stamping in puddles and the water on the tunnel floors! But it was exciting as long as his mummy and Daniel were there with him, but he liked Scott too, and bet there was something interesting in those sheds, and he couldn't wait to get there providing he could go back to the tunnel another time.

CHAPTER FIFTEEN

Daniel took them to see Scott in the sheds, and as they entered Zoe realised that they were much more than sheds. They were stone built in the stone from the quarry, and were now pleasantly light from the new windows in the roof. Scott was in the process of arranging displays around the walls of blown up photographs of various types of stone, and pictures taken inside the quarries. Against two walls sturdy cupboards had been built, on top of which were various types of green and blue stone, in addition to that there were other types of stone - granite and sandstone Zoe recognised.

"Scott, what a wonderful display! All these lovely small pieces of stone are wonderfully coloured," Zoe remarked showing her surprise.

"Yes, come over here Joss, what do you think of these different coloured stones?"

"Good, can I touch," Joss asked, already reaching for a piece of green slate which fitted in his hand and it had been polished smooth and was very tactile, and he loved the feel of it in his hand. It crossed Zoe's mind that it would make a very good missile, if held in a young hand, and she was determined to mention this sometime to Scott.

"Of course, that is for touching and feeling, but you have to be careful because they are quite heavy, and if you dropped it, it would hurt your toes," Scott said, watching with interest as Joss held the stone, and turned it from side to side.

Joss helped himself to four of the small rounded stones, and sat down on the floor to play.

"Daniel, can I borrow you for a bit," Ald Smithy said from the open doorway. "Hello Mrs Sharpe an' Joss, how'y doing."

"Fine thank you Smithy, and it's Zoe," she said, as she knew she would never get used to being called Mrs Sharpe.

"Aye lass, I recall," Smithy said with a rueful smile, and he and Daniel walked out of the building.

"Are you interested in what we are doing here Zoe," Scott said in clipped tones, as he offered a piece of pink granite for Joss to look at, and Zoe realised she had never seen him before other than well turned out. He now wore dusty jeans, and T-shirt, and his hair was untidy, and she wondered if that was because the girl who had nearly run into her and Joss on the quarry road, had mussed it up for him, and what might the situation have been for that to happen. She was punishing herself for her wayward thoughts, and she truly deserved it!

"Of course," she replied equally coldly.

"Well from the display you will realise that the slate was probably formed four hundred and fifty million years ago in the Ordovician period from volcanic ash and lava which spread across central Lakeland, but it was not just formed by volcanic debris. It is a metamorphosed rock, but it was altered from the original deposit, and the alterations created the unique properties of slate. Volcanic ash which contained chlorides giving the green colour was deposited into lagoon water, but the activity wasn't continuous, there were quiet periods, and this created the banding that is evident in green slate, and in some cases created beautiful bar markings as a result. All this made the slate easy to split. The lie of the beds of deposited material is called the bedding plane."

"And then the Ice Age created the valleys and mountains, in fact the Lake District, and the glaciers ..," Zoe interrupted him, and he looked really angry, and then caught the glint in her eye, and they both laughed, and Joss laughed too, and continued to play with the smooth stones.

"Sorry Zoe, was I boring you?"

"No, you just gave the impression that we were interrupting your work. It was really interesting, but some other time please, when Joss is not needing his tea. I should own up, I have done ancient history and geography at school, and I know where to come if I need to brush up on it, or a more in depth insight of geology. I think it's a wonderful way to get children interested in so many subjects, Joss was really excited by the tunnel, or level as Daniel explained, it was exciting and just a little frightening I think."

"He also seems to like the feel of the rocks, I had a devil of a job finding all the sea or beck washed stones. It's illegal to get them off the beaches you know. Sorry if I seemed bad tempered, it was the way Smithy called you Mrs Sharpe! I suddenly realised that I should ask you the full name of my son, if you wouldn't mind, is he only Joss or has he a second name, and is it Sharpe, Howes, or what?"

Zoe suddenly sat down on a tall stool on which Scott probably sat whilst working on the displays, she was staring down at her clasped hands, and then she looked at Joss still playing quietly sitting on the dusty floor. She smiled ruefully as he looked up at her with a smile, and she glanced hurriedly to identical eyes, which held a very different extremely enigmatic expression which tore at her heart.

"On his birth certificate it is, of course, Joshua Howes, because I couldn't think of anything else. My paternal grandfather was named Joshua, and he seemed to be the only male person that my mother seemed to admire. Neil Brown was objectionable, and Daniel was the only person around here that cared a damn."

"Father *unknown* presumably, poor Joss, some day he will want to know who his father was. Did you not know Zoe, had you been sleeping around, as at the time I didn't think you were like that?" Scott asked.

"Neither of us did *any* thinking at the time. Leave me alone Scott, you were eager enough to do so at one time. I'll have to give it some thought, as perhaps Daniel would be really pleased if Joss changed his name to Sharpe. Because now that you have mentioned it, I really don't know what they are teaching him at nursery, with regard to writing his name, maybe some people think it is Joss Sharpe already." She finished speaking, realising that she was hurting and because of that she wanted to hurt Scott. She was becoming a nasty piece of work, and she realised she must do something about it, but what!

"I think you should leave things for the time being, you are in no state to be sensible, procrastination seems to be your way of *not* dealing with matters, and in the future if for any reason he asks if I am his father I will tell him the truth."

Zoe almost fell back from the steely dislike in his eyes, and it hurt, it hurt so very much that she bent down and took the stones from Joss and slammed them onto the nearest cabinet, and pulling a very reluctant boy by the hand, she made for the door.

"Zoe, please wait, don't take it out on Joss because you are annoyed with me," Scott said quickly.

Zoe paused on the threshold. "As if I would Scott, I thought we had been getting on rather well considering. Please keep away in future, because I don't want Joss to get upset. Oh and by the way, get your girlfriend to slow down when she drives on the quarry road; she nearly ran into *me* and *your* son, as we were walking up to the quarry." She was really angry, and just stopped herself from being really nasty and saying that if Samantha had run into them then *he* would have had *nothing* to worry about.

Scott stared after Zoe and his son, she was probably quite right, they couldn't keep tearing strips off each other, it would not be fair to Joss, or do either of them any good. Also Daniel was a wonderful man, and he would certainly pick up and wonder about any friction or antipathy, or any other feelings that they didn't seem able to control.

He remembered the time that he had realised Joss was his son, and that disagreement had led to him giving her a punishing kiss, and that meant that she was quite right he should keep away. He *would* join Samantha at the local public house as she had suggested earlier, he might again see something in her that had attracted him to her when they first met! He had been disgusted at her behaviour in the stable with a client, but who was he to stand in judgement over her, perhaps it was a one off – he could understand that! At the moment he felt sick in his stomach, but he had to start to make a life for himself preferably far away from this valley of his birth. First he must help Daniel and Ald Smithy get this project up and running, it was a really good idea, and he was certain it would work, and for at least part the day it kept his mind occupied with all the necessary planning and physical work involved, and if it had not been for his preoccupation with Joss and his mother it would have been very satisfying.

Maisie was welcomed with open arms on her return by Joss and the rest of the household at Sharpe House, and they all enjoyed a leisurely celebration dinner, of Cumberland sausage, peas and mash, chosen by Joss. Next morning Daniel went off as usual up to the quarries, and Zoe, having taken Joss to nursery returned to have coffee with Maisie, and hear all the news.

"No work today Zoe, are y' not going to High Stile?" Maisie enquired.

"Yes in a little while, some of the lessons have been cancelled because the vet is coming to see one of the horses. It should be alright, but they want to make sure, and there isn't very much for me to do in the office."

"You don't fancy learning t' ride then lass," Maisie said with a smile. "Joss should learn its in't family y' know." Then she stopped speaking as she noticed her young friends pink cheeks turned red with embarrassment.

"Sorry Zoe, I meant in Daniel's family and t' family at High Stile of course, I believe them lad's are fine riders. Just as was Daniel when he was a youngster but I've not seen him riding for a long time."

"No, I've not known him to ride, since we've been at Sharpe House." Zoe agreed thoughtfully.

"Aye, well that's another story for Daniel to tell, had you not best be getting away to High Stile? *Constant occupation prevents temptation,* as my mother used to say, and so did my Bob rest his soul."

"Yes Maisie, I'd best be getting away to High Stile, when I've washed these dishes. *Better to do late than never*."

"Aye well, I've a heap of photos that belonged to his dad to finish sorting for Scott, he doesn't know who people are, or what the occasions were, so I'll be sort of busy for an hour or so. Have you any of those yellow sticky things I can write on and stick on top of't piles sorted?"

"There are some yellow stickers on Daniel's desk, why don't you do the sorting in his room, there's lots of room on the table in there because it's nice and light, and there is less chance of Joss messing things up, because he now realises that Daniel likes things neat and tidy."

"He does indeed, '*a place for everything and everything in its place.'* Maisie smiled unable to resist just one more quotation.

Maisie sorted nearly all the photographs that day, there were pictures taken of Ambleside Sports, and Grasmere Sports over the years, and the rushbearings in both villages, and the family photographs were sorted, and she left them with the yellow tags attached, as her plan was to get some used envelopes off Daniel, to put the sorted photos inside and then she would stick on the yellow labels. This was a very sensible notion, and it was fortunate that it worked so well. In actual fact Daniel was very intrigued by the piles of interesting photographs, and upon reading Maisie's explicit notes he started to put the photographs into used envelopes and stick on the informative notes, but his much appreciated help, had a consequence in the future that Maisie might not actually regret, but that she had most certainly not considered!

CHAPTER SIXTEEN

Zoe was kept busy during the next few weeks, and because the weather was warm and sunny, she spent as much time with Joss outside as was possible. He became brown and very healthy looking, as did she, but she wasn't interested very much in her own appearance. The only time she decided to take more care with her appearance was when she met the young woman that had been to see Scott at the quarry and nearly run Joss and her down. She hurried into the office one Monday morning at High Stile to find her waiting, and whilst she was waiting she was looking through the appointments book.

"Excuse me," Zoe said, reclaiming the book, and closing it was a slight thud. "What can I do for you? Do you wish to make a booking for a riding lesson?"

The young woman looked very cool and collected, and would have been very pretty if she hadn't been looking rather sulky and pursing her very red lips. Zoe wondered if Adele was aware of her presence here in the office.

"I'm Samantha Brown, and I'm waiting for Adele, she is usually around at this time, and I need to see her. I used to work with the horses, and I think I might like to help out again for a short while, and I am a good friend of her brother Scott, and will be sticking around this area for a while."

"Ms Brown, I'm not sure where Adele is today but she should be home from the school run by now, I'll ring the farmhouse for you." She rang the house, and waited as Samantha Brown moved around the small office, and then stood beside the window. Her profile was silhouetted against the sunshine outside, and although her hair looked quite dark and had a nice sheen, her profile looked rather like the animals she seemed to be so fond of, she was a very horsey type Zoe thought, and then was ashamed of her unkind thoughts. She and Scott were probably made for each other, as they were both arrogant and selfish.

Adele answered the phone in the farmhouse, and when Zoe told her who was waiting to see her she paused for a while, and then asked Zoe to ask her to go up to the house.

"Would you like to go to the farmhouse, Mrs Simpson will see you."

Samantha didn't bother replying, but went out leaving the door open, and walked confidently up to the farmhouse.

Zoe still felt ashamed of her unkind thoughts and hoped that Samantha got what she deserved, didn't she? She was a few inches taller than Zoe, and looked fit and well, and Zoe could see her as a long distance runner. The further the distance the better! God she was becoming a very nasty person, there was probably nothing wrong with Samantha at all, she was only chasing the eligible Scott Peterson. Perhaps Samantha Brown was related to the horrible 'Cruella de Neil Brown?"

Zoe decided that because of having so many uncharitable thoughts, she would refrain from having any biscuits, scones, or anything enjoyable for the rest of the day.

After a few days when Samantha didn't come near to the riding school, Zoe assumed that her request had been denied by Adele, who must have taken someone on to replace Samantha.

Three weeks later John and Adele, together with Daniel and Zoe were waiting in the Salutation Hotel in Ambleside, for their table for six to be filled. The occasion was a charity evening to raise money for the Air Ambulance, the Mountain Rescue, and local hospices. Zoe looked around the room and noticed how nice everyone looked with the men either in dinner or lounge suits, and the ladies in their evening or party clothes. Daniel had insisted that she should have a new gown, and she was very pleased with it, and Daniel had told her how very beautiful she looked, as the gown was the same colour as her blue eyes, and tonight she had twisted up her shoulder length hair and secured it with a beautiful comb, which Daniel said had belonged to his mother, and how well the old and the new complimented each other.

She was very proud of Daniel too, he looked even younger than when she had married him, now that he was well, and keeping very busy at the quarry site. Just for a second tonight when Daniel had helped her into the front seat of the car, she had wondered if she was a burden to him. Now that he was well she wondered if he would like to make their marriage into a real one, but although she loved him as a father figure, she was *not* prepared for that, and although she and Joss had provided him with a family it should have been her mother beside him giving him a satisfying and fulfilled life. Life wasn't fair.

No, life wasn't fair, because Scott was now taking the seat beside her at the end of the table, after seating Samantha Brown opposite to her. Why had she not realised that obviously Adele and John would have asked Scott and Samantha to join them. Samantha looked quite lovely in a brilliant red dress, and Scott looked gorgeous in a black dinner suit with his hair too tidy, and she only just stopped herself from moving her hand towards him.

"Sorry we are a little late, have they taken the order yet," Scott asked Daniel, presumably because he was the oldest person present, and his eyes skimmed across Zoe and she wondered if he liked what he saw, certainly Samantha must be hard to overlook in her vibrant *scarlet* colour. Pussy cat, pussy cat where have you been, her thoughts would ruin her night if she wasn't careful. She felt even worse later, as Samantha put herself out to talk to everyone, even Zoe, and she was quite pleasant.

The meal was good and the master of ceremonies was quite entertaining, and there was a short auction of goods given to make money for the charities. Daniel bought flowers to be delivered to the house for a year, John bought the services of a young lad to work for a number of days on his farm, and Scott paid a large amount for champagne, which he said would come in useful when the quarry opened for visits from schools and the visiting public, which he and Daniel agreed could be in about six weeks, and that would give them a taste of what was to come, before the end of the summer season, and then the quieter seasons of autumn and winter, would give them a chance to make any slight alterations that might be necessary.

The meal was very good, and when the tables were cleared away except for the chocolates and drinks, the dancing started, and the singer with his two colleagues providing the music started to provide music to dance to. Samantha, pulled Scott onto the floor, and he didn't seem to be too much against the idea. They danced very well together, and Adele and John joined them. Daniel said he preferred to wait for a quieter dance, with real music. He was a very good dancer Zoe found when he asked her to dance a quickstep and then a waltz. Then John asked her to dance and Daniel danced with Adele, it was an up tempo number and very enjoyable although there was no physical contact. Later Zoe was about to leave the table to go to the ladies room, because she realised that she would possibly have to dance with Scott, but she was thwarted as Daniel asked Samantha to dance, and Scott was standing before her with the expression in his grey eyes daring her to reject his offer. It was a slow waltz and she sighed and lifted her hand to be taken by his, with his other arm around her small waist, and they waltzed easily around the small wooden dance floor.

"I quite agree Zoe, this wasn't a good idea, but we might as well enjoy it," he said quietly. She was conscious of every part of his body and her own, and she had to remind herself to keep breathing. She glanced towards Daniel who was holding Samantha close, and appearing to enjoy his dance with Samantha. Daniel smiled across at Zoe, and for some strange reason she couldn't help it, she gave herself up to the music, and to her partner, as they fitted together like a pair of gloves, and it felt as though her heart would burst. It felt so right, and when the music stopped Scott held her hand tightly, but would not look into her eyes. Scott didn't ask her to dance again, and she was relieved because it was much too bitter-sweet and she was beginning to feel quite worn out.

Later in the evening, Scott looked across at his sister. "Adele, who is baby sitting the boys, as it is usually *me*?"

"John's mother kindly offered, but don't you let Elliot and John junior hear you call them babies, they consider themselves to be quite grown up. Anyway, I thought you would be coming to the dance."

"Well Samantha was very insistent, and it has been a very enjoyable evening." Scott replied. "And who is baby sitting Joss," he continued with a glance at Zoe and Daniel.

There was an awkward silence, and Samantha looked a little surprised, and Daniel looked closely at Zoe for a moment.

"Why, Maisie of course, with the help of Ald Smithy, as he and I are having a early morning at the quarry tomorrow, although it is Saturday, so I suggested he should stay over," Daniel said with a smile, and Zoe wondered if she had mistaken the awkward silence, perhaps it was only in *her* mind. Perhaps she and Scott were the only ones who felt awkward, and out of their depth. The next time Daniel said he was taking her out for a meal she would find out who they were joining, and where! Daniel continued, "Anyway I've been thinking about having the old cottage next to Sharpe House done up a bit, you know made habitable, and I thought it might suit Ald Smithy very well. He's in a council flat, and he isn't very happy, as he spends a lot of his time coming back and forth to the quarry site."

"That sounds and excellent idea Daniel, and the men who have been working on the buildings at the quarry will soon be finished, and they are doing a very good job." Scott replied thoughtfully.

"Could you see to that please Scott on Monday if possible? I am going away on Sunday for a few days, up to the Isle of Skye, if that's alright with you Zoe?"

Zoe couldn't hide her surprise and looked around her feeling quite upset. It must seem to the others present that she and Daniel did very little talking! This was the first time that Daniel had intimated that he was going away, and why to the Isle of Skye?

"Of course it's alright Daniel, why would it not be," she replied quickly.

That night Zoe couldn't sleep, she was tossing and turning in bed and she was unable to get to sleep until the early hours of the morning, it was because she was overtired, not because she wondered if Samantha was sleeping at Oak Tree Farm, or worse still *not* sleeping. Her mind was in a whirl, and across the house Daniel was also having trouble for a very different reason. He sat by the window in his room looking at the stars and the sliver of moon, as if the answer to his problems were up there. Fortunately, both Maisie and Ald Smithy, were tucked up in the rooms each side of Joss, and slept very well indeed, as did young Joss.

When Zoe awoke the sun was shining outside her window, and she heard movement downstairs and hurried downstairs as quickly as possible thinking that it must be Joss and she didn't want him to waken up the rest of the household. She tied her dressing down cord tightly around her waist, and hurried into the kitchen.

"Morning lass," Maisie said brightly, as she continued to pour tea into two cups. She then handed them to Daniel and Ald Smithy. "Just in time for a cup o' tea, before young Joss gets you running around after him."

"Thank you Maisie, I'll take a cup upstairs and have a quick shower. I thought it must be Joss in the kitchen and I didn't want him to waken anyone else," Zoe replied, and watched with some interest as Maisie passed the cup across the table, with her other hand on Ald Smithy's shoulder. She glanced at Daniel and he was watching her with a great deal of interest. She looked back at her husband, and was unable to read the enigmatic look he was giving her. Was Daniel aware of the familiar way that Maisie had with him and Smithy, and then she realised that they had all been at school together, and had not lost touch since then. Zoe quickly kissed Daniel on his forehead, and moved towards the kitchen door, but he held her hand and kissed the back of it. She was very surprised as they never showed any kind of affection usually! Perhaps that was *her* fault. It was possible that he now felt embarrassed at springing his trip up to Scotland on her in front of his friends, and he had yet to give her an explanation, although he didn't need to tell her what he was doing or intending to do, just as he never made any demands on *her* time!

"We won't be back for lunch Zoe, Smithy and I have a sandwich for lunch, and we'll make a brew at the quarry office." Daniel watched as Zoe went into the hallway towards the stairs, and Maisie watched Daniel with a worried frown on her rosy cheeked face.

"Come on you two, *'do it now, tomorrow is the day when idle people work and fools reform'* Maisie chivvied them.

Daniel smiled and pushed his chair under the table. "*Better to do late than never,"* he replied with a big smile.

"I remember mother saying that. Aye well, I don't know what my Bob God rest his soul would ha' said," Maisie sighed.

"Thou does lass, he'd a said nowt, 'cos he left that up t' thee," Ald Smith said with a twinkle in his eyes, "but he was a reet lucky bugger to have thee lookin' after 'im."

Maisie washed up the dishes looking out into the garden with a smile on her face, and then she remembered Daniel and his strange look at his young wife. Something was afoot that she wasn't privy to. She would have to stay around here a while, she somehow thought she would be needed. And having Ald Smithy and Daniel for company was quite nice too. Before Zoe had arrived in the kitchen Daniel had been explaining to Maisie and Smithy, that he was taking a few days off, and going up to the Isle of Skye, and they had both been very surprised, as that was the place in which Nell Peterson and he had planned to spend their honeymoon!

CHAPTER SEVENTEEN

Scott awoke early on Saturday morning although he had stayed at Samantha's for a late drink. He considered the evening at the Charity Event at the Salutation Hotel had been a success. Samantha appeared to enjoy the company, although at first Adele had been a little stiff and slightly embarrassed, because she had refused to take on Samantha at the riding school again, giving Samantha the impression that it was because she was fully staffed. How could his sister Adele possibly have said it was because *he* had seen her in one of the stables with one of their clients in a compromising position! He understood perfectly his sister's point of view, and just because he was finding it easy to forgive or forget that didn't mean that she had to condone such behaviour from one of her staff!

He was in the bathroom looking in the mirror and rubbed his fingers of his right hand around his chin wondering if he needed to shave again this morning, or would Samantha like the rugged dark chin look.

He looked ruefully into his own eyes in the slightly steamed up mirror, who was he kidding he had not forgiven Samantha at all, he really didn't care that much either way, but her company was quite enjoyable, and he would enjoy it until she wanted something more, which she had already intimated on one or two occasions when they were alone. He would just have to make sure they were *not* alone, and he had managed to get away last night without upsetting her too much. Except for that indiscretion she seemed alright, perhaps that was her *only* indiscretion, but the fact that he had grave doubts would seem to point to the fact that he didn't really believe that.

Perhaps after riding today, he should give the matter some further thought. He was aware that he *wasn't perfect* either, and maybe they could rub along nicely together for the time being. Before he had gone back to Afghanistan his relationship had been very satisfactory with Samantha, and he had received quite definite come-ons from two of the grooms at his sister's stables, but he wasn't interested.

He gazed into the eyes in the mirror, exactly like those of young Joss, and he hurt inside. And he wondered if the only reason he was encouraging Samantha to hang around was to prove to Zoe, that *he* could be just as happy as she appeared to be with Daniel. If that was the case then he was acting in a despicable manner, as both Daniel and Zoe were good people, but it was very hard not to get at her now and again, although he usually hurt himself just as much as he hurt Zoe!

When he arrived at High Stile, Samantha and Adele already had the two horses ready saddled. Adele watched Scott and frowned, and he wondered what was worrying her, she knew very well that he was a good rider, as was Samantha.

Adele looked on as Samantha turned her horse out of the stable.

"What's wrong with you this morning Adele, did you get too much to drink last night?" Scott asked, knowing full well that Adele had done her best last night to be pleasant to everyone around the table, and had only had two drinks.

"No Scott I didn't get too much to drink. Now this morning I gave your horse a few *oats* as a treat, so treat him gently for a while until he digests them. Now *she* has had her *oats* too, or had you forgotten?" Adele replied pointing to the filly, and Samantha riding her!

Adele walked away towards the farmhouse, and Scott frowned as he watched her. Well, it seemed that his sister was not very pleased with him, but for the moment he would leave things alone. He was not feeling very helpful himself today, and then he smiled at what his sister had intimated, she never failed to surprise him, and he had certainly got the message – she didn't approve, and they both knew the reason why!

They quite enjoyed their ride through John's fields, and took a bridle path on the west of Rydal Water, but there were far too many pedestrians walking around both Rydal Water and towards Grasmere. And who could blame them it was a beautiful day with blue sky, a few white clouds, and the water was still as a duck pond showing to perfection the reflected fells with the only ripples on the water being where the swans were upending themselves to feed underwater, or where the ducks were loudly squabbling. Scott was very definite, when he suggested to Samantha that they would return the same way to High Stile. He had realised that Samantha intended to go around Grasmere and return along the coffin route, and *he* didn't want to do that.

They turned the horses slowly, and walked sedately back the same way, every so often having to move into single file to make room for the walkers.

"Last night Zoe Sharpe looked really surprised when her husband said he was going up to the Isle of Skye, she obviously didn't know anything about his plans," Samantha said thoughtfully.

"Well, I guess Daniel has been on his own for so long and never had to consider anyone else, that he didn't think to mention it to Zoe, Maisie, or me for that matter," Scott replied, he didn't like Samantha mentioning this as it had nothing to do with her. Neither had it anything to do with him really, but he had been mulling over the same thoughts since last night. Zoe had looked quite hurt, but then she wasn't aware of the reason why Daniel might want to visit the Isle of Skye. Perhaps he was so happily married now that he could put the past where it should be – in the past!

After unsaddling the horses and rubbing them down, Scott and Samantha each walked to their own vehicle.

"See you at seven Scott, I'm looking forward to it," Samantha said happily.

"Oh, yes of course, see you at seven," he replied quickly. He had forgotten all about meeting up at the Badger Bar for something to eat. Well, it was better than cooking for himself he realised, then felt a bit of a heel. Samantha was Samantha, and it wasn't her fault that he didn't feel as much as he had in the past, and as much as she probably hoped he did!

Scott drove home, and when he arrived at the circular drive outside Oak Tree Farm, he was very surprised to see Ald Smithy and Maisie sitting at the round oak garden table, looking quite settled as if they had been there for a while. It seemed strange seeing Maisie without her apron, and it looked as though Smithy had changed from the clothes he had been wearing to go up to the quarry with Daniel.

"Hello, nice to have some surprise visitors, can I get you both a drink?"

"No thanks," Maisie said, and then realised that Smithy looked positively disappointed. "Oh, alright then, I'll go and make a cup of tea, it's too early for anything else, *a fat kitchen makes a lean will,* as mother used to say. Give us y' key, and I'll put the kettle on, and Smithy can have a bit of't cake I brought you last week if there's any left." She reached for the key, and then moved off around the house to the back door.

"What's this all about Smithy, it's really nice to see you, but I'll see you on Monday at the quarry site," Scott said with a wry smile.

"Aye well, Maisie is bothered about Daniel, she thinks there's summat up with 'im and Zoe, she can explain it all when she brings t' tea." Smithy looked across the valley, as he was only here because Maisie wanted to come. He reckoned Daniel and Zoe could manage to look after themselves. When it had all happened young Scott would only have been a young lad and Adele a few years older. And he remembered with a deep sigh how difficult it had been for Daniel's friends to keep him going, and it had taken a long time before they were not worried about leaving him on his own. Now he seemed very happy with young Zoe and Joss, and as for his health, he couldn't remember Daniel looking better!

Zoe had come across Daniel sorting out his clothes, and decided it was her wifely duty to help.

"What exactly do you want to take with you Daniel, you have three shirts and one tie, and two pairs of trousers and underwear and a jacket, on your bed."

"Well, I need some walking gear and a waterproof and walking boots. I intend to do some walking, I've a lot of thinking to do, and I reckon Skye is a good place to do it." Daniel said with a smile, relieved that Zoe wasn't giving him the third degree for not mentioning his little trip earlier. "The work up at the quarry site will soon be finished, and you now have your own car, and Maisie and Smithy will be staying here, so you and Joss will have company."

"Will you take your mobile phone, and give us a ring when you get there." Zoe asked, wondering why he had suddenly decided he needed time alone, was he regretting marrying her, and was it too noisy for him with a boy of almost four years old?

"Of course, and don't worry Zoe, I planned to go to the Isle of Skye a long time ago, and now I feel so well, I would like to do the walking I planned to do once before, and I should be back in four days."

Zoe understood how he was feeling and she kissed his cheek, as she finished packing his small suitcase, and rucksack. She too had often enjoyed time alone, and it was wonderful to think that Daniel was now well enough to take a walking holiday. Before starting the quarry project he had often taken short walks around the Lake District, but now he must feel like trying this elsewhere.

Daniel did remember to ring when he arrived in the Isle of Skye, and with having Maisie and Smithy around the four days passed quite quickly.

The only thing that Zoe felt was odd was when Adele had asked where Daniel had gone, and Zoe had informed her it was the Isle of Skye, she had looked quite pensive. But then Joss had needed Zoe's attention, and she had forgotten all about Adele's strange reaction at hearing the news.

CHAPTER EIGHTEEN

The opening of the quarry as a museum and aid to teaching was very exciting as far as Joss was concerned. He was up there as often as possible with either his mother, or Daniel and Scott. After the opening with the press, and representatives from various educational departments, where it was toasted with the champagne that Scott had bought at the charity dinner, as far as Joss was concerned it became much more interesting. He loved to see all the school children, and families who visited, as there was a play area like a miniature quarry, with heaps of different coloured stone, in different grades, in which the small children could play with toy size wagons, diggers, and tipping wagons, which was all monitored by a friend of Maisie's who was a retired teacher.

For the older school children, or children visiting with their parents, there were conducted tours of the quarry, followed by visits to the displays bringing in various additions to the geology, namely archaeology, cosmology, palaeontology the study of ancient life forms, fossils, and the staircase of time showing when the dinosaurs were on the earth, which was one of the most asked questions.

Scott was amazed at the difficulties which arose with regard to the necessary certification necessary for all the staff, or helpers, with regard to heath and safety, to obtaining certificates and going through Police checks. He had also been struck dumb, wondering how to answer when Daniel had suggested that it would be good for Zoe to make use of her degree, and how she would be an asset to the whole scheme, and after a short pause he had agreed with Daniel. But he had been of the opinion that Zoe would make up her own mind, particularly if she had to work closely with *him*.

Zoe did indeed make up her own mind, after ascertaining that Adele would have no trouble in replacing her in the office at the High Stile stables. Unfortunately she had just seen Samantha driving away from the quarry presumably after visiting her boyfriend, and declared that she would love to join them in their venture, and had kissed Daniel on the cheek, and walked out of the room, leaving both Daniel and Scott quite shocked, but in Daniel's case also very pleased.

When Zoe gave the matter some serious thought she realised that she had been underachieving at the stables, and she was determined to leave Scott and Daniel to manage as they saw fit, and she would stick to the jobs they allotted her, and also try to arrange her days to suit herself, so that she was rarely around when Scott was there.

A month after Zoe officially started working for the quarry company, both she and Scott were amazed when Daniel informed them he had arranged for an extended holiday touring parts the Mediterranean, and it was too hectic a trip for women and children. Zoe was very hurt, but was determined not to let

Daniel or Scott see how much! She rushed away to pick up Joss from nursery school, and did not return to the quarry at all that day. She helped Maisie prepare a lovely meal of roast beef, Yorkshire puddings, and vegetables, and she realised that everything including the pudding were Daniel's favourites.

"I realise you are preparing all Daniel's favourite items Maisie. When did he tell you he was going away, he only mentioned it at the quarry today, and I think Scott was as surprised as was I?" Zoe asked with a frown.

"Only yesterday, because I saw him looking at 'is new passport, and surprisingly it's a good photograph," Maisie said with a smile. "He should have mentioned it earlier to you Zoe, but I think he has only just made up his mind to go when the passport arrived." Maisie looked at Zoe and realised how very upset she was by Daniel's decision. Perhaps she thought she and Joss should have gone with him. "Oh, by the way, he has invited Ald Smithy and Scott to join us for dinner. He rang from the quarry when you had gone to get Joss from nursery. '*A good dinner sharpens wit and softens the heart,*' as mother used to say. Think on that Zoe and soften your heart, Daniel is a good man, and he cares for you and Joss. But I want to tell you something you obviously don't know. The reason Daniel went to the Isle o' Skye."

"If there was a specific reason why didn't Daniel tell me?"

"Cos he didn't want to upset you, but keeping things to yoursel' never does any good. Cum and help me set t' table in't dining room, and let me finish before you get angry lass."

Zoe loved Maisie but she was feeling quite angry at being talked down to. It wasn't her fault she didn't know about Daniel's past, it was *her mother* he had wanted to marry, not her. She was here only because he had promised her mother to

147

take care of her and of Joss, of course, and he had. He had also arranged for Maisie to stay here, and for Ald Smithy to stay in the adjoining cottage! Zoe was beginning to think she was a burden, was *that* the reason Daniel wanted to go away on holiday!

Zoe dusted off the polished oak table, and slapped down the place mats, and then she looked ruefully at Maisie. "Sorry Maisie, none of this is your fault, but you always seem to have to do the explaining. Why did Mum have to die, and why did she make Daniel promise to look after me and Joss, it wasn't fair to him or me, but I have no idea where we would be if he hadn't made that promise."

"Well '*forethought spares afterthought*,' and neither of us want Daniel to go away under a cloud. Nothing is taking any harm just yet in the kitchen, so get a couple of glasses o' sherry, and we'll have a talk, whilst Joss is playing happily and quietly with his little cars." Maisie looked across at him playing in the corner and thought what a good child he was, a credit to both Zoe and Daniel, and she shook her head in wonder, was she the *only* person around here who was certain sure that Scott was his Daddy!

She accepted the sherry and looked at Zoe and wished she could wave a magic wand to make her happy. Since she had seen the photographs of Scott as a child, she now worried about Zoe, because she was now much more aware of how they acted when they were in the same company – with great care, and with regard to Zoe with heart-ache and apprehension, but Scott wasn't so easy to read unfortunately.

Maisie told Zoe about their childhood, and what a good childhood they had enjoyed, although it was during the Second World War, they hadn't known any difference they had a wonderful time, and didn't realise they were missing certain things, such as plenty of food, and new clothes instead of hand me downs as was the case as far as she was concerned, but not Daniel as he was an only child, and his father had been unable to join up because he had flat feet, and besides that he was running a slate quarry. Daniel when he was seventeen had fallen in love with a lovely young girl named Nell. She was very feisty and high strung, and she was Nellie Peterson, she was Scott and Adele's aunt. When Zoe would have interrupted her Maisie put her hand up, she had started so she would finish! She went on to say that Nell reciprocated his love, and they became engaged. Unfortunately Nell and Daniel loved to ride the horses from the farm, and although both Daniel and her father had forbidden her to ride a particular highly strung horse, she had ignored them and gone racing across the fields. She had fallen off the horse jumping over a high fence, and she had been seriously injured when her father and Daniel had caught up with her, and she died a few days later. Daniel had never forgiven himself, because he thought *he* should have stopped her. They had planned to have a honeymoon on the Isle of Skye and go walking. That was why Daniel had gone up there recently to do what he had planned to do with Nell.

"I just thought you might understand why he had to go Zoe, not because he wasn't happy with you and Joss to take care of, but because he was unexpectedly now really well, and it was something he had always wanted to do." Maisie finished with a worried look at her young friend, as she had expected Zoe to understand, but she looked quite upset.

"I realise he might have wanted to do that, but that doesn't explain why Daniel is taking off again, so suddenly," Zoe said looking rather oddly at Maisie. "He fell in love with my mother

Charlotte quite recently, does that mean she wasn't the love of his life as I thought, because they were so happy together, and I was happy for her to at last find true love. Why did he decide to look after me and Joss, if it wasn't because he loved Mother?"

"But Zoe please…

"No Maisie, I don't understand, but I won't let how I feel spoil tonight's farewell dinner. Daniel can't help how he feels, I just wish I had known all this, because when I agreed to marry him I thought I would be able to help him through losing mother, and through the illness I had been told about by Janette, and I believed Joss would also help him. Don't misunderstand me Maisie, I am very fond of Daniel and I would never hurt him unnecessarily, and it is my own fault for thinking I understood his reasons."

"You won't do anything rash whilst Daniel is away will you Zoe. Perhaps you should let him explain himself. Oh dear what have I done, what would my Bob God rest his soul think about all this?"

Zoe walked away to be by herself, then she went and took Joss by the hand, he was with her, he was her son, she would always have that! She glanced back with a small smile for Maisie and then shook her head. Only in the last few days she had been wondering if Maisie was becoming fond of Ald Smithy, and 'my Bob' had only been gone for a couple of years, is that all love was?

The dinner was a success, and Daniel seemed to really enjoy having his small family, and his friends and colleagues around him. Zoe was rather quiet, but only Scott and Maisie were aware of this!

Later in the evening Zoe went outside for some fresh air having just put Joss to bed, because he had been rather overexcited by the festive evening and guests. She went to sit on a garden chair and look across Rydal Water. She looked at the moon shining in the water, and realised how muddy the lake would be on the bottom. Just as her life seemed to be at the moment, and was she wrong to feel so hurt and churned up inside? She must be wrong in thinking that there was only one special partner for each person!

She nearly jumped out of her skin with the feeling that someone was there in the dusk. She was quite right it was the last person she wanted to see at the moment.

"It is clear that you are trying to put on a happy face for Daniel, but you are seething underneath. It would be very nice if you could let him have his holiday without him feeling guilty. He was unwell for a lot of years and advised to take it easy, and since the operation he is truly well again. Can't you be glad for him, as are all his friends and colleagues?" Scott said coldly.

"What would you know about it Scott, you only have yourself and Samantha to think about," Zoe replied with a break in her voice for which she was ashamed of showing her feelings.

"Well you only have yourself, Joss and Daniel to think about, why can't you be happy for him?" Scott was becoming quite angry because she was upset and he couldn't do anything to help and he felt like pulling her close to comfort her, which would be a very bad idea, and he was angry because she had never before seemed to be so self orientated!

"I was thinking of my mother Charlotte, who was Daniel's fiancé because I believed he was in love with her when she was with him, and yet he goes all the way up to the Isle of Skye mourning the love of his life, your Auntie Nellie!"

"Grow up Zoe, he is now *your* husband and you should make the best of it, you obviously got what you wanted for yourself and Joss, and I can't believe you are jealous of your own mother!"

Zoe was so angry she swung her fist towards Scott, and her fist was caught *by Daniel*, who had been watching them from the shadows. What had they said, what would Daniel make of her arguing with Scott? Scott plunged his hands into his pockets and tried to keep them there, he wondered later if he would have hit Daniel, or even Zoe.

"That's enough Scott. I'd like to have a word with my wife in private. I trust you will keep things going with the business until I return in a few weeks?"

"Of course," Scott replied, and when it was obvious that Daniel wasn't moving and wanted him to leave he moved into the house, came out with his jacket and walked towards Oak Tree Farm wondering about himself – would he ever come to believe that Zoe and Joss were nothing to do with him?

Daniel sat down at the garden table, and indicated the chair opposite, and Zoe sat down knowing that Daniel had heard her discussing her mother with Scott and she was mortified.

Daniel watched her as she composed herself, and then looked him in the eyes.

"I know you heard me talking about my mother. I'm sorry Daniel but I thought you were just as much in love with her as she was with you. You made her last years very happy, and yet you go all the way to the Isle of Skye to remember your first love."

"I *was* in love with your mother, and she would have made all our lives wonderful if she had lived. It gave me pleasure to promise her to help you and Joss, which I have done to the best of my ability. I went up to Skye to say a last farewell to Nellie, my *first* love. I now intend to go to the Mediterranean where I planned to take your mother on honeymoon, to remember and say goodbye to her, and in particular Italy which is the one place that your mother always dreamed of visiting." Daniel said quietly and held out his hands, which she held across the table.

"I'm sorry Daniel, I didn't want to upset you, but I was feeling rather useless, because when I married you I intended to help take care of you when you were ill, and also to help you get over the loss of mother, and yet I didn't even know that she had always wanted to visit Italy, but of course she would never have told me that, because it was never likely to happen!"

"You have been and are doing both those things for me Zoe, both you and Joss in his own way. I want you to have a good think whilst I'm away, and you must let Maisie, Smithy, Adele and Scott help you in any way. And please take care of Joss, as I will be looking forward to seeing him when I return, because even a few weeks makes a difference in a growing boy. I also want you to get on with Smithy and Scott at the quarries, because you now have a quarter share in the business and as a shareholder your ideas will count. My Solicitor will be getting in touch with you this week. Please take care of everything whilst I'm away, which should only be for a few weeks."

"I will Daniel, and I'm sorry for getting things wrong with regard to Nell and my mother. I guess it must be possible to love more than once, I just don't know much about those things. Mother was devastated when my father left her for someone else, and I always wondered if it was my fault, but I can hardly remember anything about it now, and I guess he has a new grown up family, let's hope with someone who loves him."

"There are lots of ways to love Zoe, and you are learning all the time, and you know I love you like a daughter, and I know you and Joss love me in your own different ways. I worry that it might not be enough for you Zoe, you are young and healthy, and might need something more."

"Daniel I was unsure about everything when my mother died and left us. If it hadn't been for you, goodness knows what would have happened. Look at Joss he is so very happy, and loves it here. I'm going off to bed now Daniel, and so should you. Enjoy your holiday." She kissed him on the cheek and he patted her shoulder fondly, and they parted.

Although she was aware that Daniel would be leaving by taxi early in the morning, she slept quite well, and just managed to wave him off from her bedroom window. Daniel waved back, and then put his hand on his lap top, thinking it might be quite busy in the next few days. He was quite shocked by what he had learned recently, and hoped to put matters right!

CHAPTER NINETEEN

In the following weeks everyone worked as normal, with Scott, Smithy and Zoe at the quarries, and Maisie helping out at Sharpe House. Joss missed Daniel quite a lot, but as the days changed into weeks, he mentioned him less and less.

At the quarries Zoe now occupied Daniel's small office, and she worked well with Smithy and the other members of staff. With Scott she was cool but pleasant, as she could not forget that he had accused her of marrying Daniel for all the wrong reasons, and for being jealous of her own mother! Daniel had been very annoyed with Scott for the way he had spoken to her, but she felt she must not dwell on this, because she didn't want to come between two families who had been friends for years.

Leaving her job at High Stile had been a wrench, but she felt she would be more stretched helping with the management of the museum and having passed all the necessary tests with regard to the certificates needed to work with or around children, she felt she could gradually do more as she became more familiar with what was needed. She missed seeing Adele every day, but they managed to keep in touch by telephone, and occasionally managed the odd shopping trip, and they quite often took all the children out. It was now September and things were slowing down, and they had decided to open on Thursday through to Sunday from the end of that month, but they were still very busy and that was extended from Wednesday to Sunday. It seemed strange to have two full days off, and on the first Monday off for Zoe, she was relieved to at last get a letter from Daniel, instead of the usual email which only said where he was and what he was doing. She opened it feeling very happy, as perhaps he was on his way home again. In the letter he told her to look out for a letter from his solicitor, and she wondered why, as all the paperwork had been completed with regard to him making her a shareholder in the business. The tone of his letter seemed to show that he was having a wonderful holiday, and she was quite envious, and wondered if she and Joss might join him at some time in the future on another holiday, as she had never been out of the United Kingdom, and she hoped that Joss would benefit from such a holiday.

When she returned to Sharpe House in the afternoon, after collecting Joss from nursery school, Maisie was just getting ready tea and scones.

"Sit down lass, its quite warm for early October. Cum on Joss, do y' want a scone or shortbread?" Maisie asked him, as he obviously wanted to get outside to play.

"Shortbread please Maisie, can I go out now?"

"Well, just sit still awhile, cos I'm expecting somebody who wants to see *you*." Maisie told him with a happy smile.

"Elliot and John?" Joss, said licking the sugar off the top of his biscuit.

"No, but he is bringing something to show you and your mother, and I think I can hear him now." Maisie said mysteriously.

Joss jumped up from the table and ran to the kitchen door, and the door opened and Scott came inside carrying a small cage, with a blanket over it. Zoe's heart did its usual thump as Scott placed the cage carefully on the floor and looked warily towards her. Please not a budgie she thought, as she hated to see birds in cages.

Scott pulled off the blanket, and inside the cage were three little black puppies. Joss was struck dumb as he put his hand in to stroke them, and Zoe felt her heartstrings pull as they were so lovely, and Scott looked slightly shamefaced, aware that the damage had already been done.

"Can I have them Mummy?" Joss asked wide eyed with excitement.

"Well, *nobody* can have them yet, because they need to be with their mummy, she feeds them with her milk," Zoe said slightly repressively, with a questioning look at Scott.

"I knew you would all love to see them, they are Collie puppies, and I'm keeping one of them, and John senior said he might take one for the boys or the farm and he'll be company for Flash, and that just leaves *one* more," Scott said with a pleading look towards Zoe.

"Where's the mummy," Josh asked worriedly.

"Oh, their mummy lives at Oak Tree Farm with me, and one of the puppies will stay with her, and I wondered if there was room at Sharpe House for the other, but it would need to be looked after very carefully when it's old enough to leave its mummy? He will be ready to leave his mummy in about two more weeks."

157

"Come an' have a cup of tea Scott and a scone, and let Zoe make up her own mind," Maisie suggested with a grin.

"You both know very well that I can't possibly say *no* don't you, you both hatched this plot." Zoe said trying to resist picking up the puppy that Scott indicated. She gave in and picked up the puppy, and carefully held him out to Joss. "You must be very careful Joss, he is a baby and you mustn't hurt him." Joss sat down on the floor with the puppy in front of him, holding it very carefully, and they seemed to bond right away, Joss's eyes were wide with excitement and wonder, and Zoe thought her heart might stop as she looked into identical pleading eyes. After a couple of minutes Scott removed the puppy carefully and put him back in the cage, as Joss watched all three avidly.

Scott turned to the table, and sat down where Maisie indicated, and he looked at Zoe ruefully. "Are you sure Zoe, they seem to have bonded already, and every boy needs a dog."

"Every girl too Scott, I would have loved to have a dog, but that was never possible," and she felt a complete fool as her eyes filled with tears.

"You can share Scotty Mummy," Joss offered with a broad grin.

"So he has a name already," Scott said with a smile.

"Collie farm dogs are worth a lot of money Scott, how much do I owe you?" Zoe said, beginning to wonder what Maisie and Daniel would think if he just gave the dog to Joss!

"Nothing Zoe, but if it bothers you a lot I'll think of something," Scott said angrily, and picked up the puppies and was about to leave.

"Sit down Scott and have your scone," Maisie scolded, with an angry look towards Zoe. "What's that on the table Scott," she asked looking at a couple of letters and some circulars.

"Oh sorry, I nearly forgot, that post was left at Oak Tree Farm this morning by mistake. I don't know why they have such difficulty in sorting it properly." Scott remarked, pushing the post across the table to Zoe. He turned to watch Joss as he poked his finger through the cage, trying to make the puppies look at him. He remembered his first dog, that had been a collie too, and they had been inseparable. Whenever his parents or he and Adele had left the room at the same time, the dog had always followed him, and Adele had maintained it was just because he was the youngest, but Scott new differently!

As Zoe slit open two envelopes, Maisie pushed the teapot towards Scott, "warm up your tea Scott, then you'd best get those puppies back to their mother."

She glanced at Zoe and was shocked at the surprise, hurt and then anger as those expressions crossed her face. She went as white as a sheet and then stared across at Maisie and Scott.

"Well, what do you two know about this, because I've been living in cloud cuckoo land it would seem, together with my son and very shortly, my son's pet dog Scotty."

"What on earth is the matter?" Maisie asked with a worried frown.

"This morning I received a letter from Daniel, saying I would soon be contacted by his solicitor, this letter is from his solicitor, and it states that his client Daniel Sharpe is ending our marriage. And for my trouble he wants to give me £30,000 in settlement, but I am invited to stay here for the foreseeable future, and for as long as I wish, although the solicitor says

Daniel will be home in a couple of months, and it could be finalised by then!"

There was a surprised silence across the table.

"He is divorcing you?" Scott said in dismay, and his face was as white as Zoe's. He now realised how much she must love her husband, she looked absolutely devastated. He wasn't sure how *he* felt, but he ached for Zoe as she was in shock, and probably felt betrayed! It wasn't like Daniel!

"How else do you get rid of a wife? I would not have believed this of Daniel, before he went away he said we should both do some thinking, but this, how could he? He can stick his money, Joss and I will be leaving in the morning."

Maisie also looked devastated, and looked at Scott and jerked her head towards the door, and he realised she was demanding that *he* left! When all he wanted to do was be there for Zoe, and for Joss who wouldn't know what was happening in his safe little world! His heart had also skipped a beat as it wondered what this would mean for *him*, and then he had seen Zoe's devastation, and surely if she was the gold digger that he had accused her of being, then she would have accepted the £30,000 and be on her way to better things, but then he thought she might be determined to get at least *half* of Daniel's wealth. What was he thinking about he knew there was nothing nefarious about her, although she had been through a lot, and some of it was *his* fault. He moved away from the table and ruffled Joss's dark hair as he passed picking up the dog cage, and left very reluctantly, but hoping that Maisie could make Zoe change her mind about leaving in the morning. He had already made up his mind to bring his vehicle and park it at the bottom of the drive to Sharpe House, if Maisie was unsuccessful in persuading Zoe to stay, then she would have to get him to move his vehicle, and he would get a chance to ask her to stay! He didn't want her to take away his son, and let's face it, he also wanted her to stay it was better to see her occasionally and quite often up at the quarry, as that was much better than *not* seeing her at all! He closed the door quickly as it looked as though Joss might follow the puppies, and it hurt to think it was only the puppies he was fond of!

"Stay there Zoe, I think we need a sherry, or better still, a drop of Daniel's brandy," Maisie said and left the table, without clearing away the used dishes, and Zoe now realised that Maisie was a shocked as was *she*, and surprisingly Maisie's mother didn't seem to have a maxim to suit this particular and unexpected occasion!

"Have a sip of that lass, as I know I need one." Maisie sighed and sipped her own brandy, and then she didn't let Zoe or her mother down. "*Could everything be done twice, it would be done better,*' my mother used to say, and she was right. I know you love Daniel he is a very kind man, and he must think this is the best way forward. You, Cousin Janette and I all know that Daniel married you because he believed that was t' only way he could fulfil his promise to your mother, and I agreed w' him at the time. But, like Daniel I suppose, I've had serious thoughts about it all. You're a lovely young woman, and although you 'ave young Joss, y' must envy people like Adele, happily married for the right reason, in other words living wi' the man she loves and bringing up a family *together*." Maisie, sighed deeply and watched her young friend closely, who seemed to still be suffering from shock or was it heartbreak?

"*I* made the decision to keep my baby, selfishly I suppose, as mother was too ill to provide for us as I realise that she wanted to, it was a strain for her, and that was all *my* fault. But a willing burden is no burden at all, and I made the right decision, but it must have left me a weak and selfish person agreeing to marry Daniel, and believing it was because I could help him when he became ill!" Zoe said her voice disillusioned and weary.

"You have helped Daniel as y' well know young Zoe, and whatever y' say I think y' should take the money offered in good faith by Daniel, he's doing this for you Zoe, not for any selfish reason, and he is still looking after you and Joss. He is one of't most caring men I know."

"Well, with regard to Joss I would never take him out of reach of Daniel as I know he loves him, but I will be looking for somewhere to live with Joss, and because I know it was really for Joss, for the time being I think I will keep working at the quarry, at least until Daniel comes home. I believe he made me a shareholder for Joss, so that *I will* accept, because he also explained to me why he went to the Isle of Skye, and why he was going on this particular tour, because that was where he had intended to take Mum for their honeymoon," Zoe finished speaking and her eyes were full of tears about to fall.

"Never doubt t' fact he was in love with y'r mother, I could tell he was very happy when he used t' call on my Bob God rest his soul and me, which he often did," Maisie said worriedly. "Now lass, you'll not be running away will y' because if y' do, Daniel will be blaming *me*, and I kind of like it around here. Before you decide anything you'll have a lot o' thinking to do." Maisie finished, and now cleared the table of the used dishes.

"I won't be running away Maisie, I'll do the washing up," Zoe offered. Maisie seemed to prefer washing the dishes in the sink, but Zoe thought that she might fill up the dishwasher while she put her mind to Daniel's surprising suggestions, and then she would take Joss outside for a walk.

"Right, thank's lass, I'll be on my way out," Maisie replied hurriedly and reached for her jacket on the back of the kitchen chair.

"Where are you going Maisie, in such a hurry?"

"Well, as mother used to say *in idleness alone is there perpetual despair,* now think on that while y' doing't dishes, and I'll not be idle, I'm off to see what ald Smithy knows as he and Daniel were always blabbing to each other. But if he knows nowt I'll not tell 'im nowt." Maisie answered hurriedly, then had a second thought and wrapped up a couple of scones in a paper napkin. "He can't resist one of my scones."

Zoe stacked the dishes in the dishwasher, all the while looking across the valley and the lake, she loved it here, but she did understand why Daniel might think that she was missing out. She *was* a young woman and she *did* have needs, needs that she was aware of every time Scott was in the vicinity. She was also aware that had Scott been in this country, and this valley or if she had known he might return, then she would probably not have married Daniel. However, it had been her decision and only because she thought she would be a help for Daniel in later life. Now that he was well, he was pushing her away, but why had he decided to do this *now* as nothing had changed as far as she was aware, except that he was fit and well.

She collected Joss and realised that they were heading out of the back gate towards the coffin route and Grasmere. Was she subconsciously thinking of Scott and expecting him to be around there somewhere!

"Can we go to the hollow tree and play Mummy," Joss asked. "Soon I'll have Scotty to take for a walk, he'll like it there."

"Perhaps tomorrow Joss darling, we'll walk back and go by the lake and you can take your fishing net."

Just because she would be free to make a new life in a few months, wouldn't alter anything, she was well aware that Scott thought she was a gold digger and jealous of her own mother, but what she really needed was to talk to Daniel so that she could understand what *he* wanted!

She was surprised to see Scott's vehicle at the bottom of the drive, and was glad that they were only walking, or she would have been forced to ask him to move it, and she didn't want to see him just yet, as he would take her mind off the decisions that she would soon have to make for herself and her son. She suddenly wondered if Daniel had some needs of his own now that he was well. If that was the case then she must let him be free. Her mind was in a whirl and she didn't know what she wanted or what she must do, perhaps she should talk it over with someone who was not involved so closely in their lives?

CHAPTER TWENTY

Zoe went to see Daniel's solicitor two weeks later, having gone over in her mind everything that he had said in his letter. She arrived at his office wondering if she should have a solicitor of her own, but then thought it would not be necessary as she had decided not to ask Daniel for anything! She had been educated and given a roof of her head when she most needed it, and she was a grown woman, and should be able to manage by herself.

She didn't need anything else from Daniel as he has been more than generous already both with monetary matters and time.

A young receptionist came across to Zoe as she was in a nicely furnished waiting room. "Mrs Sharpe, Mr Joe will see you now, please follow me," and Zoe followed her as she wiggled her way into Mr Joe's office, in her high heeled shoes and pencil slim skirt, making Zoe feel that she should have dressed up for this meeting and then she wouldn't feel at a disadvantage, and indicated that Zoe should enter, as the young girl said primly, 'Mrs Sharpe.'

"Mrs Sharpe, please sit down," he said and looked up from the papers he was perusing. She could see the surprise on his young face, as he didn't look much older than her, and he looked very smart in a grey suit, but seemed quite friendly because the tie was only loosely tied, and he quickly returned to perusing the papers in front of him, probably looking for her age. He then stood and leaned across the desk to shake her hand with an apologetic smile.

"Joe Somers, I'm pleased to meet you Mrs Sharpe and I'm sorry to still be reading through the case papers, but this is my father's case really, but he is away on holiday for another week."

"Don't worry Mr Somers, I only wanted to come in to your office to say that I will *not* be accepting the £30,000 offered by my husband, but I will be staying in Sharpe House for the foreseeable future, or until I can get a home for my son and myself."

He frowned and again looked at the papers, "You are asking for much more?"

"No, I am going to let the case proceed, but I will not be accepting the £30,000 offered," Zoe replied, and he looked at her with a mystified expression.

"I have dealt with divorce cases before Mrs Sharpe, but I will need to look at this one in more depth, and I suggest that I call on you as soon as I can." Joe Somers looked rather uncomfortable, and Zoe realised that he had not looked at the file at all, and she felt rather sorry for him. "I will get my secretary to ring and arrange a date that suits you."

Zoe stood and moved towards the door, realising that he was a very attractive man, but just at the moment he was at a disadvantage, and she couldn't help but smile at his confusion.

"That will be fine Mr Somers, as I am not in a hurry. Oh, and by the way it is a proposed *annulment* not a divorce, and I understand it will only take a few weeks," Zoe said from the doorway, and although he looked like a well seasoned solicitor, she was sure that he blushed as he realised a divorce and an annulment were quite different matters!

On the way back to Sharpe House in her car, she worried and wondered. She remembered the remark made in the Post Office soon after their marriage, when a young woman was gossiping about them, and she had assumed that *Daniel* must be the father of her child. She had been very hurt at the time because she knew Daniel and what a good man he was, but managed to put this to the back of her mind, as it was nothing to do with anyone else but her and Daniel. She now began to believe that it would be better to have it all done and finished with before Daniel came home, because people who knew them both must begin to wonder why they were getting the *marriage annulled*. Cause for further gossip, if it got out, but why should it? Only the solicitors, Maisie, and Daniel's Cousin Janette and her daughters knew the real reason for the marriage, and the reason it could be annulled! Poor Daniel he had insisted they should marry because he didn't believe they should live in the same house otherwise, now he would be open for further speculation and innuendo!

During the time working at High Stile with Adele they had become very friendly, and looking back now Zoe wondered if Adele had her own ideas about Joss's father, and the reason Daniel and Zoe had married, but she had never said anything.

She was certain that Scott thought they were married in the biblical sense, and he would probably feel even more disgusted with her if he knew the truth. Why had everything to be so difficult? She now decided that when Mr Joe Somers, or his father were in touch once again, she would try to hurry things through because that would be best for Daniel and herself, and less embarrassing for Maisie, Cousin Janette, her daughters and in particular Scott and Adele!

As soon as she arrived home she rang the solicitor's office, and asked to speak to Mr Joe Somers. He was surprised to hear from her so quickly, and when she asked if things could be kept as quiet as possible, he agreed, and apologised again for not being up to date with the case. He called at Sharpe House a couple of days later, and things were discussed. One of the points he had raised was that if she was not going to accept the £30,000 then he would have to get in touch with Daniel and that would not be an easy thing to do as he was enjoying a walking holiday and moving on all the time, and in the mountains often a mobile phone would not have a signal. She could imagine his difficulty as Daniel so rarely had his mobile phone switched on!

"In that case Mr Somers, I will accept the money as I can always return it to my husband at any time. And I am only doing this to expedite matters, as this seems to be what my husband wants. I have a feeling that until these matters are finalised he will not want to return to this country. He must have a pressing agenda to which we are not privy."

"My name is Joe, as I am officially not your solicitor or your husband's, as Dad has returned and will be taking over Daniels case again. As a friend I would be very glad to advise you Zoe, sorry Mrs Sharpe. Also if anything comes on to the market that

I think may suit you, possibly a small bungalow, or well appointed flat, I'll let you know, that is if you would like me to keep in touch with you?"

"Thank your for offering, but I think everything is in hand, and until Daniel returns I shall be here at Sharpe House with my son Joss, and friends Maisie and Smithy. Obviously if anything suitable did come on the market I would be interested."

"As you predicted in this case things should move very quickly, and you could be a free woman in a few weeks. I'll keep an eye on the property market and get in touch as I think we would get on very well?" Joe Somers said wondering if he was being too forward, but she was a very attractive young woman, with or without the £30,000. Perhaps then he would find out why they were able to annul the marriage, because although Daniel Sharpe was a lot older than his wife, he was well thought of in the area, and was a very good catch.

"I don't think that would be a good idea Joe except with regard to any suitable property, but if I change my mind I'll know where to find you." Zoe answered quickly, as he had thrown her somewhat with being so forward, and just the way she was feeling at the moment any young man addressing her in such terms was a boost to her sadly mangled ego!

She was about to show him out, when the door opened and Scott came into the house with Joss, Elliot and John junior, and Scotty the collie. The place was a madhouse and Zoe quickly apologised to Joe Somers.

"No problem Zoe, I'll see you soon I hope," he said blandly, although she thought she had discouraged him somewhat with her reply.

"Scott," Joe acknowledged. Then he turned to Zoe and smiled. "See you soon I hope."

"Goodbye Joe," Zoe said without thinking and closed the door behind him, as seeing Scott had rather thrown her already shaken equilibrium.

"My, it hasn't taken you long to find yourself another suitor," Scott's voice was harsh with sarcasm.

"He is the son of Daniel's solicitor if you must know."

"I realise that Zoe, we were at school together he always was quite popular with the girls."

"Well he obviously had more charm than *I* have seen for a long time, and he is a gentleman."

"How would you know you have only just met since you received Daniel's letter. I was under the impression that you had decided to wait here until Daniel's return."

"I get the impression that if I don't do anything then Daniel will *not* return, for some reason he thinks I would be better off alone."

"You have known Daniel for a few years now, and you must have realised that he wouldn't do anything to hurt you, Joss or anyone, he is a really good man. I don't understand what is going on, but you probably will if you give it some thought," Scott remarked with an edge to his voice that he couldn't hide, but he was doing his best in front of the children. He would really like to take her by the shoulders and shake some sense into her, as she must know why Daniel wanted to divorce her!

"Joss why don't you take Elliot and John up to your room, and show them your new digger," Zoe said in exasperation, she intended to tell Scott to mind his own business, and stop trying to bully her.

"Can Scotty dog come Mummy, cos' it's not bed time yet?" Joss asked warily, he didn't like his mummy and Scott when they argued, because they did that sometimes up at the quarry, and although he didn't understand what was going on, he felt their antipathy, but he soon forgot because his mummy was especially nice to him, and often gave him a treat.

"Yes Joss, Scotty can go upstairs with you, but just for today," Zoe said quickly, and felt even more annoyed with Scott for turning her into a bad mother, what would Joss think the next time he wanted the dog in his bedroom if she said *no*? Perhaps it wouldn't really matter because soon they would be living somewhere else.

When the boys and dog left the room the two protagonists faced each other angrily.

"Scott I know Daniel is your godfather and you care about him, and I too care about him, but I think you should mind your own business, and don't try to get me to say something that isn't true. I have no idea why Daniel wants to end our marriage, but the only thing I can think of is that he has found someone else to love, after all he loved your Aunt Nell, and he loved my mother Charlotte, perhaps he has fallen in love with someone else, perhaps they are together now, how should I know!"

"Well you seem to be getting along very well with Joe Somers, and you have only just met him, or is that not the case, perhaps you met him a while back whilst visiting the solicitors?" Scott asked, but she was too angry to reply and he continued because he was also angry with himself for treating her so badly, but it had hurt so much seeing her with Joe Somers, because whilst at school they had not been friends or enemies, but they had both been good at the same things and that had led to a healthy rivalry, which it would seem was still ongoing.

"If your marriage with Daniel does end, then I will want access to my son wherever you take him, but it would be better for him if you lived nearby, not because of me alone, but because he has made friends and is really settled here."

"I will not be going anywhere in the near future because I need to work, and I have accepted Daniel's offer of shares in the business, and I intend to work to get somewhere to live with Joss. You may not like it Scott, but I have no other income, and I do think about Joss, and what is best for him. I just need you to agree to working with me for a time, without any unpleasantness," Zoe said quickly, her heart was breaking because all she really wanted was for him to say he wanted both Joss and *her*, and judging by his previous erroneous observations about her character that would not happen.

"I will not be unpleasant Zoe, neither will I mind working with you, but if you and Daniel do part, I would then like to get my name on Joss's birth certificate, and to know that you will let me see him."

"You will see him most workdays when I have collected him after school, and I agree to you having your name as his father on the birth certificate, but I don't want to hurt Daniel so we will keep that quiet. For now we will try to get along amicably," Zoe crossed her fingers behind her back, surely that should not be too difficult, she had a thought which hurt. "For some reason Adele does not seem to get along with your friend Samantha, and just for now I would rather that Joss didn't get involved with her too much. Joss has lost his grandmother, and now he'll be losing Daniel, I think that is enough upset for the time being."

"I think I can agree to that," Scott replied and he looked puzzled, and decided he must have a word with his sister Adele. "Does Adele know what is happening between you and Daniel, I don't want to put my foot in it and say something I shouldn't."

"No, but I think I should tell her tonight, because she and John are really very close to him."

CHAPTER TWENTY ONE

Scott waited during the next two work days to see if Zoe would somehow let slip that she had spoken with Adele, but nothing happened, she was plainly doing her utmost never to be alone with him. He knew that what she was doing was for the best because it was like living on a knife edge, he was always striving to be very careful what he said, because he had promised that there would be no more unpleasantness between them!

That evening he decided to go and see his sister and her husband. He needed someone to talk to, and he had known since soon after returning from Afghanistan and meeting Joss for the first time that he was his son, and by the way his sister had been acting, he thought she had come to the same conclusion but neither of them at said a word to the other! As he had expected as soon as he arrived at High Stile he was invited to stay for a meal, and during the meal he caught them both giving him interrogating looks when they thought he wasn't noticing them.

As soon as Adele brought the coffee, she instructed both the boys to go and get ready for bed, and if Elliot had any homework he was to get it all done, and report back to his parents.

"Zoe has been to see you hasn't she?" Scott said quickly. "What did she say?"

"You know what she said, she told us that Daniel wants their marriage to end, and he wants it done amicably it seems, and she wants it done quietly. However, she does seem to be very upset as she doesn't know his reason for this, as they have never had a cross word," Adele replied quietly, and Scott looked across at his sister trying to find out what she *wasn't saying*!

"You know don't you Adele, how it affects me."

"I have known that Joss was your son since the first day I met Zoe and Joss, and I gave her the job because I really liked her and I didn't want her to move away and take your son with her. You were away in Afghanistan, and I guessed that you would not know about Joss. He was born before Zoe and Daniel were married."

"I know, at first I was disgusted that she had married an older man, a man who I really love as my Godfather. But as soon as I looked into Joss's eyes, I saw myself. I first met Zoe when I helped her get her mother home when she was suffering from angina, and I carried Charlotte back along the coffin route to Mr Brown's where she was working. Well, I don't know how or why it happened, but it did, and I never forgot her. But I had never given it a thought that I might have left her with child. Not in this day and age."

"How could you Scott, her mother was seriously ill?" Adele said worriedly.

175

"I don't know what happened really, we *needed* each other, her because of her mother, and me because I couldn't get over Dad's death, and I was carrying him on the coffin route around the floods if you remember. Also, I know it is no excuse but I guess I wasn't really well, as I had to *bully my way home* from the military hospital when I heard Dad was ill. I also met Zoe on the train when I was going back, and she was going to University in Lancaster. I nearly followed her off the train, and now I wish I had." Scott finished talking and looked moodily into the wood fire sending sparks up the chimney in the homely farm kitchen.

"Well nobody was to blame as far as I can see," Adele said sagely. "However, Zoe is married to Daniel, and they seemed quite happy, and she is very upset that Daniel now wants to end it all."

"I have asked her to stay around here if possible, so that I can have access to Joss, but we'll have to wait and see what happens, the last thing I want to do is hurt Daniel, or Zoe, but I do know I want to be something more to young Joss."

"What I don't know is what you and Zoe have been to each other since you arrived back?" Adele had to ask as it had been worrying her for some time, as she had seen the strange nuances and complexities in their tense and fraught relationship.

"Nothing in the way you mean Adele, she is a married woman, and she was devastated when she received that letter from Daniel," Scott replied in a curt voice, knowing how difficult it had been to ensure what he now said was absolutely true! He had been true to Daniel and Zoe, but it had been at the price of sleepless nights and tormenting thoughts!

"Would you like to get it together with Joss and Zoe," John asked, and both Adele and Scott stared at him. He usually left such conversations to his wife!

"Well yes of course, but I don't think that is an option, she seems to be in love with her husband, although he is years older than her." Scott finished on a note of disgust.

John looked from his wife to his brother in law, and yawned and stood up. "I'll go and see to the boys, and get them in to bed." He turned back slowly, "have either of you thought that Daniel might also have seen what you two saw in Joss, and what effect that might have had on *him*, what if he noticed *after* he had married Zoe and taken Joss under his wing? I guess that Zoe never thought she would ever see you again Scott, why would she, you were a stranger as far as she was aware."

Adele stared at her husband, as he hadn't said as much as that for a long time, and it all made perfect sense!

Three weeks later Maisie sorted through the post and came across a hand written letter addressed to Mrs Zoe Sharpe, and she recognised the handwriting as that of Daniel. She walked from the hallway into the kitchen, and shook her head as she glanced at Joss and Smithy sitting at the table.

"A woman's work is never done,'as mother used to say'. Now Smithy get up't quarries and tell Scott to stay there for a while, Zoe will be late coming to work this morning. And you Joss get ready for school, and your mother will take you *before* she reads her post." Maisie said quickly, and Smithy raised an eyebrow at Maisie, fully aware of why 'my Bob God rest his soul' had never had much to say – he didn't have to with Maisie taking care of everything including him!

Joss smiled at Maisie and finished his weetabix, as Maisie had taken over from Granny Charlotte as far as he was concerned, and he liked her just as much, in fact, Granny Charlotte was just a fond memory that he talked about sometimes with Daniel and his mummy.

When Zoe popped in to Sharpe House after taking Joss to school, Maisie insisted that she should sit at the table in the sitting room and have a cup of coffee, as Maisie had lots of noisy things to do in the kitchen, one of which was cleaning the modern day stay clean cooker!

Zoe opened the letter with a small letter knife fully aware that Maisie knew it was from Daniel, and she was giving her space. Daniel's letter was written in a fine copperplate hand, the lines were straight and even, and she could never remember receiving a letter such as this. She had received one or two hand written notes, but this was something special, Daniel had taken time to think about her and Joss, and to write a lovely letter setting out his thoughts and feelings for his and their future. It was far more special than receiving an email, which he was quite capable of sending, having taken his lap top computer with him.

Venice, Italy.
September 2010

Dear Zoe,

I have felt very close to your mother Charlotte during this tour of Italy. Everything I saw in Florence (the highlight of the tour), including the superb architecture, paintings, frescos, culminating in Michelangelo's sculpture of David in the Galleria dell'Accademia I was mesmerised by, and imagined my dear Charlotte was seeing it with me, and I wouldn't be surprised if she was there beside me in the many photographs I have to show to you and Joss. It was the same in Rome, Sorrento, Pompeii, Herculaneum, Naples, Sorrento, the Amalfi Coast, Capri, and now Venice. These are all sights I would never have believed I would have the pleasure of seeing!

I realise that my last letter to you must have come as a great shock, but I would like to explain my reasons for sending it to you instead of talking to you. I guess that now the annulment is well under way, in fact, you may now be a free woman.

I helped Maisie by putting the groups of photographs that she had sorted for Scott which had belonged to his father. Amongst those photographs I saw Adele and Scott as children, and I realised that Scott must be the father of young Joss. I loved Joss before I saw that, and if possible I love him more now, because Scott is my Godson, and I have been involved in all of his life.

I have thought about things a great deal whilst travelling, and in my own way I have discussed them with my dear Charlotte. The only way that I can see to truly do as she asked and look after you and Joss, is to give you your freedom, and hope that you will find someone to love, and be loved by, even if it isn't Scott. I have already given to you and Joss a share in the quarry business, and I hope you will stay and carry on with that work. If not you will be free to do whatever you wish. I thought that £30,000 was quite a small sum and you might even consider accepting that for your future and that of young Joss. You may either keep the annulment private, or not, whatever you think will be best. Whatever happens I hope I have managed things so that you may keep your good name, as may I. However, if you and Joss are truly happy in the following years that is all I ask.

I will always be around for both of you, and my Godson and Goddaughter Adele, in the years to come, as I have never felt fitter in my life, a life which I intend to enjoy to the fullest capacity, as I have been given a second chance since the accident and operation.

If you are still living at Sharpe House when I return, I will be overjoyed, as with Maisie there, and Ald Smithy next door, everything will be as I believe it should be, in my old fashioned way! However, if you plan to move to improve your own life and that of Joss, I will be very pleased for you both, but entreat you to keep in touch as your mother would have wanted.

Today please think of me visiting St. Marks Basilica, and the Doge's Palace, and the rest of this wonderful city, as I hope both you and Joss will some time in the near future before it is claimed by the sea.

Yours affectionately, with love, for always,
Daniel Sharpe.

PS. Please give my love to Maisie, the family at High Stile, my good friend Ald Smithy, and my Godson Scott.

Zoe cried for quite a while, she had always known what a wonderful man Daniel was, and realised now that he really had been in love with her mother, and she appreciated fully everything that he had tried to do for her and Joss. The wild hope that was starting to blossom inside her must not get out of hand, there had been many things go wrong during her life, and she must not expect too much in the future. For now she would show Maisie the letter from Daniel, and she and Joss would remain in Sharpe House for the foreseeable future.

The second letter that Maisie had left for her on the small table she now opened. It was from Daniel's solicitor, Mr Joe Somers Senior, and all the paperwork was there for all to see, the marriage had been annulled, and she had changed her name back officially to Ms Zoe Howes, and her main worry was what to do with the £30,000 which had been placed in the account that she had stipulated. Perhaps that could await Daniel's return.

CHAPTER TWENTY TWO

Scott had been giving Sharpe House and it's occupants a wide berth since Zoe's accusation that either he or Maisie must know something about Daniel's decision to end their marriage. He and Zoe had both kept their distance up at the quarries, and this had not been difficult because it was the quiet season now, and they were opening only part time. He would much prefer to keep busy, as it would help keep his mind occupied, and not always thinking about Zoe, Joss and inevitably Daniel his Godfather.

He was standing on the quarry bank (now named the car park) and looked out across the Lakeland hills, as it was early morning the sun was just catching the tops of Coniston Old Man, Crinkle Crags, and to the right Scafell, Bowfell and the Langdale Pikes, and this wonderful countryside was his home, and he didn't really see himself leaving this beautiful part of the country again. His thoughts returned to his immediate problems, mainly the thought that Zoe was still in love with her husband, or why else would she be so very upset by recent events.

Now that he knew that Zoe had discussed these matters with his sister, he wanted to make contact, but it was rather difficult. He knew she was very hurt by this action by Daniel, which pointed to the fact that she loved him, as did Joss. He had to tread carefully or she might decide to leave the area with her son, although she had intimated that she would keep in touch. Perhaps the best idea would be for *him* to leave the area once again, although he doubted that the Army would want him back, they had allowed him to leave against their advice, and he had signed a paper to say that it was his own wish to leave the hospital, to spend time with his dying father, and he had returned to finish the time for which he had originally signed on.

If he signed on again he would be away for the most formative years of his son, and he didn't want to miss that, as he had missed the first two years of his son's life! Also if he left the area that would leave Joe Somers Junior a clear field as it was obvious to him that Joe was very interested in making further contact with Zoe Howes, as his sister now referred to her, casting her eye in *his* direction to see what effect her comments were having on him! It was as though his dear sister wanted a serious and illuminating conversation with him, but didn't know how to go about it.

The odd thing about all this was that Adele had said very little to him about what had transpired between herself and Zoe. Scott was upset by this, as previously both he and Adele had always told each other nearly everything. He remembered putting her right about Samantha, and Samantha had then disappeared from the area, obviously because she was herself embarrassed at being caught out with at least one customer receiving considerable extra attention, or because she was aware that Adele must know and disapprove of her behaviour. He was aware that the only reason he had started to go out with Samantha upon her return to the area in the last few months as a friend, was to show Zoe that he could still attract the opposite sex, but in actual fact, he felt rather a heel because Samantha's allure if he was totally honest with himself, now left him cold! In fact he had better sort that matter out right away, he felt a heel and he was a heel, and it wasn't fair to Samantha. He walked to his vehicle, now was as good a time as any, first thing in the morning with a very clear mind! He set off down the hill, and just managed to avoid Zoe coming up in her small Fiat car. She slammed on her brakes, and slewed into the quarry rubble on the fell side, but only the tyre made contact, and she felt the tyre slowly losing air. She glanced across in dread to see what had happened to Scott. There he was just inside the large clogs of stone which lined the outer edge of the road, with an apologetic grin on the his face, as he switched off his engine, and climbed out and walked towards her stricken vehicle. Well stricken was how she felt too, because she had thought he might be tumbling down the fell side inside his vehicle! She climbed out angrily and they met head on.

"You had better move aside and I'll see if I can do anything about changing the wheel," Scott stated angrily as he realised that she could so easily have been badly hurt!

"You were coming down the hill far too fast, you know better Scott, *you* put a twenty mile an hour limit on this road," she was breathing heavily as she was shocked as she realised the person in the other vehicle was Scott, and her heart had just recovered from a gradual painful contraction, as she breathed slowly and painfully.

"I was certain nobody would be coming up here at this time in the morning, so tell me why you are here so early."

"I tried to ring you at Oak Tree Farm, and at the quarry office, but there was no reply. I have to take Joss to the dentist this morning, and wanted you to know I would not be here until this afternoon."

"You could have tried my mobile phone, Maisie has the number," he replied angrily trying to find the spare wheel in the back of her car. He patted his pocket and realised his mobile wasn't there.

"I thought I would drive up here whilst Joss has his breakfast with Maisie and Ald Smithy. Why were you in such a hurry going down and driving so dangerously?" She demanded, as she thought he was ignoring her as he searched about in the boot of her car, lifting things out and grumbling under his breath.

"I had decided I had to see Samantha, and this seemed as good a time as any," he mumbled distractedly. Where was the damned spare wheel?

"Well don't let me stop your early morning lust," Zoe said angrily and tried to put down the car boot.

He held her shoulders tightly in anger, as her reply intrigued and aroused him, as he realised he had spoken without thinking, but she seemed even more annoyed was that because of Samantha? He pulled her close and placed his lips to hers in a kiss that was both savage and then tender. Zoe found that she was totally distracted and mesmerized by what was happening between them, and then she came to her senses and pushed him away.

"Sorry, wrong girl, I'm sure Samantha is eagerly waiting for you, don't bother about the car, I'll get Daniel's out of the garage, it is still insured and licensed," Zoe gasped out angrily, and then felt a burst if contrition, he looked so upset.

She turned tail and ran down the roadway towards Sharpe House, wondering how they could work here, with things so volatile between them. She wiped tears away from her eyes hastily, because Maisie had eyes like a hawk and missed nothing, and there was no way she wanted to upset Joss. By the time she arrived in the kitchen, she informed Smithy that she had suffered a burst tyre, and that Scott was dealing with it, and then kissed Joss, saying she would go and get ready to take him to the dentist.

Maisie watched her leave the kitchen, and then glanced at Smithy raising her eyebrows and then shook her head despondently.

"What's up Maisie," Smithy asked finishing his toast, and taking a big slurp of tea.

"You men, you see nowt, didn't yer see how white and strained that lass was, trying to look as though nothing's wrong! *Be always at leisure to do good* mother used to say, so get yourself up t' quarry and Scott. I'll have a word with young Zoe, but she'll pretend everything's alright as usual. I must mek sure her and young Joss are here when Daniel returns. In Daniel's letter he said he realised who young Joss's Dad was while looking through't photos, and, God forgive me, I left them there for him t' see, so I'm praying that everything will come out right, but right now it's not looking good, so all this bother is my fault and no body else's."

"But Maisie, '*the hand that rocks the cradle rules the world*,' and round here that's young Zoe, so it'll all come right in't end," Smithy said with a smile as it wasn't often he could come up with a saying that suited the occasion, or even had the chance, and he felt really happy as his old friend looked at him askance! He was sure of what he was saying, because he too knew the Daddy of Joss, hadn't he known him since a lad, having been friends with his father, and also Daniel Sharpe. Yes Daniel was one of the nicest men he had ever known and a real gentleman, and he prayed that what Daniel had done for Zoe was the right thing, but only time would tell.

"*A cracked plate may last as long as a sound one*' y' old begger, so no wonder y' as old as y' are now, cos' y' certainly a cracked plate," Maisie said in a huff, and Smithy left the kitchen with a big smile on his face, as he hurried off up the road as fast as a 'cracked plate' could to find Scott and see if he could help with the wheel change. Scott was a fine geologist as far as he knew, and Smithy (like Maisie's 'my Bob God rest his soul') was a quiet man who said very little but noticed a lot and now hoped that Scott was as good with his hands as he had proved he was with another part of his anatomy!

CHAPTER TWENTY THREE

Two hours later Zoe returned to Sharpe House with Joss, because she had decided he might as well go back to school for the afternoon session. For some strange reason she wanted him with her for now, as she couldn't forget that Scott had already told her he was off to see Samantha, who was obviously eager for their morning session. She now began to wonder at the feeling of anticipation she had felt upon getting the letter confirming the completion of the annulment, for some reason she had hoped that just maybe they might make Joss's future happier, her and Scott together, but now that slight hope had been bludgeoned to death, at least that was how it felt. Also she had given Scott the idea that she would be staying in the area so that he might see Joss occasionally, but that now seemed unlikely.

She decided to take Joss for a walk, and off they set, where else but the old coffin route, and at the last minute she collected the flowers out of a vase on the kitchen table picked out of the garden, and not those that Daniel had paid for every week to be delivered to the house. He was such a good and kind person and she would miss him very much!

"Can we play in the hollow oak tree please," Joss asked as he clipped Scotty onto his lead.

"Well perhaps for a little while, but first we'll go up to where we remember Nanny Charlotte, because its been a long time since we did that. Then this afternoon you will have to go back to school, and I'll take Scotty for another little walk, because I'm not going up to the quarry at all today."

She had to smile at the dog and boy, as the dog was nearly as tall as Joss now, and they were looking at each eye to eye, but Scotty never pulled on his lead when Joss was holding him, it was as though he knew he could be free if he wanted to, but he didn't, not from Joss. She now looked at the flowers in her hand taken from the vase on the kitchen table. She wished she had had time to get a proper bouquet, as they had been picked out of the garden as there were still a lot of the deep blue daisies, but her mother would understand. As she guided Joss up through the fell side to where her mother's ashes had been spread, her eyes filled with tears, she had never felt this lonely in her life, as even Daniel who had loved her mother so much, had deserted her!

Scott had left Smithy to deal with changing the wheel on Zoe's car, as now he had at last decided he must go to see Samantha, and let her know that their relationship was not going anywhere. He would apologise to her because he had known this all along, he should never have gone out with her for a second time and let her think he might be interested, and somehow he would find the words to speak to Zoe about Joss. His meeting with Samantha was not very short, neither was it very sweet, but he did apologise and in the end she told him succinctly where to go, and to whom!

Instead he returned to Smithy, who had managed to fit the spare wheel to Zoe's car, and he had moved the car onto the quarry bank where other cars were parked.

"Thank you for doing that Smithy, I shouldn't have left it to you but I had something on my mind and had to act on it." Scott said with a sigh, he was still smarting from his meeting with Samantha, because he knew she was quite right about most of what she had to say about him!

"Well, now you'd better get y'r mind around another problem Scott. Maisie rang t' say that Zoe and Joss have gone missing, at least she doesn't know where they are, because Daniel's car has returned to Sharp House, but there's no sign of them, an' young Joss should have gone back to school after dinner time. *I* have t' stay here because we have a group coming at two o'clock, all fully booked an' paid for."

Scott was aware of how his insides had been churning ever since he had nearly run into Zoe's car, and he wondered if *she* might be feeling upset at the way they had argued, and the kiss that he had forced upon her, which had made him realise what he truly needed in this life. She had literally run away from him down towards Sharpe House.

"I must go and see what Maisie has to say, they might be safely home by now," Scott said worriedly. "If they come anywhere near the quarries give the house a ring." Scott instructed, and climbed back in his vehicle, turned it around, and went back down the road as quickly as he had earlier in the morning, but this time nothing was coming up towards him!

Maisie was busy baking, and ignored the sound of Scot's vehicle turning in the driveway, and then the door being thrust open.

"Don't slam the door Scott, or you'll have everything in the oven ruined, and you usually like my scones as much as anyone." Maisie said grumpily.

"Where's Zoe, have you seen her since she took Joss to the dentist," Scott demanded, laying his hand flat on the edge of the table where it was covered in flour.

"I 'ave not, and that's not like 'er, but she looked white as a sheet earlier on, and I was a bit worried about her, but as usual she said nowt," Maisie answered and the look she gave him almost made him squirm, why should she blame him!

"Smithy says Daniel's car is back, so she must be around here somewhere," Scott replied. "And where's Joss?"

"Your *son* you mean," Maisie said, and thumped the pastry onto the table, and made the flour fly around in a white mist.

Scott felt himself go pale, as he stared at her, and then gulped for air as he watched her more closely. "Why do you say that Maisie?"

"Don't be so bloody stupid Scott, I had already worked that out, but Daniel said he too had come to that conclusion in his letter to Zoe. I thought you would have known that, as Zoe had a long talk with your Adele."

"Adele never said anything like that. I only know what Zoe said to you and me when she received Daniel's letter. I guess that is why Daniel has divorced her."

Maisie stared at him, and remembered that he had mentioned divorce when Zoe had rounded on her and Scott, believing they knew what Daniel had intended, and just for now she wouldn't enlighten him. If he wanted Zoe and Joss, then he should want them unreservedly.

"Your guess is as good as mine Scott. Are you going t' look for her and Joss, or not, or will *you finish the baking* and I'll go?" she demanded, and sniffed looking down her nose at him.

"Of course I am, but I don't know where to start. She must be walking as her car is at the quarry, and Daniel's is outside, they must be walking Scotty."

"Well then, maybe the fact that the flowers have gone out of the vase on the table here has something to do with it," Maisie replied sagely.

"Flowers, what do you mean?"

"Flowers, think about it Scott it's the anniversary of her mother's death this week, and I don't suppose Daniel has forgotten that?"

"I was away Maisie as you well know, but I believe she was cremated, and I've never seen anything in the Church Yard." Scott said mystified as he couldn't make out what Maisie meant, but he realised that she was trying to help in some way!

"Well, Daniel, Zoe and Joss took the ashes to scatter them overlooking Rydal Water, I'm not sure where, perhaps you can think o' summat. Now get away out o' here, I've seen enough of you today, I don't know what you did, but I bet it was *you* who upset her this morning." Maisie looked at him with a frown and noticed that he looked really hurt and troubled, and she was about to relent. Suddenly he seemed to come to a decision, and he kissed Maisie on the cheek, and made for the door. Now she smiled wryly, a right charmer he was, but a bit slow on the uptake!

She sighed with a hopeful smile, maybe she should go and tell Smithy that Zoe and Joss would most likely be found quite soon, as to what would happen *then* she hadn't a clue, just a feeling of hope and anticipation. *Forethought spares afterthought* her mother would have said, and she'd done plenty of thinking and worrying this morning, now it was up to someone else. She'd take a couple of scones and a flask of tea up to Smithy, he had obviously got Scott a little worried about Zoe and Joss, and she had done the same, and as Smithy deserved it she might just put a little tot of brandy in the tea! Also if Zoe did return to an empty Sharpe House with only Joss she could have a little time to come to terms with things, as they may have gone very wrong. But if she returned with Joss *and* someone else then they might need a little privacy. Ten minutes later Maisie was walking up to join Smithy at the quarry feeling quite happy, unaware that when she returned an hour later she would find things exactly as she had left them!

Joss watched as his mummy placed the blue Michaelmas daisy's in amongst the bracken, and he wondered how his Nanny Charlotte would find them cos' she'd gone to live with angels which he thought must be nice, but he felt sad because his mummy was still crying and he didn't know what to do, as Scotty kept pulling him about wanting to play. He decided to make Scotty 'sit' and they would sit together and wait. It seemed an awfully long time before his mummy suddenly looked up and shouted 'Joss.' He and Scotty both jumped up and his mummy hugged them both, but she was still very quiet and he wished she would do the smiley face they drew on the television with the mouth turned up at the sides.

"Come on we'll walk back along the coffin route to Sharpe House and you can have a little play in the hollow oak tree with Scotty, and I'll give you a note to take to school in the morning, because I should have taken you back this afternoon."

"I wanted to play football," Joss informed her, but he didn't seem too bothered because he had Scotty with him, but his reply had made her feel quite guilty.

Scotty was pulling on his lead playfully, as they made their way down a narrow pathway through the still high bracken, which was now turning various shades of yellow and brown, down to rejoin the coffin route.

Scotty went one way through the bracken and Joss another, and all three of them fell into the tall and unexpectedly strong bracken, and they started to laugh, and Scotty to bark excitedly, as Joss had let go of his lead, and he carried on down the fell side, until Scott caught him and lifted him up and came up towards Joss and Zoe.

"What is going on here, you should keep Scotty with you because he hasn't been trained yet, he might chase after sheep or lambs and the farmer might shoot…"

"Shut up Scott, don't say that he won't understand he's too young, you'll frighten him," Zoe said quickly managing to pull herself up out of the bracken. Her leg felt quite sore, but she hadn't time for that, Scott was being overbearing again, and after the confrontation this morning she was going to put him in his place, enough was enough and she had had enough!

"Mummy, I'm bleeding on two knees, and you've cut your leg," Joss said and started to cry, now that he had seen blood!

Scott sighed deeply. "I'm sorry Zoe I've been really worried about you both as Maisie said she hadn't seen you since this morning." He took her hand and pulled her up out of the bracken and turned pale as he saw blood running down the side of her leg. "You've cut yourself on last years dried up bracken it's very sharp and dangerous." He pulled her close, and just for a second or two she enjoyed being comforted.

"*I've got two* sore knees," Joss complained, and Zoe pulled away from Scott and lifted him up to cuddle him.

"Give him to me and I'll carry him," Scott demanded, and when she did reluctantly, she took Scotty's lead and they came slowly down to the footpath. "We'll go to Oak Tree Farm, it's nearer." He decided and just for once Zoe didn't argue with him as she didn't have the strength left, and besides that she had never been inside his home.

Joss looked down from a great height he thought, to watch his mummy dab at her leg with a tissue, and then she followed him and Scott with Scotty pulling at his lead and he liked being high up as it must be like riding a horse.

Zoe was trying hard to put the almost frightened look in Scott's eyes out of her mind, he had looked as if he had been very worried, and then she realised Joss was his *son*, of course he would be worried and she felt like crying again, but the cut on her leg wasn't that bad, so she must just be a wimp!

"Sorry, have we made you late for your assignation with Samantha?" Zoe said waspishly, and then wished it unsaid.

"No, as a matter of fact I have already seen her, and everything is resolved between us, so you needn't worry about it. Just let us get Joss to my house, and we can see to his sore knees!" Scott's reply was very curt, and the rest of the walk to Oak Tree Farm was done in silence.

When they got to the door the dogs started to bark, and he unlocked it without putting Joss down, and they went in. Scott placed Joss in an easy chair, and went to the kitchen to get the first aid kit. As the dogs settled down in their beds, and Scotty joined them as if he had come home, which he had! Zoe now cleaned Joss's knees with antiseptic wipes and stuck on some elastoplast, and Joss moved over to the dogs, and laid down on the carpet beside Scotty, with his arm over the dog stroking him gently.

"Are the dogs always in your living room," Zoe asked, looking round at the tall windows letting in the sunshine, and thinking how lived in and comfortable the house was. It was obvious that the whole place had been decorated since the death of Scott's father, everything looked fresh and clean but lived in, including the large and very comfortable overstuffed settee and armchairs, and a square of very soft comfortably thick carpet in the centre of the floor. She took a quick look at the fireplace, remembering that Adele had told her about it, but she had changed the subject not wanting to picture Scott there in front of the tall marble fireplace. It was still very large, but now there was a wood burning stove there, and it certainly looked homely and must be very warm in the winter months. She glanced around and saw there was also central heating. Zoe could just imagine Maisie when she visited here, as she would fit in just as well as she did at Sharpe House, Ald Smithy too!

"Of course they *live* with me, and I don't need much room for myself." Scott replied curtly, as it was the first time Zoe and Joss had been in his home, and he had hoped that she might like it, but she seemed to be finding fault with his much loved home! "I would never have given Scotty to Joss if I had believed that Daniel would not have wanted a dog in the house. You don't seem to know much about your ex husband, he always had dogs until recently."

"I am aware of that, but Maisie told me Daniel had found it too much having to walk a dog whether he felt like it or not, I guess that the angina was a trial to him," Zoe replied wondering why Scott was being so hateful about Daniel! Daniel was his Godfather after all, and they had always got on very well, she had seen that for herself.

"I'll show you the downstairs bathroom, and you can clean up your cut, your white trainer is getting slowly splashed with blood."

"I just pulled out this bit of last years bracken, can you see if there is any left in the cut please, it is on the back of my right calf - I can't get near enough," she replied showing the piece of bracken held between her thumb and forefinger. "I didn't see it until I rolled up the leg of my trousers."

He went down on his haunches all the better to see, and slowly prodded the fleshy part of the calf of her leg. "It looks clear to me, and the bathroom is the second on the left to the back of the house."

"Sorry to trouble you Scott, you obviously don't want to touch me, and I understand."

He stood up suddenly, and held her by the top of her arms. "You don't understand at all Zoe, I had to apologise to Samantha today for going out with her to make *you* jealous, or at least to realise that I too could find myself a possible partner although I didn't really realise that was why, and it was very upsetting for us both and she called me all the names under the sun. One of which was that I was not the *gentlemen* she had thought I was, and how disgusting it was because she thought Daniel was my friend. But then she doesn't know that Joss is my son, and he was on the way before Daniel married you. She knows I am interested in you, but I never said anything about your new position. Now you are divorced Zoe I want my name on Joss's Birth Certificate, and I want to be around to help you care for him and see him growing up. I should warn you Zoe that I am going to do everything in my power to get you to marry me in due course, when you have managed to get over losing Daniel, it's only fair that you should know that. The other thing I want you to know is that I never forgot you when I was in Afghanistan for the second time, and I nearly got off the train when *you did* at Lancaster Station to follow you, but I was stupid and let you go. I would have been in serious trouble with the Army, but that would have been worth it if you would have agreed to wait for me. Instead I returned to find you married to Daniel, my Godfather!" He finished speaking and Zoe could hardly believe his words, and he looked really traumatised, and her heart ached, and her eyes filled with tears at his words, spoken without any hope! But a hopeful revelation for her!

"Go and get your leg cleaned up Zoe, and think about that and I'll get a blanket, because Joss has fallen asleep on the floor with Scotty."

She was staring into his emotional grey eyes barely daring to believe what he had said but it seemed to be true, although he had never said that he was in love with her! He turned away and went upstairs and she met him on the top step as he held a small blanket over his arm. He looked into her blue eyes and they turned to green with emotion, and he pulled her close and dropped the blanket, Joss would be quite warm enough with Scotty asleep beside him! He walked towards an open door and she followed him inside, it was obviously a bedroom but unoccupied. It was clinically clean and there were two beds in there, and it afforded a beautiful view over Rydal Water, and gave them a degree of privacy, and they stood side by side drinking in the view.

"I think I fell in love with you Scott when you helped my mother, and afterwards when I followed you to thank you, it was inevitable what happened between us, if rather sudden and before we could get to know each other," Zoe said. "I was not promiscuous Scott, I just needed *you, and I still do.*"

He turned towards her, but still refrained from taking her in his arms and making love to her, which was what he wanted to do more than anything in the world!

"Zoe, it was the same with me, but afterwards I worried that it was because I had a 'traumatic brain injury' which was what my doctors were worried about, caused whilst on active service because I came home against their orders to spend the last few months of my father's life with him. But I went back, and they eventually gave me a clean bill of health. I believe that Daniel found out that Joss was my son, and I think that is why he believed it was better for you to be free, so that we could be together. I want that very much Zoe, but you seemed so happy to be with Daniel."

"He is a wonderful gentle-man, and he was going to marry my mother Charlotte as they were very much in love, but she died, and I was left with nobody and a small son to bring up, and a University debt hanging over my head, how could I work and make enough to home us both, *and* pay off my debts! My mother had asked Daniel to look after us, and he did, but he insisted that we should marry as I couldn't live in his house without causing gossip, and he even insisted that for the few days after mother died that his cousin Janette should come and stay until we were married. He has now made me free to be with you Scott, and I *need you* and so does Joss." She could hardly breathe worrying that she should have waited before declaring herself to Scott.

"Just because I gave him a puppy?"

"Certainly not, we need you to make our family complete, because I love you," she replied quietly, and as her eyes turned green once again, he lifted her up and went backwards through a door that she assumed was *his* bedroom. Soon he removed most of his clothes, and with great care and close attention he started to remove hers, and he was amazed that she seemed quite reserved and shy, but he took his time and she slowly relaxed and started to help him, then insisted that he should make sure that Joss was still asleep with Scotty, and when her mind was settled, their inevitable coming together was even more mind blowing than when Joss had been conceived, as they had time to savour their sense of euphoria and inevitable satisfaction.

An hour later Zoe gazed out of the bedroom window at Rydal Water dressed in Scott's dressing gown revelling in the slight aroma of his soap and individual scent, and felt a complete satisfaction, as Scott had shown her and told her many times how much he loved her, and she felt complete for the first time in her life, and all they had to do now was to advise Maisie, Smithy and Adele's family that they were going to be married, as nobody else mattered, except Daniel of course! But for this wedding she would be inviting her friends from University, and as many locals as could manage it. They wanted people to see how happy they were! She still felt guilty about letting Daniel take care of her and Joss, but he had wanted to do that for *her* mother! She only hoped that Scott would be alright with that!

Scott was relaxing on the bed and watching Zoe with a besotted gaze. "Give me your mobile please Scott and I'll ring Maisie she will be getting worried about Joss."

Scott lazily handed her his mobile phone. "It was Maisie who started getting me worried about you both, and also made me think about where you might be, as I hadn't been aware of the date that your mother left you so alone. I do hope that Maisie decides to stay around here when we are married."

She rang Maisie, who was at first very angry that she hadn't told them where she and Joss were, and then as she realised that Zoe was at Oak Tree Farm and was now going to *marry* Scott, she insisted on speaking to Scott immediately.

Zoe handed him the mobile phone and he tried to pull her towards him, but then he smiled and listened to Maisie.

"Well Scott lad, I'm pleased that you are going to marry young Zoe and take care of your lad. I guess you have already made the necessary promises at *least,* so there's something I want you to do. *First be just, then be generous* and this time it's what Daniel has to say, because when he wrote to Zoe last time, he also wrote to you, but he insisted that I kept it until you decided you had to marry Zoe if she would have you, and take on young Joss."

"What, what do you mean Maisie," he sat up in bed, pulling on his dressing gown handed to him by Zoe, who then started to dress quickly. Scott was holding the 'phone as if *he* was the one that had been caught out, or perhaps he felt that Maisie was already in the room rather than on the 'phone!

"Well you look in your living room in one of those nice vases on t' mantelpiece there's a letter from Daniel, for *you Scott.*" Maisie rang off abruptly hoping Scott would not let down Daniel or Zoe at this late stage, but she doubted that very much!

Scott left the bedroom, and Zoe followed him wearing Scott's T-shirt, as the dogs started to bark at the sound of him running down the stairs. He lifted down a vase, and there was nothing in it, and then he put his hand in the next vase and pulled out a sealed envelope. He now sat down on the settee and held it in his hand.

"What have you got Scott, as that looks like Daniel's hand writing?"

"It is for me alone according to Maisie, from Daniel, but don't go away because I *have* to read this."

He read it through, and then he read it through again. He then smiled at Zoe, and jumped up and swung her around as the dogs went mad, and Joss rubbed his eyes and stared at Scott in his dressing gown and his mother in a big T-shirt.

"Daniel has written to me, and it is private, but it tells me that your marriage with Daniel was *annulled* because it was in *name only*, as he promised Charlotte that he would take care of you and Joss and because of his strict beliefs that was the only way he felt that he could. Now he has found a way to make you free, because he believes that you, Joss, and I should be together, but he wants to be (as he always felt he was) your step-father, Joss's grandpa, and as always my Godfather. I guess he wanted me to make up my mind about how much I wanted you and Joss before he gave me the full details. Maisie must have kept this letter because she too wanted to make sure that I wanted to marry you no matter what had gone before!" He sighed deeply and kissed Zoe very satisfactorily.

"I promise you Zoe, that I will take good care of you and Joss, just as Daniel and Maisie have."

He closed his eyes as he held her close, she was his and his *alone*, he was happier than he had any right to be and he looked at Zoe and was amazed by the love he saw in her now green eyes - love for *him*. Now they had news for Joss, and as Scott

202

glanced at Zoe he realised that at least *she* was of the opinion that Joss would consider the news to be very welcome!

Scott took Zoe by the hand, and instructed Joss to follow them, as he took them around the four bed roomed house, with an attic room, dining room, lounge, kitchen and utility room. He was pleased when Joss decided he wanted the attic room all to himself (as that had been his room as a young boy), and Zoe had to restrain Scott from taking them outside to look around the outbuildings, insisting that it would be a much better idea if they took time to dress properly, as that would be much better than encouraging Joss to be anything other than a sensible, upright citizen, like his adopted grandfather Daniel!

Zoe and Joss did visit all the outbuildings, and found it very interesting, but they both wanted to get back to Sharpe House to see both Maisie and Ald Smithy, for an intimate celebration tea suggested by Maisie. She had also planned a telephone conversation later that evening with Daniel, for Scott, Zoe and Joss!

Three months later, there was a marriage at St. Oswald's Church, Grasmere between Scott Peterson and Zoe Howes-Sharpe, and there were three bridesmaids Emily, Jennifer and Mary (University friends of Zoe), but Elliot and John Junior thought they were too old to be pageboys but promised to look after Scotty dog! Scott's best man was his brother in law, and Joss gave his mother away with the able help of a very fit and bronzed Daniel Sharpe, newly returned from his travels. Daniel's wedding present to the couple was a beautiful album of photographs of Joss, Zoe, Charlotte, and *Scott* and his family over the years.

Any wedding guests or ramblers who might have walked the coffin route from Ambleside to St Oswald's Church, Grasmere that day would see and wonder at the ribbons and flowers decorating the hollow oak tree, and the single red rose on the coffin stone. It was Daniel Sharpe who insisted on taking the rest of the red roses in the bridal bouquet up the fell side in remembrance of Charlotte Howes, Zoe's mother, and his last love. He also remembered that Charlotte was well aware that red roses meant love, respect, courage and passion, and together they had shared all of those in their own particular way! As would Scott and Zoe in the years to come!

STORMY PARADISE

CHAPTER ONE

Morgane was leaning over the white painted wall surrounding the patio overlooking the Great Sound. She watched as the first rays of sun rose above the island to the east, bringing a brilliant brightness to the blue/green almost transparent sea. The sun felt pleasantly warm on her uncovered blond head and her bare arms, although it was only seven fifteen in the morning. She watched with pleasure as the deep pink hibiscus flowers started to open up as they felt the warmth of the sun, almost matching the colour of her cropped cotton trousers, which complemented the honey tone of her smooth slightly tanned skin. She glanced across the lawn of coarse Bermuda grass as she heard voices on the narrow road in front of the property. The voices were jovial and pleasant and Morgane liked to hear the locals chattering happily as they made their way to their jobs in the financial centre and main port of Hamilton, the capital of this lovely exotic island of Bermuda.

She smiled and waved as her cheerful and friendly helper, Benny, swung her ample figure swathed in brightly coloured cotton into the driveway, with her many gold necklaces shining only slightly more than the scrubbed brown Bermudan face. With her rubber sandals flapping as she walked up the driveway, her lined skin didn't detract from the cheerful smile. Benny returned Morgane's wave as she disappeared towards the kitchen at the back of the house. Morgane sighed, she really would have to get her act together and start preparations for breakfast for her three guests. By this time in the morning she had usually moved the tables onto the patio, inserted the green umbrellas, put on the snowy white tablecloths and set the tables ready to receive the guests, and Benny's scrumptious breakfasts.

The young honeymoon couple John and Linda, would be leaving today after a fortnight spent in these colourful tropical surroundings. Morgane doubted they had fully appreciated the islands, as they had spent most of their time in and around the chalet to the left of the house, which was next to the small swimming pool. As Morgane had only one other guest their privacy had been certain. The many white sandy stretches of beautiful beach had only been approached occasionally by the young couple, which was probably just as well as they would be returning to the United Kingdom with a *healthy* looking tan.

John and Linda arrived for breakfast, and thanked Morgane profusely for their comfortable stay, and the drive back to the airport which she had promised them in her trusty old Jeep, with the name of the house Smuggler's Cove painted on the front doors. Taxis were available, but sometimes the timekeeping of the drivers left much to be desired. John told Morgane that they had bought duty free rum, but it had not yet been delivered. She informed them that they would have to pick this up at the airport after checking in, as it would be delivered and labelled ready to be taken onto the flight with them.

Later with some difficulty, Morgane managed to get the luggage into the back of the jeep with John's help, after which he lovingly helped his wife into the back seat, and they sat together as closely as they possibly could. Morgane hoped they would feel that way about each other for many years to come. Something that was out of her experience as her mother had been an unmarried mother, but they had been very happy together as Morgane had known nothing else!

Morgane looked ruefully at the small table on the patio which was laid for one guest. Jeremy was acting true to form, and would probably arrive at his table expecting breakfast some time in the next two hours. No doubt he had been out on the town last evening, enjoying all that Hamilton had to offer! She didn't mind this too much, but the fact that he had been with them for three weeks, and had only paid for one week's bed and breakfast was beginning to worry her. He was due to fly back to the United Kingdom in another two weeks. He had supposedly come here to write, an occupation that she had yet to see him accomplish. He had informed Morgane that he was a journalist, and had decided that he would take a few weeks leave from his job, to start the book he had been planning for many years. He had a lap-top computer with him, but as yet Morgane had never seen him using it! Perhaps he was suffering from writer's block, something she had been aware her mother had suffered upon occasion. Her mother had always stayed at her computer, and persevered until some inspiration had come to her - not gone out to drink with so called friends! With a supreme effort she put thoughts of her mother out of her head. Jeremy appeared to be her present problem, she would have to think of a way to either get him writing (otherwise he might want to extend his stay) or ask him to leave. She could not afford to have him occupy a room and not pay her!

The journey to the airport was accomplished with her guests noticing things they had not had time to see, wishing they had made the effort to visit, and trying to store things in their minds to bring out and remember when they were back in the UK, and were already sorry that they had not bothered to take more photographs to show their friends. The island was only twenty-three miles long and normally a fortnight was long enough to see and experience most of the island's delights! The journey to Bermuda international airport on St. David's Island took thirty five minutes, and Morgane knew from past experience, that to exceed the twenty mile an hour limit was not an option on the narrow roads. She joined a line of very new looking taxis, and felt slightly ashamed of her old Jeep. After loading the baggage onto a trolley with John's help, Morgane hugged them both.

"I'll be pleased to see you anytime, just give me a ring and I'll hold a room for you. Or maybe you would prefer the chalet again." Morgane smiled at the tanned faces, obviously reluctant to leave their honeymoon island.

"Thank's for everything Morgane, we've had a wonderful time. We hope to come back here sometime in the future." John and Linda moved off pushing the heavy trolley, and John turned. "We won't forget the Bermuda rum. Linda's Dad will love it," he called cheerfully. Morgane quietly watched them reach the doors to the new Airport building, which opened automatically to let them through, and then closed. Seeing the doors close Morgane sighed. She had no right to feel so lonely. Her mother had left her Smuggler's Cove which was both her home and her means of making a living. She also had her mother's faithful retainer Benny, who was quite capable of running the bed and breakfast establishment single handed, and who always treated Morgane like one of her own large family. The sun was shining on the blue/green sea. Rocks and the seabed could be seen clearly, and if time were spent to stand and stare, multicoloured fish could be seen in vast numbers swimming amongst the coral and seaweed. She sighed again thinking she should be feeling extremely happy instead of not wanting to get back to the house to sort out her third, and for at least the time being non-paying, guest.

She strolled lethargically back towards the waiting row of taxis and swung into the jeep, where the hot air hit her - she had left the door open. She slammed the door, and switched on the air conditioning, the temperature should soon be more bearable. She left St David's Island and as soon as the lights were on green she started to cross the long causeway to the main island. There was a short cough behind her, and the jeep swerved, only just missing the Causeway wall on the left. The jeep slowed as she glanced behind her as she was unable to stop on the narrow Causeway. She glimpsed the figure of a hunched up man, and a pile of luggage.

"What the hell are you doing in this vehicle," she demanded angrily. There was no reply and the vehicle reached the end of the causeway and Morgane pulled up the jeep in the side of the road with a skid as she jammed on the breaks, and the inevitable dust flew up around the vehicle, and something moved from side to side in the back, and she wondered if it was her unknown passenger!

"I'm going to Smuggler's Cove, I booked a room there, the confirmation and deposit should have arrived by now. I assumed you had come to the airport to meet and greet me," he finished brusquely. He was well spoken, and his voice had a dark husky quality, causing Morgane to feel only slightly happier.

"Have you just arrived from Gatwick," Morgane asked.

"Yes, this morning," he replied his voice brusque.

"Well you had no right to just get into the jeep, and assume you would be met," she was becoming very angry. Who did this guy think he was anyway!

"Well, you might as well take me there anyway and I'll sort everything out with your employer," he replied. By the tone of his voice she realised he thought that his decision was final!

Morgane glanced at his luggage, as he must have planned an extended stay on the island judging by the amount of luggage he carried. She also saw an artist's easel. Perhaps he wasn't so bad after all. She was most definitely annoyed, but also intrigued by this man with the husky voice, who had assumed that she was the hired help. She turned and put the jeep into gear and set off on the narrow road to Smuggler's Cove. Perhaps she ought to make more of an effort with her appearance she thought sheepishly, she couldn't remember the last time she had dressed up and gone into Hamilton for a meal or for personal shopping, or just to enjoy herself! Most of the inhabitants of Bermuda made a point of looking well dressed, as did all of the visitors. No wonder he had taken her for the hired help, she must make more of her God given attributes, although she was well aware that she looked fine in her shorts or trousers and tops, with her slim five foot four figure. The fact that she had blond hair and blue eyes certainly made her look different when surrounded mostly by dark haired women. She was, however, unaware of the fact that her very quietness and serene expression made her stand out in this happy, noisily expressive and boisterous population.

"How many rooms does the guest house have to let?" asked the dark brown voice from the back of the jeep.

"Two double rooms in the house, and a chalet in the grounds," Morgane informed him, her tone of voice was meant to discourage any further questions. However, it didn't have the desired effect.

"Oh, the chalet sounds all right, that should suit me fine. At least I should get a bit of privacy. And as you are certainly a pretty girl maybe I'll paint your portrait."

Morgane was so annoyed with his arrogant assumption that she would be available to sit for him, that she ignored any further comments he made, and they were soon entering Hamilton, and driving along Front Street, where she had to stop at the traffic lights. She couldn't decide whether his last remark was a threat or a promise, as he had certainly taken it for granted that she would want this attention!

"I'm amazed, it isn't very busy in town," he remarked craning his neck to look out of the window. "I thought that you had an English policeman directing traffic."

"It will be busy enough when the cruise ships are in dock. The policeman will be on duty then, as the tourists love to take his photograph." Damn, she hadn't meant to speak to him again.

They passed through Hamilton, and drove slowly along Pitts Bay Road for a further five minutes, following a colourful horse drawn buggy with a large brown driver and two equally large tourists behind him – the poor horse seemed to be the smallest of the bunch! Morgane turned right into the driveway to Smuggler's Cove. She drove to the back of the house to the parking area under the palm trees, and jumped out slamming the door behind her. She was surprised when she turned to find he had already got out of the Jeep, and was hauling a large suitcase out onto the drive. When he stood she saw he was well over six feet tall, with an athlete's body, and she raised her eyes to meet hypnotic assessing grey eyes. He wore dark trousers and white shirt, and reached for his jacket and a leather holdall, just as her outstretched hand grasped the handle. They both pulled back immediately and Morgane wondered if he had felt the strange tingling sensation that she had when his hand accidentally touched hers. She felt confused and her cheeks felt hot. She moved aside quickly and left him to get the rest of his own belongings out of the jeep.

When he straightened up from piling his luggage and easel on the ground, she had disappeared. He looked around thoughtfully, what an interesting girl. What bone structure creating a beautiful countenance, together with the amazing colour of her eyes, he would create a lovely picture. He really would have to paint her. He moved his luggage onto the patio in front of the stone built house, and strode to the edge of the patio and looked towards the sea. There were numerous inhabited islands in the Great Sound, and across the large bay he could see more colourful stone buildings in every colour under the sun, all with a white roof, and a number were surrounded by tall palm trees, lush vegetation, and colourful flowering shrubs. It really was a painter's paradise. Although the *choice* of venue for his next few weeks painting was not his own he was well pleased, and looked forward to the completion of his unwelcome business here. The presence of the lovely young girl he had just met would make it very interesting indeed. He smiled to himself at the thought of overcoming any reservations she might have following the rather unfortunate way they had met and the unfriendly vibes he knew she felt towards him! In all his thirty two years he had not as yet been unsuccessful in arriving at a satisfactory relationship with the opposite sex, and had still managed to remain single, and mostly he had remained friends with the young women!

He heard the sliding glass doors onto the patio open behind him and turned expectantly, hoping to see the young lady that had been filling his thoughts. He was disappointed when a young man in shorts and disreputable T-shirt stepped out onto the patio. He appeared to be in need of a shower and shave. The man nodded and came across the patio, and paused alongside him beside the patio wall.

"Are you staying here," the young man asked pleasantly enough, "I have been here for three weeks and you will love it. If you need showing around the few nightspots there are, I'm the man to do it. The name is Jeremy Dixon," he finished enquiringly, putting out his hand in greeting.

Joe briefly shook his hand. "Joe. Yes, I intend staying here for a few weeks. Can you tell me where I might find the owner, Miss Maine?"

"Yes she was in reception, just inside the patio doors. She's a real honey," he said, rolling his eyes suggestively. At that moment Joe decided he did not care for the younger man, as he most definitely did not like his attitude towards women. He gave Jeremy a cold stare and then moved off into the building.

After the brilliant sunshine outdoors the interior appeared rather dim. Behind the desk the slim blond figure looked at him without expression, and she just raised her cold eyes a fraction.

Joe returned her gaze and wondered how soon he could chase that cold enigmatic look from her blue eyes, and he was very much looking forward to the challenge!

"I would like to see Miss Maine, I did write a couple of days ago booking a room."

"Nothing was in the post, but we haven't had any yet today, it probably arrived on the same 'plane that did you." She replied briskly.

"I spoke on the telephone to someone called Benny, she said there was room, but to write and confirm. This I did. We haven't been introduced, I'm Joe Lawson." He put out his hand, and when she tentatively offered he clasped hers, and he didn't want to leave go. She tugged slightly and he watched her cheeks become slightly more colourful.

"Morgane Maine," she introduced herself. Suddenly her hand was free, as he had dropped it as though it burned him. She looked nonplussed for a moment, and then moved a card towards him. "Can you fill in this form please? I presume you filled in a form on the 'plane saying that you were staying at Smuggler's Cove?"

He pulled the form towards him and clicked his pen, and started to fill in the form, he nodded in answer to her question. Morgane realised he had previously had plenty to say, had he now lost his tongue, or was he embarrassed at the way he had come on to her in the jeep?

"We have a double room in the house, or the chalet in the grounds is also available. I'll show you both."

"No don't bother, I'll take the chalet in the grounds. I'm here to paint and that should suit me fine. I'll find my own way if you just point me in the right direction."

Morgane indicated that he should turn right outside the house. She decided to let him struggle with his own luggage, as he was big enough to manage. She glanced at the form in front of her. He had not filled in his occupation, or how long he intended staying here. He was a bit of an enigma, one minute he was friendly and flirting with her, the next he was cold and taciturn. Should she have turned him away? She was going to have enough trouble with Jeremy if he didn't pay his bill soon, without inviting more! She looked again at the registration form, and saw underneath that he had left five fifty pound notes. She could not afford to turn him away. She would have to take this money to the bank, but at least she could draw out enough Bermudan dollars to pay Benny what she was owed in wages. The money received from John and Linda was already earmarked to pay bills.

Joe Lawson reappeared in front of her desk and she wondered what he wanted now! Surely he hadn't decided to leave. Maybe the chalet was not up to his standard, and her heart sank at the thought. Had he come back for his money and to say he didn't intend staying at Smuggler's Cove?

"Sorry if I was a bit abrupt just now. The chalet is perfect, having its own facilities. I will be very comfortable there," he sounded quite pleased with his accommodation. As he should be, the view was fantastic.

"I hope you took note that the water is not drinkable in the chalet. You will have to use bottled water. If there isn't a bottle there, I'll sort that out for you. You will also have to use bottled water to make tea or coffee. The water in the kitchen is drinkable because it has been treated, but in the rest of the house it is just filtered rainwater which collects on the roof and is stored in a large tank under the house."

"Thank you, everything I may need seems to be there. A very cheerful lady who introduced herself as Benny was just finishing the rooms. I will be very comfortable."

"I'll make out a receipt for your deposit," Morgane smiled in relief.

He watched her closely as the smile spread across her face, and then he straightened his shoulders, sighed, and moved away towards the chalet. He ducked his head as he went through the door, which was probably an automatic thing. His loose-limbed walk drew her attention as he walked around to the right towards his chalet. She felt her insides tighten with awareness, she must pull herself together. She smiled to herself as she was certain that Benny would have plenty to say about their new guest. She would, no doubt, describe him as a 'hunk.' Maybe Benny spent too much time with the younger members of her large boisterous family!

Morgane'a forehead creased as she frowned, she had the strangest unsettled feeling. Was it expectation or foreboding?

CHAPTER TWO

It was just before seven o'clock the next morning, when Morgane slid quietly into the pool. It was cold and she had to quickly get moving, but after two circuits of the pool the water felt quite a pleasant temperature. She swam around gathering the leaves and debris that had fallen into the pool overnight. The sun was just coming from behind the tall palm trees, and warming the front of the house. Now she had arranged a small pile of leaves on the side of the pool, which was looking quite clean, and free from the unwanted additions of the night. She swam to the shallow end and slowly climbed the steps out of the pool, basking in the warmth of the rising sun, and drawing her wet hair behind her head and squeezing out the water.

She felt a tingle at the back of her neck, and knew she was being watched. She was annoyed, she had previously taken her swim in the early evening, but had stopped that when Jeremy always managed to be there, and she was uncomfortable when he was, as he always made some suggestive remark, which always annoyed her. His unsolicited remarks had to be endured. As he was a paying guest she had to watch her sharp tongue – she really did hope that he would settle his bill without too much delay, or trouble! She glanced around and couldn't see Jeremy.

She collected her large towel and draped it securely around her. She collected up the leaves and put them into a plastic bag, and took them with her behind the house, where she disposed of them. As she drew open the screen door to the kitchen, she heard a splash and moved back towards the pool, and saw Joe Lawson taking six strokes to reach the end of the pool, and quickly turning. Maybe he was the person she had been so aware of - his chalet did overlook the pool!

Joe swam half a dozen lengths before he thought it was safe to stop and rest. He had been looking out of the chalet trying to judge how high the sun was, and had been enthralled to see Morgane rise up out of the pool squeezing the water out of her hair behind her head. This action showed to advantage her lissom perfect figure in an attractive one piece swim suit in a deep pink colour, which looked marvellous against her honey tanned skin. As she had risen out of the water, he had done some rising of his own, and the only answer to his predicament seemed to be, either a long wait, or a swim in the cold swimming pool. As soon as she had moved out of sight, he had plunged into the pool to work off excess energy.

Yesterday he had admired her and yes, he could admit to himself, desired her. What he now knew had put a different light on things, and he was not looking forward to the next few days, or weeks, or however long it took to glean the information he was looking for.

He did another six lengths of the pool then climbed slowly out, and made his way into the chalet. After a quick shower, and dressing in shirt and shorts, he switched on the kettle to make tea. He poured the boiling water over the teabag in a large mug, which he removed after dunking it up and down, and added the small carton of milk. He sipped the tea, which was too hot. He really would have to try to keep his mind on what he was doing. He picked up a sketch pad, and went outside to where a small table and two chairs awaited him in the now warm sun. He looked across the pool and garden towards the sea, and the other side of the island in the distance. There was certainly plenty for him to paint and he would do a few quick sketches. Later he picked up the mug, and was disappointed to find it empty. He wondered what time he might expect breakfast. He glanced at his watch, it was nearly eight o'clock. He flipped over the sketch pad and found on the first page a sketch of a palm tree, and the other side of the island in the distance. He stared at the second page in surprise. He stared at the distinctive bone structure of a very beautiful face staring at him from the page.

It was a very good likeness, and he held it away from him for a better look. He had not realised that his artist's eye had taken in so much detail. He looked more closely at the sketch and felt a definite feeling of relief, as he could not see any likeness in the sketch of Morgane to any other person! He glanced up to find her standing in front of him, fully dressed, and he flipped the sketch pad shut.

"Good morning Mr Lawson. You may have breakfast anytime between seven thirty and nine, either on the patio or in the dining room. Do you want a cooked breakfast, or continental?" She gave a small self-conscious smile, as her blue eyes met his grey ones. He seemed to be a morning person like herself - he seemed to be in a good mood.

"The name is Joe, Morgane. Cooked breakfast please, I'll be along to the patio in about fifteen minutes." He ran his hand across his chin, he really should have a shave. He really had no idea of the effect his morning shadow had on most of the opposite sex. What he did realise was that it was not a good idea to watch Morgane walk away from him, at least not when she was wearing well fitting cropped cotton trousers in a becoming blue with a small sleeveless top to match, and slight toe-post sandals on exquisite small feet! Did he have a foot fetish he had never known about? Up to now this lovely island seemed to have him slightly confused, and in danger of forgetting why he was here! His thoughts turned to his father, and if Morgane had seen the expression on his handsome face she would never have believed him to be a 'morning person.'

The post arrived when Joe was having his breakfast. Morgane came out from the reception area and waved a letter towards him.

"I have now received your letter and deposit. It must have arrived on the 'plane yesterday, as did you," she smiled and handed him his cheque for the deposit.

"You keep it Morgane, we'll settle up when I leave, seeing as I'm not sure when that will be," he replied, unconcerned.

The felt relieved, she had a number of bills to pay, and the spring season had hardly begun. She did have guests nearly all the year round, but she was not yet very well known, and over the last two years, since her mother's death, she had been happy just to keep her head above water. Now she thought that maybe she would have to be more businesslike, that is, if she wanted to stay on the island. There was very little accommodation on the island except for the very expensive hotels, and she wondered if because of this she was attracting the wrong kind of guest (her mind straying to Jeremy.) The honeymoon couple had booked from the United Kingdom, and Joe Lawson seemed to know of her establishment, as he had done the same. She had been relying on word of mouth - people who had stayed with her passing on the information to friends and relatives.

She had done her degree in art, and she loved to paint in her spare time. She had managed to sell one or two pictures over the two years to souvenir shops, and she had received a letter asking her to supply more, but the bed and breakfast business, with only the help of Benny in the house, took up most of her time. Benny's son-in-law helped with the garden, and her son had carried out improvements in the house, to enable Morgane to start the bed and breakfast business. When her mother had died unexpectedly at fifty four, Morgane had left the temporary job she had taken after finishing University in England, and flown to her mother's home here in Bermuda. Smugglers Cove she now owned in its entirety, but the amount of investments left to her by her mother had been a surprise. Most of the revenue received by her mother from her quite successful writing, had gone towards the house, and her mother's love of travel, and there was only a small amount left for Morgane to manage on. She could now fully appreciate the amount her mother had spent to keep her only daughter in England for her schooling, and later University!

Morgane returned to the reception desk, and safely put the cheque ready to bank. She would go into Hamilton later today. She glanced out of the window, and saw Benny giving the very late Jeremy a lecture about being on time for breakfast. As Jeremy had already guessed she would, she gave in and went off into the kitchen to prepare the meal for him. He really did take advantage of them, being late for breakfast, and also after promising faithfully to pay for his accommodation week by week, he was now two weeks behind with his payments!

Morgane went into the kitchen to help Benny. "Shall I make the toast for Jeremy?" she asked Benny, who was by now her usual happy self.

"I guess so, thanks Morgane. That boy has not paid you yet?" Benny asked, knowing full well he had not. Morgane shrugged. "Well I guess we'll have to ask my son Robin, and my son-in-law to come here. The size of those two will certainly intimidate him, he wouldn't refuse to pay then," Benny said, only partly joking.

"He'll pay eventually after all we are on an island, where could he go! My mother believed that that was why there is hardly any crime here," Morgane replied with a slight smile. She glanced at Benny, whose eyes looked big and round as she looked with meaning behind her young friend. Morgane turned, and met the cool grey eyes of Joe, who was lounging against the kitchen doorway. How much had he heard of their conversation about another guest? Morgane knew that she looked shamefaced and ill at ease. She removed the toast and stacked it in the toast rack, turning slowly.

"Can I help you Mr Lawson?" she asked briskly.

"You can help *Joe,* please. Where can I arrange for some transportation around the island?"

"Well, there are taxis, buses and horse drawn vehicles, but most people hire either a motorcycle or scooter to get around the island. I'm afraid you can't hire a car. Residents are only allowed one car per household, because of the narrow roads. There is a twenty mile an hour speed limit all over the island, so you should be quite safe on a scooter." Morgane couldn't help smiling at the consternation on his handsome face. "I'm not joking," she finished.

"Well I guess I can learn to ride a motorcycle or scooter. Will I be able to carry my painting gear on one?" he asked.

"Sure, you will. I'm going into Hamilton in about half an hour, and I can give you a lift to one of the hire shops."

"Thank you Morgane, I'll be on the patio ready when you are." He wandered off looking slightly bemused.

Half an hour later, Morgane arrived on the patio to find Jeremy finishing his breakfast, and Joe looking out to sea. Jeremy cast a baleful glance in Joe's direction, and then moved quickly into the house. Morgane thought she could detect an unpleasant atmosphere between the two men.

"Ready er...Joe?" Morgane asked, and she liked the sound of his name.

The drive to the hire shop took about ten minutes, and for the next twenty minutes Morgane had a hilarious time. She informed Joe she would wait to make sure that he found the transport that he wanted, just in case he needed to go to one of the other outlets. The manager of the hire shop wheeled a scooter out of the building, with a motorcycle helmet resting on the seat. Joe followed him, and looked strangely at the helmet, then placed it on top of his head. It sat on top of his head like a pea on a drum – it was far too small and looked ridiculous. The manager said he would find a bigger one, but to keep it on for the moment whilst he showed Joe the controls of the vehicle. Joe sat on the scooter, and when he attempted to put his feet onto the scooter in front of him, his knees wouldn't fit in and were stuck out at right angles, and man and scooter nearly landed in a heap in the road. The manager apologised profusely, and wheeled the scooter back into the garage, carrying the helmet with him. Joe glanced towards Morgane and saw that she was trying not to laugh. A bigger scooter was brought out with a red helmet, and was hardly any better than the last. By now Morgane was holding her stomach to try to stop laughing. This time Joe gave a grin, and walked into the garage with the manager. He wheeled out a motorcycle, and a full head helmet was placed on the seat. This time the helmet was a good fit and the motorcycle looked small but manageable. With his feet on the footrests his knees would stick out at a strange angle, but it was the best they could offer him. Morgane gave him a wave as she set off towards Hamilton and the bank. At least he was able to laugh at himself, not many men could she thought, still highly amused.

Morgane arrived back at Smugglers Cove, with bags of grocery and household shopping. She had been much longer than anticipated. After going to the bank to do the necessary deposits, and visiting one of the food shops, she had been tempted by a lovely chiffon dress in one of the dress shop windows on Front Street, and once tried on she had to buy it, although she had no idea when she would get the opportunity to wear it! She had just parked the jeep at the rear of the house, when she heard the sound of a motorcycle coming up the drive. Joe parked the motorcycle alongside the Jeep, and took off the helmet and shook his head with relief.

"Quite an experience," he smiled. "I think I'll like this mode of transport, I have been all the way around to Dockyard on the shore road, and found another road back. I think I've got the hang of it now, it's quite enjoyable." He smiled at Morgane, and for a moment she just looked back into his grey twinkling eyes. Her heart had missed a couple of beats, and it was an entirely new experience for her. She dragged her eyes away from his, and feeling rather hot, she returned her attention to the bags of groceries.

"Let me help you to unload," Joe said helpfully, and grabbed four of the bags, and took them towards the kitchen. Morgane followed after a moment carrying two bags, and found Joe sitting at the kitchen table with a cool drink in his hand, and laughing with Benny. He was certainly making himself at home!

There was the sound of a scooter in the driveway, and a minute later a light tap on the kitchen door, and then the sound of the screen door being opened. Benny's son Robin stood in the doorway, a big grin on his face showing his perfect white teeth. His six foot two and sixteen stone frame made the doorway look very small.

"You want the pool cleaning Morgane?" he asked. "The level is looking a bit low, and maybe we should top it up." He glanced at Joe sitting next to Benny at the table.

"Joe, this is Robin my eldest son," Benny said with pride. Morgane was a little surprised. She had never seen Jeremy introduced to the large Bermudan. Obviously Joe was already in Benny's good books, without even trying!

"Pleased to meet you Robin," Joe said standing alongside Robin, and just managing to top his tall frame. They shook hands firmly, and Robin looked at Morgane questioningly.

"Yes, Robin please clean the pool. About topping up the level, we'd better check the main water tank." Morgane replied to his earlier question, and headed out of the kitchen door. Robin followed her, and when she turned and found Joe was also accompanying them she was surprised.

"Can I see what you do Robin, and maybe do the odd sketch," Joe asked the younger man.

"Sure thing, you have probably noticed the white painted house roof. That is also a catchment area for rainwater." He pointed to a white painted cement area on the slight hill to the back of the property, which was wide at the top, and was shaped into a narrow gully. This obviously guided any rainwater towards a large grill that caught any leaves and debris, before it went into the tank under the house. "See that Joe, I'll explain what happens."

Morgane stood and watched as the two men went off up the slight rise, where Robin explained the system for collecting rainwater. They returned to the house, and Robin unlocked a small door at ground level, and then showed to Joe the large tank under the house, and they checked the water level. Morgane felt like a spare part. She decided she might as well get on with cleaning the lounge and reception area. She knew that Benny would already have started to sort out the bags of shopping. As she did her work she could hear their voices in the pool area. They must have come to a decision about the level without her input!

She was greatly surprised and quite pleased when she was finishing dusting in reception, when Jeremy arrived and handed her enough money to cover what he already owed for his stay, and for the next week.

"Thank you Jeremy, that means you are paid up until next weekend," Morgane informed him.

"Yes, sorry it was a bit late, I forgot. I'll be off into Hamilton now, see you in the morning if not before," he left through the patio doors, and she watched as he strolled down the drive. He had not bothered to provide himself with any transportation. As far as Morgane knew, he had only walked as far as Hamilton, and had not visited any other parts of the islands. So he had forgotten to pay her! She wondered if Joe had anything to do with his remembering so suddenly! Joe, apparently, didn't know when he should mind his own business. She couldn't have him upsetting her other guest. She then belatedly realised that she was feeling quite relieved that the problem had gone away for whatever reason!

Later in the afternoon, Robin came to find Morgane as she was sitting on the patio, doing the books.

"We've finished the pool, it looks good. It was only topped up with water a little. We can sort it out properly after we have had some rain." He thanked Morgane, as she handed him some folded Bermudan dollars, and he set off towards his scooter. "See you tonight," he called, and set off down the drive. Morgane looked after him with a puzzled look.

She hadn't seen Joe leaning against the side of the house. He now walked towards her. "Robin has invited me to a barbecue tonight at his mother's house, and he said you would take me along with you." She glanced into his enigmatic grey eyes. Did he really want to go to a barbecue with people he had only met today? She paused for a moment to try to steady her accelerated heartbeat. If he had come to this island for peace and quiet and to paint, he was in for a surprise.

"I'll give you a knock about six this evening, it is only a few hundred yards away, and we can walk. That is if you really want to go?" She raised her eyebrows questioningly, but when his eyes caught hers she was surprised by his look of deep concentration, and looked away slightly confused.

"Yes, I would like to go, to see what it is like to live in Bermuda, and if Benny's family have no objection, I might even do a sketch or two. See you about six." He moved off towards his chalet, and a few minutes later she heard the sound of his motorcycle going down the drive, as she tried to concentrate on her account books.

She went for a shower about five o'clock and having washed her hair, and blow-dried it, she decided to do her toe and fingernails in a light pink, which looked good against her slightly tanned skin. She dressed in a colourful sarong skirt, and white sleeveless top, and had the blouse to match the skirt ready to take with her. She wore comfortable strappy beige sandals and carried a bag to match just big enough to hold a bottle of wine, tissues, and a box of chocolates just taken out of the refrigerator for the children. Was she making this effort because Benny would be pleased she wondered? Surely it had nothing to do with the fact that Joe was going with her! When Benny had left Smuggler's Cove at around one o'clock, she was quite excited because her daughter and family were coming to join them, from across in St. George's. By Morgane's count there would be at least twelve from Benny's family alone, and her barbecues were often an excuse to have 'open house.'

With slight trepidation Morgane tapped on the open door of Joe's chalet. He came out of the bedroom, looking smart in clean shirt and shorts, and he also carried a bottle of wine. His dark hair looked freshly brushed, and he looked so good it almost took her breath away. He looked at her and his eyes seemed to darken, and it was obvious that he very much liked what he saw. He coughed slightly.

"You look lovely Morgane, the aquamarine and blue in your sarong, matches your eyes, as they keep changing colour," he said. She really was stunning and he had not meant to mention it, but she looked quite pleased with his remark, and he began

228

to wish that he had held his tongue. "Is there room in your bag for my sketch pad and pencil," he asked suddenly.

Morgane went to the table and placed her bag on it, and inserted the sketch pad and pencil he handed to her. Her eyes were riveted on the book on the table, and he quickly explained.

"I asked Benny if there was something I could read. She didn't think you would mind lending me a book. Benny told me the book is one of your mother's?" He turned the book over to look at the picture on the back cover. "You do not look much like your mother except for the bone structure. She was very dark wasn't she? Also very beautiful."

"It was two years ago that she died, suddenly. No. I don't mind you borrowing the book," Morgane said quietly. Obviously Benny had told Joe about her mother. "I'm sorry I was just a bit shocked to see it here in the chalet. She enjoyed her writing. Without it, she could never have afforded to live in Bermuda, or put me through school and University in the United Kingdom. I had just finished my final year and had taken a temporary job, when she died. She left me Smuggler's Cove, and I came over here and have been here ever since."

"Do you mean to stay and live here," Joe asked quietly.

"Until I get tired of doing bed and breakfast I suppose I shall. I do love it here, but to stay I have to have some income."

"What did you study at University?"

"Art." She glanced at him and he looked surprised. "I guess I'm not very good at it," she finished with a laugh.

"What makes you say that?" He raised his eyebrows questioningly.

"Well I haven't been able to make a living at it," she answered ruefully.

"Have you tried?"

"Not seriously. I have sold one or two paintings of Bermuda, but I don't get much time for painting."

She moved her mother's book carefully to one side on the small table, and picked up her bag, and moved towards the door with Joe following. Joe was watching the lovely picture she made as she walked ahead of him down the drive, wondering what he had let himself in for going to a family barbecue with Morgane when he ought to be keeping his distance from all these friendly people.

CHAPTER THREE

The walk to Benny's took about ten minutes, and when they arrived it was to see Benny's whole family sitting enjoying each other's company, and that of a number of friends. Joe looked slightly surprised but was welcomed warmly by Robin and introduced to everyone. The five children were having a rowdy game, which resembled cricket, on a large patch of grass outside the garden. The grown ups were sitting around the back porch, either on chairs brought out from the house, a white plastic patio set, or on the steps to the porch which ran the full length of the house. Morgane drew Joe over to a table on the porch, and they placed their offering of wine with the numerous bottles already there, which included soft drinks for the children.

To the left of the building Joe was introduced to Benny's husband, Mike, who was looking after the food cooking on the oil drum barbecue. He was a big man, now going grey, with eyes that twinkled with good humour. However, he did not have much to say - probably because his rowdy family made that unnecessary. He worked on one of the fishing boats, which took out tourists to enjoy the fruits of the sea, of which it appeared from some of the photographs hanging in the porch, there were many. Joe seemed very interested in the large marlin in some of the pictures. He stayed to talk to Mike for quite a long time, and it transpired later that Mike had invited him to join him on one of the fishing charters, providing of course that he helped, and didn't do sketches all the time!

When they arrived, Joe had had a quick word with Benny who had acceded to his request to do a few sketches. He seemed particularly interested in the children playing, with a backdrop of sea, and the curve of the island across the expanse of the Great Sound, which culminated in Dockyard which had been very busy during the last World War, and which now had two large cruise ships in the dock.

Later Joe joined Morgane as she sipped wine at one of the tables. Things were now quietening down, and the children were being persuaded it was time for bed, with limited success.

"How do they all manage here, there must only be two bedrooms? The place is only a third of the size of Smugger's Cove," Joe asked.

"They don't," Morgane smiled. "Only Mike and Benny and their youngest daughter Marian live here. Robin and his family live next door, and Jane the eldest daughter lives in St. George's with her husband and children."

"I haven't yet managed to fathom out who everyone is, but it has been a very enjoyable evening. Can I get you some more wine?" he looked at Morgane's empty glass. He looked at her closely and she was looking particularly lovely in the soft light from the electric lanterns now switched on in the porch. It was already quite dark and it was only just after eight in the evening. The smell of cooking and smoke still permeated the air. A soft glow lit the sky across the Great Sound, coming from the two large cruise ships docked there, with coloured lights twinkling, probably caused by the slight movement of the sea.

"No thanks Joe. I am about to go home. You can stay and talk with the men if you think you can find your way back to Smuggler's Cove? You have definitely made a very good impression, as they all seem to like you very much."

"Certainly not, I'll walk you back home," he replied brusquely.

"I'll be quite safe Joe, this is Bermuda."

He shook his head and looked across at Benny's now quietened family. The children were moving off to the house next door, and Robin had brought out a disc player and his sister and her husband were dancing closely together to the reggae music. Mike was having a smoke sitting next to his wife Benny, and he held her hand as she 'chilled out,' and tapped her foot to the music. Joe drew Morgane to her feet and they moved over to Benny and Mike.

"Thank you for a lovely evening," Morgane smiled at her friend.

"You're welcome, both of you," Benny replied with a grin. "I hope all our family at once was not too much of a shock for you Joe," she smiled widely, the whites of her eyes glowing in the dusk, echoing those of her husband's twinkling with merriment.

"Time you started your own family boy," Mike said as Joe turned to leave with Morgane. Joe didn't say anything and Morgane wondered if he was married with a family, her heart lurched at the thought. Although she very much liked the thought of a much younger replica of Joe! She was getting soft in the head! They had only just met, but she seemed to know him already!

They strolled along the middle of the road towards Smuggler's Cove, because the pavements were a bit uneven in places Morgane explained. There were few street lights, and luckily not very much traffic. Suddenly Joe put his hand on her arm, and she stopped walking, and she intuitively knew why. They stood quietly and listened for a few minutes to the melodious tree frogs giving their nightly performance, in the otherwise silent evening. The only sound except for the melodious performance, were the whispering fronds of palms high above them in the slight breeze from the sea, and occasionally there was the chirp of a cicada. Somehow, for a tense drawn out moment, she was being held in his arms. Then suddenly she was free and he was moving on ahead of her. She felt quite shocked. She had been waiting for his kiss, and was vitally aware that she had been willing him to kiss her! She hardly knew the man, what was the matter with her!

They finished the rest of the walk home in silence, now an almost tangible antipathy running through their veins. Each with their own thoughts, and Morgane knew *her* thoughts were chaotic. As they walked up the drive, Joe exclaimed angrily.

"It looks as though someone has broken into the chalet," and he moved quickly towards the slightly open door. Morgane arrived at the doorway as Joe switched on the light. They both looked around the room.

"There doesn't seem to have been a break-in. Nothing is missing or damaged," Joe said in puzzlement. "Maybe I left the door open." He glanced at her pale face in the harsh light. She looked upset and he knew he was to blame, as he didn't think it was from the possible break-in! "I'll see you into the house Morgane."

"There's no need," she replied quietly. Before he could move out to accompany her to the house, she had disappeared in the darkness. However, he waited outside until he saw the light go on in the house, then went into the chalet and banged the door behind him in frustration. He went to the cupboard and took out a bottle of whisky and a glass. He felt the need for a drink, something much stronger than wine. The lovely night sounds he had recently enjoyed so much, although as melodious as ever, went unnoticed. Day by day the answers he had come to these islands for became more urgent.

Next morning Morgane took her swim very early, and saw nothing of Joe! He came for his breakfast just before eight. This was much later than was usual, and he appeared to have something on his mind, and only spoke when strictly necessary to order his breakfast. Jeremy had his breakfast about nine o'clock and Morgane took the opportunity to go and clean his room. His waste paper basket was full to overflowing and she was pleased that he appeared to at last be starting the work he had intended. When she emptied the waste paper into a plastic sack, she noticed an English tabloid newspaper, folded to show a slightly unclear picture, which made her stop in her tracks. It was a picture of Joe, and the caption read "Mysterious disappearance of famous artist JDL." Morgane read the short news article. Apparently the famous artist Joseph Daniel Lawson had failed to appear at a famous London gallery, which was putting on a show of his work. His agent and friends were unaware of his whereabouts and were becoming worried. The article ended with a lot of speculation as to where he might be and with whom! Morgane kept the newspaper and disposed of the rest of the rubbish.

Morgane joined Benny in the kitchen for coffee, as she usually did around eleven. She showed the newspaper to Benny.

"What do you think I should do about this Benny?" she asked worriedly. Benny was reading the article for the second time, and slowly set the newspaper on the table.

"Nothing, Joe might just need a break. I must say it is unusual for an artist not to be there when his own work is on show, but he is a very sensible sort of man, and I'm sure he had his own reasons." She paused. "I had no idea he was so famous, he just seems like a really nice man. Maybe he wants to use some of his sketches of my family in one of his paintings," she seemed really pleased by her idea.

Morgane still looked pensive, and perused the newspaper photograph once more. "I just thought that Joe should know what is being written about him. I wasn't going to do anything with this information. The thing that worries me is that Jeremy, as a reporter, won't look at it that way. Where is Jeremy by the way?" She couldn't block out from her mind the open door to the chalet. She was certain that Joe had closed and locked it the night before when they left for Benny's home. Keys for all the letting rooms were on a board behind the reception desk!

"He said he was going into Hamilton, and left after breakfast. Joe had quite a long chat with me, and then went out to 'blow the cobwebs away' on his motorcycle, but I'm sure I heard him come back. See if the bike is parked outside." Morgane went to the window and could see the motorcycle parked in the shade behind the chalet.

Morgane walked slowly towards the chalet. The newspaper was dated two days ago, and would have arrived in Bermuda yesterday. Jeremy had already gone into Hamilton, so maybe it was too late to stop him using this information. She had to show Joe the newspaper, but she had been determined not to seek him out after the way he had acted first hot then cold on the way back from Benny's last evening!

The chalet door was open, and Morgane looked inside, and called "Joe." His reply came from outside, he was standing in front of his easel, looking out towards the sea. She wondered if he had already started to paint, and knew that not everyone liked to be watched when they were at work.

"Joe, I think you might want to see this." She handed him the newspaper, and he put down his paintbrush. He read the article through, and swore under his breath.

"Have you told anyone that I'm here," he asked, looking her in the eye.

"No, of course not, and I didn't even know you were JDL."

"Well that's all right then." He picked up his paintbrush and started to paint again, apparently unconcerned.

"I found the newspaper in Jeremy's room." He turned enquiring eyes towards her and she continued. "Jeremy is here to start writing a book, he is taking time off from his job as a reporter, in London," she informed him. Joe paused with his eyes on the horizon, and stood perfectly still, then put down the paintbrush.

"May I use your telephone please, I will ring my agent, and hopefully he can tell the press I am on holiday in Bermuda, before Jeremy rings in his story. Four hours difference, it should be about five in London. Unless you have a fax or email which would be helpful?"

"Sorry, I have mother's old computer but I haven't bothered with it, it didn't seem right some how," she apologised.

He shrugged his shoulders. "My mobile needs charging, and I never bothered because I didn't intend using it here." Morgane nodded, and they moved towards the house. She left Joe in privacy to speak to his agent, and waited on the patio. Joe was just putting down the 'phone when she hurried inside.

"Joe, Jeremy is coming up the drive with a photographer. Do you want to see them?" She looked at him anxiously. He shook his head emphatically.

"Come with me," she pulled him towards the back of the house, dropping his arm as she felt the now familiar reaction to his touch. As they moved through the kitchen she collected a bottle of water, and handed it to him.

"Joe push your motorbike further into the bushes, where it can't be seen," she instructed and waited whilst he did so. He then followed her to the rear of the white painted water catchment area behind the house, and then she slipped around the side, opening a metal grill door, partly hidden behind a hibiscus bush. He peered inside with interest, a long flight of hewn out stone steps, led towards a light in the distance.

As Joe stepped inside she closed the grill.

"I'll come and get you when I have sent them away. I'll tell them you went off painting, and won't be back until tomorrow." She slipped off and entered the house by the kitchen door.

Benny was getting ready to leave, and had told Jeremy and his friend with the camera to wait on the patio for Morgane. She smiled at Morgane. "If I were you love, I'd keep Joe down there for as long as I could. He's a lovely looking man," she rolled her eyes suggestively and walked off down the drive humming happily, her ample curves swaying in time to the tune she was humming. Morgane was not very experienced but she had some boyfriends whilst at school and university. The tantalising thoughts that Benny's comments evoked, were enough to curl and tighten her lower stomach. Wayward thoughts that she had better put out of her mind, judging by the way Joe had turned away from her last evening!

"Hello Jeremy, I see you have a friend with you." Morgane said coming out of the patio doors to join the two young men.

"Yes, we were looking for Joe. Did you know he was a famous artist, I thought he looked vaguely familiar, but never guessed he was JDL."

Morgane looked suitably impressed. "I had no idea Jeremy. Unfortunately, Joe isn't here. He took off before lunch with some painting gear, and said he wouldn't be back until tomorrow. He met a lot of people last night at Benny's barbecue, and someone must have offered him a bed for the night, so that he could continue with his painting in the morning."

She saw the look of disappointment on Jeremy's face, and the look on the photographer's face that showed he felt he was wasting his time. They seemed to believe what she said. She was surprised, as she knew she had never been able to lie, her mother had always said her face was like an open book!

"You'll have to come back tomorrow. I need the picture as proof," Jeremy said to his friend. "Give me your mobile number and I'll ring when he gets back tomorrow." Then they walked down the drive together, and Morgane assumed that Jeremy had gone back into Hamilton with the photographer.

She waited at least fifteen minutes, and Jeremy did not return. She wondered what Joe would want to do. Hide in his chalet,

239

or leave. What did it matter if people knew where he was? He had some explaining to do, as he had made her lie for him. She thought for a moment. No, he hadn't made her lie - she had done that all on her own! She went out through the kitchen door, and slowly walked towards the rainwater catchment area. She was due some explanation, or Joe could move on. She opened the grill, and slowly closed it behind her when there was no sign of Joe. He had obviously decided to do some exploring of his own. She moved slowly down the steps, the only light coming from behind her, as she moved downwards and forward towards the light at the bottom of the steps.

She knew that there were eighty seven steps, and she balanced herself with a hand against an uneven stone wall on either side. At step forty two she felt the opening on the right hand side of the passage, into a room hewn out of the rock. She hadn't been in that room since she was about twelve, she decided that she must bring a torch and inspect it one day soon. On reaching the bright sunlight at the bottom of the steps, she put a hand to shade her eyes and looked about her. The steps went from the garden at the rear of the house, following a natural fissure in the rock. In places the headroom was many feet high and in some areas the rock had been hewn away to make headroom, and it continued right underneath the road, and down to a sandy cove at sea level.

"Joe," she called out now. There were four more steps, before she reached the sand, slightly to the right of the doorway, and these could not be seen from the sea. Hence the name of the house Smuggler's Cove, which was a much later addition to the hidden steps and storage room. The small cove widened, and she found Joe sitting on a rock looking out across the Great Sound.

"What a fabulous place," he said smiling at her. "Was this cove used by smugglers at some time?" He moved over slightly so that she could join him on the warm rock. She ignored his question.

"Joe, are you going to explain what's going on. If not, you can get yourself some other accommodation. Obviously, as a famous artist you can afford to stay at one of the hotels. What are you doing here?" She sounded quite exasperated, and his eyes turned a darker grey as he gave her a close look. He sighed heavily.

"Has the photographer gone, and where is that creep Jeremy?"

"The photographer is coming back tomorrow when Jeremy gives him a ring to say you are here. Jeremy has probably gone back into Hamilton. And before you ask, he does not know of this entrance to the property, and it can only be reached by sea." She waited for him to make some explanation for the strange things that had happened since this morning. He looked out to sea, obviously with something on his mind which troubled him a great deal, and she wondered if he was not about to share his thoughts with anyone, least of all her, as he seemed extremely distracted and almost depressed! His eyes seemed to be fixed on the horizon, just where the ocean met the sky as he spoke.

"Your mother died two years ago, I think you said. She was Marie Maine the author, and before that she was quite a famous model, is that right?" He still didn't look at her directly, and seemed a bit uncomfortable with his questioning.

"That is what I told you, and yes she was a model before she started to write." Where was this questioning leading?

"Who was your father?" Now he turned to look at her puzzled face, as she shook her head and frowned.

"I don't know," she said lamely. Although she had often asked her mother, she had never told her. Morgane had even asked Benny but to no avail, although she *thought* that Benny knew. She had been with her mother as long as Morgane could remember!

Joe paused, and took her hands in his, and she looked into his troubled grey eyes, a question in hers. He really did look tormented and she wanted to comfort him, and to put whatever was worrying him right! She then squeezed his fingers compassionately and her eyes darkened as he closely watched her. He returned the pressure on her fingers, and then as if without volition, he looked away from her, across the Great Sound once again.

"Morgane, I think you might be *my half sister*."

CHAPTER FOUR

The sun was still warmly shining, the waves still lapped against the sand and rocks in Smugglers Cove, the ferry from Hamilton to Dockyard sailed in the distance followed by seabirds. The open top of the ferry seemed to be quite full with passengers, it was the direct ferry and wound its way through the small islands, some of which were inhabited, as could be seen from the palatial houses. The other ferry would call on the way back at various points on the far shore, and would take nearly twice as long as the direct ferry took to get to Dockyard.

"Did I tell you Joe that the Bermuda Maritime Museum at Dockyard is really worth a visit? I don't suppose you have been there yet," Morgane said expressionlessly. "It is housed at one of the many forts on the island, next to the sea." She stood and walked towards the sea, and paddled in the shallows, disregarding her leather sandals, which soon squeaked as she walked in and out of the lapping waves. "Come over here Joe, if you look over by those rocks where the sea is much deeper you can see the brilliant blue and green hues of the parrot fish.

It is one of the most beautiful fish we have. It is barely moving, and I bet you could easily sketch it."

Joe without his sandals, followed her towards the basking fish with the tail making a slight movement, and took her elbow in his hand. "Morgane, did you hear what I said? I said that I thought I might be your half brother." He turned her to face him, holding both her elbows, and looked closely into her blank eyes.

"That is nonsense Joe. You have been wrongly informed," she returned his gaze steadily. "We should go back to the house to decide what you are going to do, as I expect you will be leaving for London tomorrow if you can get on a flight. Jeremy is a reporter Joe, he will *not forget* about this you know. Oh, I will have to give you a cheque to repay the amount I owe you."

"Damn Jeremy, he is not important. Will you please listen to me Morgane," Joe said in exasperation, slightly shaking her elbows.

She shook off his hands, and rubbing her elbows, and set off for the steps up to Smugglers Cove. He watched as she climbed the four steps, and then disappeared through the doorway, which looked like the opening of a small fissure in the rock from where he was standing. In his frustration he flung the bottle of water that she had handed to him before he came down the long flight of steps to the cove, as far as he could into the sea. He then sat on the rock and waited for the waves to bring it back towards the shore. He had handled everything very badly, she was probably in shock. As soon as the bottle returned to shore, he would go and find Benny. Thank goodness he now knew where she lived. *He* didn't know how to handle Morgane, but Benny would. From the conversations he had enjoyed with Benny, he had discovered that Benny had been working for Morgane's mother since she first arrived in Bermuda, before Morgane was born. Why had they never told Morgane who her father was?

Joe trudged up the steps to find the grill shut, and for a second wondered if he was locked in, but on drawing it towards him it opened, and he found himself in the bright sunlight. He shaded his eyes for a moment, and then walked towards the kitchen door. He paused, as he somehow knew that Morgane did not want to see him. Maybe he should walk along to Benny's and see if she was in. He knew that Morgane could do with someone to talk to, but doubted very much that Morgane would have gone to Benny's home, as he guessed she would wait until Benny came to work in the morning. He listened and waited for a moment, but there was no sound from the house. Joe walked to his motorcycle and pulled it out from the bushes where it was hidden from sight. Just for the moment he didn't care about Jeremy, and the damage he could do, just by letting the world press know where he was. Speculation would be rife, and Joe could well do without the press hounding him at this time. Things had just quietened down after the death of his father, who in his time had been known by the press to be a good artist, with a penchant for beautiful young women! Joe blamed his father for the way the press hounded *him*, like father like son they obviously believed. Joe admitted to himself that he had known quite a number of women, and as far as he knew he had never hurt one of them - not until today.

Joe drove down onto the road, and within five minutes, he was drawing in beside Benny's spotless home. She met him at the door, outside which he paused on his motorcycle. He met her eyes, and she raised her brows in enquiry.

"I think Morgane needs you Benny," was all he said. She looked at him closely for a moment, and then dumbfounded him. She walked towards his motorcycle, wrapped her ample skirts around her legs, and climbed on behind him.

"What are you waiting for boy," she said smartly.

He started up the engine, and waited for a moment to get the feel of another person (a very ample other person) on the back of his motorcycle.

"I'm not moving unless you put this helmet on," he said to the determined woman behind him, handing her his helmet, which she put on impatiently. Whether it was legal or not, they set off and with some trepidation he drove Benny to Smugglers Cove. As soon as she alighted from the motorcycle, she handed him the helmet, then dismissed him with a nod of the head, and he headed for the chalet to cool his heels. He paced up and down the small living room, and drew his sketchbook towards him. After a few minutes, he looked at what he had drawn, and was again surprised to see that he had drawn Morgane's face, this time her eyes looked troubled and hurt. He tossed the sketchbook on the table, and went into the bedroom. Shortly after, he was swimming up and down the small swimming pool, hoping that the exercise would help him to stay away from the women in the house, until they were ready to see him.

Benny went into the house calling Morgane's name, and on getting no response, she searched the living room, patio, and bedroom to no avail. She found Morgane in the shady dining room, which nowadays was very seldom used, the only exception being when the weather was not good enough to serve breakfast on the patio. The young woman was curled up in a deep armchair, and didn't acknowledge Benny at first. Benny bent down and removed the wet sandals from

Morgane's feet, and as she took them towards the kitchen to dry, she looked thoughtfully at the young and miserable face of the girl who was almost like a daughter to her.

"I'll put the kettle on, we'll have a cup of tea," Benny said thoughtfully. What on earth had happened to make Morgane look so shocked, and what did it have to do with Joe? He obviously thought it was troubling enough to come and collect her, assuming that Morgane would want someone to talk to! Everything had been all right when Benny had left for home a few hours ago. She shrugged, a cup of tea usually helped, at least it had when her own offspring wanted to talk things over with their mother. When Benny returned to the dining room with the tray of tea, it was to find Morgane standing by the window, looking out towards Hamilton, but Benny realised that she was not seeing the panoramic vista in front of her. Benny sat at the low table and poured the tea, and patiently waited. She didn't have long to wait, and Morgane slowly returned to the armchair across from Benny, and absently accepted a cup of tea.

"Benny, you were with mother from the time she bought Smugglers Cove, and also when she returned to England for three months when I was born. Except for my secondary education and university I lived here, and you were always about and helped bring me up, as I spent a lot of time with your children." Morgane paused and suddenly looked Benny straight in the eye.

"Who was my father Benny, you were around at the time, you must know?"

Benny slowly returned her cup to the saucer, and returned Morgane's insistent stare.

"Why are you bringing that up again? You have asked many times over the years, and I told you that I didn't know."

"Sorry Benny, but I think you must know. Surely you know who Mum's friends were about that time. I expect she had boyfriends, she was a lovely person, and not at all flighty as you might expect her to be, having been a model and thrown into the company of many interesting people."

"Of course she had friends, but not one particular man friend, as far as I can remember. Quite often she had groups of friends to stay, who wouldn't, living in a beautiful place like this?" Benny looked closely at Morgane's expressive face. "What has happened to make you start to ask questions after all this time?"

"Someone brought up the subject, and I started to wonder why you had never really answered any of my questions, you usually managed to put me off somehow," Morgane said with a deep sigh. "When Mum died I looked through all the papers thinking that she might have left an explanation, but I didn't find a thing," Morgane finished, looking expectantly towards Benny.

"I suppose the someone who brought up the subject was Joe, as he is the only new arrival around here. He came to fetch me to see you, he thought you might want someone to talk to, so I came with him on the bike, I thought something dreadful had happened."

"He came to get you, and you came on his bike?" Morgane looked surprised.

"What is it with you Morgane, at first things were very frosty between you and Joe, but I thought you had started to get on quite well."

248

Morgane considered Benny's words, and felt a hurtful lump in her chest. Quite well, yes they had been getting on quite well, but there had been a definite attraction between them, on her part anyway and she had almost convinced herself that he felt it too. Now thinking about Joe made Morgane feel quite sick. *Was* he, in fact, her half brother? She thought long and hard, getting up from the armchair and pacing back and forth between the window and the table where Benny was watching her with some apprehension. If they had been kin she would know. Whatever she felt for Joe was definitely not brotherly. In truth, she felt a definite dislike for him at the moment, how could he come here and upset her safe little world, making such rash observations! He was tall with dark brown hair, and with grey eyes, and she was smallish and fair, with blue eyes, there was definitely no resemblance whatsoever!

"Come and sit down Morgane, and for heavens sake tell me what is troubling you?" Benny instructed, as though Morgane was still a child.

"Who came to visit with mum before I was born, you must remember some of them," Morgane asked in exasperation, gazing pointedly at the older women.

"Well of course I remember some of them, but she had many friends. Some were quite famous, other models, artists and photographers. You can forget the idea that she was promiscuous, she had friends, but any special men friends always treated your mother with respect. Twenty odd years ago things were much different than they are now, all this sleeping around and changing partners, I can't be doing with it," Benny said in disgust.

"Can you remember anyone named Lawson," Morgane held her breath, waiting for Benny's reply.

"Lawson," Benny paused, and glanced worriedly towards Morgane. "Maybe, yes I think there was an artist of that name, and he was here with a group of people from America. I certainly didn't think he was more friendly with your mother than any of the others present." She stopped suddenly. "Lawson, the same name as Joe?"

"Yes, Benny. Joe thinks he may be my half brother." The shocked look on Benny's face would have been amusing at some other time, but just at the moment Morgane felt as though her world was rocking and she had no control over it!

Benny had a look of deep concentration on her face, obviously trying to remember what had happened more than two decades ago.

"Wait a minute, I remember Mr Lawson now, he had lost his wife a few months previously, and he spent all his time painting. He didn't mix very much with the rest of the group. He was a bit of a loner, and kept himself to himself as though he didn't approve of the rest of the group." She stopped speaking suddenly as she looked across the room to the doorway behind Morgane. Morgane turned as she saw Benny's expression. Joe stood in the doorway, leaning heavily against the door frame.

"The timing would appear to be about right," Joe said quietly, straightening his long frame. "Sorry I didn't mean to eavesdrop. My mother died when I was twelve, and Dad took it very badly. He was away for about three months. He didn't seem to care that *I needed* him, as I too was finding it difficult to cope. I was left in boarding school, with only the occasional visit from my grandparents." He looked pale with a hard look in his normally warm eyes. "Sorry you don't need to know about that," he finished with a grim look. He took a seat opposite Benny, and Morgane paced about as before.

"He doesn't seem the sort of person I would want for my father," Morgane said her voice breaking. Joe stood and put his arm across her shoulders. Benny thought he did this to sympathise with the shock that this must be to her, hearing about her father for the first time, also that he appeared to have been too shallow to care for his only son! However, Morgane pushed Joe's arm away and moved across to the window.

"Don't touch me Joe, I still don't believe that you are my half brother, and you can cut out the brotherly-love bit, I have always managed on my own, whatever happened." She turned away from him, putting distance between them.

"Don't be stupid Morgane, you have had a shock, and anyone would be upset. You are shaking, and don't know whether to scream and shout, or cry. Anyone would want to help you over this. Is it just me you can't stand?" he asked brusquely.

Benny interrupted, "I realise now that you do look like your father. I rather liked him as he was different from the rest of them." Benny said standing abruptly. Morgane was acting out of character. She looked bitter and her expression when she spoke to Joe was that of dislike. She had obviously had all she could stand today, and Benny decided to break up the discussion. She patted Joe's arm briefly to show her sympathy, and glanced worriedly towards Morgane.

"If he was a widower, and he was my father, there would seem to be no reason why he would not admit it," Morgane said with disbelief. Her eyes looked haunted as they looked briefly at Joe. For some reason, goodness knows why, she didn't feel that he was her half brother. "Was he a penniless artist, just bumming around as you appear to be?" she asked insolently, and was immediately sorry for her harsh words.

"I agree with you Morgane, there does not seem to be any reason why he should not admit to being your father, and no, he was not penniless as he was already quite well known," Joe said briefly, looking enquiringly towards Benny. "He had sufficient to send me to boarding school," he said with a derisive twist of his lips. "What did your mother put on your birth certificate Morgane, and was your birth registered in the United Kingdom or here?"

"*Unknown*, and I was registered in England," she sighed, and turned away from him, her shoulders slumping hopelessly.

"I'm sorry this has been sprung on you Morgane, but can't you understand how I felt, it was also a big shock for me, particularly after I had met you," Joe rasped.

For a moment Morgane wanted to ask him to explain himself, but she hadn't the courage, and couldn't understand herself why it mattered so much!

"What made you come here now Joe, and why didn't you say from the outset who you were, and why you were here?" Morgane enquired, bewilderment and hurt making her voice quiet. She seemed to have lost the aggression that had her in its grip earlier. Joe struggled with the urge to take her in his arms to comfort her, and glanced at Benny who was by the open window, looking out to identify the voices they could here coming nearer down the drive.

"Joe, it's that Jeremy and the photographer back again. Do you want me to get rid of them?" Benny asked hurriedly.

"Don't bother Benny, I might as well see them, and get it over with," Joe replied resignedly. "My bike is parked where they can see it anyway. I will meet them outside. It will be nice to burst Jeremy's bubble of anticipation, when I tell him my agent has already told the press my whereabouts and that I am just taking a short holiday and there is no mystery." He glanced towards Morgane, and whatever he was going to say to her, he decided against it. "No news here then," he murmured with satisfaction as he made to leave the room to face Jeremy. He paused in the doorway and looked back at Morgane's disturbed face, and regretted the abrupt way he had approached her with his life-altering bombshell. It had to be done, and he too was trying to come to terms with the thought of her as his sister. If she was she had a right to know, but the way she was contemplating him from across the room with something almost like hatred in her blue eyes, cut into him deeply.

Joe had the satisfaction of spoiling the day for Jeremy, when he informed him that his agent had already given the press the news of his whereabouts. He had not, however, liked the reporter's suspicious look. It was plain to Joe that Jeremy Dixon had not given up on this story, although he had been slightly mollified when Joe had given permission for the photographer to take a shot of him at work outside the chalet. Joe had already put the young journalists back up when he had taken him to task for not paying his bill in a reasonable time, and now he had taken the wind out of his sails, by letting him know he was at least a day too late with his supposed news story. It would seem that whatever he decided to write would not put Joe in a good light, and just at the moment Joe would have liked to be incognito for a few months.

Joe was on his way back into the house, where he met Benny.

"I'm off home Joe, Morgane insists that she is okay, and she just wants to be left alone." She glanced at Joe, putting her head slightly to one side. "I do remember your father Joe, he was a quiet lonely man, and stood out amongst the other guests. You shouldn't be so hard on him Joe, someday you will realise what he went through, when he lost his wife and you your mother," Benny said, giving him food for thought for the rest of the evening!

"Can I give you a lift home, Benny, and thank you for coming so promptly, I knew that Morgane needed someone to talk to, she seemed to shut herself off from me, and ignore what I was trying to impart." He was still worried about her.

"No thank's Joe, Robin in coming to meet me at the bottom of the drive." She paused briefly before moving off. "You care about that girl don't you Joe?"

"Of course I do," he replied mystified.

"Like a brother?" she asked with raised eyebrows.

A car horn sounded, and she moved off down the drive to meet her son. Joe watched her leave then moved off towards the house, changing his mind on the way, and heading for the chalet. Morgane was not in a very receptive mood, and any more questions put to her would only upset her further. Besides he too needed to be alone, to mull over what Benny had said, and to think of a way to get Morgane to accept what must be, or else give him some proof to the contrary.

CHAPTER FIVE

That evening Joe had a swim, to work off excess energy, and when he at last vacated the pool, it was to find Jeremy waiting for him, sitting on one of the chairs outside the chalet. Joe sighed and would have walked by, trying to ignore the younger man.

"Can I have a word with you Joe," Jeremy asked quite pleasantly.

"Not at the moment, Jeremy, I have things to do." Joe replied with exasperation.

"I just wondered whether your father's death has anything to do with the reason you are in Bermuda," Jeremy enquired thoughtfully, but his eyes were wary, as though he was not sure of Joe's reaction to his query.

"Certainly not, why should it?" Joe could have bitten off his tongue. He had left himself wide open to further questions from the young reporter.

"It just seems strange that you should take a holiday in Bermuda, so soon after your father's death, without telling anyone your plans."

"Have you still got your father to go home to Jeremy," Joe asked briskly.

"Well yes, he is well and looking forward to when I get home, to see how I have gone on with my writing," Jeremy replied in a surprised voice.

"There you are then, how would you know what it is like to lose a parent," Joe said succinctly. "However old you are Jeremy, it still comes as a shock. What better place than this beautiful island to come to terms with such a loss."

"Point taken, Joe, but you must admit that your father has spent the latter part of his time living the high life, and enjoying the fact that he was quite famous, or should I say infamous, and able to attract many younger women." Jeremy replied with a slight grin, which smacked of approval.

Before Jeremy knew what was happening his shirt was gripped tightly around his neck and Joe held him upright against the chalet door. "Get back into the gutter where you belong Jeremy. Any such ideas written in any newspaper articles will see you in court, no matter what it costs. I'm quite sure you are aware that I am financially able to make that statement stick," he finished angrily, thrusting Jeremy away from him. He moved towards the chalet, and stopped abruptly as he heard Morgane's strained voice.

"May I have a word with you Mr Lawson."

"Yes of course Morgane. Jeremy is just leaving, leaving the island I hope," he said suggestively. He watched as Jeremy moved quickly towards the open patio doors, and disappeared into the house. He sighed and glanced at Morgane. "Mr

Lawson I notice, it was Joe earlier today." He wondered how long she had been in the shadows, and if she had heard the conversation between himself and Jeremy. He didn't have long to wait to find out.

Morgane looked behind her to make sure that Jeremy has disappeared out of sight. When she turned towards him, he was shocked by the pale, strained face that looked at him, shown clearly in the diminishing rays of the setting sun. He took his towel from his shoulders and placed it securely around his lean waist.

"What can I do for you Morgane," he asked wearily.

"Nothing I guess, I think you have already done it. Earlier today you told me you believed that you knew who my father was, and yet tonight I learn that he is dead. If I had believed you Joe, it would be quite hurtful to learn of his death just a few hours after learning of his existence. Thank you very much, for nothing." She turned so that he would not see the tears that she couldn't hold back.

Joe's arm shot out, and held tightly to her elbow, and she swung around with her hand raised intent on striking his handsome face. He blocked the blow and held her securely. He wanted to haul her close and comfort her, but knew that would be the worst thing he could do. She seemed to sag against him, but he held her without drawing her closer. This last piece of news was obviously more than she could take today and he felt guilty because he desperately needed her to believe that he was not doing this for his own satisfaction.

"Do you really believe that I am your half-sister Joe?" she asked quietly, all aggression seemed to drain out of her, and he drew away from her slightly.

"I really *don't know* Morgane, but why else would he leave you £40,000 in his Will, can you answer me that? Because it certainly doesn't make any sense to me, unless he believed he was your father. According to his solicitor and also Benny, he was in Bermuda on holiday with friends, which included your mother, at about the right time."

He watched her closely as she fought for some kind of composure. He had just sprung another surprise on her, he hadn't meant to drop this piece of information on her so abruptly, but maybe now she would take him seriously! She then spoke in a cynically flippant tone, with her fists pressed to her sides. "I certainly don't believe that your father could also be mine Joe, we are not alike in any way, and I do not want anything to do with your inheritance, you can keep it. Maybe you should get on a 'plane and return to inform your solicitor, I'll put it in writing." She said with finality.

"You can't make that decision yet. It is in trust for you until you reach twenty five years of age. You can decide what you want to do with it then. Although if you need some of it now it could be arranged with the agreement of the Trustees, of which I am one, since my father's death," he stated with unconscious authority. She shrugged her shoulders hopelessly, and stared into his drawn face. "Go to bed Morgane, the sun is going down, and tomorrow will be soon enough for any further discussions. It will be better for all concerned and you in particular, if this could be kept between us for the time being. Jeremy will have a field day if he finds out." He watched as she moved off towards the house with slumped shoulders, and hoped she would get some sleep, he was certain he would get very little himself, although he had been going through all this in his mind time and time again without getting any nearer to a solution, since the reading of his father's Will. What he had said to Jeremy was quite correct, he missed his father like crazy!

Joe locked the chalet door behind him with relief. He poured a whisky into a glass and sat, watching the huge immensity of red sky where the sun had just gone below the horizon. He hoped the whisky would help block out the graphic images he was seeing as his father had tried to come to terms with the loss of his wife (and Joe's mother) without any success. As a heartbroken twelve year old, Joe had not known how to help. His father had been a broken man, and it had not been until eight years later when he had suffered a slight heart attack, that he had decided to take life by the horns and make the best of the time he had left. This had meant a long line of lady friends who were pleased to enjoy his success with him, but none of them had managed to get him to marry them. Joe was finding it very hard to believe that he had had an affair with Morgane's mother. It had not been until after the mild heart attack that he had changed his solitary life style.

It was with an empty whisky bottle, and in the early hours of the morning that Joe eventually put out the light to try to get some much needed sleep.

For the next three days Morgane tried to avoid Joe as much as possible. She had nothing she wanted to say to him. She made sure on the few times they met, that they were never alone. Joe watched her every move, and he seemed to be letting her have time on her own to come to terms with what he had told her. As yet she had not said anything to Benny about the bequest, as she could not find any rational explanation for why she should have been left so much money by Joe's father. No wonder Joe had come over here to find out if it was possible that she was his sister, what other reason would there be for his father to leave her an inheritance? She must find the explanation, for there must be one, but why had it not come to light when her mother had died, and she had gone through all the papers she could find?

She was ready when Jeremy came to pay for a further week's stay at Smugglers Cove – she told him that she had other guests arriving and that he would have to leave. At first he didn't believe her, but her explanation seemed to be borne out with the arrival of a smartly dressed gentleman with a young woman. Jeremy saw them on the patio, and believing that they were the expected guests he packed up and departed without any fuss. Morgane was very relieved, but was uncertain whether he would actually leave the island.

Morgane felt extremely tired, and did not want to meet the new arrivals, who appeared to be making them selves comfortable on the patio. She went to her room and watched from behind the curtains as Benny spoke to them. Benny went into the house and after calling for Morgane and presuming she was not around, returned onto the patio with a tray of tea and biscuits. Morgane hoped she had not let the two rooms in the house, she was feeling anything but welcoming and would prefer to have the house empty just at the moment.

A few minutes later Joe strolled onto the patio, looking devastating in white shorts and shirt with his nicely tanned skin. He was met ecstatically by the pretty dark haired woman. She enthusiastically threw herself into his arms without reservation, and he swung her around in welcome. When he managed to untangle himself from the girl, Joe went to shake hands with the older man, and sat down at the table with them.

When it seemed that the visitors were not going to leave as they looked so settled and comfortable, Morgane decided it was time for her to depart. She badly needed some time alone, and she collected her sketch pad and left by the kitchen door. As she crept out of the door she saw Robin collecting his tools for cleaning the pool. When he would have spoken she put a finger to her lips in a silent request for him to be quiet. He nodded smilingly, and she gave him a grateful smile, as she slipped passed him and escaped through the metal grill doorway, and padded with relief down the steps to her private cove. Once on the sands she flung off her sandals and sat on the rock where Joe had sat a few days ago when he had devastated her safe little world. She dipped her toes into the seawater, but did not feel at all like sketching. She moved back onto the sand and lay down in the sun. She enjoyed the sight of the white long-tails whirling above, dipping and diving, and their distinctive call seemed vaguely therapeutic as she watched their graceful flight.

Morgane awoke with a start, and sitting up slowly she gazed out across the bay, noticing that the sun had moved a considerable distance across the blue sky. How long had she been asleep she wondered guiltily. She had left Benny to deal with the smartly dressed man and the younger women, and it was long past the time when Benny should have been on her way home to her family.

It had been patently obvious that the new arrivals were well known to Joe. Surely he should have let her know if he had friends arriving, although the way matters were between them at the moment she was not too surprised that he had not! She gathered up her sketch pad with attached pencil, and slid her sandy feet into her sandals. Trudging up the steps back to the house, she felt anything but rested. She went into the kitchen and switched on the kettle.

She swung round guiltily at Joe's noisy entrance into the kitchen.

"There you are, where have you been, I've looked everywhere for you?" he demanded angrily.

"Obviously not everywhere Joe. What has it to do with you, I wasn't aware that I had to acquaint you with all my movements," she replied waspishly. He really was the limit, even if she had been convinced that he was her half brother she would not be dictated to by him!

He moved across and reached behind her to switch off the boiling kettle, looking closely into her tired face. He took teabags out of a holder, and warmed the teapot with a little water from the kettle. Then brewed the tea, and indicated that she should sit down at the table. She thought about refusing, but couldn't summon up the energy, and sat heavily on the waiting chair. He joined her at the table carrying with him two mugs, into which he poured the tea.

"A friend of mine and his daughter arrived in Bermuda today and they came here to see me. I wanted to introduce them to you," he said heavily, whilst adding milk to the mugs of tea.

"Where are they staying," she enquired, studiously stirring her mug of tea, wondering how old the daughter was - old enough to throw herself into his arms as though she had every right and had been missing him!

"They are staying in Hamilton. I said we would see David tomorrow morning," he said flatly.

"I'll be much too busy Joe, I have a lot to do tomorrow," she murmured with a total lack of feeling. She felt very relieved that they were not staying at Smugglers Cove.

"You had better make time Morgane. David Smithson is the Solicitor dealing with my father's affairs, and along with myself is a Trustee of the money left to you by my father."

"I am not convinced that he was *my father* Joe, and you only have circumstantial evidence pointing in that direction."

"Then why did he leave you £40,000 plus accrued profits, to be held in trust until your twenty fifth birthday? The Trust was set-up twenty three years ago. Unlike me, he definitely knew of your existence?"

"Ask David Smithson, he should know," she replied tiredly.

"David only took over the business two years ago when his father died. All he has to go on are the legal papers, he knows nothing of my father's circumstances when the Trust was drawn up and the Will made." He stood angrily. "If you don't want him to come here we will go into Hamilton to see him."

"You don't believe you are my half-brother any more than I believe I am your half-sister Joe, it's just not possible." She said in desperation.

He pulled her roughly out of the chair by her elbows, and gazed into her blue eyes drowned with tears, his eyes went to her trembling mouth as he slowly pulled her towards him. His eyes darkened with intense emotion.

"Morgane, Joe, where are you?" came a shout from the front of the house.

Joe stood back, a shocked look on his face, as he returned Morgane to her chair. "Saved by the Be--nny," he murmured distractedly, and he quickly went out through the kitchen door to the rear of the house.

Morgane took in a deep breath, and pushed back her hair from hot cheeks. She was sure that Joe had been about to kiss her, and she would have done nothing to stop him! "In here

263

Benny," she called. She was very grateful for Benny's timely appearance, but not amused by Joe's strained attempt at humour.

"There you are Morgane, I wondered where you had got to. I met Mr Smithson and his daughter Jill this morning. They seem very nice people. Mr Smithson wanted to talk to me about the time that Joe's father visited the islands. I told him all I could including the fact that I never saw anything more than friendship between Joe's father and your mother. Joe's father really was a nice man, I liked him a lot, more than the people he was travelling with. Is that all right?" she asked anxiously, as she noticed the strained look on Morgane's face.

"You'd better sit down Benny. The thing that makes them almost certain that I am the daughter of Mr Lawson is the fact that he has left in trust for me the sum of £40,000 plus accruals over the years."

Benny sat in shocked silence for a few minutes trying to take in what Morgane had told her. She looked closely at the younger girl, trying to ascertain whether she was pleased or not by this windfall. Something was certainly troubling her, but Benny believed it was more to do with the fact that Joe might be her half-brother, rather than the fact that she was to come into a substantial amount of money! She had noticed, after the initial antagonism between them, that they had become much closer. This bombshell must have an enormous effect on the young newly awakened girl before her. Over the years Morgane had enjoyed the company of many friends, but Benny could not remember a time when she had shown the same reactions that she had shown after meeting Joe!

"It isn't true Benny, I'm sure Mr Lawson was not my father, and there has been some mistake somewhere." She noticed the surprised look on Benny's rounded face. "Oh, yes Benny. Joe also omitted to tell me until today that his father died a few months ago."

"If you don't believe he was your father too Morgane, why are you so upset," Benny asked quietly.

"Because Joe didn't tell me, he introduced the possibility that he may know my father one day, then a few days later he informs me he is already dead, and has left me a lot of money. I don't want any of Joe's inheritance Benny, in fact, I wish Joe, Mr Smithson and his daughter Jill would all go back to the United Kingdom. They don't belong here. We were all very happy until they came."

"Morgane, you know that Joe would not want to hurt you. It is a very traumatic time for him too you know," Benny said consolingly. She paused thoughtfully. "Morgane, I never saw anything between Mr Lawson and your mother to suggest that there was anything but a normal friendship between them. If there was they hid it very well. The male members of the party from America, were more the types to hit on your mother as she was so attractive and had a lovely personality, but she brushed them off without upsetting any one of them, that's the way she was." In remembering her good friend Benny's eyes filled with emotion.

Morgane patted the older woman's hand. "Don't worry Benny, when they have all gone back to the United Kingdom everything here will get back to normal."

"I sincerely hope so love, but somehow I don't believe that will be possible." Benny shook her head in disbelief. She had a very strong feeling that Morgane had started to mature considerably in the last few days, and that that process had only just begun.

CHAPTER SIX

Morgane sat in the jeep outside the chalet waiting for Joe, with the engine slowly turning over. She straightened the skirt of her smart navy and white dress. She had not wanted to dress up for the meeting with David Smithson in the Hamilton Princess hotel. Benny had insisted, and Morgane hadn't the energy to oppose her. She was almost certain that Benny thought that she would accept the fact that she was entitled to the money that was coming to her in just over a year's time. She glanced across to the chalet when she heard the door close with a slight bang, and Joe walked towards the jeep looking devastatingly handsome in lightweight jeans and a cotton short sleeved shirt.

"Morning," he murmured as he climbed into the front passenger seat.

Before moving off Morgane glanced at his enigmatic face. "This is a waste of time Joe, I don't want anything to do with your inheritance," she said stonily.

"We'll see about that. Dad must have wanted you to be provided for to arrange the Trust so many years ago. This meeting is arranged and David will be waiting for us." The journey into Hamilton was short and silent, and it was with a heavy heart and a great deal of reluctance that she parked the jeep in the hotel car park. She got out hastily before Joe could come round to open the door for her. He gave a little shrug and walked off towards the main entrance, where he waited patiently for her, and it was a relief to feel the cool air-conditioned air hit her as she moved inside the hotel. David Smithson was waiting for them, and Morgane was pleased to note that his daughter Jill was not with him. He shook hands with Morgane, and pleasantly indicated that they should follow him out onto the patio, where a table had been arranged for them, and coffee was served as soon as they took their seats. In other circumstances she would have liked him very much, but she felt wary of him, and felt that he was watching both Joe and her to see how they reacted to one another.

An hour later they returned to the jeep, and as soon as Morgane closed the driver's door, Joe could not contain his anger any longer.

"You really are as stubborn as a mule. You have a lovely house, and have to share it with strangers to enable you to stay here. You might as well accept the money my father has left to you. If you don't claim it in a year's time, it will still be in trust for you. Whether or not you are my half-sister, I would like to think that you are comfortable, and not having to share your house with strangers."

"Forget it Joe, I have," she replied with finality.

"David and Jill are to stay for a few days holiday, and I will probably return to England with them. Therefore, you have a few days to change your mind. Whatever you decide, you will have to go over to England as there will be papers to sign," he finished tiredly. By the tone of his voice Morgane thought he was about to wipe his hands of her, and she thought that if that were so then it would be much easier getting through the next few days, without seeing him constantly.

Upon their arrival at Smuggler's Cove Joe got out of the jeep and went directly into his chalet.

Morgane saw nothing of Joe until the next afternoon when he was out on the patio talking to Mike, Benny's husband, who had come to walk Benny home. The quiet giant of a man with grey hair and sparkling eyes, kissed Morgane on the cheek, patted her shoulder, and with a slight wave, set off down the drive with his wife. There was an uneasy silence whilst they watched the couple move out of sight. Joe moved over to the patio wall and leaned against it, with the afternoon sun behind him. He looked towards Morgane, and she wished that she could see his eyes.

"Mike seems very fond of you," he murmured.

"He and Benny have always been around as long as I can remember, and he has been like a father to me."

"At least when David and I go back to England, you will still have Mike, Benny and Robin to keep an eye on you."

"I'm a grown woman Joe, I don't need looking after," she replied hotly.

"Of that, unfortunately, I am very much aware." He paused. "I have arranged with Mike to charter the fishing boat he works on, and I'm going to take David deep-sea fishing tomorrow. Maybe whilst we are away you can consider all your options, and hopefully come to the right conclusion." Without waiting for a reply he moved off towards the chalet, leaving her to ponder over his words, not the words however that suggested she should consider her options, but whether he was aware of her as a grown woman, or the fact that she didn't need looking after!

Early the next morning she heard Mike call to collect Joe, ready for the fishing trip, and they sounded quite jovial as they set off towards the hotel where they would pick up David. The fishing boat had been moved to the hotel, and they were to set off from the hotel mooring. Morgane wondered if Jill would be accompanying them, and hoped her father would make sure she was well covered against the hot sun and sea breezes. Then had to convince herself that the thought of the young lissom body wearing only a bikini, and shamelessly sunning herself in front of Joe, was not the main reason that she hoped Jill's father would be sensible!

They were expecting three lady guests to arrive from the UK, and with preparation of the rooms for the three ladies, the morning passed quite quickly. Robin came to clean the pool, and joined Benny and Morgane for a sandwich lunch. He and Benny chatted happily about his young sons and their recent tests at school, and Morgane was hard pressed to keep up with the conversation as her mind kept wandering.

She suddenly, came back to earth when Robin remarked that his father and the skipper intended to get the boat back and moored by mid afternoon, as the weather forecast was not very good. She wandered out to the patio and looked across the Great Sound. For the moment the weather looked perfect.

When the three ladies from England arrived they were very pleased with the twin and double rooms, and after giving them various tourist brochures and providing a welcome tea tray, Morgane went down to the cove, determined to get some sketching done. She couldn't settle, and decided she would find something new to sketch, and returned to the house, and then drove off in the jeep to Spanish Point. The drive took about twenty minutes and after parking the jeep, she settled on the rocks. There was the rusty hull of a shipwreck in the foreground, and the old Fort (which was now the Maritime Museum) silhouetted against the blue sky in the distance at Dockyard, across the now slightly choppy water of the Great Sound. An hour later she felt quite pleased with the sketch, and wished she had brought along her watercolours. She put a few finishing touches to the sky, and realised that there were now dark clouds, and the sea had quite a swell. She felt slightly chilled and quickly packed up her painting things and rushed back to the jeep.

When she arrived back at Smugglers Cove, she noticed that the three guests were not around and had probably taken a taxi into Hamilton, and was surprised that their tea tray had not been taken away. She collected the tray and headed for the kitchen. It had been left as immaculate as usual by Benny, and there was a note from her confirming that the ladies had gone into Hamilton, and would not be back until around 9.30 p.m. She switched on the kettle to make herself a drink, then the 'phone rang.

"Morgane, glad you are back. Mike has just rung me to say he will be back later than expected. He is unloading the catch, and putting the fishing boat to rights. He said that it had become quite rough at sea, and the others had gone to the hospital. He didn't seem too worried but I thought I would let you know. Will you give me a ring when Joe gets back, Mike will be at least another hour before he gets home, and I can't help wondering who has been hurt?" Benny said sounding quite flustered.

"Yes of course Benny. Don't worry it can't be too serious or Mike would have said."

"You know Mike, he never has much to say. Before he gave me a chance to ask any questions he had rung off," Benny said in disgust. "If he is back before Joe I'll give you a ring."

"Yes, please do that Benny, I'd appreciate being put in the picture. Perhaps Joe will be late."

Morgane replaced the receiver, and put a glass under the cold tap, and took a long drink. Her stomach was churning and she felt quite sick. Why hadn't Joe rung, was he the one who needed hospital treatment? She glanced again at the telephone, and then shrugged, as it would only take fifteen minutes to get to the hospital. She couldn't stand around here waiting for news. She grabbed the keys, and ran to the jeep, and found it very difficult to stay within the twenty miles per hour speed limit as she negotiated the town of Hamilton and out towards the Botanical Gardens and the hospital.

It was becoming dusk, and the lights from the hospital seemed very bright. Morgane's courage seemed to have left her, and she paused to get herself together then opened the reception door and went towards the desk.

"Morgane, have you come to meet me."

Morgane turned in surprise as Joe came striding down the corridor towards her. She felt relief, and also anger that he had not seen fit to make her aware of what was happening. Forgetting, for the moment that he probably had not had much time. He took her elbow, nodded to the girl behind the reception desk, and they walked outside.

"Thanks for coming, I was about to get a taxi," he said with unconcern, as he opened the door for her to get in. He glanced at her upset face, and instead walked her around to the passenger seat."I'm sorry, were you worried?" he asked with a surprised lift of the eyebrows. He felt an unexpected curl of emotion in his chest, as he couldn't remember the last time anyone had worried about him, not since his mother had died. If his father had, he had been very good at hiding it!

Morgane stared ahead and a few tears ran unheeded down her cheeks. She glanced towards Joe who was now in the driving seat, and was surprised by the concerned look in his darkened eyes. She was relieved when he closed the door behind him, and the overhead light went out. He put his left arm across her shoulders and with his right hand he tilted her face towards him. He paused, then it was the most natural thing in the world to find his lips on hers and she was unable to stop the involuntary, automatic response, which brought an ache to her chest, and blanked every conscious thought from her mind. He lifted his lips from hers and for a fraught charged moment they were both still. Joe sat back in his seat, and she noticed from the light from the hospital windows, a pulse beating in the side of his cheek, and she realised he was very upset, as indeed was she!

"I'm sorry," they both said in unison. Joe started the jeep and the drive home was completed in silence. When the Jeep stopped at the back of Smugger's Cove, Morgane turned to Joe belatedly she felt.

"What happened on the boat, who was hurt?"

"Jill went with us, and she spent her time sunbathing up on the top deck where the skipper is, and she refused to wear a hat or to cover herself. She knew best, and David gave in to her as is usual. When it clouded over she became bored and kept wandering around from the top level, down the stairs and in and out of the cabins. We gave her the chance to bring in a tuna, but she lost the fish, and decided all fishing was a waste of time at least that was how it appeared. The skipper suggested we might trawl for marlin on the way in, which we did, because now the seas were getting a bit rough. Jill, who was supposed to stay in the cabin, decided to go up to join the skipper again, and on the way back down she got dizzy and fell. We thought she had broken her arm, but it now turns out that it is a bad sprain. She is staying in hospital overnight, because she is suffering from the effects of the sun and is quite sick. David is staying with her for a couple of hours tonight, and will pick her up in the morning." He seemed unsurprised by Jill's behaviour, and she wondered if it was because he had known her since she was a child, or if he was really fond of her now that she was a grown woman. After all girls of eighteen nowadays were classed as grown up, and the fact that she was very much attracted to Joe was plain for all to see!

Morgane put these thoughts aside as she had no right to be jealous of the younger girl.

"Would you like a hot drink, or anything to eat," she asked him warily. He didn't look as if he would rather be at the hospital with Jill – she should be pleased, but for the moment she couldn't decide what she felt, or what she thought she ought to feel, everything was up in the air and she felt really tired and upset, but she must not show Joe how much!

"I'm starving, could you manage a bacon sandwich, and a hot drink. We only had bottled water or beer to drink, and sandwiches, on the boat. Except for Jill's accident, we had a wonderful day, even though it was cut a bit short by the weather. David says he will be coming over again, mostly for the fishing but also for a holiday." Joe said wondering if he was trying too hard to be normal.

Joe put on the kettle, and took a seat at the kitchen table. Morgane put four rashers of bacon into a pan, and sliced a couple of bread buns in two, and placed them on a plate. The bacon was soon ready and Morgane placed the bacon buns in front of Joe."Are you not having any," he asked.

She shook her head, the last thing she felt like doing was eating. She sat and watched as he enjoyed his buns until he pushed away his plate, and smiled his thanks. It seemed very homely and right that they should be sitting together in the evening, and when forbidden tantalising thoughts started to enter her head, she pushed back her chair and stood.

"Maybe you would like to take your drink with you to the chalet," she suggested quickly. He glanced at her face, and also stood.

"Sorry Morgane. You don't have to worry, I won't touch you again. That was a big mistake, but you looked so vulnerable, and I guess I wanted to comfort you."

"So you think I was to blame, for becoming emotional. I suggest you go back to the U.K. with your friends David and Jill," she suggested forcefully.

Just then voices could be heard in reception, and Morgane went to wish the ladies good night and to see if there was anything they needed. When she returned to the kitchen it was empty, and the plate and mug had been washed and left on the sink.

Morgane left a night light switched on, and went to her room. She took a quick shower and suddenly didn't feel like sleeping. She moved over to the window and gazed out towards the sea.

Stars and moon were shining, and it would have been a wonderful evening for lovers. She stared towards the sea, and listened with pleasure to the euphonious sound of the tree frogs and insects giving their nightly recital. If she had to leave the island she would miss these wonderful night sounds. That still did not give her the right to accept the money that had been left to her to make her life easier. She still didn't believe that she had a right to it. She didn't believe that she would have felt the way she did about Joe if they had been related! She lay on the bed and slammed the pillow against the headboard, did she really believe that they were not related, or was it just wishful thinking? She was too tired to think anymore. Tomorrow she would talk again with Joe, one thing was certain, they would both be much better off with some distance between them, at least that of the Atlantic Ocean!

The next morning Benny came bright and early, and Morgane apologised to her for not ringing her back last evening. It hadn't mattered because Mike had been home within the hour and able to relate the happenings of the day. Benny had a few choice words to say about young women who were too full of themselves meaning Jill of course, and in particular husbands who only made short phone calls home!

Joe had an early breakfast and as he was smartly dressed, Morgane assumed that he was meeting David again. Morgane heard his conversation with Benny from the kitchen. It turned out that he was on the way to the airport.

"I managed to get a flight back today. David and Jill will be following me in a couple of days. I did my packing last night, and if you would order me a taxi Benny I'll be on my way to David's hotel, and then the airport."

"Morgane will take you Joe, you have a lot of luggage. I can manage the other three guests myself." Benny was obviously very sorry to see Joe leave, Morgane could hear her give a sniff, and knew that the corner of the apron would be used to wipe her eyes. Benny was so open and felt that there was no need to hide her emotions. Morgane was feeling so tight that she thought she might snap! Had she really meant it last evening, when she had suggested that he should leave with David and Jill?

Morgane walked out to join them on the patio, and saw that Joe's luggage was all packed and ready to go. She knew she could not refuse to give him a lift, as Benny would want to know why.

"I heard you talking, I can give you lift to the airport Joe," Morgane offered stiffly. "I will also need to return some of your money you overpaid."

"No need, we can sort out finances in the future. I notice you have other guests, and there is no need for you to give me a lift. I can get a taxi, because I have to see David on the way to the airport." He said with finality.

Benny reached up and kissed his cheek. "See you again soon Joe," and she went through to the kitchen.

"Goodbye Morgane. Take care of yourself and Benny. Also Smugglers Cove. I have got used to the place now, and the people. However, I'll see you when you come over to the U.K. to sign the various papers. Whether you decide to take the money or not, there will still be a considerable amount of paperwork." He gazed at her steadily, then kissed her briefly on the cheek, and stared for a moment into her emotion filled eyes. "You see Morgane, I can't be trusted, only last night I said I would never do that again." He picked up some of his luggage and went off down the drive towards the gate.

Morgane felt absolutely shattered. She had known that the time would come when he would leave the island, and last night she had told him to do just that. However, she wasn't ready. She felt totally bereft, and definitely more lonely than she ever had before!

When the taxi arrived at the gate to pick up Joe, Morgane was already in the small shower attached to her bedroom. This way she could cry if she needed to and no one would know, or even care. God she was feeling sorry for herself, but she couldn't watch Joe leave the islands.

CHAPTER SEVEN

The next few weeks seemed interminable. Morgane found it a real effort to get up in the morning and help Benny with the household chores, usually because she had trouble sleeping. They had plenty of guests to keep things ticking along nicely, but for the first time since starting the bed and breakfast business, she would have preferred to have the house and chalet unoccupied. The guests were as nice as they had ever been, but she had to force herself to be sociable and to take time to help with advice as to which parts of the island they should see. Never before in her twenty odd years had she had to remind herself to put a smile on her face.

It was Robin, whom she was helping to clean the pool, that brought this to her attention, by asking her what was wrong with her, and what had happened to the cheerful lass he had known for years. She decided to put Joe to the back of her mind and to concentrate on the day to day running of the business, and by doing so she might make a better job of running the bed and breakfast, and then she could forget all about money! This worked during the day, but at night she had considerable difficulty in controlling her wayward thoughts.

On the day of Joe's departure, she had hidden herself away until after lunch. When she had seen Benny at lunchtime it was to find her excitedly perusing a large painting, which she had found in the chalet. It was a painting, by Joe, and portrayed Morgane coming out of the pool. Morgane thought that it was very flattering but was not at all pleased when she found that Benny had asked Robin to hang it in the lounge. Whenever she was in the lounge she was aware of the painting, which reminded her of Joe. The painting was of the very highest standard, but it was the subject that Morgane was doubtful about. There was something about the painting that made her uneasy, particularly the eyes, perhaps it was the level of intensity shown in the face. As the painting had been hung for a number of weeks now, she had decided that once Benny left for home after lunch, she would take the opportunity to remove it, and placed one of her own paintings in its stead. Benny could hardly object to Morgane hanging one of her own paintings in her own lounge! She covered the painting carefully and slipped the bundle into the back of her wardrobe. As soon as she closed the doors on it, she felt that she had taken the first step to getting her life back.

As if to prove the point, that afternoon she visited St. George's after taking two guests to the airport, and managed to sell two of her paintings to an art shop. She had dealt with Mr Granger the proprietor before, but today he seemed very eager to have the paintings. He also asked her to bring him any other paintings she wished to sell. Since Robin had pointed out that she was not her usual happy self, she had set aside more time to paint. Whilst painting, she put everything except the canvas in front of her out of her mind and she was sure there was an improvement in her work. This seemed to be borne out by the request from Mr Granger for more of her work. As she handed them over to him she took a good look at them, and saw that they had more depth than the ones she had previously painted. In the last three months she had experienced a wide variety of emotions all new to her, maybe that was the change she was seeing in her own paintings.

Morgane was taking her leave of Mr Granger when a young man came through from the house. He came forward to join them and Mr Granger introduced him to Morgane, as his younger brother Simon, on an extended holiday from New York. He was slightly taller than her, quite good looking in his obviously American T-shirt and shorts, and seemed really pleased to be introduced to someone around his own age. He seemed pleasant enough, with his hazel eyes, tanned skin and brown hair tinted at the ends to blonde by the sun. When he asked her if she would like to go for a drink with him, she refused pleasantly, saying she had other places to visit in St. Georges.

After leaving the art shop she walked across the bridge onto Ordnance Island, and looked with interest at the Cruise Ship docked there. She decided to do a sketch of the Deliverance, a replica of a sailing ship built in 1610. From there she moved slightly and sketched the famous ducking stool, once used to duck disorderly persons.

She was looking inland from the island into King's Square, which was thronging with visitors, and looked particularly colourful with flags flying near the Town Hall, and the beautifully painted houses behind the square and the town. She made quick notes of the colours, and soon packed away her pad and pencils, slinging her bag onto her back, and returning to the jeep parked in the square. She noticed the stocks and wondered if she had time to do a sketch, but decided Benny would be sending out a search party if the didn't get herself home.

Lately Benny had been unlike her usual self, demanding to know where Morgane was going and what time she would be back. Maybe it would be a good idea to get Benny more help in the house, if she was going to take more time to paint. She would mention it to Benny when she got home, Benny might already have someone suitable in mind, and it would be nice for Benny to have more time at home with Mike and her extended family. She had been coming to Smugglers Cove since her mother had bought it, maybe she wanting a change, or to retire. The more Morgane thought about this, the less she liked the idea of Benny retiring, but she must now be in her late fifties, and Morgane had never before wondered if she might wish to retire. It was a very thoughtful girl who arrived back, and with relief found that Benny was in the garden talking with Robin, who was cutting back the very prolific exotic plants near the parking area. She watched mother and son, and wondered how to approach Benny tactfully to ascertain whether she wanted more help in the house, and what her future plans were. She castigated herself for not thinking about this before now. She regretted that she had been so selfish as to assume that things would go on to suit *her* indefinitely. This would need careful handling, the last thing she wanted to do was make Benny think that she was too old to manage. Joe would have known what to do. Where had that thought come from? Since when had she needed someone else to help with her decisions!

Morgane joined Benny and Robin and admired Robin's tidy work on the exotic plants.

"Are you sure it's cut far enough back?" he asked Morgane, thoughtfully looking at his pile of cuttings.

"You usually decide that for yourself Robin, of course it's fine," she said with a smile. "I'll put the kettle on."

"Not for me Morgane," Benny said briskly. "I'll be getting on home, as I just thought I'd wait until you got in." Morgane watched her as she strolled down to the road and turned right, after joining two ladies who just happened to be walking her way. She could hear their laughter as they chatted happily on their way home. Most of the locals knew everyone in their immediate vicinity.

"Tea in five minutes Robin."

When Robin joined her in the kitchen he found her sitting with her head in her hands, and an open letter in front of her. He watched her for a moment then sat down at the table opposite her.

"Is there a problem Morgane?"

She sighed and lifted her head and pointed to the letter on the table. "It looks as though I have to go to England, to settle some legal business." She got up from the table and poured the boiling water into the waiting teapot. Well at least she now had a good reason to suggest that they should get some help in the house. "I'll give your mother time to get home, and then I'll give her a ring, so that she can try to think of someone who could come and help whilst I'm away. Someone will have to stay in the house, if not, I'll have to tell some of our guests that we can't accommodate them."

"I'm sure that won't be necessary, one of us can stay here," Robin offered thoughtfully. "Our Auntie Maggie has just finished at the nursery school, maybe she would do it. She is the widow of Dad's brother, the one that was lost overboard in the hurricane two years ago. Mum will know what's best. Maybe she and Dad would stay here."

"I don't want to disrupt the family Robin. I'm not booking a flight until everything is settled. I see you have your mother's shopping in the van. If you could mention it to her when you drop it off for her, she could decide what *she* considers the best option. I don't want to go, but they will only keep writing until I do, so I might as well get it over with."

After Robin had left to go to his mother's, she read the letter once more. It was from David Smithson and there was no mention of his co-Trustee. Maybe Joe would be busy or away. There was a definite feeling of anticipation and dread within her. She had decided it would be better if she did not see Joe, but the thought that she might, had started a restless feeling, which was proving hard to control! She had just been getting her wayward feelings under control, and now she felt that she must get away as soon as possible, in order that she might put her mind to settling down again as soon as the got back home. If by then she had found someone to help Benny in the house, then she could get back to her painting, which she felt was a necessity to keep her mind off other things. She was much too young to brood and be miserable, she should pull herself together and get on with her life, and if that meant going to London to get that over with, then go she must.

She needn't have worried overnight, as when Benny arrived in the morning everything had been arranged. Her sister-in-law would love to come and live in the house and help look after the guests, that is, if Morgane approved. She certainly did, she remembered meeting Maggie at one of Benny's many picnics.

She was a lovely lady who didn't stand any nonsense from the children, but they still loved her! Because of her age she had been forced to give up the nursery work, and Morgane was sure that she would be very good at coping with the bed and breakfast trade. Particularly, with Benny's help. Benny, of course, would be left in charge of the property and business.

Morgane was reluctant to get her tickets booked, but knew that if she refused to make the trip then David Smithson, and possibly Joe, would come over to the islands. In his letter David Smithson had said that the Trust would pay for her ticket, but as yet Morgane had not yet decided whether she would accept the offer. She had decided, however, that she would not accept the Trust money. It was now September and she would not be twenty five until next year.

The day of her departure dawned sunny and bright, which was the opposite of the way Morgane was feeling! Robin had insisted on taking her to the airport in her jeep, and he was taking over the driving of guests to and from the airport during her absence. She fully realised how lucky she was to have Benny's family, all eager and insistent upon helping her. Her eyes filled with tears as Robin drove away, as she had never felt quite so alone in her life. She had known Robin all her life and had missed him and his family when she was sent to school in England, and it was time she grew up! She picked up her one suitcase, and walked into the airport to check in for her flight. One suitcase was more than sufficient to take her few clothes. She would have to buy some warm clothing when she arrived in England. Her last visit to the United Kingdom had been nearly five years ago, when she had returned to the islands after getting her degree. The warm clothing she had then was now either too much out of date, or did not fit.

As the British Airways 777 took off from Bermuda International Airport, the sun was almost setting in the west and she watched through tear filled eyes, the shadow of the aircraft on the aquamarine sea, looking like an enormous whale following them. In approximately seven hours they would be landing at Gatwick, in the early hours of the morning.

She was surprised when she was awoken by the stewardess, asking if she wanted breakfast, she hadn't expected to sleep. She was about to refuse a meal when the smell of it reminded her that she must have missed the evening snack or meal. The last thing she remembered was trying to concentrate on the film that was being shown. They had a good landing, and it took a while for everyone to disembark.

She trudged along following the crowd of fellow passengers, quite a number of whom she knew by sight. She tiredly took the long walk from the gate where they landed through passport control, to the baggage claim area. She was lucky, her case was one of the earliest onto the luggage carousel, and she walked briskly through Customs. She had been led to understand that there was a shuttle train from the airport to London, and she must ask someone the way.

"Morgane, over here."

She looked around in bewilderment, and her eyes met Joe's familiar grey eyes. Her heart thumped then increased its rhythm, and she suddenly felt hot and confused. Her hand on the handle of her suitcase was removed and its place taken by Joe's. He picked up the case and with a hand under her elbow he led her out to the car park. Morgane was very much aware of the attention he commanded as they moved outside the building. She wondered if the small crowd knew who he was, or was it just his air of authority and good looks that attracted attention? They were already in the car when she saw a flash, which lit up the interior of the chauffeur driven car, and she realised that she had been shielded by Joe's large frame.

"Is that the press, did they get a picture?" she asked in surprise.

"Nothing they can use, they didn't get a picture of you anyway," Joe said, his voice full of satisfaction.

"I'm sorry Joe I didn't think you were followed around by the press, except Jeremy in Bermuda, of course. I didn't need to be met at the airport, but if you had insisted you could have just sent a car."

"If I had sent a car for you, would you have climbed into it? It's not three in the morning yet, where would you have gone?" He sounded annoyed. She supposed he had every right to be annoyed with her. He had come to meet her at the airport in the early hours of the morning, been hounded by the press, no doubt, and she didn't seem very appreciative of the effort he had made.

"I'm sorry, I do appreciate you coming to pick me up, but it was unexpected. I didn't know that you were aware that I was arriving tonight or in the United Kingdom. Or should I say this morning."

"I do keep in touch with David you know. We are joint Trustees."

Morgane was unable to stifle a yawn, and she slumped tiredly against the back of the seat, and gave a shiver.

"You are cold," he stated the obvious. He leaned and tapped the glass behind the driver and indicated that the heat should be turned on. He removed his jacket and easing her forward he put it around her shoulders. She was about to refuse when the look in his eyes warned her not to bother. She snuggled into the

286

warmth of his jacket, feeling comfortable and cared for, and didn't wake up again until the car came to a stop. She found herself leaning against his warm body with his arm about her shoulders. She wanted to stay just where she was, but struggled to a sitting position and demanded to know where they were!

"At my London flat, where else could you go at this time in the morning?" he asked. "It is the obvious place for you to stay, as you needn't pay for a hotel. Although if you insist, I'm sure the Trust will pay for it."

"I don't want anything off you or the Trust. However, I will come in if you don't mind until a more reasonable hour."

Joe shrugged his shoulders and looked exasperated. The driver opened the door for her and she stepped out into the chill air, still wearing Joe's jacket. Joe opened the outer door to the building, and the driver put her suitcase in the hall, and nodded to her with a kind of respect, as he left. They went up to the top floor in the lift, and Joe dropped her suitcase on the floor and indicated that she should go inside.

She stepped inside and looked around with interest. It was a beautiful flat, and judging by the large windows would have a good view over the city. The furnishings were modern and looked very expensive. She wondered if this was the place that he entertained his many women friends. She assumed that he had many women friends, as the press seemed to follow him around looking for stories. Also his father, according to Jeremy, had latterly fully enjoyed a single life!

"Sit down Morgane, I'll make you a cup of tea." Joe said moving off towards a large room, which she assumed must be the dining room and kitchen area. He indicated a comfortable armchair, and pressed a remote control machine and the flames in the fireplace gave off a lovely comforting warmth. When Joe returned with the tea she was having trouble keeping her eyes open. She dutifully and gratefully sipped her tea, and when she had finished she set down the cup and saucer on a small glass topped table.

"Bed I think," Joe said decisively.

She stood quickly and was about to berate him, when he gave a crooked smile, and indicated a room to the left. "I have two bedrooms Morgane. You can use that one."

She coloured with embarrassment. "No Joe, I'll stay in the chair. I won't use a room for just a few hours."

"Where do you think you are going to Morgane? David Smithson didn't say you had a room booked."

"I will be staying with friends," she replied with determination.

"What friends?" he asked with disbelief.

"Friends I was at University with. I telephoned and they were pleased to offer me a place to stay as long as I am in the city."

He was silent for a few moments, obviously taking in this surprise news. He shrugged and looked at her closely. "It would appear that anywhere will do rather than stay in the same flat as me," he said with reluctant acceptance. When she didn't reply he continued. "I'm being picked up at nine o'clock this morning, and so I'll deliver you and your suitcase to your friends. That way the driver will know where to pick you up tomorrow to take you to David's office."

"I imagined you would drive yourself. Thank you Joe, I appreciate your offer of accommodation, but I will be better staying with my friends. One of them works at City University and works from home three days a week. Therefore, someone will be there to let me in the flat. I'm feeling really tired, I *will* use the bedroom if it's no bother."

"I usually do drive myself, but picking you up at the airport at such an early hour meant that I had not had any sleep. I won't be able to drive you to David's office the following day because I have to be at the Gallery." Joe picked up her suitcase and opening the bedroom door set it on the floor inside, and indicated that she should enter. He indicated the en suite bathroom, and strode back into the lounge. As she closed the door she watched as he poured himself a stiff drink, switched off the warm flames in the fireplace, and moved off towards another door, which she assumed was the other bedroom. She stood with her back against the closed bedroom door and took a deep breath. She had not anticipated spending the night with Joe sleeping in the adjoining bedroom. He was still as devastatingly attractive as she remembered. Had she not learned anything in the last few weeks since he left the Bermuda islands? There was time for about three hours sleep before the car would arrive to pick up Joe. She would feel much better about everything if she could just get to sleep!

CHAPTER EIGHT

Next morning Morgane heard Joe moving about in the flat, and although she still felt very tired she pushed herself out of bed and had a refreshing hot shower. She had pulled out of her suitcase a change of clothes, including trousers and a light fleece, which she thought were warm enough. Her hair was damp from the shower, and she realised she had not packed a hairdryer.

She opened the bedroom door and encountered Joe with his hand raised ready to knock. "I've made coffee and toast, that's all I have in for breakfast," he said apologetically. He appeared to be lively enough even though he must have lost a few hours sleep. Perhaps because he was used to just sleeping a few hours!

"That's fine thank you. Joe, do you have a hairdryer I could borrow, my hair is damp from the shower?"

"In my bathroom, it's a fixture I'm afraid. You will have to dry it in there." He seemed unconcerned, but she moved through his bedroom to the bathroom with certain misgivings.

As she thought, the bedroom and bathroom were furnished to his masculine taste. The latter smelled of the soap or cologne that she associated with him, and which had been comforting when she had been wrapped in his jacket earlier this morning. She put the dryer on full heat, not wanting to prolong the time spent in that most intimate room. When she joined him at a breakfast bar in the kitchen, he poured a cup of coffee for her.

"How are Benny and Mike, Robin and the rest of their family," he enquired. His interest seemed genuine, and not just an enquiry to ease the tension between them.

"They are all fine thank you."

"I hope it won't be too difficult for Benny to cope, or have you closed Smugglers Cove until you get back?"

"No Benny is in charge. She has her widowed sister-in-law to help her. Maggie will be living in Smugglers Cove at least until I return."

"That seems a very good plan. We will have to make a move soon, as the car will be here in a few minutes. How do you feel, no jet-lag?"

"I feel a bit tired, but I'll stay awake for most of the day, then by tomorrow I should be feeling all right. If you are short of time Joe, the car could drop you off first at the Gallery."

"No, there's time for you to be dropped off first."

Morgane wondered how he could possibly know that, as she had not as yet told him the address! She collected her suitcase, which was immediately taken from her by Joe, and they went down in the lift. In the lift he insisted that she should have one of his cards, giving his address and various telephone numbers. She accepted the card but thought that it would be most unlikely that she would use it.

Half and hour later they were driving down an avenue looking for the address of her friends. It turned out to be an old town house, which had been converted into flats and, of course, the flat she was looking for was on the third floor. As there was no lift Joe insisted on carrying her suitcase. No doubt, he was intent on seeing that the flat was a suitable place for her to stay!

She rang the doorbell, which was quickly opened, and a man of roughly twenty-five years, with dark curly hair and a warm smile, slipped his arms around her and twirled her around, ending with a warm kiss on her cheek. "Morgane you look fantastic. It's great that you can stay here for a couple of weeks. We have lots of catching up to do." He then saw the tall man beside her, holding her suitcase.

"Martin, this is Mr Lawson, he is a friend of the solicitor I have come to see. Joe this is Martin Brent, we were at University together." Morgane looked at Joe's face, which was a picture. He shook hands with the younger man, lifted the suitcase he had lowered to the floor, and carried it into the flat. Morgane was extremely annoyed, as it seemed he was determined to get a look at the flat. She glanced around and could see nothing to indicate that Martin shared the flat with his wife, who was already out at business. Serve him right, if he thought she was sharing with Martin alone, she was not going to acquaint him with the true circumstances!

Martin looked closely at Joe. "I think I know you Sir, aren't you the painter Joe Lawson?"

Joe nodded, and quickly took his leave of them. He banged the outer door hard behind him. Martin Brent had called him *Sir*. Very respectful, but Joe was feeling a lot more than five or six years older than the younger man. He had not been prepared to meet a *male* friend of Morgane's. However, he did seem a nice young man and the area he lived in was quite a good area. He had to curb this idea that he was Morgane's protector, and the stab of jealousy he had felt when Martin greeted her so heartily would also have to be curbed. Still there would be no harm in checking out Morgane's friend. He would put David on it as soon as possible.

Martin used as his office the small single bedroom, to which he retired after they had shared a cup of coffee, and talked about old friends for over an hour. Morgane then decided to go into town to do a little clothes shopping. She bought some knee high boots, a warm skirt and a couple of jumpers. Later she had a sandwich in a small cafe, and enjoyed people watching for an hour. By that time she was feeling extremely tired, and went back to the flat, to await Mary's return from business. Mary had taken a design course at university whilst Morgane took art, and Martin an AI course.

Morgane received an excited welcome from Mary, and very soon she had been brought up to date with the marital status of their group of friends, and what they were all doing with their lives. After a couple of hours it seemed as if they had never had the Atlantic Ocean between them!

"What have you been doing apart from running your home Smugglers Cove as a bed and breakfast establishment?" Mary wanted to know, and Morgane suddenly realised that she did not want to tell anyone, including her closest friends, the real reason for her trip back to England.

"Oh, I do quite a bit of painting. The island is beautiful, and I am never short of something to paint. In fact I have managed to sell a few paintings, and have been asked for more."

"That's wonderful Morgane. When you rang you said you were coming over here to see a solicitor. How long will it take, your legal business? Both Martin and I would love you to stay at least a few weeks. You have asked us many times to come over to stay with you in Bermuda, and we might just take you up on that invitation, as soon as Martin had achieved his Master's Degree. He should get a boost in salary, even if he continues his research job, and we should be able to manage the air fares. As it stands at the moment for the price of the fares we could have a fortnight's holiday anywhere on the continent."

Mary was as dark as Morgane was fair, and her hair was cut quite short, and she had the most piquant, expressively pretty face. She was rather petite, and sat in the chair opposite Morgane, with her legs curled up on the seat, with the inevitable mischievous smile. They both sipped from glasses of white wine, and being already tired, Morgane found it very potent. She realised how much she had missed her friend, and remembered fondly the long chats into the night they had enjoyed whilst rooming together, before Mary and Martin had married.

"You don't have to remind me Mary, how much the air fares are," she replied ruefully.

"Martin said JDL the painter dropped you off this morning, what's all that about," Mary asked and settled down further into her chair comfortably. Wanting to know, no doubt, how and where they had met.

Morgane felt very guilty, she would not lie to her friend, but until things were sorted out definitely between her and Joe, she preferred to keep the real reason for being here to herself.

"Oh Joe stayed in the chalet in the grounds at Smugglers Cove, and he happens to know the solicitor that I have come to see. He did quite a bit of painting whilst he was there. He kindly picked me up at the airport this morning." There was no need to tell Mary how early the flight had arrived! She yawned, suddenly realising how tired she had become.

"Sorry Morgane, you should be in bed. Martin said he had shown you the spare room, I hope you will be comfortable there. I'll be working tomorrow, I can't take time off just yet, I have been working on the window displays and I must make sure they are just right. It's only three months to Christmas! I understand you will be seeing the solicitor in the morning, so we will be able to have a chat again tomorrow evening. However, we'll all go out for a meal to celebrate your arrival." She kissed Morgane goodnight, and wandered off into the office to join her husband, carrying her wine with her.

The next morning Morgane was awakened by Mary, as she popped into her room with a welcome cup of tea. "Are you joining us for breakfast? We only have cereal and toast, is that enough for you?"

"It certainly is, and thank you Mary. I'll join you when I've had a quick shower. I'll have to be ready in an hour, as they are sending a car for me at nine o'clock."

After breakfast, Martin and Mary left together as Martin was going into the university to work today. They had insisted that Morgane should have a key to the flat so that she could let herself in whenever she wanted. Having cleared away the breakfast dishes and tidied the kitchen, she wandered down to the front door, so that the driver would not have to come up the flights of stairs. She felt quite smart in her new boots, warm skirt, and fashionable skimpy sweater. She carried a jacket, and was pleasantly surprised by the warmth of the September sun when she arrived in the small front garden. The birds were singing and flitting about in the avenue of trees, and it didn't feel at all like being in the city of London. A couple of minutes later the car drew up in front of the flats and her heart gave a thump as she saw that Joe was waiting in the back seat. She had been prepared to meet him at the solicitor's, thinking he would want to see David first, and would meet her there.

"Good morning Morgane. You look suitably rested," he clipped. She almost smiled thinking that he seemed surprised, maybe he thought she would be tired after a night suffering from jet lag and/or unbridled passion! She stared at him for a moment, and then quickly moved her eyes from his. He looked wonderful, and he was dressed in a suit suitable for the city. It didn't seem to matter what he wore, he still had this unsettling effect on her equilibrium.

"It's a waste of time Joe, as I still haven't changed my mind. I am not convinced you are my half brother, and as I have no intention of accepting the money The Trust is spending money on me unnecessarily."

"Have you brought your passport with you? David will need proof of identity. As you are not twenty-five yet, you needn't make a final decision. There are just a few documents for you to read and sign today."

It appeared that he was about to explain further, but his mobile telephone rang, and he spent the rest of the journey talking to 'Karen' at the gallery exhibiting his paintings. Morgane wondered if Karen was one of his (according to the press) many girlfriends! Morgane was determined to ignore him, and spent the journey watching the traffic, which seemed even busier than when she had spent time at university just a few years ago. It made her return to Bermuda in a week or so, seem very welcome indeed. She doubted if anyone in the city had ever heard of a twenty mile an hour limit! The car drew up in front of a large office block, obviously housing many businesses, and the vestibule was very grand and sumptuously furnished. Joe drew the attention of the girls behind the reception desk, just by walking passed, and Morgane wondered if perhaps she had become invisible! In the lift Joe gave her a close look, obviously wondering what she was smiling about. She wondered if he thought she had been protesting too much about the inheritance, and now that her birthday was getting closer her professed principles would disappear, and she would gladly grab the money offered!

Morgane was welcomed to London by David, who was just as nice as she remembered from his visit to Bermuda. All his suggestions, regarding tests, and further enquiries into the possibility of Mr Lawson being her father, the signing and witnessing of documents, all went amicably Morgane decided, at least as far as she and David were concerned. However, Morgane did not waver in her determination. She refused to change her mind, and when the meeting was over, David Smithson, said goodbye to her showing a reluctant acceptance of her wishes, and a good deal of respect. The one thing she did not believe was when he said that his daughter Jill had sent Morgane her kind regards!

Joe, however, was not in a very good mood when they left the office, his fists were clenched and she wondered if that was to stop him from shaking her. His brow was deeply furrowed, with his eyes coldly assessing as they looked at her moodily. Any other man would be pleased that he was not about to lose such a substantial sum out of his inheritance. On the other hand, maybe it was not a large sum to him! Just at that moment Morgane would willingly have boarded a plane back to Bermuda. She didn't think his iron control over his feelings would last much longer. She was, therefore, greatly surprised when he insisted he was taking her to lunch. The car dropped them off at Joe's flat, and he took her elbow with determination as though he thought she would not accompany him up in the lift to the top floor.

Joe walked into the flat and asked her if she wanted to freshen up. She moved into the bathroom, it was bliss to have a few moments alone. No doubt the lunch, with Joe almost silent, and most definitely disapproving, would seem interminable.

When she came out of the bathroom it was to find that Joe had changed into a comfortable sweater and designer jeans. She had imagined they were going to lunch in a restaurant in town. She gave him a questioning glance.

"These are more comfortable than the suit. I'll be driving for a while, and lunch will be ready when we get there."

"Where?" She wanted to know.

"Wait and see. You have had your own way all day today, however much it disrupted things, now it is my turn."

"I hope we will not be too long, I am going out for a meal with friends this evening," Morgane informed him briskly.

"Don't worry, as I'll have you back in London in good time. As I too have commitments this evening," he returned expressionlessly.

They took the lift, and when the door opened it was to the garage which was below ground level. Joe helped her into the shining and comfortable silver Mercedes, and thereafter concentrated on his driving. After half and hour Morgane again began to wonder where they were heading. Joe was undoubtedly a very good driver, and soon they left the motorway and were in the countryside. They slowly travelled through a small village, which was very pretty indeed with the trees changing to their autumn colours, and the sun showing to perfection the myriad cottage, and formal gardens. They turned into a drive, and after a couple of minutes arrived at a large stone built house.

"This doesn't look like a restaurant, where are we," Morgane demanded.

Joe ignored her and parked the car in front of the large front door, which quickly opened and a smiling woman came down the two steps to greet them.

"This is Mrs Watson, my housekeeper, who has kindly prepared lunch for us. This is Morgane Maine, a friend of mine from Bermuda," Joe introduced the two women. "We'll have lunch now please," he smiled at his housekeeper, who smiled back and indicated for Morgane to follow her. They moved through the house (Morgane with a strong feeling of reluctance) and onto a large patio at the rear of the house, where a table was ready for them.

"I'll show you the downstairs cloakroom, Ms Maine, and then bring in the lunch right away," Mrs Watson offered, with a smile.

"Morgane please," she instructed the friendly woman, and following her from the patio. She would deal with Joe in a minute! She gave him a cold glare, which he completely ignored. After tidying herself in the cloakroom, she moved back onto the terrace, where Joe was sitting at the table reading a newspaper. She sat at the table, and after a glance around to make sure they were alone she addressed him coldly.

"What are we doing here?"

He slowly put down the newspaper, folding it carefully. "I thought you should see where my father lived. It is, of course, my home now. After we have had a bite to eat, I'll show you his studio. He spent most of his time here. As you can see it is a large comfortable home. You needn't bother about your small inheritance if you decide to accept, it will not leave me short of anything." He looked at her angrily, and then his face changed to a smile as Mrs Watson arrived with cold meats and salad, and chatted to him about the weather, and how well the garden looked! Morgane sat and fumed, and wondered if the friendly housekeeper was aware of the circumstances, she would not have been surprised if Joe had discussed the situation with her, they were on such very friendly terms.

Morgane did her best with the meal, but mostly pushed the food around on her plate, and was glad when the meal was over.

"Thank you Mrs Watson, that was very nice, but I'm afraid I wasn't very hungry," Morgane apologised. Joe indicated that she should follow him and he set off along the terrace, where she reluctantly followed. They came to a large building in the grounds, which turned out to be his father's studio.

"Do you use this room for *your* painting?" Morgane asked Joe, already visualising him hard at work on a portrait. The light from the large windows and skylights was perfect. He nodded, but did not offer to show her any of the canvases stacked up against the walls. She had not wanted to show any interest in the canvases but because he seemed reluctant to show them to her, she was disappointed.

"What medium do you use?"

"Mostly oils, but I do watercolours and pastels too," he murmured. He seemed thoroughly fed up and she thought he was probably wishing he had not brought her here to *his* home, and that of his father. She wondered for a second if her own love of art was inherited from her father, whoever he might be, and swallowed hard. She could scotch that idea right away, her mother had been artistic, but had used writing as her means of expression!

Joe turned, looking at her closely, and caught her miserable expression. He should never have brought her here, as it had been an ill conceived idea. Every time he came home, he would remember her in these surroundings. As if everything was not difficult enough, he had to complicate things further for himself. He would forget about showing her the rest of the house and grounds, the sooner they were on their way back to London the more relieved he would be!

"I guess I shouldn't have brought you here Morgane. I thought if you saw where my father lived, you would realise that the amount left to you would not deprive me in the least. I would like to think you had something behind you, and you could forget about the bed and breakfast business. Benny and Robin can't be around all the time and I don't think you should be doing it without someone else around."

"Stop trying to run my life Joe, it has nothing to do with you. You are not *my brother* or my keeper, and I will do what I like." She turned quickly, and in doing so knocked against a table full of brushes, pallet knives and bottles of fluid, which crashed to the floor. Paint thinner splashed across her skirt and boots. "Now look what you made me do," she said in despair, and her eyes filled with tears of exasperation. He picked up a paint rag and the look she gave him dared him to dab at the paint thinner at his peril. She brushed a hand across her eyes, and he took hold of her elbows and held her still, and was

301

shocked at the antipathy he could see in her eyes. She was held by the look of speculation narrowing his eyes, as he held her still, and the air became charged, and she saw his eyes darken.

"I wish I was home in Bermuda," she gasped brokenly. He suddenly stood back, and she bent down to start picking up the brushes, then took up the rag and dabbed ineffectually at her skirt.

"Leave the damned brushes," he demanded, moving purposely towards the doorway. He turned suddenly. "Are you hoping that the good Martin will follow you to Bermuda?" he finished sarcastically. He was fighting a losing battle, he wanted to pull her into his arms and make her forget everything and everyone but him!

"He might just do that Joe," she replied. He stared at her for a moment then moved out of the studio, and strode across to the silver Mercedes where he waited impatiently for her to join him.

She slowly closed the studio door, and followed him. He didn't open the car door for her so she did it herself, and as soon as she was seated and had done up her seatbelt, the car shot off down the drive.

"I should have thanked Mrs Watson," she said angrily, and was totally ignored as he switched on some music, and there was a very uncomfortable atmosphere in the car all the way back to London. He parked outside her friends flat, and she was surprised when he followed her up to the door. She took out her key, but Martin must have seen them arrive, and quickly opened the door for her. She thanked him, and turned to Joe, but he was already on the stairs making his way back to the car. She did not see him again during her short stay in London.

As Joe took the steps two at a time his mind was in a whirl. He sat quietly in the car for a few minutes before driving off. He had been shaken by their traumatic confrontation in the studio. He had no right to try to run her life. He knew what he should do, that was to encourage her and Martin. Martin seemed a very reliable person, young and attractive to the opposite sex. He seemed to have a good job, a job that enabled him to work from home for part of the time. Morgane could do a lot worse! He decided to let matters take their course, without his input, not that Morgane would allow him to put his oar in anyway. She certainly had a mind of her own, and only seemed to believe what she wanted to believe. Was it women's intuition that made her so adamant in her beliefs? Whatever the outcome of any further investigations into the matter by himself and David, she still had a right to the money as it had been willed to her by his father - whatever his reason was for so doing. She really was incredibly stubborn, and all he wanted for her was for her to be able to live more comfortably, and to be able to do the things that she wanted, like her painting, instead of having to run her home as a bed and breakfast business. Comfortable and pleasant as it was for her customers! All this ruminating was not, of course, strictly true. He did want all those things for her, but he also wanted to be a part of her life. To give full rein to the primeval gut-response that they seemed to share, and see where it led them! Before this could happen he had to ascertain, without any doubt, the fact that they did not share the same father, as Morgane adamantly believed! He was running short of ideas. David had suggested that they investigate as far as possible the rest of her mother's many friends of twenty five years ago, and to put this in motion David was interviewing a private investigator. And the first job for the investigator would be to go through the mountain of correspondence his father had left behind him. Joe straightened his shoulders, and drove off into the rapidly fading evening light, the best thing he could do for her was to give her some space. Let her enjoy her break here in London. There was quite a lot happening in his own life, maybe he should concentrate on that for the next week or so!

The next morning Morgane rebooked her flight home, deciding a week with her friends was long enough, any longer and they might regret asking her to stay with them, she didn't feel that she was very good company just at this time. She knew that Mary was worried about her introspective friend, and had accepted Morgane's explanation last evening when they went out to meet their university friends, that she was now suffering from jet-lag. However, she could not bring herself to talk to anyone, even Mary, about the possibility that Joe might be her half-brother, she would not and could not, believe it! Whatever there was between them, and there was something at least on her part, it was certainly not brotherly. She also worried that if it was proved so, the press would find out and Joe's life would be made a misery, and the only way to put a stop to the inevitable speculation, would be by telling the truth, as far as they could. They needed some proof one way or the other, and soon!

CHAPTER NINE

Morgane broke her news that she had booked her flight back to Bermuda the next day, and at first Mary and Martin had been disappointed, but Morgane pointed out to them that she didn't want to leave her business for so long. It would not be fair on her friend Benny and her sister-in-law. They reluctantly accepted this explanation, and after a further invitation to visit the islands and stay with Morgane, they promised to come to stay with her after Martin had secured his Doctorate.

The next few days were full and very enjoyable. She spent time with Mary at her job in a large department store, and was even offered a job by her very pleasant departmental boss! Morgane didn't know whether this was a genuine offer, but it was, nevertheless, satisfying to receive such an offer.

It was the moments spent alone in her small bedroom that were the worst to bear. Joe kept coming into her mind unbidden. Every day she thought that he might appear in person, but he did no such thing. She wanted to apologise for the way she had behaved when he had taken her to his home for lunch. It had felt so right to be there part of the time, and she had been interested in Joe's father and where he had lived, but it had just been because he was Joe's father, not because she thought he might be *hers* too! She was sorry they had parted on a note of dissension. She was well aware that underneath Joe's surface hardness there was a depth of artistic sensitivity. Maybe he was hurting just as much as was she, by this period of uncertainty they were both going through. Maybe he just wanted to get on with his life, have all the legalities ironed out, and then there would be no need for him to be obligated to her any further. Was she being a stubborn fool? Maybe she should take the money and run all the way back to Bermuda, and put a line under this whole sorry business! If it were that simple, she would probably have already done so.

The only blight on the rest of her days in the UK was a surprise visit from Jill Smithson. She was in the flat alone, when the doorbell rang. At first she ignored it thinking it must be for Martin, but he was working at the University today. When it rang for a second time, and the ringing was prolonged, Morgane left her bedroom where she was trying to decide how she would pack everything into the one suitcase, now that she had bought new and heavier clothes. She answered the door, and was almost pushed aside as Jill Smithson strode into the flat, without being invited! Something had obviously upset the younger girl, her red lips were almost pouting, and her brow was furrowed, and her eyes flashed a warning. She looked only slightly shamefaced, as Morgane quietly and politely closed the flat door, and indicated that her visitor should take a seat.

"Dad gave me your address because he thinks I've come to show you around, but I haven't," she said aggressively.

"That's quite all right Jill, I already know my way around London," Morgane replied raising her eyebrows in enquiry.

"I don't know why you are here in London, but you are ruining everything. Joe promised to take me to the opening of his exhibition at the Gallery tonight, but he has now left a message saying he can't. I've been looking forward to it, and have even bought a new dress. I suppose he is taking you," Jill said accusingly, and Morgane could see that she was very near to tears, and even more besotted with Joe than it had appeared in Bermuda!

"No Jill, I am not going to the opening of the exhibition. I didn't even know it was today. Maybe you should contact Joe and ask him why he has cancelled?"

"I don't know where to find him, I've been ringing around," Jill replied haughtily.

Morgane almost felt sorry for the unhappy girl. "Look Jill, I haven't seen Joe for days, and don't expect to see him anytime soon. You should ask your father, he may know where Joe is."

Morgane knew that whatever she said to the girl whilst she was in such distress was not going to help, and she was determined to believe that Morgane was somehow to blame for her disappointment! Jill stood up, dabbed her eyes with a tissue and grabbed her bag from the chair. "Joe and I are meant to be together, so if you are in this country because of Joe you can forget it. I know he will be relieved when you have gone back to Bermuda." With this parting shot, she swept out of the flat, and Morgane could hear her footsteps running down the stairs.

Had Jill heard Joe and her father talking? It was quite possible that Joe did wish her back in Bermuda. Nevertheless, being told this by a third party was not easy to bear. She almost regretted the fact that she had already brought her flight home forward, as she didn't like the idea of either Joe or Jill thinking she had done this because of anything they had said! Was Joe really in a relationship with Jill? There would only be about twelve years difference in their ages, in this day and age that was not unusual. In Bermuda Morgane had been aware that Jill fancied herself in love with Joe, but had assumed that it was just a teenage crush. Maybe it was more than that, as asking her to accompany him to the opening of his exhibition was not the best way to discourage her. She must concentrate her utmost will and put these unpleasant thoughts out of her mind, she would not let them ruin the last few days she would have with her friends.

A week later it was Martin's turn to answer the door, and invite his visitor into the flat. What did Joe Lawson want *here*? Morgane never had explained how they had become friends, except that he had spent a little time in Bermuda?

"Would you care to sit down, and could I get you a drink," he asked the older man pleasantly.

"No thank you Martin, I haven't much time." He looked around the flat questioningly. "Is Morgane out?"

"Out! Yes, you could say that! She flew back to Bermuda a couple of days ago. It seemed a shame that she had to shorten her holiday as it was lovely having her to visit. There was so much to catch up on, as she hasn't been over here since her mother died. I think I've persuaded her to get an up to date computer, it's so much easier to keep in touch with email. It will be good for her business too." Martin sounded quite pleased with himself.

As well he might. Joe felt really jaded. She had left without getting in touch – it showed him just how much she thought about him, her unwanted inheritance, and David Smithson! He smiled ruefully at Martin. "I'll better let her solicitor know."

"Oh, she seemed to think everything had been sorted." Martin said vaguely. He had a thought. "Look at this Mr Lawson, it is one of Morgane's, what do you think? It will be lovely to see this beautiful place in the not too distant future."

Martin indicated a painting, obviously of Bermuda, although the view was not familiar to Joe. He considered it carefully. She really was very good, and he had no doubt that she could make her living at painting, if she set her mind to it. She must consider Martin to be a very special friend!

"Call me Joe," he instructed Martin. "You should hang on to that painting Martin, it really is very good."

"I sure will," Martin said pleasantly, as he escorted his unexpected and illustrious visitor to the door. Knowing someone as well known as Joe Lawson, could only help Morgane if she decided to concentrate her efforts in the world of art!

Morgane returned to Bermuda with a definite feeling of homecoming. Unfortunately, she was not expected and Maggie, Benny's sister-in-law, was still in residence, and the house and chalet was full with six customers who were staying for a fortnight. Maggie had the decorators working in her own house, and Morgane insisted that she could not return there until it was finished. Morgane, as her bedroom was already in use, set to work with a will to get the two rooms under the eaves of the house, which had only ever been used for storage, into some sort of order so that she could make herself comfortable on a folding bed. Maggie and Benny were both keen to help, although Morgane was worried about them using the folding steps which gave access to the attic rooms.

In actual fact, the rooms were quite large, and storage boxes and odd pieces of furniture were stored in one room, and Morgane found that the other was plenty big enough for her bed, small dressing table, her easel, and painting materials. She felt very private and almost cut off from the rest of the house. Robin helped move the heavily filled boxes and pieces of furniture, and came up with the suggestion that a couple of large opening windows in the roof would provide ample light for her to paint in comfort. The roof lights, they decided, would not interfere with the main purpose of the roof, which was a catchment area for rainwater. He also suggested that storage space could be built round the edges of the room where head-room was much less. This work was soon put in hand, and the rooms became light and airy and a pleasure to use. The views over the island and sea were breathtaking, but Morgane had spent as much as she possibly could for the moment. The ideal thing to do would be to have a new staircase built leading to the new rooms, as there was plenty of space on the second floor landing. Rashly Morgane decided they should go ahead with this.

Robin and Benny kindly helped Morgane to go through the storage boxes, and after a couple of days there was much less to store. Morgane could not decide whether she was relieved or disappointed, when they did not come across anything of her mother's such as correspondence or photographs. It had been the obvious place to look for some clue to disprove or prove Joe and David Smithson's theory as to the identity of her father!

During this activity the only times that Morgane had time to think about Joe, and the problems he had brought into her life, were easily pushed aside, only to return in the evenings, which were now becoming shorter. The weather was still quite hot, and they were doing good business, and it was with relief that Morgane realised that Maggie, although her own house was now fully decorated, was happy to stay on and help with the business. She had become quite used to seeing Benny every day and also to be close to Benny's large family. Her own daughter and son had moved away from the islands, and both were married and living in America. Unfortunately they only managed to visit once or twice a year.

Morgane was glad of her new found freedom, and enjoyed long days moving around the island painting until her heart was content. Or as content as it ever was these days! Joe and the associated problems came home to her every night, and her brain whirled around and around, going through every scenario. She could not admit to herself how she felt about Joe, she knew the thought of him made her chest ache, and he was never far from her mind, she only knew that she could not accept him as a half-brother! There were so many contradictory emotions, that every morning she felt even more confused. She longed every night to get a good nights sleep, but her feeble attempts were always thwarted, and left her weary and anything but her usual happy self. Benny, of course, noticed all this and became more and more worried about her young friend. She was very glad that Maggie seemed settled in Smugglers Cove and gave no sign that she wanted to move back to her own home.

After her brief instruction from Martin one wet afternoon in London, on the use and helpfulness of a computer in business,

Morgane decided that she really could not do without one. She really would like to be able to contact Martin and Mary, and her other university friends. Besides since university she was not keeping up with the times, and needed to be dragged into the new millennium! Benny and Maggie both informed her that they wanted nothing to do with the 'new fangled thing' and that she would have to use it alone. After a couple of instances when Robin had to send his eldest son around to 'put Auntie Morgane right' she decided to take some much needed lessons in the use and operation of the computer. She found it very useful thereafter, and very soon wondered how she had managed without it!

Three weeks later she received a letter from David Smithson. She opened the letter and looked immediately at the headed paper. She caught herself up quickly, as she had been looking at the heading expecting to see Joe's name and maybe his email address. How stupid could she be, he was only a Trustee, along with David Smithson, of the Trust dealing with her alleged inheritance. She then read through the letter, and pushed it absently to one side, there was nothing in it to interest her! Attached to the letter was a cheque for £15,000, the latter being sent at the discretion of the Trustees for her immediate use. It had been sent to her now rather than making her wait for the full amount when it became due to her on her twenty-fifth birthday, but it was left unheeded in the 'in' tray on her desk in reception.

The bill for the new up-to-date computer, for several hundred dollars, was also left in the said tray. When this was found by Benny, together with the cheque for £15,000, she offered to deliver the cheque in full settlement for the computer, and put the substantial cheque Morgane had received in the bank. She was even more worried about Morgane's state of mind when a post-dated cheque was handed to her for delivery to the computer company, and the cheque for £15,000 was torn in two and dumped unceremoniously into the waste paper basket! Later in the day Benny salvaged the torn cheque and put it away safely. No doubt, in the next few days Morgane would change her mind at least Benny very much hoped she would. Benny felt a strong need to talk things over with her sister-in-law, Maggie. For now she would hold her tongue, and try to get Morgane in a receptive mood one day, and have a good talk with her, and perhaps she would find out what had happened during Morgane's trip to London. Although back a few months now, she had not said anything about her trip, nor had she mentioned Joe at all, even when Benny had brought up his name in conversation a number of times.

Morgane continued with her painting, and whilst cleaning the attic rooms, Benny looked at the picture on the easel. She recognised the view as one from the private cove at the foot of the steps down from Smugglers Cove. She found it strangely disturbing, with strange clouds and a menacing sea, which was surprising as the Great Sound is only open to the sea on the most western side, and usually reasonably calm. She also noticed that the large picture painted by Joe, had been removed from Morgane's wardrobe in the room Maggie was now using, but it was still wrapped securely, and stored facing the wall, together with one or two of Morgane's own paintings.

At the weekend, the new guests had arrived and were making themselves comfortable, and Robin was cleaning the pool. He watched as a brown haired man with the tips heavily blonded, with a dark tan, and looking quite scruffy with a T-shirt with the arms ripped out, and baggy shorts and sandals, strolled leisurely up the drive with his hands in his pockets. He looked carefully at the house and the grounds with a keen intelligence, and the look on his face was almost smug. For some reason he reminded Robin of Jeremy, the reporter, although on the surface they looked totally different. He saw Robin working by the pool, and walked nonchalantly over to him.

"Is Morgane in?" he asked brusquely. "If so, tell her I would like to see her."

"Who shall I say wants to see *Miss Maine*," Robin said continuing his long sweeps across the pool with a net, efficiently catching anything floating on the surface.

"Just say Simon Granger is here," he instructed in an offhand manner.

Robin did another two or three sweeps across the pool then slowly emptied his net, and set it carefully against the pool rim. Simon Granger - he remembered him from school, he had been a year or two lower than Robin, but always in some sort of trouble, and not very well liked by the other boys. He was nothing like his elder brother, who Robin knew quite well, being around the same age. He hadn't seen or heard of Simon for years, and he wondered where he had been. By the odd sound of his drawling voice, it had probably been America, probably New York. Robin was both intrigued and troubled by his turning up here to see Morgane, and decided to keep to himself the fact that he remembered him from school. Maybe it would give him some sort of edge against him in the future, should it become necessary, for he didn't care for the speculative way he was looking around the house and grounds, or the fact that he appeared to be on first name terms with Morgane. He knew that his mother was worried about Morgane

314

just at the moment, and he had been keeping a close eye on her himself lately, she appeared to be so vulnerable, and walked around the place as though she was weighted down with worries. He didn't think his mother and Morgane had any secrets from each other, and he preferred to leave it that way – he thought he knew his own lovely wife Chrissie, but she never failed to surprise him. Robin took his time putting his net to one side, and after asking Simon to wait, he ambled across to the house. He hoped that Morgane had taken herself off painting, but when he called up the stairs she answered him, and came to join him in the reception area.

"There's a chap here to see you, says his name is Simon Granger," he told her and was pleased when she looked puzzled. "He asked for you by your first name," he finished with disapproval.

Morgane thought for a moment. "Oh, I remember, I met him when I was in St. George's, selling some paintings. He is Mr Granger's brother, I wonder what he wants? Would you please tell him I'll be out in a few minutes."

Robin nodded, and turned away to leave by the kitchen door. He hoped Morgane was not going to make the effort to tidy her hair, or whatever women did, when called on by some man. When she came out, if she thought he would make himself scarce she was in for a surprise. He wasn't going anywhere, as long as Simon Granger was around the property. If he remembered correctly, Simon had never had any special friends, and no wonder, he was always in trouble and often managed to put the blame on someone else's shoulders. He knew better than to tell Chrissie what she should do, as it might just have the opposite effect. He thought that Morgane would not be any different, so he had to hope that whatever had brought Simon here would not bring him here again! Anyway he wasn't going anywhere. He was going to work on even if he was late home, he would stay until Simon Granger had left Smugglers Cove.

CHAPTER TEN

Morgane met Simon by the pool. He looked much the same as he had when she met him at his brother's shop. Maybe his tan was darker, but the hair highlighted to blonde was very attractive, even if contrived by the use of a bottle! The hazel eyes still seemed very friendly and attractive.

"It is nice to see you again Simon. What can I do for you," she enquired, rather intrigued by his appearance here because she was sure she had not given him any encouragement when they last met.

"My brother wondered if you would have any more paintings for sale, not just at the moment, as things are slowing down. In a couple of months or so?" he smiled with all the charm he had practised to perfection. He had forgotten what a beautiful girl she was, and looking around again he thought she must live very comfortably. Smugglers Cove looked well tended with the exotic gardens surrounding the house. The views across the Great Sound were extensive and took in the large horseshoe curve of sea from Dockyard to Spanish Point. The temperature today was very pleasantly warm, much more to his taste than the blazing hot sun when he had first met Morgane Maine in St. George's. He felt excited by the prospect of getting to know her better!

"Yes, I have a few finished paintings, but I'll get a few more together and then take them for your brother to see. He certainly has the knack of selling them."

"I'm sure they sell themselves Morgane. I really like your work, and am thinking of perhaps taking some of it back to the States with me, as I have a few contacts there. It could be the start of something really big. What do you think?"

"I don't think I'm ready for that yet Simon. Maybe some time in the future," she replied pleasantly.

"Well you think about it, I would be pleased to help you get established over there." He finished rather smugly. And then paused with a charming smile, "tell you what, how about letting me buy you dinner tonight, and we can talk about it. When we met in my brother's art shop, you said you would have a drink with me sometime in the future. This is it," he finished triumphantly.

She was a loss for words for a moment or two. She had said, 'maybe' she would have a drink with him in the future some time. He really was rather persistent. However, she didn't want to upset his brother, who was managing to sell quite a few of her paintings, which helped quite a bit financially.

"Not dinner," she replied. "Perhaps you have time for a glass of wine," she offered belatedly, when he looked disappointed. He cheered up immediately.

"Yes, I'd like that. Where shall we go?"

"I haven't much time, if you would like to wait on the patio, I'll fetch a bottle," she offered, indicating the front of the house. They walked together towards the patio, whilst Simon admired the view, and Robin still by the pool, chewed his bottom lip in annoyance. Chrissie was going to have something to say to him when he arrived home later than expected, but he wasn't leaving Morgane alone with Simon Granger! He knew he was being irrational, but there must be something wrong with a boy that had no friends, besides he hadn't liked Simon's attitude earlier when he had requested to see 'Morgane.' Robin continued his work in the garden. He could hear their voices, although he could not hear what was said. He was relieved when Simon departed, and he was able to pack up his tools and make his way home to his family.

Morgane had quite enjoyed different company, but wasn't sure whether she wished to see Simon again. She regretted the fact that her few friends on the island were either married, and thus otherwise engaged most of the time, or now worked in the UK or America, and were seldom on the island. She had been very lax in not keeping in better touch with them, but being single it was not often that she was now invited to join them, and it was her own fault because she had started to refuse invitations over the last few months. She realised that she had relied too much on the invitations from Benny and her family where she felt comfortable, and knew that she was not being set up to meet blind dates!

Two weeks passed uneventfully, and after taking two guests to the airport for their return home to the UK, before crossing the causeway, Morgane drove the jeep up to St. George's Island. She drove through Ferry Point Park to settle herself comfortably overlooking Whale Bone Bay, where she intended to make sketches for more paintings. The structure of the rocks around the access to the shore, were very interesting, and there were very few people about, and it would make a very good painting. The day was warm and sunny, and the park was not very busy with tourists, and she settled down comfortably to sketch, with the added benefit of not having people trying to look over her shoulder! For a further sketch or two she moved on towards the Martello Tower, and an old gun emplacement. The light was good, and she was surprised when she heard her name being called. She turned in surprise, to find Simon on his way to join her. At first she felt slightly annoyed at being disturbed when her sketching was going so well, then felt guilty for these feelings.

She acknowledged Simon, and he came and sat quietly beside her whilst she finished her sketch. She was pleasantly surprised that he managed to sit quietly and let her finish her work. He was so quiet she almost forgot that he was there. As she started to pack up her belongings, he insisted on helping, and joined her as she started to walk back to her jeep.

"Have you given any thought to our discussion the other day? I really do have some contacts in the States who, I'm quite sure, would be very interested in marketing some of your work?" He asked eagerly.

"I'm afraid I haven't, I am quite happy just selling to your brother, and I also have an outlet in Hamilton, it takes me all my painting time to keep them satisfied," she replied apologetically.

"The more success you have, the more time you would have to paint, you could leave the bed and breakfast business to be run by someone else," he suggested helpfully. "Oh, the other thing I meant to say to you was that I rang Smuggler's Cove this morning, and a person who said her name was Maggie, told me that you were painting in this area. I wanted to ask if you could provide me with accommodation for a couple of weeks. My brother won't have room for me in the immediate future?"

She didn't know how to reply, and wasn't pleased at being put on the spot by Maggie. Simon must be all right, he was Mr Granger's brother, and it was the quiet part of the year with regard to the bed and breakfast trade. However, she did not want to be continually pressed to let him handle the selling of her paintings! They were personal, and she was the one who would decide what to sell and what to keep. Having turned him down in this respect she didn't feel that she could also tell him she did not want to accommodate him. It would only be for a couple of weeks.

"If you would like to give me your telephone number, I'll check about the accommodation, and let you know." They had arrived at her jeep, and she opened the back door to put in her painting materials. She opened the front doors to let the air circulate, she had only been painting for an hour or so, and the inside of the jeep felt as if it had been closed up for the full day. She pushed back the blond hair with a warm hand, it really was very hot, hotter than she would have expected for a November afternoon. She glanced at the sky, it looked perfectly normal, and there had not been any word of a hurricane or even inclement weather.

"Thank you Morgane. You are a life saver, and it will be nice to stay near Hamilton for a change." He laughed and gave a pleased smile. Suddenly he leaned forward and kissed her on the cheek. She was taken aback, but he seemed so pleased and happy, she didn't like to make a fuss. He handed in to the back of the jeep the last of her belongings, and she banged the door

321

shut. As she turned there was a flash, and she put her arm up to shield her face in surprise.

"You looked so lovely stood there with the sea behind you, in your white shorts and top, I had to take a photo," he said with a charming but unrepentant smile. "It was lucky I managed to find you in the park, I might have missed you."

Morgane slowly got into the driving seat. He was showing a little too much interest for her liking, she would have to think of a way of telling him pleasantly, that she wasn't interested in anything but friendship.

"Would you mind giving me a lift to the bottom of the hill, where you could drop me, and I'll walk back to St. George's," he asked with a cheeky grin, and he was inside the vehicle and sat comfortably in the front seat before she could answer.

She shrugged her shoulders, and raised her eyebrows shaking her head a little. She started the engine and drove slowly down the hill towards the main road, where she stopped for Simon to get out, where he blew her a kiss of thanks, and was off along the road towards St George's with a slight swagger. She watched him go and shook her head, he really didn't seem very old, she had been certain he was in his middle twenties, or thereabouts. No, she didn't want to compare him with Joe, poor Simon didn't stand a chance! She should really ask Joe about marketing her paintings, that is if he thought they were good enough, but it was much better if there was no contact between them, life would be much simpler that way. He and Jill Smithson might by now have declared themselves! She didn't really believe that this would happen, she thought that Joe would go for an older, and more sophisticated type! She was almost relieved when she arrived at the drive to Smuggler's Cove and had to put her mind to other things.

Maggie was sitting in the shade beside the chalet, watching as a young couple, their latest guests, were enjoying themselves in the pool. She smiled at Morgane, who joined her at the table.

"A Simon Granger rang for you, I hope you didn't mind but I said you were out painting somewhere near Whale Bone Bay. Benny said I shouldn't have told him, was she right?" Maggie seemed a bit disgruntled, obviously disliking the fact that she had been reprimanded by Benny. Morgane was at a loss as to what to say, she didn't want to upset Maggie, even more worrying was the thought that she might upset Benny.

"Well he did find me, and he did hold me up for a while, but it didn't matter. I have full confidence in you Maggie."

"I'm pleased that you have confidence in me," Maggie said with a sniff. No doubt, the sniff was for Benny trying to tell the confident nursery teacher what to do! "I'll go and put the kettle on for a nice cup of tea," she finished with a smile, and strode off into the house through the kitchen door.

Morgane spent some time talking to the guests, and then went to the kitchen to join Maggie, who was buttering scones to go with the tea. She indicated a chair, "Just ready, I made these scones earlier they've just cooled down lovely."

They enjoyed the scones and tea, and Morgane decided she had better remove her painting gear from the jeep. As she was about to leave the kitchen she was called back by Maggie. "Just a minute Morgane, I took a telephone call when you were talking with the guests. He said he had already spoken to you, and I took a booking from Simon Granger for two weeks, he will have a double room in the house. It's nice to know at least you have confidence in me Morgane," she smiled to herself, removing the cups and saucers from the table and placing them carefully in the sink.

Morgane continued outside and put her head in her hands. How had this happened? She was a wimp, and far too worried about upsetting Benny or Maggie, and now she would be lumbered with Simon staying in the house for a fortnight. She had nothing against him, but she would rather the room was filled with two guests, who were not going to be interested in *her* whereabouts! What she really felt like doing was to go up to her rooms at the top of the house, and draw up the ladder, so that she could be completely alone. It had been a big mistake to take out the ladder, and put in a permanent staircase. That too had been her own idea, to make access easier for Benny and Maggie.

When Robin heard that Simon was coming to stay for a couple of weeks in the house, he was so upset that he decided to have a word with his mother. Who in turn explained to Maggie, all the reservations that Robin had about Simon Granger. Four days later Simon moved into Smugglers Cove, and for the first two days of his stay, Morgane never saw him. She was amazed and suddenly felt much more confident. She had been wrong about Simon, he was not intent on pursuing her, he had just been friendly, and it was good to help out a friend.

On the third day of Simon's stay in the house, Morgane arrived home from an afternoon painting, to find him on the patio, with a bottle of wine and two glasses. He rose from his seat when the jeep pulled up at the side of the house, and waved for her to come and join him. He smiled and indicated the seat opposite to him.

"I was beginning to think you didn't live here any more," he said, as he poured her a glass of red wine. Red because he had decided to wait until she arrived home, whenever that was, and

324

the wine was rather warm, although he had kept it under the shade of the umbrella.

"I have been rather busy," she replied, knowing full well that she had not. She just hadn't been around when he was, she had not purposely kept out of his way!

She pushed her hair behind her ears, and lifted it from the nape of her neck. "It really is unseasonably hot."

"When we have finished the bottle we could have a dip in the pool. That would cool you down."

"I might just take a short dip in the pool, but I'm sorry I won't be helping you to finish the bottle, it's rather too early in the day for me. However, this glass of wine is very nice, thank you." They chatted amiably for about half an hour, and then Morgane said she would see him in the pool shortly. Simon looked very pleased, as he stood as Morgane left her seat and moved into the house. He quickly finished the bottle of wine, and went off to change for his swim. However, he was very disappointed when he arrived at the pool to find Robin painting the window of the chalet, which overlooked the pool. The painting took just about the same length of time that it took Morgane to arrive by the pool, looking drop-dead gorgeous in her one-piece suit, have a short swim, and move off back into the house. A few minutes after she had left, Simon pulled himself out of the pool, and glared at Robin. Robin gave him a bright smile, and went off towards the kitchen door.

A couple of days later, Simon had not seen Morgane again, except as she drove off in the jeep. The suspicion he harboured that he was being systematically watched by the three staff, and was not going to be left alone with Morgane, seemed to have become a hard fact, when he was unceremoniously jostled as he tried to take a photograph of Morgane sitting by the pool. If

Robin, that big ape of a man had not been so intimidating Simon might have questioned him about it. He was sure that Morgane had no idea what was going on, and he smugly decided he would wait and outwit her overbearing staff, and he did have over a week left of his stay. To tell the truth he had a grudging admiration for the effort that they had all put into it, which up to date had been quite successful. However, Simon Granger was too clever by far for these minions employed by Morgane, just as he was too clever for his only brother and he was well aware that he was on to a good thing here at Smuggler's Cove!

That afternoon he stayed in his room and made his plans. He watched as Robin came back from the shops and after delivering the goods he then, after ascertaining that Maggie was in, gave his mother a lift home. Simon was even more determined to outwit them, now that the simple souls thought everything was going well. It did not occur to him to wonder why they were going to so much trouble, and what the reason was, for as far as he knew they didn't know him!

He went into Hamilton later, and knew that none of the people at Smuggler's Cove had been aware that he was inside the house, nor had they seen him leave the second time. He strolled nonchalantly along Pitts Bay Road towards Hamilton, in quite a good mood. He would later meet an acquaintance in the Par-la-ville Park, and hoped he would learn something to his advantage. Later when he returned to the house he would make a point of having a talk with Morgane, as he had yet to persuade her to part with some of her paintings, so that he could take them with him, and hopefully make some much needed money. He had been mooching around Bermuda for long enough, and he was really looking forward to enjoying the amenities of America quite soon. Bermuda was fantastic, and he should know, he was born here, but it had lost some of its appeal when he had arrived home again without a dollar to his name. His brother had not been a bit of help. He had put him up for a few weeks, then decided it was time for his younger brother to go back to America, just because he had converted a couple of very old clocks which had belonged to the parents into much needed dollars! Meeting Morgane had been a bonus, as she had a lovely home, and was a marvellous painter, besides she really was something to look at herself, and his ability to charm women came naturally to him!

Robin waited outside the old Perot Post Office for his mother, she had insisted he must bring her in this afternoon to get a letter posted, and it must go today! When she arrived back and heaved herself into the van, she looked quite flustered.

"You OK mother," he asked.

She paused for a moment, and then replied that it was the heat, and they'd better be on their way home soon, she had dinner to prepare for his dad. She remained quiet for the drive home, but seemed preoccupied.

CHAPTER ELEVEN

Benny waited a couple of days, and then watched for the post. She had written to Joe to inform him about the cheque that Morgane had torn up, and that she, Benny, had retrieved from the waste basket. No doubt Joe and David Smithson were aware that the cheque had not been cashed, but surely they wouldn't have sent it if they had not come to some agreement? She also had mentioned that Morgane was not herself, and was working at all hours at her painting. She kept taking herself off for hours at a time, and Benny believed she was not sleeping very much. She had lost interest in the business, which was surprising as at first when she had returned from the United Kingdom, she had buckled down and had made various improvements to the house, and the work must have been quite costly. Benny felt many conflicting emotions, mostly guilt at having written to Joe. She felt she had let Morgane down by eliciting Joe's help behind Morgane's back, but why not, as there was a possibility that Joe was her half-brother, if he was, then he was her only relative! The cheque had not been the main reason she had decided to write to Joe, it was the fact that Simon Granger had made himself comfortable at Smuggler's Cove and that she didn't trust him at all. He was up to no good, and she had already felt that without the warning from Robin about his unworthiness. She had also heard him trying to persuade Morgane to part with some of her paintings, which he intended to sell in the States, and she really thought that if Morgane allowed this, she would be seriously ripped off – if she got any recompense at all!

She had posted the letter to Joe, c/o David Smithson. When she had been walking back to the parked van and Robin, she had been shocked to see two men standing in the park, alongside one of the stone seats, slightly shaded by the palm trees and hibiscus bushes. The shock was not that two men would discuss things in the park, but that the two men were Simon Granger and Jeremy Dixon. Surely it was too big a coincidence that they should be acquainted! Was Jeremy Dixon dissatisfied with the explanation Joe had given him as to why he was in Bermuda? Was he still intent on getting a story, and hoping to use Simon to help him get it? It was quite possible that they had met when Jeremy had last been on the islands.

Normally Benny would have tackled Morgane about all this having known her through the years she was growing up, before and after her mother's death. But just for the moment she knew that she would not get through to the younger girl, who seemed to have shut herself off from everyone, and preferred to keep her own counsel.

Most of the last two nights, Benny had worried what the best course of action would be, and Mike after losing rather a lot of sleep, suggested that she got one of the grandchildren to send an email, or she should telephone London herself. When Joe had not replied in a couple of days, Benny decided that she would telephone the solicitor, David Smithson, and leave a message for Joe, as she did not have his telephone number, it had not been written in the visitor's book when he registered in the spring.

Benny went to reception and removed the letter and cheque Morgane had received from David Smithson, and this time took a note of the telephone number, and replaced them. She was lucky and was able to speak with David Smithson, and felt much better when he said he would contact Joe. She did feel much better now that the ball was not in her court alone, and waited hopefully for a telephone call from Joe, which, unfortunately, did not materialise during that day.

Morgane gathered a couple of her paintings, her sketch book and bag, and ran down to the jeep. She had to get away for a while, and decided to take the north coast road towards St. George's. She wanted to do a sketch or two at Palmetto Park or maybe Flatts Inlet. She started the engine and saw in the side mirror Simon running out from the patio area, but ignored his wave, she wanted to be alone today, without any hangers on! He was becoming a nuisance, and she wished wholeheartedly that she had been more honest with Maggie, when she had taken the booking! It was a bit cloudy at Palmetto Park, and she moved on to Flatts Inlet. The tide had turned and the water was swirling under the bridge at the Inlet, and she watched a couple of American tourists, trying to fish in the fast running seawater. Had it been a day when the children were not at school, they would have been jumping into the water and enjoying the ride into the inlet, where they were always watched carefully by the older men enjoying their pipes and gossiping in the sunlight. She did a couple of sketches and then returned to the jeep and drove on towards St. George's.

Mr Granger welcomed her, and was pleased to take the paintings from her for sale. They chatted amiably for a few minutes, and Morgane asked him if he had enjoyed the company of his brother.

She was surprised, when his smile froze, and he looked out of the window for a moment, and then returned to face her with a look of resignation, tinged with disappointment.

"I'm afraid things didn't go too well. He only comes home when he wants something from me. I don't think he will be back." He smiled wryly, and changed the subject, saying that he would be glad to receive any further paintings she had for sale in the future. He escorted her out of the shop, and she wandered around the square, wondering what had gone wrong between the brothers. Obviously Mr Granger was not aware that his brother was still on the islands. She went into a cafe by the bridge, ordered coffee, and sat and pondered the situation at length.

The next morning was the end of the two weeks for which Simon had booked his room, and when asked by Maggie to settle his bill, he promised to do so at lunchtime when he had spoken with Morgane. Maggie was not worried as she would be in the house all day, and would keep an eye on him.

Robin worked in the garden during the early morning, and was worried when he received a call from his wife Chrissie, asking him to come home, as their son Robin Junior was unwell. He was not too worried as his mother had been ill last evening, but said it was nothing to worry about, but she would take the day off as Maggie was quite capable of managing.

331

When he arrived home Chrissie was adamant that they should take Robin Junior to the hospital to get him checked over, he seemed to be suffering more than his grandmother. Both he and his wife were worried as young Robin had never suffered any of the usual childhood illnesses, nor had his daughters who were at school where these were sometimes picked up.

Benny rang Maggie to make sure that she was well, and was pleased when Maggie said she would look after things at Smugglers Cove and not to worry. She insisted that she could manage perfectly well, two guests had left earlier in the morning and Morgane had just now returned from the Airport after dropping them off. Maggie found Simon on the patio, and told him that Morgane would be down in a few minutes.

She went to the bedrooms and changed the beds, and took the bedding into the utility room to do the washing.

As soon as he heard the washing machine start up in the distance, Simon left the patio and started up the stairs, Morgane quite often spent a lot of time painting in her rooms at the top of the house. He looked around with interest, so this was where she generally spent most of her time, time he was sure she spent there so that she wouldn't be disturbed by anyone. Recently he had received the impression that she didn't like him being around, and he was determined to make a last ditch attempt to get her to allow him to stay on. He was getting desperate, as the money received for the sale of the antique clocks taken from his brother's home had now run out. He needed some of her paintings to get the means to buy his ticket to the States. He was surprised when she wasn't there, and returned to the patio, just in time to see her disappearing into the chalet, outside of which she had set up her easel.

Morgane collected a bottle of water and turned to find Simon standing in the chalet doorway, with the usual charming smile on his face. She stood for a moment, tightly holding the bottle of water, waiting for him to move. When he didn't she indicated that she wished to move out of the chalet.

"I've been trying to get a word with you Morgane, but you never seem to be around. I thought I might stay on for a few more days, to give you time to decide if you would like me to market some of your paintings, I'll get a good price?" He looked at her with a confident smile, standing with one hand on each door jamb, making it impossible for her to move out of the chalet.

"I'm afraid that won't be possible. We are fully booked," she replied, hoping he was not going to prove difficult, and would move away from the doorway. Suddenly feeling rather cold, she placed the bottle of water on the table, and pulled on her cotton sweatshirt, which she had been carrying.

"I looked in the book in reception, you appear to have no one in for the next week, I realised that Maggie wouldn't be up to speed on the computer yet," he said thoughtfully, and didn't move an inch.

"Well, I did tell Maggie we would do some cleaning, and a bit of decorating, if she kept a week free. She must have decided on this week." The charming smile disappeared from his face, and his eyes turned cold. He clearly didn't believe her!

"That's a shame Morgane. If you get some of the paintings ready, I'll get out of your way."

"I haven't any paintings to give you. The paintings I have finished for sale, I left with your brother in St. George's. He seems to be under the impression that you have already left

Bermuda." She replied, acutely conscious of his change of attitude towards her. He frowned unpleasantly, and she realised that she had been ruthlessly manipulated into letting him stay here, and was almost certain that he had no intention of paying for his room. Thank goodness for Robin, he was here to work in the garden this morning. However, she had no intention of letting Simon know the unsettling effect he was having on her, now that he seemed to challenge everything that she said.

He grinned unpleasantly. "My brother only *hopes* that I have left Bermuda. I haven't done anything wrong. How can it be wrong to sell a couple of items that belonged to my parents? Unfortunately they were not as valuable as I hoped, and I will have to stay on for a little while longer. At least until I have enough for my air ticket. Play your cards right Morgane, and I might even help you decorate for my keep." He moved towards her, and she retreated out of reach. "You have been keeping me at arms length for long enough, you know perfectly well that you are a very attractive woman, and that I am interested in more than friendship. You have been parading around in your shorts and skimpy tops, just to be noticed," he said with a threatening voice, and a cynical twist of his lips.

She was shocked to the core, how could he have received that impression, she had never at any time given him reason to believe that she had any interest in him other than as a passing acquaintance. She swallowed feeling very nervous she must not let him see how much his attitude affected her, and must strive to appear calm and unemotional.

"That is not true Simon I have done absolutely nothing to give you that impression. Will you please go and settle your bill with Maggie, and leave as soon as possible." She could hear the bravado in her voice, and hoped that he would not pick up on it!

"No, I'm not going anywhere, not yet anyway." He moved towards her, and pushed the hair back from her face with a slightly shaking hand. "You mussed up your hair when you put on your sweatshirt."

She tried to move under his outstretched arm, but he gripped a handful of hair, and her scalp stung with the force of his hold.

"Robin," she shouted at the top of her voice, now thoroughly frightened but there was no answer. Simon held on and just grinned. He swung her around by her hair, and she gasped in pain as he pinned her against the wall with his hateful body. "How the mighty are fallen, where is your knight in shining armour now, the very famous Joe Lawson." He smiled as he saw the surprise momentarily chase the horror from her blue eyes. "Yes, Jeremy told me about him, and asked me to try to find out why he had been here at Smuggler's Cove, as he reckons there is something going on that would be of interest to the press. I might even make enough for my air ticket, if you tell me what you know," he suggested with a sneer.

She tried to hide from him the consternation she felt that he even knew about Joe. "There's nothing to tell," she said with renewed determination. "Get off me," she shouted as the pressure of his body became even more hateful. "Robin, come here a moment please."

"There's no point in shouting for Robin, he went off in the van towards his home half an hour ago, and Maggie is doing the washing with the machines at full volume, she won't hear you. Relax and enjoy yourself, I intend to." He made a determined effort to try and subdue her, and she made a concerted effort and coaxed her tense muscles to loosen momentarily, then when he was not expecting it she pushed him as hard as she could. He held on to her and in so doing he hit her across the cheek with a stinging blow.

The next thing he knew he was face down looking at very close quarters at the coarse Bermuda grass immediately outside the chalet. His arm hurt abominably as he was hauled up again with it bent behind his back, and then he was falling through the air and landing with a splash in the swimming pool. His ardour had certainly been cooled, and when he surfaced he realised the shock and shame he felt at his own behaviour, and he prayed that Morgane was not hurt too badly. He had never hit a woman before in his life, he would never have believed he could behave so badly, and he almost felt like letting himself sink into the depths of the pool. How could he sink so low, and he wasn't thinking about the water in which he was floundering. However, when he surfaced again, it was to see the indomitable grey haired Maggie, holding a large piece of wood, and he could tell by the threatening sight she made that she would bludgeon him if he tried to get out of the pool. Slightly slimmer than Benny, she looked strong and wiry for her age, and the look on her face had made many a youngster in school think twice about disobeying her! She never took her dark eyes off him, and he could hear Maggie talking to the man behind her.

"You must be Joe, see to Morgane will you, I would love to deal with this young man, I just hope he gives me the opportunity," she looked threateningly into the pool.

Joe had arrived a couple of seconds too late to stop the slap that Morgane had received, and he had felt the blow just as much as had she. He dare not move towards the man in the pool because he was frightened of what he might do to him. He had never been a violent man, but his feelings now churned up his insides. His heart felt like breaking as he met Morgane's deep blue eyes. She looked so hurt and confused.

"Morgane, it's me Joe," he said quietly, moving close to her. She looked even more confused if that were possible, and then she blinked in surprise, and put her hand up to her cheek.

"Don't look at me Joe." She paused, closing her eyes, then she burst into tears, and he just made out the words "I'm glad you are here," as he took her in his arms, and she cried against his chest. He took a tissue from a box on the window sill, and she started to mop up the tears.

"Your suit Joe, I'll ruin your suit," she murmured as she noticed how he was dressed. Even in her state of extreme distress, her heartbeat increased as he held her tightly against him.

"Damn the suit, what's going on here?" he asked furiously.

"I'm not sure," she sobbed against his chest, as he soothed her by stroking his hand up and down her shaking back. He put his hand under her chin, and looked into her dark distressed eyes, and heaved a big sigh.

"Come into the house with me Morgane, I have a telephone call to make. Benny's sister-in-law seems to be a wonderful woman, but I would rather we got the police to come and sort out the lout in the pool, because I'm not sure I can keep my hands off him." He slipped his arm under her legs and lifted her, and walked off towards the house. As they passed the pool, Simon was still bobbing about, near the steps, but he was not game to try to get out of the pool. Maggie stood aggressively above him, as though daring him to try it! Morgane looked back over Joe's shoulder, and thought what a picture it would make. The sun was directly ahead, and the pool looked silver.

The head bobbing up and down looked black, and the silhouette of the elderly lady wielding a big stick was a picture in itself. The tall palm trees, looked very exotic, and there was a slight breeze moving the palm fronds back and forth against the blue sky with the odd frothy white cloud looking soft as cotton wool. Was she going mad? What was wrong with her? She closed her eyes against the bright sunlight, and just for a moment forgot the scene behind them. She crumpled the wet tissue, and wrapped her arms around Joe's neck, tucking her head under his chin, and revelling in his nearness. If she was in shock, maybe that wasn't a bad thing, as Joe was here, he was holding her close, and she felt safe and secure, and more content than she had for months. He pushed open the kitchen door with his shoulder and moved slowly into the house. It took all the control he could muster, and all his willpower to even think about moving away from her slight, shaking body.

CHAPTER TWELVE

Joe stood Morgane on her feet, but kept his arm around her whilst he drew the telephone towards him.

"Don't get the police Joe, just tell him to go away and not come back," Morgane said breathlessly. "It will be more trouble than he's worth."

She was completely ignored as he dialled and stood back and waited, as he looked into her worried eyes. He had an odd look in his eyes, and it made her feel uneasy. Surely he didn't think that she had encouraged Simon in any way. She had ignored him as much as she possibly could, without being rude and unpleasant. Joe must have spoken to the police, for he put down the telephone, and indicated that she should take a seat at the kitchen table. She sighed deeply as whenever they sat together at this table they seemed to have some sort of misunderstanding! She felt bereft, as his hands left her shoulders, and he moved to the kitchen door.

"I'll be back in a minute, I must just check on Maggie and your unhappy suitor. Then maybe you can give me some explanation of the situation." His tone was enigmatic, and she wondered what he was thinking. She was also extremely embarrassed that poor Maggie had been drawn into the situation, and also the police. As for Joe, she could hardly believe that he was here. Why was he here, had he brought proof of some kind with him? Was today to be the last day of uncertainty? She stood up, and although feeling dizzy, she moved as quickly as she could to the stairs, and climbed up to her room, and closed the door thankfully.

She climbed onto the bed, and after a couple of minutes she heard what must be the police motorcycle coming up the drive. She put her head under the pillow to drown the sound. Soon she would be ready to go downstairs again and face the questioning. The trouble was she didn't have many answers!

Joe found Maggie standing as he had left her, ready for action. The bedraggled young man looked very unhappy and was shivering as he sat on the steps of the pool, with his lower half still submerged. Just then a police motorcycle arrived, and the vehicle swung around with a flourish, ready for departure, and a very large policeman possibly in his mid thirties walked with interest to join the trio at the poolside. He removed his sunglasses, and the white of his eyes, and the little bit of grey at his temples looked very white against his dark skin. He had had a very boring day, but this looked as though it might be interesting! He looked closely at the man in the pool.

"Well, hello Simon. Still managing to get into trouble I see," he remarked quite pleasantly. Simon stood, and walked stiffly out of the pool, it was the first time that he could remember being pleased to see the police! He was very wary of the old woman, and not at all certain that she would not carry out her threats, if he moved. He was surprised when she patted the policeman on the shoulder, and smiled into his craggy face.

"Nice to see you boy! You seem to have done all right for yourself, and I always knew you'd turn out fine. It seems a long time, but I had this lad in my class at school." She smiled at Joe, whilst indicating the policeman, and then shook Joe's hand. "I'm Maggie, you must be Joe, pleased to meet you. Good timing Joe!" She moved off towards the house and turned back to give further instructions. She indicated Simon. "*He* can use the shower and dressing gown in the chalet, and get out of his wet clothes. I'll go and put the kettle on to boil, you Joe can come inside until the police car gets here."

The policeman gave a rueful smile as he glanced at Joe, "Sounds all right to me. She always was right you know. Anyway she will, not doubt, let us know if the young lady needs to see a doctor. We can get some of the preliminary questions over, before the car arrives." He indicated the chalet, and taking the cold and bedraggled Simon by the arm, marched him inside. Soon the shower could be heard, as Joe waited outside for a moment, and then followed Maggie as instructed!

He was desperate to see Morgane, but had to think about the consequences. How much did Maggie know about Morgane and himself, she was obviously aware of his existence, from what she had just said. How much had Simon and Jeremy found out? Probably nothing, it would be conjecture on their part, and they would he hoping for a pay-out for a story. They probably had no idea of the real possibilities. As soon as he had received the message from Benny, via David Smithson, he had booked the first available flight, which had arrived this morning. It had arrived on time, but they had a long wait to reclaim their luggage. He was sorry that he had not been able to get here sooner, and then Morgane would not have had to deal with Simon on her own.

He noticed the tools, left by Robin by the side of the drive. It was not like Robin to leave his tools lying about - it looked as though he had left in a hurry. Where was Benny? He must have a word with her before he spoke to the police. The main thing was to make sure that Morgane had not been hurt, and then to try and keep her name out of any investigations the police deemed necessary. It was imperative that he and Morgane should finally find out the truth about their relationship, things could not go on this way. They were both in limbo, neither able to get on with the rest of their lives with this hanging over them.

He walked into the kitchen, and found that Maggie was again organising things to everyone's advantage.

"Please nip upstairs Joe, and make sure Morgane is all right. I went up before, but she must still be in shock. Tell her not to come down until she is ready. Oh, please tell her I have rung Benny, and she and Robin will be here shortly. Benny wasn't well this morning, but feels fine now. Robin had to take his son to the hospital, he really wasn't at all well, and they think it may be chicken pox, so they've brought him back home for his mother to look after. You can't be too careful with children. Off you go then." She looked at him for a moment, as he stood there, was he bashful, she was under the impression that they knew each other well.

"Where is Morgane, Maggie, I understand there have been a few renovations since I left?"

"Quite right, sorry, she's on the top floor, there's a new staircase, follow that." She quickly poured a cup of tea, and handed it to Joe. "Take this with you, she probably needs it. As soon as Benny gets here I'll send her up to Morgane. She won't be satisfied until she has seen her."

Joe paused outside the bedroom door at the top of the new stairs. It was not a good idea that he should visit her in the intimacy of her bedroom, but he had to know if there was anyone else, besides Benny, that knew of their circumstances. He had already decided that the policeman in charge of the investigation would have to be made aware of *all* the circumstances, but surely he could bring charges against this Simon character for non-payment of his accommodation bill, rather than bring Morgane's private life into the public eye. For him self he was no longer bothered, the press could do what they liked, but again he would prefer to keep Morgane out of the limelight. If Simon had a history of violence, then it would be another story altogether.

"Morgane, can I come in? Maggie has sent you a cup of tea," Joe tapped lightly on the bedroom door.

"Come in," replied a muffled voice. Joe opened the door, and slowly entered. She was sitting up on her bed, with her head in her hands.

"Are you all right," he asked worriedly.

"Yes thank you Joe, just a slight headache. He pulled my hair, and caught my cheek with his hand. But I don't want to press charges. Nor do I care about the money he owes for his room, I just want them to send him away."

She reached for the tea, and started to sip it gratefully.

Joe moved her hair slightly back from her cheek, which was now looking red, and which would probably come out in a bruise by tomorrow. He drew in his breath, and suddenly moved over to the window.

"I don't think he should get away with that. For all we know he might make a habit of it. We will wait and see what the police say, and I think you should see a doctor, and if necessary get it photographed." Just for that moment Joe wished he had smashed his fist into the man's face, instead of throwing him into the pool!

He watched as she sipped her tea. Her hair was dishevelled and her long lashes were spread across her cheeks, both of which seemed to be highly coloured. He felt like moving over to the bed, and taking her in his arms, and running his fingers through her long golden hair. Instead he moved into the next room through an archway, and started to look at the stacked canvasses, and a few water colours.

"It is quite private up here, and seems a good place to paint," he said looking out of the window towards the swimming pool at the side of the house. "Did you find the picture I left for you?" He stopped and picked up a painting, removing the blanket covering. "I see you did," he finished thoughtfully. He considered this to be one of his best paintings, if not *the* best!

"Benny hung it in the lounge, and I didn't want to keep looking at myself," she said apologetically, coming into the archway between the two rooms, gingerly trying to get the brush through her long hair.

He seemed to ignore her apology, and continued to look through her paintings, and right at the back, he found the one she had done of him. He walked over to the window with it to get the light. Morgane disappeared into the other room, covered in embarrassment. What a cheek to think she could paint him, because she had not the talent to do him justice she thought to herself!

344

"Why are you here Joe, I wasn't expecting you?" He appeared in the archway.

"What do you suppose would have happened this afternoon if I hadn't turned up?" he asked cynically, he frowned, and paced up and down with his hands deep in his trouser pockets.

"I didn't encourage him you know," she replied quickly, "I had given him no reason to believe that his attentions would be welcome. I have kept out of his way as much as possible, it was unfortunate that Maggie let him the room, but she thought she was doing the right thing. Rather than upset anyone, I thought the two weeks would go quickly, but they seemed to go on forever. Thank you for what you did." She realised how tardy she had been in thanking him, when Robin hadn't come to her call for help, she had been in deep trouble. The consequences of Joe not being there didn't bear thinking about!

Joe continued his pacing, and Morgane wished he would stop, it was most unsettling. Eventually he stopped, and stared out of the window, then he turned and his intense eyes studied her.

"Benny wrote to me, about the torn up cheque. I wasn't worried about that, as we could always issue a new one. She also mentioned your new suitor, and was worried because she thought you might let him take some of your paintings, also that he might be bent on taking advantage of you with regard to your letting him stay here. I thought she must have got things wrong, because you already had Martin, who I believed was coming over to stay with you at some time. I called to see you at his place, but you had already left the UK. He seemed mightily pleased that you were going to get a new computer and, therefore, you would be able to keep in close contact. That's why, David Smithson and I decided that the cheque

345

would be useful to you." He stood and gazed at her enquiringly.

She squirmed a little inside, feeling ashamed that she had let Joe think that she and Martin were more than good friends. She looked at him, and wondered if he could tell, from her face, how guilty she felt.

"Martin and I are just good friends. I assume that Mary wasn't there when you called. Mary is also a very good friend. I was a bridesmaid at their wedding, soon after we graduated." She was unable to tell from his cool expressionless eyes what he felt about this news. "I'm sorry I should have explained the situation at the time, but we weren't on very good terms just then."

"I see," he said coldly, and she wondered if he did! He continued after a short pause. "I had not replied by then to Benny's letter, and she telephoned David at the office. She explained that she had seen Simon Granger in Par-la-ville Park in Hamilton, talking very seriously with Jeremy Dixon. I then began to wonder if Benny was correct and that you were getting close to Simon and had told him about our possible relationship, and more importantly, the money you are to inherit. I should mention now, Morgane, that the amount you will receive will be vastly more than you are probably expecting. It has been invested for a considerable time and very well indeed."

"I was never close to Simon. I wasn't interested in him, and I never told him anything about my private life, or you. Simon was born in Bermuda, and has been staying with his brother. He could have met Jeremy during his holiday here, and if Jeremy is on the island again, it could be that he is still trying to work out why you were here. Here you are *again*, that should give him more cause for thought."

It now seemed to be her turn to pace the room, and she joined Joe by the window. Just then a police car drew up in the drive, and two men got out of the car, one in plain clothes.

Joe turned to Morgane, and placing his hands on her shoulders, looked into her worried blue eyes. "Don't say anything Morgane. I will have a word with the chap in charge, tell him the situation as best I can and hopefully, neither Simon nor Jeremy will find out what they so urgently want to know. The policeman who arrived on the motorcycle knew Simon, who apparently has been in trouble with the law before. I'll go down now, and you follow in a few minutes. Is that all right with you Morgane?" She nodded and he turned and left the room.

As she continued to look out of the window, Robin arrived in his van, and helped his mother out of the passenger seat. Benny had been unwell this morning, but where was Robin when she needed him? He seemed to be there every time she had turned round over the last two weeks. She waited a few minutes then after a quick look in the mirror (her face didn't look too bad) she thought she had better make her way downstairs ready to make her statement to the police.

She met Benny on the landing, puffing her way upstairs. Benny pulled her into her arms, after looking into her wan face. "You all right luv? This should never have happened. If only I hadn't been unwell, and Robin hadn't had to take Chrissie and Robin Junior to the hospital, this would never have happened."

"Are they all right, what happened to Chrissie and little Robin?" She felt guilty for putting herself before Robin's family, even if only in her thoughts.

347

"Don't worry Morgane, they are fine. Chrissie thought little Robin had a fever, and at first they didn't bother, because I had been unwell, but I was getting better by the minute, they thought he must have something similar. But he seemed to get much worse. As it turns out he may have chicken pox, and they have sent him home. If it is then I suppose the rest of the children will get it."

"Thank goodness it isn't anything too serious," Morgane replied with relief, and they started back down the stairs.

"I haven't spoken properly with our Maggie yet, where was she, she promised to look out for you?" Benny huffed.

"Is that what you have all been doing, looking out for me? I did begin to notice that there was always someone around, except when I took off in the jeep to do some painting. I must admit, Benny, I was rather glad about that, as I didn't relish being left alone with Simon, he was becoming rather pressing about the paintings, and seemed to be there every time I turned around." She smiled gratefully at Benny.

"Well it was Robin who remembered Simon from school. He was a bit younger than Robin, but was always in trouble, and never had any friends, as he always did something to drive them away. Apparently he was selfish and a bit unpredictable, to put it mildly. I admit I didn't like him when he arrived here, and that was before Robin told me about him."

"He told me today, when I refused to let him take any of my paintings, that he had been asked to leave by his brother. You know, Mr Granger to whom I have been selling some of my paintings. That's where I met Simon. Apparently he took some things from the family home and sold them, keeping the money for himself presumably. He said all the money had gone, and it seems he had no intention of paying our bill." Morgane replied trying not to think of their recent traumatic confrontation in the chalet. She was dreading facing up to the people in the room, but derived a little comfort from the thought that Joe would be there. It didn't bear thinking about what might have happened if he hadn't turned up just at that time. She shivered, and Benny squeezed her shoulders before they went into the room to join the others, who were all sat around the kitchen table with Maggie in charge!

She had the feeling that the police were pleased with the fact that they had some function to perform. Not much happened except for traffic accidents on the islands!

CHAPTER THIRTEEN

On entering the lounge, Morgane was relieved to find that Joe seemed to have arranged everything with the police officer, and Simon was already being escorted to the police station to be charged. Apparently, he had asked for his brother, in St. George's, to be contacted and he was now on his way to join them. The police officer with the motorcycle took a statement from Morgane, who insisted that Simon should not be charged with actual bodily harm, as she refused to be seen by a doctor. She insisted that the blow she had received was a mistake. However, he would be charged for none payment of his bill, and his brother had also intimated that he would be making a complaint about the taking without permission of the two antique clocks. Morgane was relieved to find that she would not have to attend the Court Hearing as Simon had admitted both offences. He had also promised his brother that he had learned his lesson, and would like to stay on the island and get a responsible job!

A few days later Morgane received two letters, one from each of the brothers, apologising profusely, and thanking her for not pressing the more serious charge. She was grateful that things would now be resolved and she hoped that Simon would be true to his word, and not offend in the future.

Joe stayed on in the chalet, and spent most of his time, during the next two days, touring the island on his hired motorcycle. She had hoped that things would be easier between them, but since the dramatic day of his unexpected arrival this was not the case. He had not brought any of his painting materials, and even though Morgane had said that he might use any of hers, he had not as yet taken her up on this offer.

He had not mentioned how long he would be staying on the islands, and she decided that neither of them would be able to get on with their lives as they should, unless something was resolved. She realised that she had been the one to state that she did not believe there was any chance that she was Joe's half-sister and leave the matter there, but that had not resolved anything. She must ask Joe to put things in motion to find out one way or the other without delay. Now that Joe's father was dead she wasn't even sure that there was a way to do this.

In the late afternoon, Morgane could not settle to painting, or cleaning, and decided to take a last swim for the season. Robin intended to empty the pool very soon, to start any necessary renovations. A few tiles needed replacing and there was quite a bit of re-grouting necessary. The day was warm enough, but the water felt quite cold. However after a few quick lengths, it felt quite pleasant. The exercise was welcome, and twenty minutes later she climbed out of the pool feeling much better. However this feeling of well-being was soon to be dissipated.

She wrapped herself in a large towel, and stopped to look at the darkening sky, a swirling wind seemed to be rising and the palm fronds above showered the pool with debris. She gave a shiver and was moving towards the house, when she heard the sound of the motorcycle hired by Joe. She hadn't realised it before, but she must have listened for it over the last few days, because she had no doubt as to the driver of the machine that she could hear on the road outside the property. She paused, and Joe turned the corner into the drive and parked next to the house.

Although there were a lot of pressing matters in the UK which needed his attention, Joe had decided to stay in Bermuda until he was convinced that Morgane had recovered from the bad experience with Simon Granger. He removed his helmet and light waterproof jacket, and placed them on the machine. He watched as Morgane walked towards him, and even wrapped in a large towel, he struggled to keep the physical awareness he felt under iron control. The last thing she needed was another unwanted suitor. A very unsuitable suitor to boot!

"You need to get inside Morgane, there is a cold wind," he said as she walked towards him.

"I know, but I think it is time we had a serious talk Joe. Things can't be allowed to continue as they are," she had been bolstering herself up all day to finally admit to Joe that she had been wrong, and no amount of sticking her head in the sand would resolve anything! "I have been thinking and..."

"Hardly the time or place Morgane. When you have showered and changed would be more appropriate." He sounded quite harsh, and she again wondered if Joe thought she had played hot and cold with Simon, and was partially to blame for what had happened? She was aware of her own feeling of guilt, which probably brought these thoughts to her mind. Guilt for not wishing to upset Maggie, when she made the unwanted booking and, therefore, letting things take their course when she should have told Simon he could not stay. She had never felt at ease in his company, which had always been thrust upon her, never at her own instigation! "For your own good will you go and get dressed?" he said through gritted teeth, with unconscious authority. This was like a red rag to a bull, now that she had at last plucked up enough courage to confront him, instead of just pushing everything to the back of her mind and hoping it would go away!

He put his hands on her shoulders and held her at arms length. She now felt extremely humiliated. Did he think she was now coming on to him! Blue eyes blazed furiously at him. How dare he think she was so easy! Antagonism blazed between them, as she caught his speculative eyes on her angry face. It seemed a long time, but could only have been a second or two that they glared at each other, when his eyes lifted from her face and he looked over her shoulder. Then she too heard the sound of a motor vehicle.

Morgane turned from Joe, to see the taxi come to a halt, and before the driver could open the door, out stepped Jill Smithson, with her usual look of distaste as she glanced at Morgane, whom she then ignored. Her manners left much to be desired!

"I haven't booked in yet Joe. Where do you suggest I stay," she smiled lovingly at him. "The Hamilton Princess?"

Morgane looked on as Joe moved towards the girl. She wasn't sure whether he looked relieved or pleased, by the timely intrusion. However, she had to admire the tenacious way the other girl pursued Joe! She felt at a definite disadvantage as she looked at the beautifully clad younger girl, as she tossed her head to make her dark hair shimmer in the weak sun. Morgane wrapped the towel tightly around her shivering body, and patted her wet hair with the corner of the now damp towel.

When Joe turned he found that Morgane had disappeared into the house. He helped Jill back into the vehicle, and got in beside her. After a couple of seconds the vehicle turned in the drive, and then drove off towards Hamilton.

Morgane ran quickly up the stairs, and into the shower, where she would not allow tears to join with the strong stream of warm water. She was furious with herself and Joe. It seemed that he didn't want to hear what she had to say, whilst all the while he had badgered her to agree to take the money, and to do anything to resolve the situation. Now she wanted to settle the situation once and for all, he seemed to have other more important things to deal with, like Jill. He would have to make the next move, as it would not come from her! Her resolve was hardened when, as far as she knew, Joe did not arrive back at Smuggler's Cove that evening. She should know she had been awake most of the night.

The next day brought sunshine and heavy showers, with a brisk wind.

Benny came for a couple of hours in the morning, and wanted to know where Joe was. Maggie informed her sister in law, that he had a girlfriend staying at the Hamilton Princess, and he had rung to say he didn't want breakfast. Upon which information Benny did not comment, but gave Morgane an old fashioned look which could have meant anything. They were all enjoying a morning cup of coffee, and Morgane finished hers and moved over to the sink with her cup and saucer.

"I think I'll go and get a few sketches done, if you don't need me here," she said looking out of the window at the now sunny sky. Their only guest at the moment was Joe, always supposing that he chose to return.

"Don't stay out too late." Benny advised. "Mike thinks that the weather might get a bit rough tonight, or tomorrow. He is not as convinced as the TV people that the hurricane will miss the islands. I'll just go and get the lamps checked over, and get the candles around the place. If Mike is right then we may need them if the hurricane does move this way, and the electricity goes off again."

"Thank you Benny, I won't be late. I've heard about the odd hurricane hitting the islands, but that's never happened when I've been here. Usually they seem to be in the Caribbean, or southern states of the United States of America."

"Well if it looks as if it might get close, I'll ask Robin to come back and help you prepare for it." Benny said thoughtfully.

"There's no need, I'm sure Maggie knows what to do, we can manage everything between us. Anyway Robin will have his own home to prepare, and yours of course." She glanced at Maggie requesting her agreement.

"The media don't think it will come this way, but I do know what to do Benny," Maggie said confidently, as she looked out at the blue sky.

"Well, I'll be getting back home to Mike. The charter fishing boats are not going out today. See you both tomorrow." She pulled on a cardigan, and collected her shopping bag.

"I'll give you a lift home Benny, and then I think I'll go along South Shore Road, and stop at Horse Shoe Bay. I believe there are a lot of jelly fish coming ashore, and I've only ever seen one or two of the Portuguese man-of-war. If I remember correctly they are a nice purple colour. I might get a different type of picture for a change." Morgane said as they went out to the Jeep.

"Watch out for the long tentacles, they are really very dangerous. Whatever you do, don't touch any."

"Oh, Benny I won't do that. I'm only going to look at the ones that have been washed up, and I know, they can still sting."

They travelled in silence until Morgane turned the Jeep into the parking area near to Benny's home.

"Have you and Joe been arguing?" Benny asked, watching her young friend's face carefully.

"No more than usual Benny, we seem to rub each other up the wrong way. I do appreciate the fact that you contacted Joe, and also that he came over here. I also intend to get things sorted out as soon as possible. That is, when he has enjoyed his little holiday with Jill Smithson. He never did say how long he was staying."

Benny climbed down from the Jeep, and looked as though she would reply, but instead she gave Morgane a speculative look, then waved, and headed towards the house and Mike. His grey head nodded in acknowledgement, and he waved to Morgane from the side of the house, as she drove away.

She drove back passed her home and towards Hamilton, making sure that she did not look towards the Hamilton Princess Hotel. The ride along the South Shore Road was accomplished on very quiet roads, and she pulled into Horse Shoe Bay car park, to find there was only two other vehicles. She gathered her sketch pad, and walked along the sands, where the sand was slightly humped which showed how high the tide had been. She saw many of the jelly fish with the blue/purple bladder like float, and sketched and made a note of the colours she wanted to remember.

Retracing her steps she walked along towards Jobson's Cove. The small cove was surrounded by enormous rocks, which were sparsely covered with exotic shrubs, and architectural-like succulents. Steps had been cut into the rocks, leading down to the water level in the large rock to the right of the cove. The water in the cove was still, as the opening to the open sea was only a couple of metres wide. A few weeks ago this little cove would have been populated by many families swimming and sunbathing, today she was the lone occupant. It was an excellent place to snorkel, and particularly safe for children. She removed her sandals and walked from the warm sand into the shallow water, which felt surprisingly warm. Inside the cove she noticed that the water was a clear aquamarine where it was shallow, and through the opening to the sea the water was as blue as the sky.

She collected a clear plastic box from her bag, and walked back into the water, and held the box in the surface of the water. She almost jumped back in shock as she saw the small black and white fish, now looking much bigger as magnified by the box and water, but it was the small worm which had made her jump, and now looked like a snake curled up on the sand! She stood and made a note of the colours she had seen. As she moved off she just missed standing on one of the jelly fish tentacles. She was shaken by the near miss as without attention she could have been seriously ill, or worse!

As she walked back through the sand dunes to Horseshoe Bay, she was surprised to see that the sky was now grey with clouds. Towards the west they seemed to be much darker, and she wondered if the hurricane was, in fact, coming this way. The swell of the sea seemed to be much more noticeable. She got to the jeep and noticed that the other vehicles had already departed the car park. She drove along the South Shore Road back towards Hamilton, and the roads were very quiet, but the threatened hurricane seemed to be passing them by. The wind was quite strong, but manageable. However, she was relieved to be back home at Smuggler's Cove and she wondered if Joe was safely in the Hamilton Princess Hotel, entertaining Jill, there was no sign of occupation in the chalet. She glanced at the house where Maggie had already put on many of the lights.

Maggie suggested they had better close the wooden shutters to the windows, and make sure everything in the garden had either been tied down, or put safely away, even though the hurricane appeared to passing them by, they would still get the strong winds and possibly a lot of rain. At least they would get well stocked with a good supply of water. Maggie also lit one of the lamps, and made sure that candles were handy, and the means of lighting them was to hand. She also filled two large flasks with boiling water.

The wind was now much stronger and getting louder by the minute as they heard the heavy rain join in the cacophony of sound. According to the television they still maintained that the hurricane would pass Bermuda. Morgane was upstairs in her room, having changed into a track suit for extra warmth, and looked out to the chalet. Thinking that if there was a light, she would definitely go out and ask Joe to come into the house where it would be much safer. There was no light. She then realised that the upper floor shutters on the back of the house had not been closed and fixed. Obviously Maggie didn't think the wind was that bad. Still Morgane thought she would keep an eye on things.

A couple of hours later Morgane admired the way Maggie took the whole thing in her stride. She had her cup of cocoa as usual, and made her way towards the stairs, pausing by the telephone, which she lifted up and listened to with interest. She put the receiver down immediately. "Thought so, the 'phones are already off. That means the computer will be off too I suppose. I don't much like mobile 'phones but I guess they can be useful." She smiled and continued on her way to bed, with a smothered yawn.

An hour later, the wind was still howling, and debris was being blown against the shutters of the windows. Morgane decided she would go to bed and try to listen to some music on her earphones that would blot out the noise of the storm, and also take her mind off Joe. Where could he be? First she went to the kitchen door at the back of the house, and confirmed for herself the fact that the front of the house was getting the brunt of the storm, and thankfully all the shutters were closed on that side.

She was about to close the door, when she noticed the silhouette of a figure on the drive, nearing the chalet. She closed the door behind her, and went towards him.

"Joe, come in the house, it will be much safer." She could hear the relief she felt at knowing he was safe in her own voice.

"I had to come to check that you and Maggie and the property were safe," he called to her over the wind, which suddenly seemed much louder. There was a loud grinding sound. They both turned towards the sound, and Morgane thought she was going dizzy, as one of the large palm trees at the bottom of the drive seemed to be moving at a strange angle.

There was another loud crack, and as if in slow motion, she moved towards Joe and he was coming towards her. She felt his arm around her back as they hit the ground, and seemed to roll over and over, and although they stopped moving, all around them the top of the palm tree seemed to take forever to settle on the ground. Morgane felt winded and very sore where the spiky brown husks seemed to be in her hair and covering her body, except where Joe protected her. She lifted one arm but could not push aside the heavy weight of palm fronds above her. "Joe, Joe, can you hear me. Are you all right?" but there was no answer to her anxious cry.

Tears of frustration squeezed from her eyes. Something was very wrong, she couldn't see anything, but could feel everything, every ache and pain, particularly her heart thumping. She tried to pull herself together as she concentrated on trying to hear or feel Joe's pulse. She was lying on one of Joe's arms, and his other arm lying across her left side felt ominously heavy.

CHAPTER FOURTEEN

Morgane slid her hand down Joe's arm until she came to his wrist, and with considerable effort she moved her fingers into the position where she thought she should feel his pulse. She was unable to feel his pulse, she was probably in the wrong position, and gave a whimper of dread. She then felt his hand move and grip hers tightly. The relief she felt was intense, and tears ran unchecked down her grimy cheeks, but she couldn't move to wipe them away, and besides that they were in complete darkness.

"Are you hurt Morgane, I must have been momentarily stunned," he said into her ear, the wind and rain were still making a deafening noise around them.

She tightened the muscles of her legs and arms. "Everything seems to work, I just ache all over, but can't move much at all, we seem to be trapped. What about you?" She felt him trying to move, with a little success. "Joe I can't see anything at all. What is going on?"

"Just after I noticed the tree starting to fall, the lights went out in the house. They have probably gone out all over the islands. The tree seems to have fallen behind us, between us and the house. We will have to try to push our way out from under it. Can you move forward at all?" By now his voice seemed quite normal, and she was beginning to relax slightly.

She pushed her arms through the rain sodden palm fronds in front of her body, and pushed against solid rock. They were trapped between the fallen palm tree and solid rock!

"Solid rock Joe." Her hands were still feeling around as much as she could. "I think we are pressed against the bottom of the water catchment area. I can hear it running down into the grid and overflowing."

"What about the door. Can you feel the door down to the cove?" Joe asked with a small degree of hope in his voice.

"Wait a minute," she said stretching her hand as far as possible to the right, and her fingers wrapped around part of the cold ironwork door. "I can't reach up to the door opening. With our luck it will be locked. If not we can push it open, as it opens inwards to the steps," she replied in desperation.

"If I can raise the branch immediately above you, do you think you can reach it?

"I'll try, but don't strain yourself Joe, someone will find us eventually."

"Not until it comes light. If Maggie had heard the tree crash down, she would have been out here by now. She must sleep very deeply and just as well as she does everything else. On the count of three I'll try to lift the part of the tree holding you down. Hold on to the door if you can, I don't want you falling down the steps. Ready?" He was already drawing in deep breaths in readiness.

She nodded, then realised he couldn't see her. "Yes, ready when you are, but be careful Joe."

Joe counted slowly, and on the count of three she scrambled into a kneeling position, and reached the door, which swung open in front of her, causing her to fall forward, and her hands landed on the second step. She clasped tightly with one hand on the open door, and swung her legs around, then holding firmly to the door she managed to get a foothold, and stood upright.

"It's open Joe, I'm on the steps, can you follow?"

She heard the tree falling back into its original position. "When I get my breath back," he gasped hopefully.

"Joe, you will have to be careful. I'll hold the door as near closed as I can, you mustn't fall down the steps. The first few steps are wet and slippery. We'll have to hold on to each other, each of us holding the side, step down as one, or we might push each other down. You know how steep the steps are." Now they were almost safe she was beginning to panic. She had a fluttering feeling in her chest, they might have been better just waiting for the tree to be moved in the light of day!

She felt the door move, and then his arm was securely around her waist, and they clung together for a while. She revelled in the warmth of his body next to her, but was conscious of the water running down her back, and could feel it dripping off his chin onto her cheek.

"Forty two steps down to the right, is the room the smugglers used. We'll be more comfortable in there, at least the room will be dry," she said with relief removing only one arm from around his waist as they slowly moved down counting the steps. "It is about a metre to the right, and it opens up into a room, but the doorway is quite low for you, don't knock yourself out Joe. It's a pity we haven't a torch, or some kind of light. Forty two, can you feel the opening?"

"Yes, well done Morgane. We may have a light if there are any candles in here, as I have a lighter if it's still working as it must be wet through with the rain and wind." They shuffled forward, not losing contact with each other.

"But you don't smoke," she said with surprise.

"Ah, but I occasionally light other people's."

This remark, brought Jill into her mind, and she almost removed her arm from around his waist. Almost. Joe's hand was against the roof of the small tunnel, and when he felt the free space above his head, he slowly stood up with a relieved sigh, keeping contact with Morgane.

On the second attempt the lighter worked, and Morgane quickly found a candle in a holder, and shaded the candle with her hands as Joe lit it. The warm glow was very comforting. Soon they had three candles lit, and could see the contents of the room. Morgane moved to a metal chest, but it was locked, and after a quick search in the dim light, she realised there was no key to be found. She had been hoping they might find something inside to wrap themselves in. She was now shivering and wrapped her arms around her upper body, to try and generate some warmth. Joe removed his thin damp jacket, and wrapped it around Morgane's shoulders.

"You need that," she objected, but he pulled it tight around her and indicated that they should sit on one of the boxes. It was filled with books and journals, which fell out onto the damp floor when he tipped the box on one side, so that they might both sit down.

"Were you aware that these old books and papers were in here," he asked with interest, "they seem very old and smell quite musty like an ancient church," he said turning one over towards the candle so that he might read the words on the front. "It's some sort of ship's manifest. I'm sure the local Museum would be very interested in reading these." He lifted them off the damp stone floor, and placed them carefully on another box filled with similar books.

"Come here, we will have to keep each other warm, we could be here a few hours," he said squinting at the watch on his wrist in the candlelight. "According to this, if it's still going, we could have another six hours or more to wait before anyone gets the tree moved."

Morgane nestled in to Joe's side, his arm was welcoming across her shoulders, and she laid her cheek on his chest, and one arm around his waist. "I don't suppose you have your mobile with you Morgane?" he asked, his warm breath welcome on her forehead.

"No, it's on the kitchen table, but I don't suppose we would get a signal from in here anyway. We won't have been missed yet, seeing as Maggie is sleeping through the storm. If she sleeps in after daylight, we could always go down to the cove, and see if there are any boats about."

"We may have to wait Morgane, people could be hurt. We have been very lucky we could have been killed or seriously hurt. I can't hear very much from outside, the storm could well have passed over."

"You were stunned for a few seconds Joe, you could suffer from a delayed reaction, let me see your eyes," she ordered, and gazed into them with the help of a candle she held up. She couldn't decipher the expression she saw there, and put her cheek back onto his chest in confusion. She now felt totally aware of their closeness, and just for the moment decided to go with the flow, and make the most of the relief and pleasure she felt in being so close to him. They needed each other just now, whether they were half brother and sister or not!

"I take it they are normal, not rolling about," he said and she could hear the smile in his voice, as his arms tightened around her comfortingly.

"Joe. When I came out of the pool the other day, I only wanted to tell you that I was ready to do whatever you wanted to try and determine once and for all whether *your father* was also mine. I got the impression that you thought I was coming on to you, and I thought you had got that idea because of Simon. I never did encourage him you know. I never gave him any reason to think I would welcome his advances." She waited for him to answer, but the last thing she wanted was to start another argument with him. Not when they seemed so comfortable together!

His arm tightened around her, and when she would have looked at him, he moved his hand to keep her head pressed against his chest. "I never did believe that of you Morgane, I know you too well. What I was struggling with was the thought of your lovely body, so scantily clad underneath that towel. You must know how much I am attracted to you, and at least for now, we can't do anything about it. I'll get in touch with David Smithson, and get him to contact the medical men, and see what can be done. I have no way of knowing whether Dad ever had a DNA test, and I'm not at all sure that if we had blood tests it would prove anything. Now that is out of the way, try and get some rest." He sounded jaded, and she knew that if they had not been in such an intimate situation, he would not have explained his feelings. He had not, however, found it necessary to explain his pleased smile upon the arrival of Jill.

She would not previously have believed it of him, but now it seemed to her that anyone in a swimsuit who was reasonably attractive would have received his attention.

She must have dozed, for when she awoke, she was still held close to his chest, but they were both stretched out on three of the boxes, which Joe must have placed close together. He had tucked her body in front of his, and she revelled in the warmth of his long body against her own. He was breathing evenly, and she realised he was asleep. She relaxed, feeling at least partly warm and comfortable, and slept until Joe shook her awake.

She sat up and rubbed her eyes. "Is it morning?"

"Yes, the storm is over and if you listen you will hear Robin and Mike cutting up the tree with a chain saw. They shouted down the steps, hoping we were safe inside. Maggie had them up at the crack of dawn, as soon as she saw the tree and realised you were not in your room."

"Was it bad, was anyone hurt?"

"Two or three people with broken limbs and a number of trees are down. Apparently, all the trees fell, and the electricity went off with the same heavy blast of wind. Most of the storm missed the islands, and I have been down to the cove, and was amazed to see a lovely sunny morning, with only a slight breeze, and a bit of debris on the shore line. Maggie was out there, and wouldn't move until I answered their calls. She says she is making breakfast, and the water is good and hot. The electricity has been on for over an hour now."

"That sounds wonderful, I'm longing for a hot shower." she felt a bit guilty, she had been wearing Joe's coat all night. "You must be cold Joe."

"I admit a shower will be very welcome. There's only one problem, the tree falling broke some of the windows in the chalet, and Maggie says I have to move into the house."

"Fine, we are very lucky if we only have a few windows to replace and a palm tree to cut up and dispose of." She paused. "What about Jill at the Hamilton Princess?"

"What about her? When I left she was enjoying the attention of *most* of the male guests."

She wondered if he was really as happy about that, as he sounded! However, she would worry about that when she had inspected Smugglers Cove and had breakfast and a hot shower!

Much later, the box of books and journals that Joe had carried up from the smuggler's hide-away, was on the centre of the kitchen table. The books and records were very old, and Morgane was sure that they must have belonged to a much earlier owner of the property. Her mother had not known about their existence, at least she had never mentioned them.

Maggie, Benny, Mike, Robin, Joe and Morgane all sat around the table, each perusing part of the find. The items in the box appeared to be over two hundred years old. Joe glanced across at Morgane, who was totally engrossed in the book she was perusing closely.

"You will have to do something to preserve these Morgane, they need proper conservation," he said catching her eye. He seemed perfectly well, having had a headache tablet after getting cleaned up, and moving his belongings from the chalet to the house. The others seemed just as enthralled, as Morgane knew she would be, if she could just forget that Joe had received a blow to the head, whilst protecting her, and she was constantly watching to make sure that he was not suffering any after effects.

"Do you think I should contact the Maritime Museum?" she asked, her mind already made up. "There could have been a building here before this house."

"Brilliant idea, ring them now," Joe seemed really excited by the find. "Robin and I will bring up the other boxes, as they might be just as interesting as this one." He caught Robin's eye, and they set off out of the kitchen door with great enthusiasm. She smiled, and went to telephone the Museum, as luckily the phone had been restored at the same time as the electricity.

Morgane was put through to the curator of the Maritime Museum, who listened with interest when told about the find, and also the location. She described a number of the papers and journals, and the curator was so excited that he suggested a visit to the house, and a visit to the "site," as he called the room hewn out of rock. He promised to call the next day, and when told of this, Joe continued to look through the artefacts, with the help of Robin and Mike whenever they could spare the time. Unfortunately for Robin a lot of debris had to be cleared, both at Smuggler's Cove and at his own and his parent's home.

Although invited to have dinner with them, by Maggie, Joe declined the offer and disappeared in the direction of Hamilton. Morgane was pleased that he had not invited Jill to Smuggler's Cove, for just at the moment she felt too pent up with current events to put up with jealousy and threats such as those delivered by Jill in London. Jill's determination to win Joe over had certainly not diminished. Morgane did not know what to believe any more. Joe had admitted an attraction towards her but that was all, and that would not have happened if they had not been forced into each other's company for most of the night, and part of the day!

She heard Joe return to the house that evening. She had not been aware that she had been listening for him, but once he had arrived she enjoyed the best nights sleep for months. She certainly made up for the lack of sleep the previous night.

The next day the curator arrived and she directed him down to the cove and to the hidden room. He was enthralled with what he had seen, and was equally excited about the journals and papers. With Morgane's agreement he rang the Bermuda Archives, and within twenty minutes the woman in charge was equally enthralled. After spending a couple of hours inspecting as much as they could, they suggested that the three boxes should be taken to the Archives where they would be safe, and Morgane would be welcome to come in and watch the progress made in documenting everything. Also that whatever happened to the finds in the future would be her decision.

The next day she invited Joe to go along with her to the Archives to see what progress was being made, and where the artefacts would be stored. He seemed very pleased with the invitation, and they spent a very interesting three hours there. He did not mention Jill, and Morgane wondered if she was still on the island. Also Joe had not said how long he intended to stay. If she asked him he might think that she wished him to go! She was in such an emotional turmoil at the moment, that she didn't know what she wanted!

That evening Joe invited her out for dinner, and Maggie overheard them, and declared that was a lovely idea, now she could take the opportunity to spend the evening over at Benny's, as there were no other guests. Morgane had been about to refuse, but now agreed to go, how could she disappoint Maggie! In truth, she wanted to spend an evening alone with Joe, but felt that this would be storing up trouble for the future. But just for now she would live for the moment and hope for the best.

Joe ordered a taxi to pick them up. When he met her at the foot of the stairs, he stared at her, and seemed a little stunned. He then said that the silver grey chiffon dress was almost as beautiful as was she. He then walked her carefully to the taxi without touching her! Minutes later, the taxi drew up outside the Hamilton Princess Hotel, and Morgane shrank back into the seat. She had been right all along, as she was in for a big disappointment. No doubt, they were here to join Jill! Her first evening outing for months was going to be a complete waste of time and effort!

They entered the large dining room, and it transpired that Joe had reserved a table for two overlooking the Great Sound. He did stop momentarily at another table for two, where Jill and a handsome young man were about to dine. Morgane received a very cool nod of acknowledgement from Jill, but her companion jumped up immediately, and Joe introduced him to Morgane. His name was Dan and he seemed completely enthralled with his dinner partner.

Morgane thoroughly enjoyed the dinner shared with Joe, and they talked none stop about the artefacts they had found, painting, fishing, the islands, and everything except his father and themselves. They both reached for the salt at the same moment, and he wound his fingers with hers, and exerted a warm pressure. He watched with a bemused smile as her cheeks took on a pink glow, and she lowered her eyes to her plate in confusion. She was slightly embarrassed, goodness, she was in her twenties not her teens!

When Joe's mobile rang, he apologised and moved out of one of the doors leading to the patio, to take the call which he said was from his agent in London. Within seconds Jill came to the table, and occupied his seat.

"He still wants me you know, he just wants me to go out with someone younger for a time. Then when we get together he will be sure that he is not too old for me, and I won't regret settling for one man, without having known anyone else." She smiled unpleasantly, and quickly returned to her table, as she saw Joe coming back into the dining room. Jill was still the arrogant, self-interested girl she had proved to be earlier during her first visit to the islands, and also in London. Morgane could see why Joe would not want to settle down with someone so young, until he was sure that she would not regret it later. Being able to understand his reasoning, did not make it any easier to bear. Maybe he was truly in love with Jill, and felt only physical attraction for Morgane Maine. When Joe returned to the table, the ease between them vanished, and she could see from his puzzled face that he had no idea what had happened to cause this change! Soon he suggested they leave, and he asked the waiter to get them a taxi. When they arrived at Smuggler's Cove, she offered to make him a drink, which he declined. The evening that had started out so well, it seemed was a great disappointment to them both.

The next morning at breakfast, Joe asked Morgane to sit with him a while, she joined him at the table. Her heart missed a beat at his look of extreme tiredness, and his eyes were coolly aloof.

"I will be booking my flight home today. My agent wants me back in London, which is understandable as I did leave quickly without making any arrangements. Jill is leaving on Thursday

372

evening, I might as well go on that flight, and deliver her safely to her father."

"Oh," she said quickly, he heart sinking into her sandals at the thought of Joe leaving the islands again. She had no right to expect anything else, as he had his own life in the United Kingdom, which did not really include her, because she certainly believed she was *not* his half sister!

"I will be seeing David as soon as I get back, and if there are any tests to be done which will help prove your parentage, I'll let you know. I'll leave you a card with my telephone numbers and email address, although I seem to remember giving you one before in London! I would like to hear what happens with the items we took to the Archives in Hamilton. They could prove to be very important to the history of the islands. They could even go back as far as 1609 when Admiral Sir George Somers discovered the islands by mistake." He smiled briefly, "I'd better go and put Maggie in the picture about when I expect to leave. Will Benny be in today, as I would like to see her before I leave?"

"Yes." She mentally shook herself, could she only answer in words of one syllable?

"I'd like to make sure I get to say goodbye to her," he said fondly moving towards reception. He paused. "Do you mind if I take you up on your offer to use your painting materials. I'll be leaving the motorcycle with the hirer today. I may as well stay around and paint, that is if you are sure you don't mind." She nodded, all the while wanting to shout "Joe don't go." She pulled herself together and ran up the stairs to her room. She quickly tidied everything personal away, and made sure that the paints and canvases were easily available, just in case Joe came to use them. At the last minute she slipped off her well worn sandals, and slipped on a smart pair of shoes. She was going shopping in Hamilton and if she had time, intended to call at the Archives in the Museum, to catch up with the progress made.

The weather was pleasantly warm and after collecting the shopping, she decided to get it back home quickly. She went upstairs to collect some tissues, and realised that Joe *had* been painting. She collected the tissues, and noticed the worn sandals askew on the polished wooden floor, and she straightened them and placed them neatly under the end of the bed, out of sight.

Her visit to the Archives was unfortunately rather short, but very interesting. As she was leaving the curator brought her a large brown envelope, in which she said were numerous letters, probably of a personal nature, that were addressed to Marie Maine, whom they assumed was her mother. Morgane was mystified, as she had never known her mother go into the small room, certainly not as long as she could remember. She had herself gone into the small room many years ago, whilst playing with her school friends and they had found it very exciting, but her mother had at all times been either writing, or entertaining friends like Benny, who lived locally.

CHAPTER FIFTEEN

Morgane arrived home, with the packet beside her on the front seat of the jeep. At the time of her mother's death, the solicitor had dealt with her mother's Will, and he had been in possession of all the relevant papers. Although Morgane had searched through the house, she had found nothing else of interest.

As far as she knew, and with what Benny had told her, from when Morgane was quite small her mother had lived a fulfilling but quiet life. She had spent most of her time on Bermuda, writing. She had been quite a prolific writer - she had a daughter to bring up and educate. Sending Morgane over to the United Kingdom for her secondary, and University education, must have been very expensive. This Morgane had accepted, but now she wondered if her mother had not lived such an idyllic life as it had appeared at the time!

She called in to the kitchen to make sure that all the groceries had been put away, mainly the frozen food. Maggie, as usual had done her job well. She then went upstairs to her rooms, telling herself that it was not to see if Joe was in the room painting. If that was her reason, she was disappointed because he was no where to be seen. She was about to leave, when she noticed her sandals were not under the bed where she had placed them neatly. They were on the carpet, slightly askew as if she had just kicked them off. Very strange, she could have sworn she had straightened them earlier.

She sat on the bed and looked inside the package handed to her by the curator at the Archives. There were numerous letters addressed to her mother, and they were tied up with red ribbon. Suddenly she was completely still. Could they be from Joe's father! Her stomach seemed to reel at the thought, and she quickly went to the kitchen for a drink of water. She returned to her room, and still could not open the letters, as her fingers were all over the place. Benny, she must find Benny. Maybe Benny would recognise the handwriting on the envelopes. She couldn't bring herself to open any of the letters.

Should she post them on to David Smithson, let him deal with them? On the other hand they might have nothing to do with Joe's father, and that could prove to be very embarrassing for everyone concerned.

"Morgane, dinner," the sound of Maggie's voice, echoing up the stairs, made her jump. Then as though she had received a reprieve, Morgane returned the letters to the brown paper envelope, and slowly went down to join Maggie for dinner. The last thing she felt like doing was to eat!

Maggie was pouring a glass of wine, when Morgane joined her in the dining room. The table had been set for three, but there was no sign of Joe and she realised she had gained a little time to try and get her churning emotions under control.

"Joe went to see Benny, he is catching the flight tomorrow evening, and he wanted to say goodbye to her and Mike. Also Robin, if he is around. I'll keep his dinner, as I can always warm it later if he hasn't eaten."

So, he *was* going back to the United Kingdom with Jill. Morgane felt guilty at the jealous feeling that this information arose, what right had she to feel jealous? Also it was most unfair to think that she could wait and read the letters after he had left, he was as anxious to find out the truth as she was herself. If he did marry Jill, then he would also want his finances settled, and would have to explain to her the reason for his trips to Bermuda, and the place that Morgane now played in his life. She was being selfish, and the letters would have to be read, *whatever* they contained.

She pushed her plate to one side, and surprised Maggie by going towards the telephone and once connected, asked Benny if she might visit her.

"Sorry about the meal Maggie, but I'm not hungry. I'm going out for a while."

"I gathered that from your telephone call. What do you want to go over to Benny's for at this time of night?" Maggie couldn't stop herself asking.

"I'll tell you in the morning Maggie. I need to show Benny a letter I have found, and I need to see her tonight."

She ran up to her room, and chose the letter showing the earliest date posted. That would be sufficient for Benny to see, with a little luck she would be able to identify the writing on the envelope, or letter. As she was climbing into the jeep, she suddenly stopped. She was expecting Benny to identify the writing on an envelope that had been hidden away for twenty-five years, and it was a lot to ask! She shrugged and started the engine, as she did not now want to wait until morning.

She drew the jeep to a stop in the parking area near to Benny's house, and sat for a few moments enjoying the sight of the waves on the shore in the distance, and the tree frogs and insects making their nightly music. It soothed her, and she walked slowly to the open door, with Benny's large frame silhouetted against the lighter interior, wondering if she should just have ignored the letters, but that would not be fair to Joe, as they just might prove something one way or the other!

"What's all this about love, what's worrying you," Benny said drawing Morgane into the living room, and indicating an easy chair.

Morgane smiled at Mike, who was busily sucking an empty pipe, his eyes twinkling with good humour.

"Do you want me to disappear for a few minutes," he asked Morgane quietly.

"No Mike, do stay. You might be able to help, as you must have been with Benny twenty–five years ago, as Robin is only a year older than me." She paused, and drew from her pocket the envelope, which she silently handed to Benny. Benny perused the envelope carefully, and looked directly at Morgane.

"Where did you find this?"

"The archive people found a number of letters in one of the boxes we found and took to them for appraisal. They thought these looked private, and gave them back to me today."

"I don't recognise the writing. However, I can tell you that it was not written by Mr Lawson, he used a very artistic copperplate hand, really neat. That was what you wanted to know wasn't it?"

378

Morgane felt a great feeling of relief, and sagged in the chair. "Would you mind opening the letter Benny?" Benny accepted the knife that Mike passed to her, which she did not need, as the letter had already been opened, and presumably read.

"Do you want me to read it?" She paused waiting form Morgane's reply. She read the letter through after receiving a nod from the younger woman who sat with her hands clasped tightly together. She raised her eyebrows at the contents, and then smiled, and handed the letter to Morgane.

"You'd better read it, as it's from an American gentleman. Neil Hammond. I remember him. He was one of a group of people who visited often. They were friends of your mother when she was modelling clothes."

Morgane slowly read the letter, and then read it once again, a wild hope was slowly growing within her, she couldn't be sure from one letter, but her mother and this Neil Hammond had definitely been more than friends.

"This could be what we have been looking for Benny, do you think it *is possible*?"

"Definitely," Benny said with a smile, and glanced at the puzzled look on her husband's brown face.

"Did Joe visit you earlier," Morgane asked quickly.

"Yes he left fifteen minutes before you rang to say you were coming over. You probably passed him on the road, as he was walking, and said he wanted to hear the tree frogs' nightly recital once again."

Morgane put the letter in her pocket, smiled at Benny and gave her a quick hug, and then kissed Mike on the top of his silver curly hair. "You had better explain what is going on to Mike, he looks a little mystified. See you tomorrow Benny."

She drove back to Smuggler's Cove finding it hard to keep to the speed limit. How had she missed Joe, or had he possibly rung for a taxi and gone to the Hamilton Princess? What if he had packed his belongings, and gone there for the night! That would be terrible as she really wanted him to be here, and to see for himself what these letters contained, as they just might be what they had been looking for!

She entered the kitchen, and looked for the plated meal which she knew that Maggie would have covered with film and left near the microwave. There was nothing there, and she felt relieved. Joe might be in his room, but for now she wanted to read one or two more of the letters. She could yet be disappointed.

She made herself take a shower, and prepare for bed, and then settled down to read the letters in date order. It seemed to her, from the long loving letters, that her mother and Neil Hammond had, in fact, been lovers. Was he her father? Her emotions were all over the place, and she couldn't read any more of the letters alone. She left the bed and put on her robe, gathered the letters, and set off down the stairs to the next landing.

Joe lay on the bed in his robe, the light was still on, and the book beside him was unopened. He shielded his eyes with his arm across his brow. It was almost an hour since he had heard the jeep return to the house. Where had Morgane been going at that time of night, he wondered? She had passed him on the road, as he was about to turn into the drive. She had looked as if she was on a mission, and he had been greatly relieved when the jeep returned. He glanced at the suitcases on the small settee by the window - he would have to finish packing in the morning. His mind returned to the unpleasant interview with Jill earlier in the day. He must have a word with David, who thought the sun shone out of his beautiful daughter. Joe hated to disabuse his friend, but unless he held a tighter rein on his daughter she could end up in trouble with some man or other. However, Dan seemed a nice enough young man, she could do much worse.

There was a light tap on his door, and he scrambled off the bed, pulling his robe around him. What could Maggie want at this time of night he wondered as he glanced at the travelling alarm on the bedside table – it showed eleven fifteen. He opened the door slowly, to find Morgane standing in front of him, without makeup, her blond hair slightly ruffled, looking about fifteen years old. He drew in a quick breath, which was a great mistake, as he could smell her own particular clean and enticing scent. His first impulse was to take her in his arms and carry her over to the bed, but he held the door only partly open.

"What can I do for you Morgane, whatever it is can't it wait until morning?" he asked his tone anything but welcoming.

"It possibly could, but I can't do this alone, I need you to help," she pushed passed him, and went to sit on the side of the bed. Joe remained standing by the open door.

"Come over here Joe, shut the door we don't want to disturb Maggie, she likes her sleep." When he didn't move she glanced at his disturbed face. "This affects *you*, Joe." He wondered with a deep sigh if she knew how much!

"Look Joe, the people at the Archives found these letters in one of the boxes we took for them to peruse. They are letters to my mother, and they are not from your father. I have read four of them, but I thought you had a right to look at them too. It looks as though my mother and Neil Hammond were in love, during the year before I was born. This could let you and your father off the hook Joe. I took them to show Benny because I didn't want to open them, as I was frightened of what they might contain. Benny knew at once that they were not from your father, as he had lovely clear copperplate writing. She says this Neil Hammond was a frequent visitor, along with other friends from the States."

By now Joe had moved over to the bed to sit down, and when Morgane stopped her explanations, he started to read. She waited until he had finished the fourth letter, then handed him the next. "We can go through the rest together," she said happily, now that she had his full attention. He slipped his arm around her shoulder, and they continued to read. Then the strangest thing happened. Morgane fell asleep, and Joe pushed her gently onto the bed, and lifted her feet up to make her more comfortable.

She awoke slowly, and it took a few seconds to remember where she was! She looked around and caught Joe's eyes as he watched her.

"Sorry, how long have I been asleep?"

"Three hours, you must have needed it," he said with a smile. "Have you ever heard of this Neil Hammond before Morgane?" She shook her head, and Joe continued. "He was an extremely prominent man in American government and society, and he and his wife lived almost celebrity lives. Did you notice I said was, I'm afraid he died seven years ago, leaving a wife and no other family."

"How do you know all this Joe, I've only been asleep for three hours," she interrupted him, trying to inwardly digest what he was telling her.

"Email, and the Internet," he admitted. "I have been using your computer."

"How could you do that you don't know the password?"

"Well, I put in Benny, Mike, Marie, your date of birth, and then *tree frogs together with various numbers* as I know you love to hear them. Four hours time difference, Morgane, which means that David is already in his office."

"Oh Joe, if he was my father, I'll never get to know him," she said sadly, feeling almost guilty at the happy feeling that she was trying to keep back, at least until Joe finished telling her what he had found out about this Neil Hammond. Joe leant forward and took her hand in sympathy.

"The other news is, that in one of the later letters he tells your mother that he had requested my father to accept a sum of money, to hold for you, which my father was going to pass to you if ever you needed it. If that didn't occur then he would Will it to you. Dad must have decided the Trust Fund was the best way to do this. I just wish he had explained everything in his will. I guess he just forgot about it. In that same letter to your mother he also makes it painfully clear that he would have left his wife and come to your mother, but she wouldn't let him. It would have been the end of his career in politics, and besides that, your mother had met his wife and liked her very much. My father agreed to do this for his friend, because if Neil had given the money to your mother it might have been discovered, as at every election time the opposition would have loved to find some sort of scandal. If that payment was discovered it was for a painting bought from my father! Just then my father was still mourning his wife and my mother, and didn't care either way."

She was quiet as she took in all this information. "Joe, you must have suffered all the time since your father died, wondering. Now you know your father was just doing a friend a good turn. Please don't feel bitter about it. Jill will understand everything when you tell her." He looked puzzled for a moment, and then shrugged.

"You are a wonderful person Morgane. Your first thought is for me, when it should be, after realising your biological father is already dead, that you can now accept the money that he left to you, with the help of my father." He sat down on the bed beside her, which promptly sent every thought out of her head!

"Morgane I desperately need to kiss you, and please remember, I am *not* your half-brother as you have maintained all along," his eyes stared into hers, and what he saw there he accepted as her invitation for him to kiss her. As soon as their lips met, so did their bodies and they clung together as if they would never part. She felt the dark potent magic in the room. Soon she was pressed against Joe's strong, lean body, and she felt as if she had come home. He was a very attentive lover and was building up feelings she had only ever imagined, and then some! Months of frustration and need overcame them, and they couldn't get enough of each other. When they became one, she gave a little cry, and he stilled in surprise. Then he remembered the complimentary items in the top drawer of the bedside cabinet. Then with protection and great care he brought them both to fulfilment. She felt as though every beautiful colour she had ever seen turned a glowing pink, and settled about their entwined bodies. She positively glowed, with his body heavy against hers, and it was the most wonderful feeling in the world.

"Are you hurt, I never guessed it would be your first time?" he asked her in wonderment, it was hard to believe as she was such a beautiful girl with a friendly disposition.

"I feel wonderful Joe. I am just a bit worried about Jill." She paused not knowing how to carry on, she didn't want to spoil this wonderful intimacy between them, but she had to know if there was any truth in what Jill had said.

"Forget Jill, there was never anything between us, but I'm afraid it took her a while to believe that. In the end I told her I was in love with *you.*"

She was silent for a moment, filled with emotion. "Do you mean that Joe, really, but shouldn't I have been the first to know?" She was about to tell him what Jill had told her, then thought better of it.

"I think I fell for you on the day we met, but when I found out your name, I had to curb any inclinations I had in that direction. These have been the most traumatic months I have known in my life. I was jealous of Martin, because you never told me about Mary. I was also jealous of Simon, when Benny rang and told me about him. I was desperate, I was hundreds of miles away, and I couldn't get here fast enough. As it happens I was just in time." He cupped her face between his hands and kissed her gently on the lips. "Have you something to say to me Morgane?"

"I was attracted to you on the first day too, but couldn't understand why you were blowing hot then cold. I knew for certain that I loved you when you told me you thought I might be your half-sister. I was devastated at the thought, and for quite a while couldn't take it in, but in my heart I thought you couldn't be, or how could I feel the way I did." He kissed her until they had to come up for air. "Do you really love me Joe, I find it hard to believe. You have been so strong in not giving in to the attraction that we both felt?"

"Do you want proof. Come with me." He pulled her off the bed and put her robe around her shoulders, and slipped on his own robe, and then bundled up her pyjamas and handed them to her. He took her from his bedroom, up the stairs to her rooms. She looked around and could not see anything that might prove that he loved her.

He walked to the easel and took off the cover. The painting, left to dry, was of nothing but a patch of wooden flooring, and her worn sandals, slightly askew as if she had just kicked them off. He must love her to want to paint those old sandals just because they were hers!

He drew her towards the bed, lifted her robe off her shoulders and let it fall to the floor, "I know of a much better way to prove it to you, but first you have to promise to marry me as soon as possible. If you say yes, then we can email Martin and Mary in London and ask them to come over here for the Wedding with all expenses taken care of, and any other friends. And we will get Benny and Maggie to arrange a wedding breakfast at one of the hotels, as soon as I find a Vicar and Church to marry us, and as I have never seen so many Churches painted in so many lovely colours on a small island, *you* can make the choice. Will you marry me Morgane?"

"I will Joe, as soon as we can. But what about you, you have none of your friends over here?"

"I'll have Martin as my groomsman, and I'll have Benny's son Robin as my Best Man, and I'll need my solicitor here to make sure everything is above board, we don't want any misunderstandings about *our union* in the future, not like our parents!"